FINDING
Casey

Paperback ISBN: 978-1-7362248-5-4
Electronic ISBN: 978-1-7362248-6-1

Published by Nathan Jarelle
P.O. Box 3004
Upper Marlboro, Maryland 20772
www.natejayreads.com

FINDING
Casey

PART OF THE BEYOND POETRY SERIES

Nathan Jarelle

Washington, D.C.

Author's Preface

I seriously contemplated the direction of the *Beyond Poetry* series about midway through the second book. It grieved me to watch Junior and Casey go their separate ways, but nothing lasts forever in this cruel world. Friendships dissolve, time passes—people move on. It's hard letting go, and I struggled letting go of Junior and Casey in order to expand the depth of the series so that each succeeding title solidifies its salt. *Beyond Poetry* really is beyond poetry.

For years, Casey Haughton's life was plagued with disappointments—some of which were subtly mentioned throughout the first two books. I hoped that readers would feel compelled to learn more about the origins of each of the central characters. I felt an immense connection to these titles which will gift the series with new bodies of work for many years to come. And it is my pledge (and honor) to deliver on that promise.

Finding Casey unfolds five years prior to the events of the first book. Therefore, there is no linkage to Junior yet, as Casey was still struggling to find her stride in life during that time. Her sweet but loquacious character was always challenged. These challenges began in her troubled childhood. Her story is a punishing reminder of how merciless and indiscriminate life can be.

Sincerely,
Nathan Jarelle

If you or someone you know is experiencing suicidal thoughts or a crisis, please reach out immediately to the Suicide Prevention Lifeline at **800-273-8255** or text HOME to the Crisis Text Line at **741741.** These services are free and confidential.

Unlovable

Little Casey moved in with her Auntie Patty and Uncle Benny shortly after her mother's death when she was just nine years old. Her mother's name was Janice. She once had long, beautiful natural hair but Casey had never seen it due to her mother's heroin addiction. The drug dried out her hair and fried her mother's veins until she eventually overdosed on the bathroom floor inside their Newark, New Jersey apartment. Casey's father was a street hustler known around town as Boots. She never knew his first name since the coward barely visited, although they shared the same last name, Johnson. Boots dropped Casey off at school one morning and never returned. So, when the school phoned Casey's auntie and uncle and told them what'd happened, they took her in.

Patty and Benny rented a tiny one-bedroom apartment in Brownsville-Brooklyn, New York. They didn't have central air, so during the summer months they'd use fans and frozen bean bags from the grocery mart as a reprieve. Their place smelled like feet and cigarettes most of the year except during the cold months when they used a space heater to warm up.

Little Casey looked different than most of the children on her block. She was cute but overweight with a pot belly, green eyes, pale skin, and goldish, crinkly hair. She was born white as snow due to her albinism. Children teased and mocked her because of it. "Momma said I'm Black, even though my skin is white. It's called albinism," she explained once to a group of skeptical juveniles. "Y'all ever heard of it?" she asked.

"Nope!" *Whop.* A girl socked Casey in the eye and pushed her into a patch of mud. "Man, you ain't Black. Stop tryin' to be like us, white girl."

Casey howled all the way home, holding her inflamed eye. "They hit me!" she cried, breathing heavily. "I can't believe they hit me!"

Aunt Patty placed a slab of fatback on her niece's eye to cease the swelling. Casey's aunt used a lot of fatback that summer—those damn kids were so cruel to her. They hurled rocks, sticks, and other objects at Casey or chased her home after school. Once, a boy found a used condom on the ground and put it in her hair. Children would even throw things onto her balcony to discourage her from coming to the park. "Get back inside, ugly!" Her chubby cheeks sagged with glum as she'd watch the other kids play. To cheer her up, Uncle Benny bought Casey her first ever board game, *Operation.* "C'mon, I'll play with ya. I'll be your friend," he said. Little Casey lit up. She finally had a friend.

Every day after school, Casey played her favorite board-game with Uncle Benny. She'd crack up laughing each time the buzzer went off on him. Sometimes, Uncle Benny would do it just to make her laugh. "Oh, you think that shit's funny, huh?" *Bzzzz.* Casey would crumble to the floor, weak with hilarity. Aunt Patty would bake her niece cupcakes and even make her lemonade. One time, Uncle Benny hit the buzzer while Casey was drinking and lemonade gushed from her nose.

At night, Casey slept beside her auntie while Uncle Benny took to the couch. She'd awake some nights to find him standing in the doorway of their master bedroom making odd gestures. "Uncle Benny?" she'd call to him. "Is that you?" His silhouette would then quickly disappear.

One day, while Aunt Patty was at church, Casey was alone with her uncle in the apartment. She had just finished her homework and was practicing on her boardgame before Uncle Benny called her over. "Do you ever leave that game alone?" he asked. "C'mon over and sit with me for a little bit." Casey left her game and bounced beside him on the sofa. Uncle Benny placed his hand onto her fat little leg and started to rubbed it. "I'm really happy you're here, Casey." She looked up and noticed Uncle Benny was grinning at her.

Every time Aunt Patty wasn't home, Casey noticed her leg or other private parts were explored by him. The fourth time it happened, she got up to leave but Uncle Benny pulled her arm, causing her to stumble backward onto him. What she felt next frightened her.

"Let go of me!" She fought him. "I'm gonna tell Aunt Patty!"

"No the hell you ain't!" He wrestled with her. "I'll whoop your little ass if you do."

Casey bit her uncle on the hand, freeing herself, ran into the bathroom and locked the door. For two hours, Uncle Benny alternated between picking at the lock, and trying to sweet talk Casey out of the bathroom. She hid inside their gross tub, trembling with fear.

"Goddamn, you." He jiggled the handle. "Open this door, right now!"

"No, I'm gonna tell Aunt Patty what you did."

Uncle Benny began kicking at the door. Casey covered her ears and screamed at him.

"You're scaring me. Stop it!" she whimpered.

When Aunt Patty arrived home, Casey bolted from the bathroom and into her auntie's arms.

"Aunt P-P-P-Patty," she stuttered, barely able to talk. "You gotta help me! Uncle Benny keeps touching me, and I don't like it. Please make him stop."

"You'se a damn lie. Patty, I told that girl to put away that game and finish her homework. Know what she did? Bit me on my hand—look." He showed off his bite mark. "God knows, I ain't touch her, Patty. Little brat has been gettin' out of hand every time you leave."

Aunt Patty slapped her niece across her face. *Whap.* Casey held her hot cheek in shock.

"How dare you sit up there and accuse your uncle of such a thing? I won't have it!"

She stormed over to the closet and returned with an extension cord snaked around her fist. She yoked Casey by her arm and beat her so badly that even Uncle Benny had to intervene. Afterward, her little chunky limbs were covered with red lashes. The markings were so painful that it hurt Casey to bathe or put on clothes.

Everything changed after the bite incident. There were no more cupcakes, lemonade, or board games. Believing her niece was a heathen in need of saving, Aunt Patty beat Casey over minor things: leaving her coat at school, not finishing her dinner, or not knowing how to do her homework. She'd beat Casey sometimes until holes appeared in her underwear. She flew into a rage once when Casey refused to eat her pig's feet dinner.

"Girl, get in here!" She pointed down at her angry slippers. "Right-damn-now."

Casey slinked from the sofa and sauntered into the kitchen as if she was headed to see the executioner. She looked down at her feet, afraid to look into her aunt's cobra eyes.

"Why'd you throw my food away? Huh?" *Whap.* "I told you about that shit. Now, pick my goddamn food out of there."

Fighting back tears, Casey reached into the garbage with her bare hands and removed her uneaten dinner. She stood there, holding her fleshy meal in her hands. Patty dragged over to the table and shoved a plate in front of her.

"Now, eat," she said. "We don't waste no food 'round here."

"But I don't like pig's feet," Casey protested. "Please, don't make me eat it. I promise, I won't throw nothin' else away."

When Aunt Patty lunged for the extension cord, Casey aborted her complaint and began to eat. She clipped her nose and shuddered as she sucked down the rubbery cartilage. Aunt Patty even made her drink the greasy juice at the bottom of the bowl.

The next day at school, Casey complained to her teacher that her stomach hurt. "Please, Miss Edelman." She danced and winced. "I really gotta go. I can't hold it anymore." Miss Edelman sent Casey back to her seat. Minutes later, Casey's stomach erupted down her dress. She squealed in embarrassment as kids teased her. Her negligent teacher hauled her down to the nurse's station with two fingers and whisked her inside.

"I can't deal with this nonsense right now; I'm trying to teach."

Casey was still crying as the school's nurse began working on her. The lady peeled away her pasty clothes with scorn.

"Good Lord. What'd you eat last night? Here, let's get you out of this stuff."

When the nurse touched Casey's shoulder, she yelped in agony.

"Owww—owww!"

The nurse backed off. She pulled Casey's dress back and noticed her hideous scars.

"How did this happen?" The nurse growled. "Is someone hurting you?"

Little Casey was too afraid to answer. She was scared if

she told the nurse what had happened, Aunt Patty would find out and get her again. Less than an hour later, the principal, a cop, and a social worker showed up at the school to investigate her scars.

"Casey? Sweetie?" The nurse dropped onto one knee. "Honey, can you please show me your scars again? Please, Casey?"

Reluctant at first, Casey showed off her scars to the group as they sighed with collective displeasure. She even pointed at a mark beneath her chin from a dress shoe her aunt once hurled at her. Aunt Patty and Uncle Benny were both arrested, and Casey was placed into the State's care. She'd never have to worry again about eating out of the trash or locking herself in a bathroom to get away from her sick uncle.

Little Casey wandered through foster care for the next few years, bouncing from home to home. Despite an address change, the kids were still the same. She was bullied and harassed constantly by her peers. While living in Queens, kids chased her down at recess one afternoon, took her sneakers and knocked out her front tooth. In Harlem, girls pinned Casey onto the ground and cut her hair with scissors. "You fuckin' freak." *Snip-Snip.* She hid her patchy hair beneath hats for months until her hair grew back. She returned to Brooklyn (by way of Flatbush) and was literally run out of the neighborhood for saying "nigga" at the playground. When Casey tried to explain herself, the kids jumped her. "Stop tryin' to be like us. Go hang with your white friends!" It crushed her so badly, she ran away from home and slept in the subway for three days. A transit cop found Little Casey eating out of the trash and took her in. Her exhausted social worker, Mrs. Newman, provided a solution. "I think I know just the place, Casey," she told her. "We'll get it right this time."

Casey had just turned thirteen when she moved in with the Haughtons in West Fellers, New York in June of 1978. She was a sweet but scarred kid with gappy front teeth who seldom smiled or talked. She trudged up the driveway behind Mrs. Newman as they approached her new home. The suburbs of West Fellers was vastly different than the city, she quickly noticed. There were parks with tall trees, friendly-looking kids, and the town was free of hookers and graffiti. Casey thought she was dreaming. Her new daddy worked as a lawyer in Manhattan. He was tall, educated, handsome, and easygo-ing. Her mother was a special education teacher, soft-spoken, loved to laugh and had the prettiest smile she'd ever seen.

Casey also had a sister now too: Courtney. She was a lanky girl who wore Chuck Taylors with striped knee-high socks. She wore pigtails and glasses. Casey discovered right away that Courtney was different from most kids she'd met. Her pleasantness caught Casey off guard. As Courtney hopped down from her Stingray bicycle to greet her with a hug, Casey shoved her to the ground. Courtney looked back at her parents, stunned.

"What is *wrong* with you?" Courtney barked at Casey. She sucked her teeth and returned to her bicycle, dejected.

Casey looked over at Mrs. Newman, confused.

"I don't think Courtney wants to fight, Casey," she said. "Why not give her a chance?"

Casey looked over at Courtney, noticed her long face and went back to re-introduce herself.

"Sorry I pushed you," she apologized. "I ain't use to other kids, you know, likin' me and stuff. You can push me back if you want to."

Courtney hugged her a second time.

"It's alright." She shrugged. "I probably shouldn't have run up on you like that, anyway. So, what's up? You wanna ride bikes? There's this park up the street. Man, everybody goes there."

"Can't. I ain't got no bike," Casey sighed. "I can walk with you, though."

Courtney jetted around back and returned with a brand-new Stingray bicycle the Haughtons had bought in anticipation of her arrival. The bike was even her favorite color green. Casey's jaw touched the pavement.

"Holy shit. It's greeeen."

The Haughtons laughed at her excitement. Mrs. Haughton walked over to greet her new daughter and straighten her bicycle bell.

"Welcome home, Casey. I heard you like cupcakes. Can I bake you some for dessert? Do you like fried catfish?"

"Cupcakes?" Casey showed her missing tooth. "I *love* cupcakes. Catfish, too!"

"Great. Maybe when you get back, we can talk about that

smile, too? I know a dentist who can help. Wouldn't you like to smile more? Your dad and I would love to see you smile more."

Casey looked at Mrs. Newman, puzzled by her awesome family.

"Run along now, Casey." Mrs. Newman patted her pumpkin head. "I'm gonna stick around and speak with the Haughtons for a bit. I'll be here when you get back."

Casey was still cheesing as she cruised down the driveway with her new bicycle.

"C'mon, Casey, let's go!" Courtney waved her on. "C'mon-c'mon."

"Be back by four, girls," their daddy spoke up. "Wouldn't want your fish to get cold."

"We will!" The girls chimed, cruising up the summer pavement.

The Haughtons were a well-respected middle-class Black family with a stellar reputation throughout their town of 3,400 residents. They were the example family that even white folks who lived there aspired to be, and they were a humble bunch. They loved sci-fi movies, carnivals, museums, and they liked to hang out at the pool. Mrs. Haughton was able to pull some strings at a local dentist to have Casey's gappy teeth fixed for half the cost. The Haughtons bought her new threads and a matching pair of Chuck Taylor sneakers to match Courtney's. For a while, the girls were dubbed "The Chuck Girls" around West Fellers, known for their matching kicks. The Haughtons even had Casey's last name legally changed from Johnson to Haughton. With her gorgeous new smile (and family), Casey's face was upturned more than ever before. She teared at the results one night. "Wow," she looked herself over. "Is this all real?" Casey had her own bedroom, her own closet, and most importantly, the Haughtons had central air, and their place didn't smell like feet and cigarettes. Across from Casey's room was the hallway bathroom which she shared with Courtney. The girls acquainted themselves by doing each other's hair and debating their favorite songs. Courtney loved to talk and would ask a thousand questions. She'd wince as the bristles on Courtney's comb yanked her kinky hair.

"So, how'd you lose your tooth?" Courtney once asked. "Did you get in a fight?"

"Yeah, you could say that. I got jumped while I was—ow—living in Queens—owww." Casey weaved. "Do you have to comb so hard?"

"Well, if you'd quit moving, it probably wouldn't hurt so much." Courtney went back to combing her sister's head. "So, why'd they jump you?"

"Who knows? All I know is, I'm just tired of getting beat up—ow."

Courtney placed her comb on the sink. She bunched Casey's fluffy golden hair in her hands and tied it in a pony tail.

"Well, you won't have to worry about anyone bothering you again. If it happens, just tell me, and I'll beat them up."

On Courtney's bedroom door was a poster of Michael Jackson, her celebrity crush. Every night before bed, she'd kiss her lover on the lips. One night, Casey tried to kiss Courtney's poster and caught a pillow upside the head. *Whap.* "Get your own husband." *Whap.* Courtney blasted her again. Casey grabbed her pillow and went after her. They whacked each other silly until their daddy finally put his foot down. "Alright, girls, that's enough," he yelled from below. With their giggles behind them, the girls yielded for the night. Casey had been there just shy of three weeks, but to her it felt like three years. She fit perfectly into the Haughtons' world. The family had a basketball court in the driveway where she'd practice her shot after school with Mr. Haughton. Some weekends, the Haughtons would bike together on a nearby trail and Casey would lead the pack. "It's on you, sweetheart." Mrs. Haughton would yell from the back. "Wherever you wanna go." Casey would give her family a nod of acceptance and pedal up the rocky surface, her eyes glassy with thanks.

That summer, Courtney taught Casey how to fish, pick berries, catch lighting bugs in a jar and how to backflip out of a swing set from high in the air. She even showed Casey what to do when her menstrual cycle happened—no one had ever showed her. She also helped Casey with her pronunciation of tricky words.

"It's not *rur-roll*, Casey, it's *rural*," she corrected her. "Take your time."

Casey sounded like a hungry stomach trying to pronounce the delicate adjective.

"Rurr? Rur-roo-roo—I can't do it. There's no way I can

say 'rural.' Oh, shit. I got it!"

Courtney had impeccable dialect for a teenager, and she never used foul language. One afternoon, Casey came home mad after a group of girls harassed her at the park. She thought she had escaped her old miserable life in the city but was mistaken. Courtney was lying in the family's hammock out back listening to Janis Ian.

"They made fun of me!" she hyperventilated. "They called me ugly. They said I bleached my skin. I ain't did nothin' to those girls, Courtney—nothin'."

Courtney turned off her radio. She stepped into her Chucks, retrieved her bat from the garage and went hunting for the culprits down at the park. Casey shadowed her from behind, glancing at the bat the whole way there.

"That's them." She pointed at the bleachers. "Hey, what's the bat for?"

Courtney marched over to the rowdy group of girls, breeching their conversation, and struck the metal bleachers with her bat. *Bang.* Wide-eyed, they scurried from the ringing steel.

"Y'all motherfuckin' bitches!" she cursed. "Leave my sister alone, or else I'm gonna smash your heads in with this bat. Understood?"

The group all nodded simultaneously.

"Good," she said. "Have a nice fucking day, ladies." Courtney then whacked the bleachers repeatedly like a lunatic and walked off. Casey co-signed at the end. "Yeah!" She ran to catch up with her sister.

Casey couldn't've imagined Courtney had a mean streak about her. She cursed again once during the school year when her math teacher gave her a B– on her exam.

"Can't believe that cunt gave me an eighty-*three!*" She crumbled up the paper and hurled it at her Michael Jackson poster. "Fuckin' jerk-off—I worked my ass off on that god-damn test."

Casey crashed to the floor, laughing.

The sisters were the perfect duo. They were born the same year and month in June of 1965, although Courtney was a few days older. They loved cupcakes, green, Michael Jackson, and all the same television shows. Courtney was book smart and Casey upped her sister's street credibility by teaching her the latest slang. "Too proper, that won't work. Put some bass in it. You gotta be like, 'Yo, son, whatcha lookin' at?' And if somebody starts trippin', just say, 'Yo-yo-yo, squash that.' Got it?" Courtney jotted the reformed dialect inside her journal.

"Courtney? Noooo. Don't write it down, you dork—just say it."

"Alright, I will. Give me a fuckin' break."

"Yeah… hell, yeah—that's what I'm talkin' about!" Casey celebrated. "But look, don't say 'alright', like a dweeb. It's a'ight."

"Ate?"

"A'ight."

"Oh, hot? I gotcha."

"No, man. It's a'ight. Like, *a'ight,* where we goin'? You got it?"

Courtney wrote it down in her book. "A'ight… got it."

A'ight

By the girls' sophomore year of high school, their relationship started to change as Courtney was now dating. She'd abandoned her knee-high socks for makeup and had posters of Marilyn Monroe on her bedroom walls. She was attractive, athletic, and captain of the cheerleaders at their school. Casey was captain of nothing. She was overweight with a pimply face and wore excessive skin creams to cover her blemishes. She'd trot down the hallway behind Courtney with her books smothered against her chest, waiting for some jock to finish asking out her sister. Courtney would turn around, surprised to see her still there. "Casey? What are you doing?" she'd giggle, ashamed. "Later, okay?" Casey would slog down the hall afterwards with her whale spout hair, feeling stupid. She envied the attention Courtney received.

Meanwhile, Casey was still being buttonholed over her albinism. Kids put gum on her locker handle or would shoot spitballs at her in class. She was self-conscious about her skin condition and refused to change into her gym shorts during P.E. because her legs were so bright and plump. Not to mention, the scars from her aunt's extension cord were still visible—at least to her. One day, it got so hot, Casey forfeited her insecurities and paid for it when kids poked fun at her clumpy white knees. She hid beneath the bleachers and cried. They teased her about that, too. When she later complained about her troubles, Courtney blew her off. "Everybody gets teased. It's high school for cryin' out loud, Casey." The rejection ate away at her. Casey got so fed up after a while, she stopped going to school and started hanging out in Brooklyn.

The first time Casey tried marijuana she didn't want to but worried that if she said no, she'd get teased again. She placed the joint up to her lips, took a puff, and coughed like crazy, but the kids didn't make fun of her. "What'd you say your name was again? Susie?" one boy asked her.

"Do I sound like a fuckin' Susie to you?" she growled. "It's Casey, ass wipe. Get it right and keep it right." Her new friends all laughed at her delivery. She had a way with words and could go with the best of them. Before long, Casey became part of a wretched crew that smoked trees, skipped school, stole from street vendors, shot guns at empty bottles, and lingered in the bowels of Brooklyn's toughest neighborhoods—places that would make the Haughtons shit. Mr. and Mrs. Haughton approached Casey about her behavior after finding a half-smoked joint inside her dresser drawer.

"C'mon, Casey, we don't need this stuff," Mr. Haughton reasoned with her. "Look, I was a kid once too—I get it. I'm not angry, okay? But I don't want to see this stuff anymore."

"You won't." Casey shrugged. "It was just a little… I don't know."

"Do you want to talk about it?" Mrs. Haughton offered. "We're here for you, okay? If you ever want to talk, Casey. I'm here."

Casey wiped her eyes. "I know. I won't do it again. I'm sorry. I uh… I think I wanna lay down for a while, though."

The Haughtons took away Casey's joint and walked off.

By junior year, Casey became rebellious and withdrawn from her family. She punched out a girl down at the park in West Fellers, breaking the kid's nose. She popped another kid at school and followed her crew Uptown to rage war on a gang of Harlemers. Her reputation quickly grew and despite her frumpy appearance, she had a mean left hook. The few times she was at school, she was down in the principal's office. She once got suspended for flipping off her science teacher for asking why she hadn't been to class in over two weeks. "Shut the fuck up, bitch. None of your goddamn business." The class oozed at Casey's crudeness, but the Haughtons didn't. Her anger came pouring out one evening at dinner as the family confronted her repulsive behavior.

"You are out of control!" Mr. Haughton ripped her. "I talked to Mr. Strickland. He says you haven't been to his class in days. You get your tail into his class, or else."

"Or else, what?" Casey challenged him. "Fuck Mr. Strickland, and fuck that school, too. Th'hell with all this phony-ass shit, man."

Mr. Haughton slammed his hand onto the table. *Bang.*

Dishes floated into the air.

"Get up," he lunged for her arm. "Get up from my table, right now. Until you act right, you will not eat at my table!"

"Well, maybe I don't wanna eat at your table anymore." Casey began to cry. "Maybe I'll just leave, and I won't ever come back here. I don't fit in, anyway."

Casey popped from her chair and ran from the house.

She marched up Benjamin Avenue until she reached the bus stop for Brooklyn. Once there, she sparked up a cigarette. Minutes later, Courtney came cruising up the street in their daddy's car (another low blow since their parents refused to let Casey drive due to her grades). Courtney shut off the motor and jumped out.

"Girl, you better get in this car. Are you crazy?" She closed the door. "Why'd you flip out like that? What's gotten into you?"

"I'm tired of everyone telling me how to live my life. Do this, Casey. Do that, Casey. From now on, I'm gonna do what's best for me."

"That's not gonna work, you know that." Courtney grabbed at her arm. "Now, c'mon. Let's go home before Dad kills you. Quit acting stupid."

Casey shoved Courtney onto the pavement. The fall was worse than when the girls first met.

"I'm doing things my way from now on. Stay outta my way, Courtney."

She boarded the bus to Brooklyn, leaving her sister there on the ground.

Later when she returned home, her father was standing on the porch waiting for her. He eyeballed her, turned and went back inside. She could tell he was losing hope with her.

Casey's bitter attitude wrecked the Haughton kingdom over the coming months. She'd fight with her family and was disrespectful. She'd hang out late and would even steal money from her parents to buy marijuana. She hated Courtney during that time for being so damn perfect.

Casey was also struggling to comprehend her sexual orientation. While lounging with her crew in the city, she tastetested a kiss with another girl and liked it. She summoned Courtney to her room later that night to tell her about it and was blown off. "Five minutes, I promise. I'm wrapping up some stuff for our junior class picnic this summer." Courtney never came back to hear the story. She was too busy being sworn in as class president with all her superlatives and good-girl bullshit. Their contrasting natures eventually drove them apart.

The Haughtons tried everything to help Casey. They hired a counselor, but she wouldn't go. They proposed home-schooling, but she threatened to leave if a teacher showed up. She preferred her old hood in Brooklyn and the cats out there, even though they were just as likely to be cruel to her. Some days, her crew paid her to perform sexual acts. She'd leave feeling disgusting and would cry on the way home. One night, Casey was so fed up that she attempted to end her life by leaping in front of a train, but she slipped on a patch of ice, spraining her foot. Casey told her family she fell at school. She felt pathetic and failed at everything it seemed, including how to properly kill herself.

In April of 1982, two months shy of her 17th birthday, Casey went with two of her male friends to rob a convenience store. She played lookout from the outside as her cronies ransacked the place and pistol-whipped the owner. "Where the fuck's the bread?" *Whap.* Casey's heart flickered as police cars came shrieking down the block. She dashed inside the mom-and-pop shop to alert her gang. "Shit, y'all, one-time—one-time!" Casey and her crew all scurried toward the back. They pushed and kicked at doors, trying to escape. "Fuck, it won't open!" She ran toward a lone door at the end of the hallway and lunged at it. The door gave way, launching her out into the alley and into the arms of awaiting lawmen. She was arrested alongside her friends and taken down to the precinct where she was photographed and booked. Their score was a meager forty-two dollars.

The sounds of clicking doors, police blotter, and swinging keys made Casey nervous as she retraced the steps which led to her involvement in the robbery. She computed the math inside her head to figure out that for forty-two dollars she'd put her freedom at stake. Lucky for Casey, she was still a juvenile. She placed her forehead onto the table, picturing the disgust on the Haughtons' faces upon learning of her involvement. The longer the cops kept her confined inside that small room, the more she thought about her decision to tag along. She had two loving parents, a sister, savings for college, and a car if she could improve her grades. She was near her breaking point when suddenly the door swung open and Courtney ran in to console her. The girls embraced like lovers seeing each other for the first time in months. Their parents stood at the door. Their faces said it all.

"Courtney, I'm scared. What was I thinking, going up there with those boys?"

Courtney comforted her right away. "Shhhh, it's okay. You made a mistake. We'll get through it—just like everything else." Courtney pressed her head against Casey's. "I love you, sis. C'mon, let's get out of here."

Mr. Haughton interrupted their reunion. "Casey's not coming back with us, Courtney. Let her go."

The girls looked at each other, panic etched on their worried faces.

"What are you talking about? Why not? Daddy, what are you saying? Mom? Mom, what's Dad talking about? Why can't Casey come home?"

The Haughtons joined hands. "A few weeks back, your mother and I relinquished our parental rights. We released Casey into her own custody. Casey isn't our responsibility anymore. She'll be seventeen in a few weeks, she can look after herself."

The girls both squealed as a team of deputies entered the small room to take Casey away.

"So, you're just going to give up on her? Just like that?"

"I had to!" he protested. "Stealing. Cutting class. Smoking. Drinking—now this? I really am sorry, Casey, but I can't allow this to go on inside my house anymore."

As the deputies closed in, the girls backed themselves against the wall and locked arms. They wept like slaves being separated at an auction as cops tore the two teens apart. Casey could only make out blurred images of Courtney as she struggled to break from her father's grip. Cops dragged Casey away through the double doors, ignoring her sister's cries. For years after that, if Casey listened hard enough, she could still hear Courtney calling her name.

One

Casey's plea agreement for her part in the robbery was fifteen years. It was the best deal the state could offer the endangered adolescent. If her case had gone to trial, and she was later found guilty, she could've received double the time. The Haughtons refused to mortgage their home on the hope that a better lawyer could get Casey out of trouble. The deal she got was a sure bet that someday she'd see light again, and with good behavior, she could make parole in between. She stood before a judge teary-eyed and covered in bright jailhouse scrubs with her hands shackled in front of her. "New York Department of Corrections" was imprinted across her back. Courtney gasped during her sentencing. Fifteen years meant that Casey would miss many milestones in her life: prom, graduation, and the celebrations of her eighteenth, twenty-first, and thirtieth birthdays. She peered at the embroidered seal on the paneled walls behind the judge's bench, wondering what awaited her on the other side.

In the wake of Casey's delinquency, the Haughtons' reputation quickly dissolved around West Fellers. Neighbors supported the family at first until details of the robbery were made public. The Haughtons' good reputation deflated soon after. Neighbors showed up at the house to shame them. In the aisle at the grocery store, a man chastised Mr. Haughton. "You're that punk father who let his kid rob a liquor store," the man said. "You should be ashamed of yourself!" Days later, a vandalizer spray-painted "NIGGERS" on the family's garage, and Courtney was removed as class president at her school.

Isolated from them, Casey didn't know any of this. All she could think about was that she was going to prison. The walk to the barred bus that awaited Casey behind the courthouse was paralyzing. Her legs stiffened and her mind was so weary with fear and disgrace that she collapsed onto all fours and had to be escorted to her bus. The pain had depleted her ability to walk or think coherently. Over and over, she replayed the sentencing inside her head. *Fifteen years*, she thought. Without parole, Casey wouldn't see daylight until she was thirty-two years old. She crumbled again as she saw the iron windows of her bus which would transport her to Esseltown, New York, a small township near the Canadian border. She piled into her seat and pressed her head against the glass.

The small settlement reminded Casey of a segregated setting during the Jim Crow era. She gazed from her bus window, seizing the sights and sounds of freedom before paying her debt to society. The farther Casey got from her city, and the more rural the passing glimpses, the more restless her mind became. *Where are they taking me?* Even if Casey could escape, it wasn't smart to consider. She didn't know where she was, or how to drive a thirty-five-foot bus. Not to mention, the driver was encased behind a steel cage which prevented inmates from accessing the wheel, and his partner aboard carried a large shotgun. Beside Casey was her convicted neighbor, staring ahead with a cold look. Her eyes grew with surprise as she looked down at the woman's killer hands. She sat back in her seat, observing the hopeless offender with a side-eye as the bus rolled onto the prison's campus.

The exterior of the St. Agnes Reformatory Center for Women ("SARC") looked like a torture chamber from the Victorian era. Pointy cupulas lined its domed roof. Its gargantuan structure was just as threatening. Rifle-wielding guards patrolled the towers. A dried reddish film leaked from the windows as if a victim had attempted to escape before being cornered and cannibalized. Casey imagined a humpback man with one eye named Igor, lurking throughout the facility. The driver cruised toward the gate and lowered his window to chat up the gatekeeper.

"Got some fresh meat for you, Ed. Fresh from New York City," the driver chuckled.

"New York City?" Ed repeated. "Well, then, let's not keep the warden's pussies waitin'. He ain't too patient when it comes to his fun."

Casey panicked. *Pussies? Fun?* The iron gate ticked like a faulty rollercoaster at an amusement park as the driver proceeded inside the complex. He shut off the motor and turned to formally greet the sixty condemned passengers.

"Okay, listen up!" He spoke with presence and authority. "I need one single line out there on that blacktop. Once there, wait for further instructions. Welcome to St. Agnes, ladies."

The driver unbolted a large padlock from the front of the bus which connected each rider to their seats. Casey lifted her foot as the big rusty steel chain snaked past her ankle. She stood up and waited her turn to exit the bus. Outside, she caught a glimpse of a hat belonging to a colossal male guard pacing across the blacktop. A closer look revealed the guard was a female. She had large biceps with huge thick veins. She reminded Casey of "Thunderlips" from the movie *Rocky III*. The brickhouse woman plodded onto the bus to order the remaining passengers off—she even sounded like Thunderlips. "What the fuck are you all still doing on my bus?" the woman hissed. Inmates crashed into one another, trying to get the hell off. No one wanted any part of the snarling, husky guard.

Outside, convicts filed onto the blacktop shoulder-to-shoulder as curious prisoners watched from behind a tall, spiny fence. They hooted and hollered—some even made gestures that were sexual in nature. The harassment was nothing new to Casey since she'd spent her life evading bullies. "Hey, you!" A woman pointed at her through the fence. "Yeah, bitch. I'm talkin' to *you*."

Casey shifted her eyes to the left. The heckler looked to be around fifty years old and was missing the top front row of her teeth. Casey wondered if the Haughtons' dentist back in West Fellers could help. "You ever had pussy before?" the woman asked her. The deranged inmate stuck her tongue through the wired fence and wiggled it at her. Casey shuddered and look straight ahead. Meanwhile, Thunderlips marched up and down the blacktop, sizing up her meal. She wore the rim of her Stetson hat just above her sunglasses and stood over six feet tall. She paraded around the arrivers there before stopping in front of a scrawny brunette-haired felon. The innocuous offender appeared to be all of 115 pounds soaking wet. Thunderlips doubled her in both size and height.

"Th'hell are you eyeballin' me like that for, convict? Huh?" *Whop.* She belted the petite inmate, putting her to sleep. She then dragged the sleepy inmate by her top until it tore from her back as spectators cheered on the barbarity. "Yeah, Sarge!" one inmate yelled. "Give those bitches a warm welcome!"

With onlookers egging her on, Thunderlips went down the line, flattening newcomers at random to the delight of staff and long-timers. The attacks were all arbitrary as both guards and inmates wagered cigarettes to see who'd be left standing. "How about this one here?" *Whop.* She blasted another. Even the bullies Casey faced back home as a kid showed some kind of mercy. Lucky for her, Thunderlips injured her hand after punching out six or seven inmates. She fanned away the pain before snatching her clipboard from the ground. "Welcome to your new home," she said. "For those of you left standing, head down to intake." Casey stepped over a napping felon and hurried inside.

Intake was even more dehumanizing. Casey and her group were accompanied into a sweltering loading bay full of sick male COs (Correctional Officers) donning latex gloves. Thunderlips entered a short time after and stopped at the front of the line. She snapped her bitchy fingers at Casey's group. "Strip!" she demanded. "I wanna see some skin inside this bay!" Casey and her fellow riders took off their garbs. Casey was so shaken up from the blacktop, if she could, she'd hand Thunderlips the skin off her back, too. Her eyes brimmed with fear. She was merely a kitten, locked inside a cage full of big cats.

One by one, perverted COs violated the new arrivers. They poked and prodded as they examined their cavities, searching for contraband. The cuter the inmate, the more poking and prodding they received. Casey numbed herself when it was her turn to get searched. The process was simple but invasive. "Open your mouth. Lift your tongue. Side to side. Turn around. Raise your arms above your head. Spread your legs. Squat. Cough. Stand up. Lift your foot. Next foot. Very good. Next prisoner, step forward."

Another CO then ushered Casey into the next bay where she was forced to shower in front of another nosy guard. "Good 'nuff," the man said. "Get over to property and pick up your stuff." Naked, wet, and shivering, Casey was escorted down to clothing and issued new scrubs, a pillow, mattress pad, and a blanket that smelled like sex. The sounds of alarm bells and trampling feet solidified to Casey she was a long way from West Fellers. Prisoners goaded the freckled-faced kid as a guard led her to her cell, they threatened to christen her when the time was right. A scar-faced woman gave her the most grief. "Fat-ass bitch." *Toof.* The lady spat in Casey's face. "You on my block now, ho." Casey flicked the gunk from the side of her head and continued down the corridor to her cell.

"In there," the woman CO pointed. "C'mon now, don't get all scared on me."

Naked and with spit particles still stuck in her hair, Casey hurried past the guard and into her cell. She entered the crammed space and looked around at the impenetrable walls and zoned out. *Holy shit. I'm in prison.* The guard who directed her inside yelled down to the gate operator. "Yo, Gil, close it up!" Casey's iron door emerged from the wall, barricading her inside her eight-by-ten asylum. She dropped her things onto the bed and rushed to the door.

"Please, don't go!" Casey whimpered. "I'm only seventeen. I'm just a stupid kid. What am I supposed to do?"

The CO trimmed her eyes at Casey.

"Do you believe in God?"

Casey thought hard about that question.

"I-I-don't know," she stammered. "Why? Should I?"

"I wouldn't, if I were you," the CO said. "There ain't no God here." The CO turned and left, leaving Casey speechless. She ambled over to her dull cot, dressed herself and slowly made up her new bed. She walked over to the stone wall and touched its rocky surface. Reality jolted her as she backed onto her cot, covering her mouth. The thin mattress felt like an ironing board. She sat there, contemplating her young life. Overwhelmed, she draped her blanket over her head and howled quietly so no one could hear her.

Letters

Casey cried a lot during her first six weeks at St. Agnes. The regret crippled her. At first, Courtney would drive six and a half hours one-way across the state every other weekend to visit her inside a supervised room with guards mounted at every exit. They'd hold hands and exchange tears before guards separated them at the thirty-minute mark. For Casey, the thirty minutes felt like three. "No, please, five more minutes!" COs ignored her request and upended the girls' visit. It broke her each time when Courtney had to leave. "I'll see you in a couple weeks, Case," she'd say. Casey would watch her sister turn at the end of the hall before returning to her cell, devastated.

Courtney's letters were the only thing that gave Casey hope during those first six weeks. In the letters, Courtney would often apologize to her for being aloof during their high school days. Her letters would typically begin with an *I'm sorry* or some other kind of shamefaced opening. And no matter what, all of Courtney's letters would end with, *See you soon.* She'd draw little butterflies at the end of each message before buttoning it with her signature. Courtney would mail Casey a box full of their old summer pictures from when they were both thirteen. She once sent a coloring book the two had shared. *We never did finish this,* Courtney wrote. *Maybe you'd like to?*

While Courtney seemed determined to repair the damage with Casey, the Haughtons were less enthused about their felon-daughter. The air felt dead whenever Casey would call, and her father was short with her. "Well, I appreciate the call, but Courtney's not here right now. She's at *school,*" he once emphasized. Mrs. Haughton was a tad more forgiving. "Yeah, Casey, we didn't forget about your commissary—we'll get around to it." Cased started timing her calls to coincide with Courtney's schedule. She sniveled into the phone one afternoon while explaining the cold treatment she received from her parents.

"You just gotta give 'em time, Case," Courtney advised her. "They'll come around, eventually. Right now, it's still early. It's hard on us all."

Casey thumbed her eyes.

"Well, I hope so. I mean, you're the only one who visits me, you know. I feel like shit each time I call my own house. It's just so hard being away from y'all. I'm struggling in here, Court. It's like, some days I don't know if I can make it."

Casey seldom brought it up, but St. Agnes was its own erratic world. During her first week, Casey saw an inmate die over a honey bun. That same week, she watched another inmate get stabbed during a card game. There were fights every day—brutal fights—with minimal intervention from correctional staff. Most of the COs were just as atrocious as the inmates they policed. Some instigated fights between rival female gangs to keep convicts divided, and the male COs often solicited inmates for sex in exchange for perks. Offended, the female COs would take out their frustrations on the prisoners. The prettier inmates were isolated or punished for asinine violations: showering a minute longer than the allotted three minutes or failing to stay in a single-file line. The water at St. Agnes was unsanitary and as many as three or four inmates would share one shower head at a time. Inmates passed their time by playing cards, dominos, chess, checkers or hanging out in the communal areas. Casey passed her time by writing letters and reading law books, hoping to find a chink in her conviction worth exploiting.

By October, Casey's communication with Courtney seemed feint. Desperate, she called home looking for answers.

"What's going on?" Casey asked her mother. "I sent a letter to you and daddy a few weeks back—I still need money for my commissary. I can barely afford cigarettes. And where's Courtney? She barely visits me—and her letters are short."

Mrs. Haughton exploded on her. "Look, now isn't the time, Casey. Nobody's worried about a commissary account at some goddamn jailhouse right now. Okay? We have lives."

The Haughtons' silence kept her on edge. *Are they finished with me?* Casey wondered. She lingered out in the yard puffing on Kools, plucking butts into a patch of dewy grass, thinking. Her eyes filled with hopelessness as she surveyed the towering, gated walls and realized she'd spend the holidays couped inside of a steel box. When Casey did finally catch Courtney, she had more to worry about than what decorations to hang around her cell. Courtney stammered through the call.

"D-d-doctors found a tumor on Dad's lung, Casey," she stuttered, barely able to get it out. "I would've told you sooner, but… I-I-It's not looking too good."

The fact that Courtney had kept their father's diagnosis a secret made Casey sick.

"Well, why didn't you tell me sooner?" Casey swiped her damp cheek. "I know I can't do much from in here, but he's my father, too. How long has he been sick?"

"A little while, I guess. He started having stomach pains right around the time you… look, all I know is that it's getting hard to keep a smile on my face and act like everything's fine when it isn't. I feel like I gotta be the strong one. Mom isn't taking it so well."

"Well, you know I'm here for you guys, right?" Casey spoke up. "You know that right?"

Casey's eagerness was met with silence. She was miles away and not returning to West Fellers anytime soon.

"Look, I gotta go. Call me later," Courtney said. "I'll tell you more about it."

"You do believe me Courtney, right?"

Courtney hesitated.

"Of course… We'll talk soon."

Casey held the phone long after Courtney hung up. She closed her eyes and tapped the device against her forehead, bummed. She was useless to her family from behind bars. She returned the phone onto its hook and slogged back to her iron box to lament her pitiful existence.

Each time Casey called home, her father's condition had worsened. She'd read through Courtney's cute letters but skipped the parts about their father's cancer. She was still adapting to the black-heartedness of prison life after serving only a few months. Meanwhile, her world seemed to be coming down all at once. Two weeks passed before Casey worked up the courage to call home again. By then, she was barely sleeping and so windswept about her situation that she was depressed. She coddled the phone beside her head, anxious of what bad news she'd receive next. Courtney's voice buckled as she provided the latest update.

"Doctor said the cancer spread. He'll be lucky if he sees the new year."

Casey placed her head onto the phone box and exhaled into the receiver.

"I just don't get it. Where did this all come from? she asked. "Is it my fault? Am I the one who made him sick?"

"Casey—"

"No, don't sugarcoat it. It's my fuckin' fault!" she blamed herself. "If I'd never went to that stupid-ass liquor store with my stupid-ass friends, I'd be home."

Courtney didn't say anything, but she didn't disagree, either.

"Dad wants to talk to you, hold on."

Casey's mind flashed to the good times they'd shared when the Haughtons were a family—carnival visits, weekends in Manhattan, s'mores in the backyard, and catching lightning bugs in a jar in July.

She cleared the lump inside her throat as Mr. Haughton answered the line. The man was barely intelligible, he was so weak.

"Hel-hel-lo?"

"Dad?" Casey began to cry. "Dad, I'm so sorry. I screwed up. I'm supposed to be home."

"You already are," he said.

He never said he forgave her, but it felt like forgiveness to her. He chuckled before choking on his own humor as a violent cough ripped through the line. He was so sick, Casey could hear it when he laughed. She paid her respects to the father who'd given her the home she'd never had by calling every day for weeks. Before long, the cancer depleted Mr. Haughton so badly that he could barely talk. Casey would call the house some days just to talk to him—his hearing was still sharp.

"Hi, Daddy. You know I love you, right?" she'd say. "You gave me a home to feel proud of, and you taught me the meaning of family, when I didn't know what that was."

He replied with a grunt. *Mmph.*

Casey continued. "I know, Daddy. I think about it all the time… I just really hope you can forgive me for what I did some day."

Out in the yard, Casey sat on a wooden bench in her prison scrubs with her head dipped down at her socked flip-flops, a cigarette wedged between her fingers. She looked around at her co-inmates, some of whom were serving life sentences and wondered if she'd ever make it home.

On Friday, November 5, 1982, Casey called home to read her daddy a poem she'd penned all Thursday. She was hardly a poet but felt it in her heart to write. She dialed the house four times without any luck before finally getting through just after six that evening. She could tell by the sound of her sister's voice that things were worse than before. "He went last night," Courtney told her. "I'm sorry, sis—I really am, but we gotta keep the line clear. Mom's expecting a call from Dad's sister in Minnesota. We'll talk later."

Knees tucked into her chest, Casey sat on the floor of her cell with her back pressed against the wall. Beside her on the floor was the poem she'd written. She looked over at her blue handwriting, swept her damp face, and removed a lighter from her pocket to burn it. She tilted her daddy's poem, intensifying the blaze until the paper turned brown.

Casey looked up at her barred window into the fall clouds. Losing her father was one thing, but *we gotta keep the line clear* was equally as painful. She couldn't even grieve alongside her family during a call.

Mr. Haughton's passing gutted Casey. She rotted inside her cell for days, curled in a ball on her cot. The walls of her tiny living space closed in, smothering her. Her small world had just gotten smaller. A lifer serving time for murder passed by Casey's cell, noticed her catatonic state and offered her some advice.

"Been noticing you the past few days. You good, youngster?"

Casey glanced over at the elder convict and returned to her withdrawn state.

"Yup," the lady said. "I know that look. That's the kind of look when things at home ain't right—I've been there a couple times myself. It ain't pretty."

Casey crawled off her cot and over to her cell door.

"I just lost my dad. How do I get through this?"

"You don't. It never really goes away. It just gets buried behind the walls of time after a while—almost like in here. After a while, the concrete just covers up everything."

Casey crossed her arms and returned to her cot. She faced the wall so that the woman wouldn't see her crumble.

"I did a lot of that, too," the convict said. "Look, if you're gonna mourn, learn to mourn with a hobby. If you don't have one, get one. That's the only way you're gonna make it in here. Life's gonna happen whether you like or not." The wise woman walked off.

Casey took the murderer's advice. She returned to the library but not for law books to reexamine her case. She instead requested copies of old newspaper clippings, magazines, and other discarded publications from the past. She used the little money she'd accumulated in her commissary to buy glue and a pair scissors. For hours, Casey sat in her cell and collaged. It wasn't pretty, but it was better than a slow death. Her first picture was an elephant made of scraps from old *Jet* magazines. Seeing her creativity offered a hope she never knew existed.

Collages

Thanksgiving came and went without the festivities. Casey spent her holiday trimming items from magazines and *New York Times* papers from 1978 and '79. The time period made her smile; it was the same year she and Courtney had become sisters. She carefully trimmed out pictures of their favorite shows like *Good Times* and *Three's Company.* Casey even found a picture of Michael Jackson. She giggled as she kissed his shiny jheri curl—it reminded her of the girlish crush Courtney had on him. Their favorite movies: *Paradise Alley, Jaws 2, Grease,* and *Halloween* with Jamie Lee Curtis—Mr. Haughton had taken the girls down to the old drive-in. Casey pasted the severed pictures onto a white poster board and hung it inside her cell. A passing CO scoffed at her art.

"Th'hell is that supposed to be, Haughton?" The guard laughed at her.

Casey looked over at the sloppy watchman and returned to her new hobby. Her eyes said "fuck you," but her mouth didn't move. She could feel the man staring at the back of her head.

"Jesus Christ, Haughton. Are you planning on going through all those old magazines? I guess that's what boredom does to the mind, huh?"

Casey ignored the patronizing guard and continued working. The CO sucked his teeth at her and moved on.

As a little girl, Casey never dreamed she might be creative, but deep down, she was. She collaged through 176 newspapers (she kept count) and 109 old magazines—the oldest she found dated back to the 1920s. She felt silly about her new hobby, but it eased the tension she felt brought on by her father's death and it emancipated her.

Meanwhile, south of Esseltown, her homelife was in disarray. She called home one afternoon in early December to check on her family and was silenced by a tone she thought she'd never hear.

"I swear, Casey, I'm gonna kill your sister one of these days," Mrs. Haughton ranted. "You really ought to talk some sense into her."

"Why? What'd she do?"

"What didn't she do? She's been cutting school, hanging out late, and smoking boat. She thinks she's so slick—get this. Last night, she showed up inside my closet and was watching me through the walls while I was trying to sleep. Damn girl is driving me nuts."

"I'll talk to her."

Casey waited a day for the tension to ease at home and called the next day to chew out Courtney. She blasted her sister without recourse.

"What the hell, Court?" she barked at her. "Smokin' boat? Cuttin' school? Look, I know things have been hard since dad passed, but damn. And what's this I hear about you hiding inside the closet while mom is trying to sleep? Yo, that's creepy—don't be doin' that. If you wanna smoke something, try weed. Word, boat is a *whole* other animal. Trust me, I know."

"I'm not on boat or taking any other drugs, Case. Where'd you get this junk from?"

"Mom said you've been hangin' out inside her closet. Look, I know you probably don't remember much of what you did, but don't fuck with that shit—it's dangerous. Smoke weed instead, okay? See, weed is from the earth and—"

"I am not on drugs, Casey, what are you..." Courtney stopped herself. "Ho-ly shit."

"What? *What?*"

"Just the other day, mom accused one of the neighbors of the same thing. She said she thinks Mr. Reynolds is after her."

"After her? The guy had his feet amputated in Vietnam. He ain't gettin' after nobody."

Casey hung up the phone that afternoon feeling worried about her mother's state. She was halfway through her first year at St. Agnes and slowly adjusting to her barred world. Between prison stripes, grief and family drama at home, her collaged world remained unsteady.

Casey had witnessed a lot of grisly things as a kid growing up in the city, but St. Agnes took the cake. COs were brutal, prisoners were impractical and assistance with mental health was nonexistent. One inmate from 4B gouged out her eye at breakfast with the sharpened end of a tooth brush. A woman in 5D signed her death warrant by scaling the fence out in the yard. "Halt!" A guard screamed from the PA system in the tower. Prisoners cheered on the shit-show, providing the climber an audience. Casey was having her morning cigarette at the time and reading a letter from Courtney before stopping to look up. The guard raised his rifle at the climber. "Get down from there, or else I'm gonna shoot you down," he threatened. The woman continued climbing, ignoring his orders. There was no chance in hell the woman could've possibly escaped, by Casey's estimation. The fence was too tall and she was nearly out of breath and not even close to the middle. Even if the climber had made it to the top, a row of razor-sharp wires awaited her, followed by a second tall gate with even more barbed wire.

The guard in the tower eventually obliged her. *Blam.* The shot jerked Casey involuntarily. All the cheering and hype ceased as the woman fell onto the sandy asphalt. Chatter permeated throughout the yard as if bystanders there didn't know that a hot-shit rookie was sitting in the tower with a rifle, itching to try out his new toy.

The woman's name was Annette Marsha Lewis. She was fifty-six years old with two kids and an ex-husband. According to the rumor mill, she'd been convicted in 1948 for strangling her cousin for sleeping with her then husband. She perished a short time after being shot and was buried on the prison farm. Her tombstone was a cross made with two pieces of shitty PVC pipe held together by a bootstring. Instead of writing her name, guards jotted her prisoner ID number. Casey penned the horrific ordeal in a letter to Courtney. *Girl, you won't believe this sick shit I just saw…*

Casey found it difficult to turn a deaf ear to her mother's eerie condition. The phone calls were weirder and Mrs. Haughton's proclamations of Courtney hiding inside her closet changed to Courtney now trying to kill her.

On Christmas morning, Casey called the house to wish her family a Merry Christmas and didn't get an answer. She called the day after, and the day after that but still couldn't get through. Courtney showed up at the prison days before the new year. When Casey entered the visiting lobby, she noticed her sister's frazzled hair and anxious bug eyes and quickly sat down. The expression on Courtney's face made it clear that she hadn't slept in days. The girls held hands as they talked.

"She ain't right, Case. Mom ain't been right since Dad died."

Casey rubbed her sister's hand. "What's happening to her?"

"She's up all the time at night, mumbling to herself—I can hear her through the wall. I'm afraid she might hurt herself." Courtney fought back tears. "The doctors think she's got some form of psychosis going on. Plus, the bank is threatening to take the house. Our mortgage is behind."

"Is there a way you can talk to 'em and let 'em know what's going on? I mean, shit, there must be something they can do?"

"Banks don't care, Casey. They just want the stupid money. Mom's been with Dad since she was fourteen—*fourteen*. I'm so worried about her. I can't even leave her by herself. I had to get Uncle Artis to watch her just so I could come visit you. It's like… I don't know what to do anymore, you know. Between this and school, I feel so overwhelmed."

The girls spent the rest of their visit strategizing how to get their mother help until a CO interrupted them. The guard banged the butt of her metal baton on the girls' table.

"Time's up, Haughton. Let's start gettin' back."

Casey clasped her small hands together.

"Please, ma'am," she begged. "May I have just a couple more minutes with my sister? My father died last month, and my family is going through a lot with that."

The CO looked at her. "Girl, I don't give two shits about your father or your mother," the guard sniped. "You're a piece-of-shit convict. Now, head back to your cell. NOW."

Casey's jaw tightened with rage. If it wasn't for Courtney gently stroking her leg beneath the table, she would've lunged at the guard and ended up in solitary confinement. She bit her tongue.

"It's okay, Case," Courtney told her. "I've got to get going, anyway. I'll come back to visit another time. Call me tomorrow."

Casey eye-fucked the merciless guard. She rose to her

feet slowly. The female CO gave her a smirk, bitching Casey in front of her sister.

"Th'hell you lookin' at? You got a problem, convict? Take it up with the warden. C'mon, let's go. Hurry up, before I ban all your visits."

The guard walked off. Casey clenched her fist to go after her before Courtney quickly interfered. She grabbed Casey by her face.

"Do-not," Courtney whispered. "They're just trying to break you, Case, remember that." She pecked Casey on the cheek and left.

When Casey returned to her cell, she went ballistic, crying and cussing. She destroyed one of her collage sets, ripping it in half. She lifted the mattress from her cot, hurled it against the wall and punched her mirror above the sink, spider-webbing the glass. High on pain and rage, she bellowed, "Fuuuuck!" Casey wanted the guard's head on a stick, but more than ever, she wanted to be home where she belonged. She collapsed onto her cell floor, broken.

Doctors classified Mrs. Haughton's diagnosis as dementia, anxiety, and depression as a result of her husband's death. Courtney classified their mother's condition as the symptoms of a broken heart. Gloom ensued over the next several months as Mrs. Haughton slowly deteriorated. In a letter dated Tuesday, March 8, 1983, Courtney penned, *I think she wants to die—* Casey shoved her sister's letter beneath her cot along with the rest. She returned later that evening to read the rest of it. *—The other day, I came in from school and* *found her standing at the stove with the pilots all burning, but nothing was on them. She was completely naked. Graduation can't come soon enough. At least that way I can be home more to help.* Courtney's letters triggered Casey so badly that she stopped reading them. During an April visit, Courtney arrived at the jail with more devastating news.

"Mom's gonna be in a home for a little while until things get better. It's the only way to—"

Casey rose from her seat in disbelief. She walked over to the window and pressed her forehead against it.

"Well, what else I was supposed to do, Casey?" Courtney asked.

"How long?"

Courtney deflated. "I can't say. Hopefully not long. Her sister is comin' in from Chicago. My guess is until she gets better."

"Gets better? Lately, it seems like nothin' has gotten better with me still in the picture. Everything is just all *fucked* up."

"Please don't do this right now, Casey."

"Do what? Apparently, I've done more than enough over the past year."

"What's happening to our family right now isn't your fault," Courtney explained to her. "That's not why this is all happening. It's just… life stuff. Dad got cancer because it runs in his family. Mom's going through her spell because she's upset about Dad passing away—c'mon."

Courtney joined her at the window and reached for her sister's hand.

"I'm goin' crazy—not being able to be there for y'all." Casey wiped her eyes. "I can't believe I stuck myself in here like this. Feel like I just wanna roll over and die."

"Well, you can't."

"Why the hell not?"

Courtney's eyes teared with desolation. "Because… then I'll be all by myself."

Casey looked at her. She tightened herself up in that moment and played the role as the responsible, sturdy sibling. She grabbed Courtney by her sweet head, pulled her sister onto her shoulder and kissed her hair.

"C'mere-c'mere. I got you." Casey placed her head onto Courtney's and left it there. It was hell trying to keep her family together from behind a thirty-foot wall wrapped in barbed wire. She barely had time to console her sister before two CO dicks showed up to separate them.

"Time's up, Haughton."

"Just a couple more minutes. C'mon, guys. Gimme a break with this shit—"

"You heard what my partner said! Visiting hours are over. Now move along before I write you up and have your visitations banned for ninety days."

Casey exploded.

"Well, write me up then, motherfucker!" Her lips foamed. "Show some compassion for once? Can't you see what's goin' on?"

Courtney stepped in. "Casey, just go. Call me later."

"No, Courtney, no!" she fussed. "I'm not reading any

more letters. I'm not calling you on the phone. I'm not gonna sit here a-a-and just watch my life fade away. I'm going home with you today, and nobody's gonna stop me. End of story."

"You can't, Casey. You just can't."

"Why the hell not?"

"They'll kill you!" Courtney seeped inside her tired hands as loathing guards looked on at the two. "You wanna help me out? Go. Go before something happens to you, too. Go, Casey!"

Casey thumbed at her eyes and turned to leave. She stopped at the door to somberly acknowledge her sister's weepy goodbye. An apathetic guard nudged her from behind.

"C'mon, Haughton, let's go."

Casey dropped her head and moved along.

Next of Kin

A week before Mother's Day, May 1983, Casey flipped on a CO during cell inspection and lost both her phone and visitation privileges. A guard provoked her wrath by dumping a box filled with old photos of her and Courtney from their childhood.

"You punk-ass bitch! You did that on purpose!" She lunged at the guard.

The ill-advised move cost her four weeks of contact with Courtney. They held up her calls and confiscated all her old and new mail as if she was part of some sort of trafficking conspiracy. At the end of their baseless investigation, her letters and memorabilia were returned. Casey thumbed through her dated stack down in the prison's property section in front of the same guard who'd gotten her into trouble weeks earlier.

"Oh, I almost forgot." With a smug look, he removed a new, already-opened envelope from a batch of seized mail. "I'd call home, if I was you."

As Casey reached for the letter, the guard moved it.

"Now, what do you say?"

Casey sighed with defeat. "May, I please have the god-damn letter, sir? Please?!"

As the CO finally gave up the letter, Casey snatched it from his hand and bolted down the corridor to the nearest phone to call home. The line rang nearly a dozen times before Courtney finally answered. Her melancholic tone was immediately noticeable.

"Courtney? Courtney, it's me!" she panted, still out of breath. "I just got your letter, I haven't had a chance to read it yet, but I got it. Is everything okay? How's Mom doin'?"

Courtney breathed into the receiver.

"No, Casey. Everything is not okay. Where've you been?"

"It's a long story—fuckin' asshole guards. I'll tell you more later. Where's Mom? Is she still in a home? How's her recovery?"

There was a long pause. "She's dead, Casey. Mom passed away about two weeks ago. She had a bad fall—doctors tried everything they could to—"

The phone sagged in Casey's hand, crashing onto her shoulder. In less than a year, she'd lost both her parents. She couldn't believe it. Whatever grain of hope she had left for her future was gone.

"Courtney, listen… sis, I am so sorry that I couldn't—"

"You weren't there for me," Courtney interrupted her. "This whole time. You said you'd have my back, and you didn't."

"I tried, I really did, and I'm sorry." Casey split in half. "I called. I sent letters—I did the best I could despite my circumstances."

"Your circumstances? Like getting yourself locked up and leaving your family here to pick up the tab in your absence? What about *my* circumstances, Casey? What a way to say thanks to the sister that took you under her wing when you were a broken bird still learning to fly." Courtney's voice gave out. "I gave you the SHIRT from my back, and you left me all BY MYSELF!"

The phone was silent. Casey searched for the right words to express her culpability but came up short. Losing her parents was hard, but nothing cut her worse than the guilt she felt for leaving Courtney hanging. She felt just as worthless as she had on the day of her sentencing.

"I need time." Courtney swallowed. "A lot of time, and I need some space."

Casey exhausted into the line, overwhelmed. Her voice was so fractured she could barely talk. The pain sliced into her like a razor.

"Okay," she squeaked. "I understand."

Click. Courtney hung up on her. Casey returned the phone onto the hook and stuffed her hands beneath her armpits. She stared at the wall in disbelief, shocked by how quickly her life had changed in under a year. A fellow inmate tapped her on the shoulder from behind. "Are you gonna use that?" Casey moved to the side, allowing the impatient convict to use the phone. By her estimation, she wouldn't need a phone for some time. She gathered what debris was left of her wrecked heart and returned to her cell.

Two

Behind a pair of ugly bifocal glasses, Casey put the finishing touches on a miniature doll house inside her cell. Her tedious but delicate masterpiece had taken her 8,583 popsicle sticks to create. It took her 402 days—slightly over a year's worth of work. She had begun her project last June to commemorate her birthday. She glanced over at the wall and marked "finish" on her 1989 calendar. Seven years had passed since her ill-fated conviction.

With her glasses shoved over her round face, Casey operated diligently, unperturbed by St. Agnes's mayhem. Her wooden doll house was the spitting image of her teenage home back in West Fellers. Regretfully, the Haughton house had sold for cheap during the fall of '84, shortly before Courtney joined the United States Army and moved away. Off in the distance, a pair of screechy carts pushed up the corridor. *Wednesday,* she thought to herself. Wednesdays were mail days at the prison. Weeks ago, she'd sent Courtney a letter and was still waiting for her reply. The girls' contact had faded over the years. The inmate pushing the cart stopped in front of Casey's cell. "Sorry, Haughton. Try again next week." The woman pushed along. Casey returned to her doll house, not surprised.

For seven years, Casey and Courtney had traded barbs. She'd apologized a lot at first, begging for her sister's forgiveness like a dog persisting for treats. She called, she wrote letters, she'd even send money from her commissary. *Just wanted you to know I'm thinking about you, and I hope you've been thinking of me just the same.*

Courtney sent a dry response two months later. *Thanks. I'm holding on. Hope you're well.*

Casey reread the letter for days inside her cell, hoping to find a *love* or *miss you* somewhere in Courtney's nifty handwriting. Dejected, she returned the post card to its original envelope and placed it beneath her pillow.

Following their mother's death, Casey sent letters and would call often despite their adjourned relationship. In October of '84, Courtney sent Casey a photo of herself in her army uniform. She was stationed in Fort Bragg, North Carolina at the time. On the back was the caption: *Trying something new!* Casey's eyes filled with surprise. *North Carolina?* She had to wait another month before Courtney finally left her a number to call. Their first conversation didn't go over well.

"So, when was I gonna be part of this discussion? North Carolina?" Casey fussed. "Are you fuckin' kidding me? Why not just mail me your ass to kiss while you're at it?"

"What are you talking about? I'm nineteen years old,"

Courtney shot back. "If I wanna leave New York to start a new life then that's what I'm gonna do. I don't need a damn permission slip from you, Casey. I'm in North Carolina. Deal with it."

Casey sucked her teeth. Courtney sucked hers.

"Real mature, Courtney. Yeah, just pack up and drop off the map like you don't have a sister still living in New York. What about the house?"

"What *about* the house?" Courtney hissed. "I sold it."

"You SOLD our HOUSE?" Casey raised her voice, drawing the attention of a passing guard. She lowered to a whisper. "You sold our house? How could you do that?"

"What else was I supposed to do? It's not like you were around to help."

"So, you leave New York and send me a picture of you in North Carolina as a 'fuck you?' Is that it? Well, fuck *you*, Courtney."

"Fuck me? No, fuck *you*, Casey. The world doesn't stop just because you go to jail."

The girls sat on the phone in silent dispute.

"So, now what?" Courtney asked.

Casey flicked her shoulders. "I don't know," she said. "Guess I just have to get used to you not wanting a sister anymore. Should be easy to do considering the little we've spoken over the past year, don't you think?"

Courtney gasped. "You know what, I don't have time for this nonsense. I gotta go."

"Yeah, I'll bet you do."

Casey lived a strict routine throughout her bid at St. Agnes. Her day started at 5 a.m. every morning for formal count by the prison's captain. Counts happened in the mornings, late evenings, or at random. Convicts working the kitchen had to be up by 3 a.m. since inmates hit the cafeteria to eat by six. There were two breakfast shifts: 6:00 to 6:45 a.m. and 6:45 to 7:30 a.m. The food was shit—you wouldn't feed it to a dog: lumpy oatmeal or grits, biscuits that could be used as a blunt object, toast, undercooked meat, and a blueberry or banana muffin. Coffee and fruit drinks were served on a first come, first serve basis, and the utensils were all unsanitary with speckles of yesterday's meal still visible. The water tasted like it had come from a toilet.

After breakfast, inmates with jobs reported to work. Assignments included: cook, barber or hair stylist, maintenance, tattoo shop, clerical work, infirmary, library, laundry, laborer, mail room, wood shop and manufacturing (where Casey was assigned) and landscaping duties. All assignments were under supervision. COs carried on their person handcuffs, a radio, a leather slapjack, and a cattle prod for troublesome inmates.

Lunch shifts were 11:00 to 11:45 a.m. and 11:45 to 12:30 p.m. Workdays ended at five on the nose. Inmates were allowed a shower, recreation time in the yard, gym or library. Working inmates earned $0.21 per hour, Monday through Friday, and the money was automatically deposited into each inmate's commissary account bi-weekly. A bottle of lotion cost $3.05. Hair conditioner averaged $2.08, and a stick of women's deodorant was $1.58. It took Casey two weeks' worth of pay to cover two feminine products.

Dinner was served from 6:00 to 6:45 p.m. and 6:45 to 7:30 p.m. After dinner, inmates had the option of attending class or other developmental activities such as anger management, alcohol or drug rehabilitation classes, or poetry and book clubs. Casey chose neither. She spent her free time in the lounge area playing cards or watching TV with other uninterested convicts. At 8:15 p.m., the prison conducted its final head count and by nine (depending which captain was working) all inmates were secured inside their cells for the night.

Casey hated her job in the woodshop, but she needed it to earn wages. She cut and sorted wood using a machine. She wore a white construction hat with bifocal eye protection, gloves, and a fluorescent safety vest. She was a genius at distinguishing the different wood types.

"Yo, Haughton." An older inmate appeared behind her one day with two slabs of wood. "Which is which?"

Casey rubbed her double chin, looking over the two pieces. "Hmph… This one's oak," she pointed out. "And this one should beeee walnut—with mahogany."

The lost inmate thanked her and returned to work. Despite her usefulness, Casey had a short fuse. She was fired from her first job as a cook for blowing up on her supervisor. "Look, I ain't no damn Aunt Jemima, man." Casey tossed her apron into the garbage. "You want pancakes? Make 'em yourself. I'm out."

Casey's second job was in the laundry center before she

was fired from there, too. Same reason: her dirty mouth.

"You want *me* to handwash this nasty-ass blanket just because the washer is down? For cryin' out loud, it's got cum juice all over it. What am I supposed to do with that?"

"But it's your job—"

"Yeah, *was* my job. Here you go." Casey untied her apron and handed it to the boss.

Casey wouldn't have gotten the job in the wood shop if it hadn't been for her girlfriend, Sheena Washington. The two met during a card game in the spring of '85.

"So, you shot at two people inside a mall and only got eleven years?" Casey asked. "I should've had your lawyer. How'd you pull that one off?"

"Easy," Sheena giggled. "I missed! Do you really think I would've got eleven years if I had hit those girls I was aiming for?" She threw down a queen of spades, laughing at her own misfortune. "That was all God."

Casey and Sheena became thick as thieves. Originally from Chicago, Sheena Washington had run away from home when she was fourteen and fled to New York with dreams of becoming an actress. Like Casey, Sheena ran into the wrong crowd and ended up in prison. She was a cute, petite woman with brown eyes and long hair (which she kept long to cover a large scar at the base of her head). Less than a week after they'd met, Casey had a job in the woodshop and by the second week, the two were seeing each other.

The first time Casey had kissed a girl was when she was fifteen. She did it for money at the time. The crew she was hanging with in Brooklyn double-dared her and offered her ten dollars to kiss another willing participant. Growing up, she'd always had questions about her sexuality but was too bashful to fully disclose her feelings. She wrestled with her prerogative for years. Surrounded by women in the huge iron box, the choice was easy to make.

Her first uncoerced kiss happened when she was twenty years old. She and Sheena were sitting out in the yard beneath the watch tower when her friend and workshop colleague stole a sweet kiss. Casey's pale face turned red with delight. The kiss made her heart strings tighten, and her skin prickled with the crawling feet of ten thousand lady bugs. Reluctant at first, she tittered and returned an amateur kiss, unable to hide her beaming grin.

"Why'd you stop?" Sheena placed her hand over hers. "What you so scared of?"

Casey covered her face. "I don't know. I just... I don't know."

Sheena lapped her again... and once more on the neck for good luck. Casey turned her head, pink with giddiness. Sheena ran her fingers up Casey's arm and fondled her neck. She giggled and tilted her head to the side.

"Ayeee, okay, a'ight!" she screeched. "Quit lookin' at me like that," she cheesed.

"You scared of me?"

"No, I ain't scared you. Now, shut up!"

Sheena got up from the bench and extended her hand. "C'mon, let's go."

"Where we going? I gotta be back at the woodshop in a little bit."

"No shit, Casey. Now, will you please just c'mon? Stop being so scared."

Casey reached out to take Sheena's hand, allowing her friend to guide her throughout the prison and into an unchartered area of their weary institution.

From the Other Side

"**H**ere they come, y'all, look!" A lifer pointed through the wired fence from the courtyard at an ugly white bus as it made its way onto the campus.

"Fresh meat, ladies," a CO yelled from the loudspeaker. "Let's give our guests the standing ovation they deserve, yes?"

Casey and her fellow convicts out in the yard swarmed at the gates, awaiting the arrival of the bright-eyed novices to start their bids. Casey was in the middle of a card game and left to join the fun. Rookie felons piled onto the blacktop in a single file line. Casey grabbed the gate and shook it like a maniac. Before long, Sheena showed up to participate.

"Girl, you have no idea how much I was lookin' forward to this," she told Casey. "Guards said they got another bus coming in Thursday and Friday of next week. I can hardly wait!"

"Me neither," said Casey.

Thunderlips showed up on the blacktop with her customary hat and began whacking out inmates, the same as she had done seven years earlier. COs and veteran inmates both celebrated the cruelty. It was funny at first, watching new felons double-over in agony or collapse onto the pavement. Casey wagered two cigarettes that Thunderlips's hands could hold up. She hit one felon so hard that the poor girl struck her head against the ground and suffered a seizure. The kid reminded Casey of Courtney during their high school days. The grisly sight ceased her celebration.

"I'll be at the table if you need me."

"Why? What's wrong?" Sheena asked. "I thought you loved first days?"

Casey looked over at the pile of spilled bodies on the other side of the gate. She shook her head and walked off.

"Here's your two cigarettes. I'll be over at the table."

By July of '89, Casey had been an inmate for seven years at St. Agnes. She had gotten used to her routine, made a few friends and enjoyed a few activities which helped to past the time. Life in the box was easy compared to the outside. She had a roof over her head, three square meals, a job, girlfriend and a peace of mind. She was pitifully comfortable amidst the chaos happening all around her. Sheena and her cronies showed up at the table after the shit show by the gate. Casey was shuffling a deck of cards with her back facing the crowded fence.

"Yo, why'd you leave?" Sheena asked. "You good?"

Casey tapped the cards against the table. "Deal up."

She divvied her cards to Sheena and the other players there. Just as she began reviewing her hand, a CO rushed over to get her.

"Got a visitor, Haughton," the guard informed her. "Thirty minutes—not a second longer."

Casey looked over at Sheena and the other players, confused.

"Visitor? For me? Sorry ladies, gotta run."

Casey placed her hand face down onto the table and got up to leave. Across from her, she could see the air leave Sheena.

"Who is it, Casey?" another player asked.

"Who *else?*" Sheena threw up her hands. "Her army-brat sister, Courtney."

The group groaned with displeasure as Sheena continued to complain.

"She's such a flake," she continued. "What is she even doing here?"

Casey kissed Sheena on her jealous lips and headed inside. "I'll be back."

Sheena had hated Courtney from the moment Casey first mentioned she had a sister. Courtney had visited twice since their parents had passed. Her last visit was two years ago, but the prison went into lockdown before the girls could see each other and she was forced to leave.

When Casey entered the visitation area, she glanced throughout the loaded room and noticed her elegant sister dressed in her army uniform, seated toward the back. She returned to the hallway, out of breath. Seeing her sister after a long while always made Casey's heart clatter. It reminded her of staring in the face of her idol or favorite celebrity—she needed a minute to gather her thoughts. Courtney's grace was like a mirror reflecting back at Casey, showing her how much of a piece of shit she truly was. She pep-talked herself into going through with the visit. *She's just your sister. She ain't no better than you.* Casey straightened her collar and hair before entering. Courtney glowed from across the room. Her pictures throughout the years never did her justice. She rose to her feet as Casey walked over to greet her.

"Hey," Courtney said softly.

Casey returned the favor. "Hey. Long time, no see."

The girls hugged awkwardly before taking their seats.

"What are you doing up this way?" Casey asked her. "Couldn't believe it when a guard told me I had a visitor. Seems like forever."

"I'm in town on business. Thought I'd ride up since I'm not usually out here much these days. How you been?"

"Livin' the dream."

"Yeah?" Courtney giggled. "Wish I could say the same. Army's been rolling me all throughout the country like a bowling ball since basic training. You get my letter?"

"Which one?"

"The one I *sent*." She cut her eyes at Casey. "I bet you didn't even read it."

Casey played with a spot inside of her palm, a guilty habit she picked up as child whenever she was in hot water. Courtney shook her head at her.

"Wow, Case. I mean, just… wow."

"Okay, I didn't read the damn letter. I don't know, I just… I get all emotional and stuff when I read—you know how I am. I just haven't felt up to it. Now, what are you really doing up this way? Esseltown isn't a military township, from what

I recall. What'd you think, I'm stupid? Now, are you here for me, or do you have a hillbilly boyfriend nearby named Cletus that you haven't told me about yet? Which one is it?"

"Both, actually," Courtney laughed. "But his name isn't Cletus, it's Uncle Sam, and I *am* here on business which is what I wrote to you about. You would've known that if you read it."

"Well, I didn't. So, what'd you write? C'mon, I only got a few minutes. The guards carry cattle prods now, and I don't feel like gettin' zapped. Spill it."

"Fine." Courtney cleared her throat. "I'm moving back to New York in August."

Casey gave her sister an incredulous look. "For real?"

"Yup. For real." Courtney nodded. "The army offered me two choices: Biloxi or Brooklyn." Courtney weighed her hands. "I'm not sure how safe the South is for a sista—even as a sergeant in the army, you know."

"Yeah, well, Brooklyn ain't exactly a cakewalk either, Courtney."

"True, but at least I can be closer to home where I'm comfortable and not have to worry about someone spittin' in my coffee or angry townsmen tying me to a tree."

The thought of Courtney moving back to New York should've excited Casey, but it didn't. She'd lost hope for a life on the outside and hadn't given much thought of getting out. In prison there were no bills, taxes, jobs or expectations to pursue the "American Dream." In prison, *everybody* was a piece of shit—including the guards.

"Well, I'm glad the army accommodated you, Courtney," Casey told her. "Shit, you can't beat living for free, whether it's in Mississippi or New York."

"I wouldn't say it's free, Casey—nothing's free. That's a load of crap."

"Yeah, well, you've got your philosophy, and I've got mine."

"If you're scared of the outside world, just say it."

"Why don't you kiss my fat ass? What if I say that instead?"

"Dammit, Casey," Courtney raised her voice. "Why do all our visits or calls have to end like this? Two sisters shouting at one another?"

"That's because you think you're better than people."

"Pleaseeee, I do not. What are you even saying right now, Case?"

"I'm sayin' that you should've never left New York in the first place—that's what I'm sayin'. You couldn't even tell me. Suddenly, you're in North Carolina with army gear, a hat and a big stupid rifle on your shoulder, you fuck. You act like you were the only one grieving after Mommy passed away."

"Yeah? Well, I wish I had that big stupid rifle right about now—I'd put it up to your forehead and pull the trigger until the *goddamn* thing was empty!"

A team of guards surrounded the girls as they continued to bark at each other. Casey had Courtney's beautiful face so contorted with anger that her eyeballs were bulging from her head. They fussed at each other through the rest of their visit before guards intervened.

"I think this visit is over, ladies. Wouldn't you say so?"

Teed off, Courtney grabbed her bag and left. The two battled over the last word like children.

"Yeah, that's it, run! Run, like you always do," Casey yelled from the visiting area. "Give my regards to Uncle Sam. I hope he cums all over your face… in Biloxi!"

Courtney gave her the finger. "Well, at least I *can* go to Biloxi. Where you goin', huh? Nowhere! You'll be ninety-five years old before you even know what cum on your face feels like!"

"Fuck you."

"Fuck *you*."

Casey kicked open the door leading back to the yard.

Before lights out, Casey sulked in front of a janky television box watching *Golden Girls* alongside Sheena in the common area. On and on her girlfriend went: Courtney this. Courtney that. She yapped, picking at Casey's scar. "I mean, why would she even come here in the first place? It doesn't make any sense."

Sheena had more than just good looks; she had the biggest mouth Casey had ever seen, and she was undoubtedly as jealous as they come. She threw an angry fit once when Casey showed her a picture of Courtney smiling in her army uniform. Sheena had suspected Casey was cheating on her and snatched the picture from her hand.

"Who the hell's this—you seein' her over me?"

Casey took back her photo. The two were hanging out inside her cell at the time. "She's my sister. Chill the fuck out." Sheena had no chill when it came to her relationship or any other instance when she felt threatened. She flipped out when Casey showed her a box full of letters and old pictures dating back to 1978. Now, Sheena was jealous that Casey knew Courtney longer than she'd known her—Casey couldn't win. Every call, letter, visit or contact Casey had with Courtney, Sheena put her nose in it.

"So, about this Mississippi thing," Sheena mentioned.

Casey side-eyed her. "What about it?"

"Do you think Courtney is dumb enough to even consider Mississippi after today?"

"Courtney's not dumb, Sheena," Casey replied. "She may be a lot of things, but she ain't dumb. If the army's giving her a choice, she's moving to Brooklyn. It doesn't matter to me, either way. I could care less."

"Well, I think she'd be better off in Mississippi. What does Courtney know about the city? She's a brat from the suburbs. They'll eat her alive out there in BK—she's not like us. She's a cornball and a sellout—probably grew up listening to Led Zeppelin and Lynyrd Skynyrd."

Casey glanced over at Sheena, shook her head and went back to watching TV.

"Well, it's true, right?"

"Is what true?"

"Is she not the biggest cornball you've ever seen? Didn't you tell me once she put on a pirate hat and dressed up as Pippi Longstocking for Halloween? Who does that?"

Casey handed off the remote to Sheena; she'd heard

enough. She stood on her feet, yawned and made a tyranno-saurus noise as she stretched.

"That was 1978, Sheena. It's not like America gave Black kids a lot of alternatives for Halloween during those days. Give her a break."

Sheena cut her eyes at Casey.

"Well, I'm sorry, but there's no way in hell I'd dress up as Pippi Longstocking—ever. Why are you always takin' up for that trick whenever I dog her? I thought you were on my side?"

Casey pulled Sheena onto her feet and kissed her. She slipped her hand beneath her scrubs and squeezed her petite rump. Her girlfriend giggled between smooches.

"Leave my cornball sister alone for once, will ya?" Casey kissed her goodnight and headed up to her cell.

As she turned to leave, a brawl erupted between two inmates on the second floor. Two convicts were entangled in the corner, both had each other by the hair, jockeying for leverage and position—high on adrenaline and rage.

"Get off me!" one of them shrieked. One of the ladies pulled out a shank from beneath her pants and jammed it into the other's back, repeatedly. Within seconds, the victim's white T-shirt turned red and her grip loosened.

"Quit stabbin' me, bitch!" the victim panted, out of breath.

COs dressed in riot-style gear stormed into Casey's cell block and lobbed a stun grenade. The bright blast blew out the TV and made Casey's ears ring.

"Everybody down, now!"

Casey planted her belly across the floor along with the

other disoriented convicts on her block. She looked up and noticed a guard with a shotgun pointed at her. The guard chambered a slug before placing his foot against her back. "Don't move, Haughton!" Casey didn't cough. The violence she'd gotten used to. But the stun grenades, being treated like a second-class citizen and having her possessions tossed during inspections—she never got used to that. She looked over at Sheena, wondering what was on her girlfriend's mind.

Sheena was grinning at her, amused by it all. "Some crazy shit, right? Yo, you think homegirl's gonna make it?"

Casey gave Sheena a dubious look. She pressed her face into the floor. *I gotta get out of here.*

Three

Casey mulled on the brutal fight for days after it happened. It bothered her more than any of the other muggings she'd witnessed there. Later that week, she visited her case manager in the front office to inquire about her parole eligibility.

"Name? Date of birth? Last four of your social?" the clerk asked her.

"Haughton. Six-seventeen-sixty-five. Last four: two-five-zero-six." The clerk plunked Casey's info into the system. She glanced at her to verify her identity and began typing again.

"September."

"September? Really?" She lit up with hope. "So, *this* September, right?"

The woman returned to typing on her computer. She looked up at Casey then went back to typing again. She rose from her desk, moseyed over to a large printer to retrieve a heap of papers, returned and handed them to her. Casey flipped through the stack and looked at her, confused.

"What's all this?"

"Your parole forms. You have to apply for it first. You might want to get started soon. A lot of inmates are putting in—the wait time could be crazy." The woman placed a pen onto the counter. "Can you have this back to me before lunch?"

Glee appeared on Casey's face as she swiped the pen.

"Lady, I'll have it back to you before God finds out."

Casey took a seat at a table in the back and went to work. It took her fifty minutes to complete the packet. She returned to the counter and handed it to her case manager. The woman flipped through her booklet and pointed at a blank line. "You forgot to sign here." Casey scribbled her chicken scratch and gave it back to her. The clerk nodded at her. "Great. One sec, dear." The clerk left Casey at the counter and went into the copy room and returned with a photocopy. She handed the xeroxed stack to Casey.

"You'll be notified of your hearing date in the future. I'd lookout for it."

"Hearing date?"

"Yes, you have to go before the board. You don't just sign a bunch of papers and go home." The clerk laughed at her. "A panel reviews your case and prison history to determine if you're fit to return to society."

"What are you talking about? Of course, I'm fit to return to society." Casey combated. "I'm not a fuckin' serial killer for crying out loud. I robbed a liquor store when I was seventeen—it's not like I went around slicing up kids with a chainsaw or anything."

"Then you should have no problem convincing the parole board of your eligibility." The clerk smiled. "Have a good day, Miss Haughton."

"Wait, what am I supposed to say at the board? Who's gonna be there?"

"Good day, Miss Haughton."

For four nights, Casey laid on her cot replaying the gruesome scene inside her head from the other evening. She couldn't rid the image of the assailant's blade plunging into the victim's back. The visual was burned into her memory along with the regret of her poor choices. Next to her on the bed was her paperwork from the clerk's office. She looked up and noticed a guard watching her. Casey quickly put away her forms. "Goddamn, can I have a little privacy here?" The CO snickered at her and walked off.

Prison politics at St. Agnes were devoid of democracy for staff. COs hustled an overlapping twelve-hour shift, six days a week. Day shift was from 7:00 a.m. until 5:00 p.m. Evenings were 3:00 p.m. until 1:00 a.m. Midnight crews worked from 9:00 p.m. until 7:00 a.m. Each guard was allowed two thirty-minute breaks. The warden's favorite personnel were assigned to nicer details such as protective custody (a.k.a. "PC" or "Punk City"), infirmary duty, or never worked weekends. The rest were assigned to the yard, general pop, or maximum-security. For COs working the latter, inmates were crankier and more volatile. They spat, bit, hurled shit, and did other abhorrent things. A rookie guard once got the shit kicked out of him by a woman in maximum-security. The lifer then dragged the inexperienced guard into her cell prompting a wild stand-off. The inmate was eventually subdued, and the guard was rescued, treated, and later fired. Fights happened all the time between COs and inmates. If any guard was seen by a superior getting squashed by an inmate, they were either fined, fired, or placed on suspension. The pay there was terrible, and the benefits subpar. Not to mention, there were interoffice relationships amongst staff and some COs even dated inmates. The more Casey stewed over her situation, the more she realized how badly she needed to get away from it all.

Casey stood at the phone box with the receiver in her hand, one morning. With her future in the hands of the state, she swallowed her pride and dialed Courtney. She twiddled the line cord around her fingers as she waited for her sister to accept the call. She was stationed in Missouri at the time. She brimmed with relief as Courtney showed up on the other end.

"You know, you've got some kind of nerve calling me," Courtney fired first. "I should've blocked your call."

"I know, and I'm sorry. I was a real jerk the other day."

"You're a jerk every day, Casey."

"Well, I don't mean to be. Look, how many times do you want me to say that I'm sorry? I get like that sometimes, but I don't really mean anything by it. It's all just… stress from being held up in here so long. You know I appreciate you coming up here to see me—you know that. I miss you, Courtney. What more do you want me to say?"

Courtney blew into the receiver.

"What-do-you-want?"

"Well…" Casey fiddled at the phone cord. "I could be eligible for parole soon. I sent the paperwork up a few days ago. I'm supposed to have a hearing."

"So? What's that got to do with me?"

"Well, I was just thinkin' that, you know, the last time you were here and everything, you said you had a few options on the table."

"What are you asking me, Casey? What options?"

"Well, I was thinkin', you know… options like… like returning to Brooklyn. Were you for real?"

Courtney sat in silence.

"Are you asking to move in with me?"

"Me? Hell no! Girl, are you crazy? Of course, not… well, yes—but not like you might think," Casey changed her answer mid-flight. "Just until I can get things in order, you know, temporarily."

Courtney mulled again.

"I don't know if I like that idea very much—you living with me. I have to think about that. I need some time. I'll get back to you."

"Well, how much time do you need?" Casey pressed her. "I could go before the parole board any day. I gotta tell 'em somethin', Court."

"Good. Tell them that your sister needs time to think things over because her younger sister is an asshole. Did you get that? Do you need me to repeat it?"

"No, Courtney. I think that I can manage to—"

"Tell. The. Parole. Board," Courtney repeated to Casey as if she was slow, "That. Your. Sister. Needs. Time. Should I write it in a letter for you to post up around your cell? Or would you prefer a smoke signal?"

Casey lost it. "See, why the *fuck* you gotta talk to me like I'm five or some shit?"

Courtney hung up on her.

It wasn't a "no" or a "yes," but Casey liked her chances, either way. She wore a glimmer of hope on her sleeve the rest of the week. Two Wednesdays later, the prison's in-house mail carrier handed Casey an envelope from the parole board. The packet had already been opened as expected. Casey had miraculously received an official date for her hearing—even the carrier was shocked.

"Congrats, Haughton! Usually, those things take months before you receive a response."

Casey's girlfriend was less than optimistic about her chances for an early release.

"Well, I wouldn't get my hopes up on gettin' out of here anytime soon," Sheena told her. "You know how the system is. Wouldn't want you to be disappointed."

"Yeah, but there's still a chance, right? Hell, I'll take that. I spoke to Courtney about it. She said she might let me crash at her place until I get back on my feet."

Sheena rolled her eyes. "Like I said, I wouldn't get my hopes up."

"You said that already, Sheena."

"Well, I'm just trying to protect you from getting your feelings hurt. Even if you do make it out, you don't have a job, money or even a high school diploma. You think somebody's gonna hire you? An ex-felon? Big waste of time, if you ask me."

Casey stared at Sheena, wondering whether her sorrowful monologue was genuine. It didn't take her long to see through the mist. "Well, I didn't ask you. So, there you go. Either way, I'm going up before that board. Just keep the parole stuff between us. Don't let it out the bag, Sheena."

"You really think they're gonna let you out? You're an even bigger fool than I thought."

"Fine, let me be a fool. Damn, Sheena. Aren't you even happy for me?"

Sheena stubbornly played in her hair, avoiding eye contact.

"You know what? Fuck it." Casey stuffed her letter back inside her envelope. "Forget we even talked about it. I guess I'll have to look out for my own best interest from now on."

Casey took her letter and her feelings and stomped off.

The Hearing

Casey's hearing was set for July 17, 1989, at 9 a.m. She entered the room and bashfully took her seat across from the three-person board. Deciding her fate was a retired judge from New Jersey, a criminal psychologist, and an ex-state trooper from New York. Brawny COs stood near the door like bouncers at a night club. Casey could feel them eyeballing the back of her head.

"So, how old were you when you were molested by your uncle?" the shrink asked.

"Young, that's all I can remember."

"Did it happen more than once?" the trooper chimed in.

Casey coiled her head at the ex-cop. "Once is more than enough, sir," she said. "Yes, he did it several times."

The board stopped to record notes before the judge intervened.

"Tell us more about your childhood."

Casey crossed her arms. "Well, there isn't much to tell. I'm originally from Newark. My parents were both drugheads. So, I lived with my aunt and uncle for a while until that no longer worked out. From there, I skipped around in foster care before moving to West Fellers."

"Did you have any friends growing up?"

"Not really."

"Why not?" the trooper asked.

Casey's heart began to race. She bounced her knee to try to ward it off. Her eyes glittered as she recounted the horror she'd experienced from her peers.

"Miss Haughton?"

"Yeah, man, I heard you." She swiped at her tear ducts. "No friends."

The panel paused to record notes, leaving her in the dark. They shielded their faces behind manila folders before peppering Casey with more intrusive questions.

"Talk about your state of mind on the day of the robbery."

"What's there to talk about? *My state of mind*—I didn't have one," she said. "If I did, I wouldn't've gone. There was no state of mind."

"Well, where was it? Why didn't you have one?" the judge asked.

Casey rolled her eyes. By then, she was so fed up with the interrogation, she no longer gave a shit and started shooting from her hip. She moved toward the edge of her seat.

"Well, in order for you to understand my state of mind— or lack thereof," she sassed them, "I'd have to take you back to where it all started. It's hard for me to do that."

"Why is that?"

"Because I'm sitting in a room full of people who

obviously didn't have to travel down the same path that I had to. So, you'll never understand. I'm not here because I wanna be in here, Your Honor. I'm in here because it's obvious that path was a dead end. I'm here today because I'm hoping you'll allow me to somehow go back the way I came and find a new route to take."

The board stared at Casey, lost in her give-a-shit attitude. They deliberated for nearly two minutes before grilling her with more tough questions.

"Do you have any family here in New York, Miss Haughton?"

"Yes, a sister," Casey lied. Courtney was still stationed in Missouri at the time and undecided about moving back to New York, not to mention her moving in. "We talked, and if all goes well here today, she says I can live with her." Another lie.

"Where does your sister live?"

"Brooklyn," Casey lied yet again.

"Can you provide a contact number for her?"

Casey gave the panel Courtney's full name and her telephone number. She went for a few brownie points at the end of her hearing by walking over to shake each board member's hand. She raced to the phone afterwards to alert Courtney of her mischievous deed.

"You *what?*" Courtney screamed into her ear. "Girl, what the hell is wrong with you? I am still in Missouri, Casey. I haven't even been out that way to look for apartments yet—if I decide to come at all. Why would you set me up like that?"

"I had to. It's the only way I can get out of here." Casey

covered her mouth over the receiver. "I gotta have a New York address, otherwise I'm not eligible. C'mon, Courtney. Please, just work with me."

"Work with you? You're lucky I don't kill your ass." Courtney pulled her hair out through the phone. "That is so selfish—I can't believe you would do that. You go back in there and you tell them the truth."

"I can't. They've adjourned—"

"Then fucking readjourn them!" Courtney shouted. "Goddammit, Casey! You really screwed me this time, you know that?"

Casey pressed the phone to the side of her head.

"Courtney," Casey whimpered. "Please, I'm beggin' you. Son, straight up, I saw this chic get shanked the other night—I can't stay here anymore. I gotta get out of this place, man, for real. Son, I will iron your uniforms every day, wash your car, rub your feet—whatever you want. Don't leave me in here. Besides, you don't want to go to Mississippi. Yo, they be burnin' crosses in people's front yards, a-a-and they got racism, confederate flags, and big-ass dogs with swamps and crocodiles. Man, even the crocodiles be racist! Please, sis? Pretty please?"

Courtney blew into the receiver as Casey continued to whine.

"Stop whining, shut up. God, I hate when you do that," she interrupted her. "There ain't no such thing as a racist crocodile, Casey, now knock it off."

Casey shut right up, allowing her sister to think.

"First of all, let's get something straight. You do *not* make any life decisions for me. I make my own decisions. Is that understood?"

"I got it, Court."

"Good. Get this. Living with me is going to be worse than anything you've ever experienced at St. Agnes. You're gonna follow my rules, pay half the rent, go back to school and perform charitable work which I deem appropriate. You're not gonna watch TV all day and loaf around at my place playing cards or making houses out of popsicle sticks. You're gonna work. Got it?"

"What kind of charitable work do I have to do?"

"I don't know yet," Courtney growled. "It might be kissing my ass."

"Girl, I'll *wash* your ass, if you help get me out of here."

"Damn straight. Number three—this one's a biggie. If I get one phone call at my job, or if the cops show up at my place, you're done. I'll drive you back to St. Agnes myself."

"Fine, I'll behave. You won't have to worry, I swear to God."

"Swear to me! You're an asshole, Casey, do you know that? I'm already gettin' gray hair because of you and we don't even live in the same house. What a pile of dog shit, man. You're like a little tick, sucking the life out of me."

"I know."

"Yeah, you ought to know! You better hope I find something I like in the next thirty days, or else I'm gonna rip your heart out, Casey. I'll do it, you know I will. They'll be giving me the electric chair after what I do to you."

"I know. I love you, Courtney—"

"Fuck you. You love yourself," Courtney continued her rant. "You whore. You moron. You idiot. You imbecile. I wish I was in the same cell with you right about now—I'd take that popsicle house and break it over your head."

"I know, sis. But look, I gotta go. I'll call you later."

"Don't you hang up this phone, Casey. I'm not through with you yet! I'm not through—"

Casey returned the receiver onto the hook. She placed her head onto the box and exhaled with relief. She couldn't help her grin, knowing her days at St. Agnes were soon coming to an end. An inmate tapped onto Casey's shoulder from behind. She turned to look and noticed a surly convict standing behind her. "Are you done with that?"

Casey gestured at the woman, inviting her to the phone before happily returning to her cell.

Betrayal

Casey's paperwork bottlenecked during August of that year, following her hearing. That was stressful enough, but she also noticed the other inmates yapping at her more and giving her a hard time. Meanwhile, she struggled to stay off the guards' radar.

There were clerical delays in her parole process which infuriated her. "We regret to inform you that we have still not received…" It was commonplace at St. Agnes for an inmate's parole process to get pigeonholed. The worst case was a prisoner there named Bethany Hamilton. Her paperwork went missing seventeen times before she was finally released. Casey had no intention of being a resident at St. Agnes any longer than she had to. She entered the mailing room one morning and spoke to an elder convict about the discrepancy.

"You know, Haughton, if I was you, I'd stay away from that girl you've been hangin' out with—Sheena. I'd bet she's behind all this. Girl couldn't hold water if her life depended on it."

"What makes you say that?" Casey asked. "I know Sheena runs her mouth from time to time, but she really is a sweetheart."

The lady looked at her. "You mean to tell me that I know your girlfriend better than you do?" The woman laughed. "You're more naïve than I thought, Haughton. Do yourself a favor: watch your ass. You've got a long way to go before you get out of here."

On a Sunday, Casey was turning through an *Ebony* magazine on her cot, admiring the many different hair trends throughout the year when St. Agnes's riot team showed up, ready to toss her cell. She quickly sat up, confused.

"Can I help y'all?"

"Need you to step out, Haughton," one of the guards said. "I know you're hiding drugs in there. Just let us know where they are, and this'll all go peacefully."

Casey went off.

"Drugs? What drugs? she squawked at them. "Man, I don't keep any drugs in here. What the hell is all this?"

"Still gonna need you to step out so the team can conduct a full search. We have reason to believe you might be in possession of a large quantity of—"

"What reason do you have to believe that I am in possession of anything other than the skin on my back? Y'all ain't got shit else better to do than to screw with me on a Sunday?"

"Please step out, ma'am."

Casey launched into a childish tantrum as she scooted from her bed. She snatched her magazine and busted through the guards.

"So fucking stupid—outta my way, move—MOVE!" she snarled at them. "Hurry up, let's get this over with."

The guards torpedoed Casey's cell. On her sink was a small box she used to store her precious memorabilia from over the years. COs dumped it onto the floor. They used box cutters to slice open her mattress and pillow and turned her bedframe upside down, looking for narcotics. On Casey's window sill was a box of Little Debbie cupcakes she'd purchased from the commissary. They trampled her favorite snack, leaving frosted coating throughout the rubble. Another CO picked up Casey's childhood home made of popsicle sticks and looked it over.

"C'mon, man. Don't do it," she pleaded. "Just give it here, I'll take it. I'll—"

The guard dumped it onto the floor, shattering it.

"Oops!" The guard laughed and returned to trashing Casey's cell with his cronies.

In the end, no drugs were recovered. Casey sifted through the piled wreckage for any valuables left intact. Rage washed over her as she stood over her possessions. She lifted what was left of her wooden doll house and dropped it into the debris. Her precious photos were creased and covered in boot prints, and her letters were torn in half. Her bed had been stripped, and her mattress was full of puncture marks. The riot team had even confiscated her bodywash products and stolen her last three cigarettes. She restored what was left of her ragged bed and sat on it. She thought back to what the mail carrier had told her a few days ago about Sheena and went looking for her girlfriend. With her fists clenched, she headed out to the yard where Sheena often played cards.

"Sheena! Yo, Sheena?" Casey stormed across the courtyard. A smirk appeared on her girlfriend's face as she walked up. A crowd of nosy convicts encircled the two, urging them to fight.

"COs just trashed my cell over some contraband bullshit. You know anything about that?"

"What are you talking about?" Sheena grinned. "Why do you think I said anything?"

"Because you got the biggest mouth up in here, that's why. You've been jealous of me ever since I told you about my parole hearing. From now on, stay the hell out of my way, Sheena, and maybe I'll think about letting you live."

As Casey turned to leave, Sheena pushed her from behind, forcing her to the ground. Dirt flew into her face and nostrils, making it hard to breathe. Casey reminisced back to her bullied childhood.

"Let me live?" Sheena removed her earrings. "I'm from the South Side of Chicago—you know I don't play that shit, Casey. C'mon, get up. C'mon, West Fellers, what's up? You ain't no real hood chic like that. I'll rock your world, Casey, and you know that shit."

Casey glanced around at the crowd of inciting influencers, her face covered in both sand and embarrassment. She rose to her feet, dusted off her clothes and spat into the turf.

"Go to hell, Sheena." Casey walked off. "You gonna get yours one of these days."

It was the shrewdest decision Casey had made in seven years. Behind her, Sheena continued to chirp, desperately trying to goad her into blowing her only shot at escaping St. Agnes.

"Dyke-ass bitch," she scoffed. "That's why you're gonna end up right back here with the rest of us. You ain't no better. Yeah, I'll see you when you get back."

Casey gave her ex-lover the finger and kept going.

Casey's parole paperwork continued to delay and she feared for her safety. One morning at breakfast, she found a shard of glass in her oatmeal. In her chicken noodle soup, at lunch, was a mouse's tail. She hurled the disgusting bowl at the wall and stormed off. Inmates laughed at her misfortune. One evening after work, she was on her way to the showers and noticed a group of girls plotting near the entrance. Casey didn't know the girls but was sure the girls knew her. She took a raincheck instead.

Her voice quavered as she vented to an elder mail sorter working the desk. "I'm being sabotaged, Doris," she complained. "They're trying to kill me, but at the same time keep me alive. I don't wanna die in a place like this."

"You won't," Doris told her. "I will, but you won't."

"How can you be so sure?" Tears welled in Casey's eyes. She hadn't slept in days, had barely eaten and could still taste the mouse's tail she'd found. The elder woman reached across the counter and grabbed Casey by her round face.

"Breathe, dear… breathe."

A tear rolled down Casey's cheek. "I'm trying, man, but it's hard—"

"Shhhh," the woman quieted her. "What's the matter with you? Don't you have any faith, girl? Don't you believe at all?"

"How can I believe when bullshit keeps happening to me every-fucking-day—"

"*Shhhh.*" The woman silenced her again. "Believe, girl." Doris finally let her go. "Now, at my age and my health, Lord knows, I don't make many promises. But you'll be on your way out of here soon. Now, hand it over."

Casey sagged her shoulders. She handed Doris an envelope with her parole paperwork loaded inside. Doris took the package and placed it into the outgoing pile.

"My life is in there, Doris," Casey told her. "This is the fifth time I've mailed it. Please, I am counting on you." She cleared her lungs and left, leaving her fate in Doris's hands.

St. Agnes resumed its normal bustle throughout August and into September. As the weeks went by without a word from the parole office, Casey fell into despair. She zoned one night over her situation and lost it. *I'm gonna die in here.* The next day, the prison went into lockdown after inmates assaulted a guard and stole a set of keys from the main office. For three days, Casey was held up inside of her cell with minimal food or drinking water as she waited for COs to track down the culprits responsible. Once the shutdown was lifted, she jetted down to the mail room to check on her package and noticed a new face at the counter.

"Oh, Doris? Yeah, she's down in the infirmary. She ain't been feelin' too good. Not sure what envelope you're talkin' about. Can I help you with something else?"

Casey shook her head and walked off. She returned to her job back in the woodshop with a worried mind. Her day was punctuated by frequent smoke breaks where she envisioned rotting away just like Doris. She used her lunch-break to explain the deception over the phone to Courtney. "You probably won't be seeing me anytime soon—at least not as early as I thought." Her throat thickened with emotion. "They're trying to bury me, Court. They want me to die in this joint."

Courtney cheered her up with humor. "Yeah? Well, they'll change their minds after they smell your gas. Shit's worse than napalm," she said. "Okay, I gotta go. Call me when something good happens, for a change."

Casey hung up and returned to work.

On a Wednesday, Casey was playing cards with herself when she overheard the mail cart being pushed up the corridor. She threw down her stack and rushed to her gated wall, but the cart continued to roll along. "Sorry, Haughton. Not today."

Casey returned to her cot with her shoulders collapsed. She swatted at the cards, sending them flying throughout her tiny cell. She crashed onto her bed, smothered her face with her pillow, screamed and kicked her feet like a child.

"Uh, Haughton?" the carrier called to her.

Casey quickly sat up. Her hair was a mess, and her face was red with awkwardness.

"Sorry, must've been at the bottom of the stack. Here you go."

Casey soared over to take the opened package. Her eyes scrolled down to the bold print: ***You are hereby officially released on Monday, September 25, 1989, under the following conditions…*** She gasped in shock. After seven tiresome years, Casey was finally free. She squeaked and squalled, jumping up and down to the dismay of the carrier.

"Girl, are you crazy? Do you know how many women in here are lookin' for a letter like yours? Keep your good news to yourself, Haughton. Don't show your hand. Not in here."

The carrier cut her eyes at her before moving on. Casey quickly folded up her letter, placed it inside her shirt and went back to pouting like a juvenile.

Four

The iron turnstile shrieked as Casey Haughton emerged from St. Agnes Prison on Monday, September 25, 1989. Wearing blue jeans, sneakers, and a faded MTV T-shirt she'd found in the prison's donation center, she exited the grim facility and looked around. The relentless mountain air carried her hair sideways as she gawked at the gray, forested hills looming in the background. Their silky, smooth texture reminded her of a famous oil painting. She'd arrived at St. Agnes seven summers ago as a shy, overweight teen with sun-kissed freckles scattered across her round face. At twenty-four years old, she was starting from scratch with a felony conviction under her belt.

Across the lot, a bus dumped a batch of rookie inmates onto the worn asphalt. Veteran convicts lined the fences to welcome the group. "I want her—yeah, you!" An elder inmate pointed at one of the newcomers. Casey remembered standing on both sides of that fence and vowed not to miss either side. She strolled over to the huge gate and showed the guard there her release papers. The man paired her prison

ID card with her circular face and lifted the towering wall. It screeched just as it had when she arrived there at seventeen.

"Good luck, Haughton," the guard told her.

Casey continued through the dilapidated archway without response as the doors slammed against the pavement behind her. The sound made her shudder at the thought of serving a life's sentence. Immediately to her left, she noticed her sister, Courtney, dressed in denim, leaning against a blue Chevy Chevette on the side of the road. She looked like a hip parent waiting to pick up her kid after school.

"I told you that you didn't have to come," said Casey. "I could've caught a cab down."

Courtney looked at her.

"Cabbies up here don't drive down into the city. Besides, I figured I'd saved you the trouble." Courtney walked over and embraced her. "Uhm, *hello!*" she said.

Casey grabbed her back. "Hey, Court." She smiled. "Sorry, if my manners aren't up to par. I've been livin' under a rock the last seven years."

"Duly noted."

Just as the girls finished their weird hello, a whip of chilly mountain air cut beneath Casey's T-shirt. She stroked her bare arms.

"Cold?" Courtney asked.

"Freezing. You got an extra jacket or something I can wear?"

Courtney went into her trunk. She fetched out a tie-dyed hoodie from a black duffel bag and handed it to her. Casey quickly put it on and looked up at her, surprised.

"Oh, my God, what are you still doing with this thing?" She stretched out her arms as she looked it over. "You got me this for my birthday. Can't believe it still fits."

"Fifteenth, if I recall." Courtney smiled at her. "It's my airport blanky. I sleep in it when I'm on the plane. It's warm and has a lot of room."

"A lot of room? Wow, low blow. Well, I do need to lose some weight."

Courtney shook her head. "You never were that confident." She patted Casey's face. "Well, we better get going. We've got a long drive ahead of us."

Casey placed her bag in the trunk and closed it. She hoped their awkward exchange earlier was just an aberration.

The trip back to the city started out quiet between the two sisters. Casey stared out the passenger window into the passing world as Courtney cruised down the interstate. She was still processing freedom on the outside. The sky and its puffy clouds had a peculiar tint. The passing trees reminded her of the world she'd left behind. The thought put Casey at war with herself; she was a nobody again. As an inmate, she'd had a steady job earning twenty-one cents per hour as a woodshop operator. She'd had a cot, TV, hobbies, access to a library (which she seldom used since she hated reading), a place to sleep, and three hot meals. In the free world, she was a convicted felon. Reality smashed Casey in the face as she thought of all she had missed out on during her time away. Suddenly, it dawned on her. *What do I do now?* She glanced over at Courtney in the driver's seat, watching as she pushed down the highway doing seventy, humming to Stacey Lattisaw.

"Hey, can you pull over for a second? I think I'm gonna be sick."

Courtney eased her Chevy onto the gravelly shoulder. Casey unbuckled her seatbelt and sprang from the car. Overwhelmed, the thought of where her life was headed made her ill. She fetched for her cigarettes, tossed one into her mouth and sparked it. The soothing nicotine calmed her anxious mind. Before long, Courtney got out to check on her.

"You ain't sick." She closed the door. "You just wanted to smoke."

Casey exhaled. "Well, how else was I gonna get you to pull over?"

"Well, can you smoke in the car? I want to get back before rush hour."

"Rush hour?" Casey chuckled. "It's New York City, Courtney. It's always friggin' rush hour there. Did Uncle Sam make you forget? Just give me a second, will ya?"

"One… Now will you please come on?"

"I-just-need-a-minute," Casey spoke through her teeth. "I feel bad enough as it is that you have to ride home beside a total stranger."

"You're not a stranger, Case."

"Well, I feel like one!" she raised her voice. "I've been locked up for seven years of my life—let me have my damn cigarette, why don't you? Just leave me be. God, I feel like I don't even know who the hell I am anymore."

Courtney placed her hands onto her sister's trembling shoulders.

"Your name is Casey Theresa Haughton. Your birth name is Carmen Johnson, but not a lot of people know that about you. You live in Brooklyn, New York with your sister, Courtney. You both share the same birthday month, June. Your favorite color is green. You love cupcakes and fried catfish, and at night, you like to sleep with the TV on because it makes you feel like you're not alone." She held Casey by her Moon Pie face. "You may have forgotten who you are, but I didn't. You're a bitch sometimes, but no doubt about it, you *are* my sister."

Casey giggled with gratitude. Courtney laughed too.

"How come you know so much about me?"

"Because I'm your sister, dummy, I'm supposed to," Courtney sniffled.

Casey placed her head against Courtney's. Their heart-warming ceremony was soiled by the horn of a rambunctious truck driver. They laughed and wiped away each other's tears.

"Son, you be mad ugly when you cry, you know that?" Courtney chuckled.

"Fuck you," Casey laughed, drying her eyes. "Dang, you sure know how to pull at the heart strings, Court. We *are* sisters."

Courtney took Casey's cigarette. She dropped it onto the rocky asphalt and stubbed it with her tennis shoe.

"C'mon, I wasn't finished. I still had half of stick left—what the fuck?"

Courtney ignored her complaint.

"How about some new habits? Maybe I'll loan you some of my books from my old base in Fort Bragg. I used to read a lot of Langston Hughes my first year. Yooo, I heard they just built a school after him somewhere in the city. It's supposed to be some special kind of school for gifted kids. I was thinkin' maybe we could check it out on the way home?"

Casey picked up her squashed cigarette, looked it over and flicked it out into the roadway.

"I don't care about no Langston Hughes right now, Courtney—or some school—or any of your old books from Fort Bragg. That was my last cigarette, you know?"

Courtney opened the passenger door and gestured for Casey to get in.

"Off you go," she cheesed at her. "Welcome to your new life."

Casey crossed her arms and plodded into the passenger seat.

The Haughton Girls

With their hatchet buried somewhere along the busy interstate, the girls spent the rest of their long drive jamming to old tunes and reminiscing. They somehow managed to pick up where they had left off before Casey went away.

"Son, remember when you beat up Sophina Proctor at her house because she winked at your boyfriend? We were in ninth grade, right? Damn, that was funny."

"Ha-ha hell." Courtney's face tightened. "I'm still pissed about that. Skank-ass bitch."

"*Courtney?*" Casey laughed out loud. "Man, you sound like me. I go away and come back and you talk worse than I do. You never cussed like this before. What'd the army do to you?"

"What didn't they do? Sophina had it coming though, Casey. She knew I was into Marc, and then she tries to act all innocent. We made up at graduation. She's got like three kids now, I heard."

"Kids. Ugh. I couldn't imagine being a mother or just around kids, period."

Hearing about their old classmate's motherly duties made Casey realize just how much she'd missed out on. She helped herself to the glovebox and fingered through a collection of Courtney's cassette tapes. Her eyes widened upon finding the single "Smooth Operator" by Sadé.

"Son, you got Sadé?"

"Who doesn't own a Sadé tape these days, Casey?"

"Me—I ain't got one."

Without permission, Casey popped in the cassette and cranked up the volume. She grinded her hips and snapped her fingers as if she was on the dance floor at some hole in the wall night club. Courtney harped on her dancing right away.

"Girl, what was that? You call that dancing? Here, take the wheel."

"No-no-no, wait-wait-wait!"

Courtney let go of the wheel. Her '81 Chevy drifted across the freeway, nearly plowing into the guard rail. Cars beeped and flipped her the bird as she quickly took back the wheel.

"Don't you know how to drive?!"

"No, I never got my driver's license!"

The girls laughed at their close call. They rocked from side to side, grooving to the tunes of the popular music artist. Courtney had no rhythm at all. She danced like a white girl learning the Electric Slide for the first time. Casey sat back in her seat, unimpressed.

"What?" Courtney stopped herself. "What's that look for?"

"Man, you can't dance worth a shit."

"Shut up, I can dance."

Courtney ejected her Sadé cassette and turned on the radio. "Wanna Be Startin' Somethin'" by Michael Jackson was playing on the station. The girls set aside their rhythmic differences and danced together again. Courtney rolled down all the windows in her hooptie and turned up the volume. They rocked from side to side, shucking and jiving in unison as they floated down the highway doing eighty-five. When Courtney sung one side of the chorus, Casey followed through with the other. The girls didn't miss a step.

By nightfall, the sisters were less than an hour from home. A collision between an eighteen-wheeler, and a minivan slowed their momentum. They slinked down the interstate in bumper-to-bumper traffic before an exit spared them. Courtney whipped into a gas station lot. She handed Casey a wrinkly twenty-dollar bill. Casey gently pushed her hand away.

"I'll get it this time." She winked at her. "I had a little dough in my commissary. So, how much does it take to fill up this piece of shit, anyway?"

"Um, excuse me. My car ain't no piece of shit, thank you very much. I drove this bad boy all the way from Roanoke, Virginia to St. Louis, Missouri."

"Roanoke, Virginia? What were you doing way down there?"

"That's where I bought it. It's so nice there, Casey. You'd love it."

Casey rolled her eyes and went inside. She entered the gas station, still humming to Michael Jackson. She picked up a bag of barbeque chips, cigarettes, and a soda before heading to the counter where a balding middle-aged man with a funny-shaped head was reading the paper. Casey handed the man twenty dollars. "All of this and the rest on six, please." The clerk bagged her unhealthy snacks and whistled to himself. Casey couldn't help but notice his wrinkly scalp and snorted. The whistling suddenly stopped as the man looked up at her.

"What?" he barked.

"I ain't say nothin'," she replied. She noticed the name "Wilkinson" on the man's shirt. "Nice name. I like that." The man bagged her goodies, not taking his eyes off Casey and handed it to her. As soon as Casey made it back to the pumps, she came apart.

"Oh my God. Courtney, you missed it!" She clutched her stomach. "You gotta see homeboy's head. Take a look."

Courtney peeped from behind the pump.

"Jesus. How does he put on his shirts? What does he do? Step into them?"

After gassing up, the girls returned onto the freeway. Casey leaned back in her seat and propped her feet out of Courtney's window. She shoved a hand full of potato chips into her mouth and wiggled her kicks. Freedom was blissful.

"So, tell me about your pad, Court."

"Pad? English, Casey. Do you mind? What the hell's a pad?"

"Your home. Your house. Your crib. Your humble abode. Son, I bet you got a fat crib. Fuckin' waterbed. Paintings on every wall. I bet you even got one of those naked Greek statutes with the little dick," Casey giggled. "I bet his balls are out on your coffee table inside your living room."

"Don't worry about what balls go on my coffee table, okay?"

"So, there *is* a pair of balls in your life, I see." Casey sat up. "I knew all that career-woman shit was a farce. What's his name?"

"There are no Greek statues or balls inside my apartment, Casey. I'm just trying to focus on me right now, you know. Maybe you ought to do the same."

"Encroachment—defense." Casey motioned like an NFL referee. "Five-yard penalty—still third down—did I hit a nerve or something?"

"Enough with the jokes, Casey. I'm serious. Do you even know what your plans are? You're sitting on a pot of gold with this parole thing, and I just want to be clear that we're on the same page. The world's not the same as you last remember it."

"I'm a convicted felon, Courtney, not an idiot. Of course, I know that. Son, I just did seven years at one of the hardest prisons on the East Coast and lived to talk about it. I think I can handle myself out here."

Courtney's face straightened with worry.

"I'm talking about the dope, Casey. Yo, people are dying out here—it's bad. Look, we're a long way from home out here in Brooklyn. It ain't West Fellers, that's all I'm saying."

"Dope is everywhere, Court, not just in Brooklyn. Shit, girls were getting high back at St. Agnes all the time. Guards too."

"Really? How? I thought they intercepted things like that?"

"Are you kidding me? Drugs are a billion-dollar industry. Everyone's in on it. I wouldn't be surprised if the army was involved in that shit, too."

"Army? That is the most ignorant thing I've ever heard. The army's not funneling any drugs. You're just talking out of your ass now."

"You wanna bet? How's that shit gettin' here in the U.S. then? Where's it coming from? Someone has to answer for that. Drugs make too much money, and anytime there's money involved, you know the government is behind it. So, what are you gonna say now, huh, that the government isn't hiding a cure for HIV/AIDS or cancer? Wake up, Courtney. There's too much money on the table for our government to not know what the hell is going on."

Courtney blew her off.

"You've been hanging around too many of those jailhouse lawyers, Casey. Don't worry, we'll get you squared away."

Casey shook her head and went back to eating her chips.

Home Sweet Home

Casey couldn't believe her eyes as Courtney's Chevy turned off the main roadway and onto Noet Avenue. The block looked like a tryout for extras in the film *Night of the Living Dead*. The morbid city street was embattled with hookers and dope fiends. Courtney's tree fresheners swayed from side to side as her tires grinded against a section of gravely pavement. Sleepwalking drugheads pervaded the corners, walking on unsteady legs before congregating beneath the awnings of commercial buildings, teeth missing from their shifty mouths. Occasionally, a hooker appeared on the sidewalk, looking for a pay day. At a traffic light, a man with a prosthetic leg hobbled in front of Courtney's car with a spray bottle in one hand and a squeegee in the other. He sprayed and cleaned Courtney's windshield without her consent.

"Shit, I shouldn't've come this way." Courtney wound down her window and shooed him off. "Excuse me, sir?" She waved to get his attention. The man continued to clean her car. "No-no-no. No, thank you. Thaaank you. It's clean. Okay, I'm good." The man wobbled back to the median strip to wait for the next car. The light changed soon after, pushing the girls further into the city's darkness.

The area where Courtney lived was a far cry from West Fellers and reminded Casey of her old Brooklyn apartment as a kid. The unfinished pavement was stripped and rocky. Tenants loafed throughout the lot, blasting Public Enemy, Big Daddy Kane or other obnoxious tunes from their sub-woofers, puffing on spliffs as kids popped wheelies on their BMX bicycles. Courtney's building stood twelve stories high and was about as dark as Casey's past. To the right was a rusted fire escape and large dumpster. Nosy tenants plastered to their balconies, yelling at their neighbors across from them. Courtney backed her car into a spot and shut off the motor. Her lot was barely visible in the dark.

"Welcome home, I guess." She shrugged unenthusiastically. "At least it's close to work. Maybe someday I can afford one of those big townhouses over in Fort Foote."

"What are you talking about? It's home, Courtney. Can't be all that bad."

"Oh, it's bad," Courtney laughed. "C'mon, my back's stiff, and I need a shower."

Casey followed her sister across the busy lot. A group of men hanging out behind the trunk of a Ford Pinto stopped to wolf at Courtney's flawless physique. Up ahead, Casey noted a group of teenagers loitering near the main entrance, blocking the sidewalk. One of the kids was sporting a Kango hat and wore a baby-blue tracksuit with Adidas sneakers. He clowned behind a pair of bug-eyed shades and fake gold chain. A large boombox thumped from his shoulders. The kid looked to be about sixteen or seventeen, the same age as Casey when she was arrested. As the girls approached, the kids all moved except for the rowdy teen. He hogged most of the sidewalk, indifferent to them as they tried to pass.

"Excuse me, young man," Courtney said politely, but he didn't budge. "*Excuse* me, young man."

The kid tipped his shades at her. "You gotta say the magic word, sweetheart." He went back to clowning.

Casey stepped in front of Courtney and turned off the boy's radio.

"She said move the fuck out of her way! Can't you hear?" she barked at the boy.

The boy's peers all laughed at him. The kid removed his hat and placed it at his heart.

"Yo-yo-yo, sweetheart. What's all the static for? I'm just tryin' to get this here fly lady's digits. You're breaking my heart."

Casey looked the boy up and down, unimpressed. "Boy, get the fuck outta my face. A'ight? I'm not in the mood. Now, MOVE."

The boy slid from the girls' path. He mumbled as Casey bypassed him.

"Fat-ass, white bitch."

Casey's head quickly spun around. She returned to the foul-mouthed boy as Courtney lugged on the tail of her sister's hoodie, trying to contain her angry mass. The soles of her sneakers dragged against the pavement.

"No, Casey, no!"

Casey marched over to the disrespectful teen and stood in front of him, unafraid. He towered her by at least six inches.

"What'd you say? I'm a fat *what?*" Casey tilted her head. She pointed her finger into the kid's face. "Play with somethin' safe, homeboy, don't play with me. I'll hurt you out here."

"You won't do shit."

Casey stepped closer to him. "You sure about that?"

"Casey, let it go." Courtney intervened. "He's just a kid."

Casey glared at the rude boy, not blinking. She'd served time beside cold-blooded killers and could sense the kid was full of hot air. The boy looked over at his friends for validation and carried on.

"You heard me the first time," he said. "I called you a fat-ass, white—"

Whap. Casey slapped the kid hard across the puss. His Kango hat spun on his head like a cartoon character. He held his boiling cheek.

"Th'fuck you'd hit me for?!"

Whap. Casey slapped the other side, sending his hat floating to the ground. His crew laughed and paraded around him as he rubbed his tender mug in disbelief. Casey fanned her scorching hands, not taking her eyes off him. She picked up his Kango and placed it onto his bonehead.

"Now, say somethin' else! I'll kick your dick off, kid. Are we good?"

The kid's eyes blurred with embarrassment. He shook his head. "Yes, ma'am."

"Good. Now, the next time you see any adult comin' up

this sidewalk, you move your little nasty body out of the way. Don't be all disrespectful and shit." Casey looked over at the boy's crew and offered them a piece of her. "Y'all need your asses kicked too?"

"No, ma'am," they chorused.

Casey looked the boy up and down and walked off. Behind her, she overheard Courtney apologizing to them.

"Sorry, guys. Please don't sue me—I can't afford it." She followed Casey inside the building and cornered her in the hallway.

"Girl, what the hell is wrong with you? Why'd you hit that kid like that?"

"What's wrong with *me*? Did you hear what that little turd called me, Courtney?"

"Of course, Casey, I was there. He's just a kid. Look, you can't go around—"

"He's an asshole," Casey raised her voice. "Oh, please. Don't look at me like that, Courtney. I didn't even hit the boy that hard. He's lucky I'm tired. I would've knocked him back about two grades."

Courtney exhaled at her grumpy sister. She stuffed her hands inside her bag, pulled out her keys and stormed off.

"I just moved here, you know. I don't want any problems."

"Neither do I. But I'm not about to let some little wet-dream-havin', can't-even-grow-a-full-mustache little bastard with a boombox walk all over me, either. Now, where's your apartment?"

The inside of Courtney's building reminded Casey of her

old projects back in Newark. The walls were peeling and in desperate need of repainting. In the middle of the floor was a black garbage can to capture a bad ceiling leak. The large bin was nearly full. Down the hallway, a snaggle-toothed resident sat on a chair with his skinny legs crossed, sucking down a bottle of Colt 45 Malt Liquor. Beside the elevators was a security guard, asleep at his desk. The girls bypassed him. "Usually, he's awake," Courtney sighed and called for an elevator. Seconds later, a car came rattling down the shaft. The gears shrieked as the door slowly jerked opened. The inside smelled pissy and the button for the seventh floor didn't light when Courtney pressed it.

"You can't go around cracking people just because they call you names, Casey," Courtney told her. "You're on parole, remember? Besides, it's childish."

"Seriously? As many people as you've beaten up in your day? Sophina Proctor. Sarah Cunningham. Kevin Ford. Anna Bell—shall I go on? Don't make me out to be the monster here."

"Sophina was in the ninth grade... with us. Sarah was a year older. Kevin touched my butt. Anna called mom a whore. My point is that everybody was our age or older, Casey. What I just saw was a grownup bullying a little kid."

"Did you see how tall that boy was? What was I supposed to do? Suck it up and walk away?"

"Yes!" Courtney raised her voice. "You know, I sure hope I don't regret this whole idea of us living together."

Casey's jaw hung to the floor. She followed Courtney off the elevator and down the hall, still pleading her case.

"C'mon, Courtney, don't do me like that… are you even listening to me? Look, I had to show that little punk what's up so that he doesn't try to get over on us again. If I upset you, I'm sorry. Okay? I promise, I won't be any more trouble."

Courtney stopped at her apartment door and turned around.

"Am I gonna be alone again?"

"What?"

"You have no idea the pain I felt after you went away," Courtney said. "Seven years, Casey. Now, I need your word that you're gonna take this thing serious and not get caught up out here."

Casey exhaled with compliance.

"Okay, I'm sorry. I'll try to keep a lid on things. I promise." Casey held up two fingers and cheesed. "See, scouts' honor."

Courtney fixed her fingers.

"You're missing one," she winked. Courtney unbolted apartment door and stood to the side. "Welcome home, sis."

Five

The scent of lavender which permeated throughout Courtney's apartment was a contrast to the moldy wretch of St. Agnes. Her one-bedroom sanctuary reminded Casey of an upscale spa somewhere in Midtown Manhattan. The view from her balcony was silencing. Buildings staggered the nightly backdrop with lights like little curious eyes. In the corner sky was a fluorescent moon. Its bluish tint eclipsed the balcony, revealing her plant addiction. Begonias and pansies dangled from her apartment railing. The flowers were almost as pretty as Courtney was. Inside, her carpet was neatly groomed with fresh vacuum tracks and traces of Arm & Hammer deodorizer still present. Her furniture was so fresh, it looked as if it'd been delivered an hour before the girls got there. The kitchen? Spotless—not a crumb or dish in sight; her apartment looked like a model condo from a *Better Homes* publication. Casey made it halfway across her sister's rug before Courtney stopped her.

"What's that look for?"

Courtney looked down at her sneakers.

"Oh. My bad." Casey stripped off her sneakers and placed them near the door. Her socked feet melted through the plush surface.

"Daaamn, Court," Casey looked around. "Didn't know you were livin' like this. Son, this is dope. I would've never guessed by the hole in the ceiling, down in the main lobby."

"Yeah, well, don't get used to it. I'm renting."

"For how long?"

"I don't know, I haven't decided. I guess until those kids out front find out what car I drive and steal my hubcaps." Courtney lowered her eyes at Casey. "If I had it my way, we'd live on base."

"So, why don't we?"

Courtney placed her bag onto the couch and trotted over to the icebox.

"The army's not a Holiday Inn, Casey. Only spouses and dependents can live on base. Plus, your felony doesn't help us out any. Want a drink?"

"You got any Heineken?"

Courtney fetched two ice cold Heineckens from the fridge. She plucked both caps before rejoining Casey in the living room. The girls toasted in celebration and began to sip. Casey looked down at her socked feet and noticed her big toe was sticking out. Courtney's eyes soon followed.

"Ever heard of Fruit of the Loom? Hanes?" she teased her. "So, when did they start serving beer in prison?"

Casey took a satisfying sip and wiped the fuzz from her mouth.

"I started before you, remember?"

Casey continued her tour. On the coffee table, she noticed a family portrait. She lifted its oak frame to get a closer look. Her heart murmured as she traced her parents' faces with her finger.

"One of our last shots." She deflated. "We took this a month before I... went away—that's so sad. Sometimes it doesn't even seem real, what happened to them."

Courtney appeared beside her. "Tell me about it. After Mom and Dad passed, and with you gone, there weren't many options for me. So, I hooked up with a recruiter and decided to join—I had to do something since college was no longer an option. After the house got sold, I was homeless for a short time before I signed up. Best move I could've ever made."

Casey looked down at the photo again. She couldn't believe Courtney had been homeless.

"Look, Courtney, there's something I need to tell you. I, um... not a day goes by that I don't think about... everything, you know, and I wish sometimes I could just wave a magic wand and make it all disappear. It's just so fucked up because in my mind, I *know* I'm so much smarter than what happened seven years ago, but I just—"

"Casey, it's over," Courtney interrupted her. "It's not 1982 anymore. Shit, in a few months, we'll be in a whole new decade. Let's try to look forward from now on."

Casey's eyes gleamed as she returned the photo onto the table. Courtney lifted the frame and changed the temperature. Once upon a time, laughter was the girls' medicine.

"Son, look at your fat-ass head. Looks like a beach ball."

"Fuck you," Casey snickered, wiping her eyes. "God, I was such a train wreck back then."

"Car wreck, yes. Train wreck is a stretch."

"How would you know? You were too busy lip-locking with Marc before you dumped him and started dating Mike, the 'baseball star'." Casey air quoted. "Did he ever go pro? Is his brother still around? The cute guy that used to look like El DeBarge?"

"Who? Ramsey? Girl, Ramsey's gay! You didn't know that?"

"Get the fuck outta here—are you serious?"

"I can't believe you didn't know that, Casey. Everybody and their momma knew that Ramsey was gay. He batted for both teams."

"A switch-hitter, huh? Well, the more the merrier, that's my philosophy."

Courtney gasped. "Wait a minute. You're bisexual, too?"

"I never told you that?"

"No, you didn't. I mean, it's okay, but I never knew that. Well, I had my suspicions, but by that time, you'd already been sent away."

The girls shared a tragic giggle as Courtney finished the last sip of her drink.

"Well, my dear, I need a shower—and it's late. There's some Dominos in the icebox, in case you get hungry. We'll catch up more tomorrow."

Courtney tossed her empty bottle into the trash and

headed to the back for the night. Before she could get far, Casey stopped her.

"Court, hold up. One last thing before we turn the page." Casey took a deep breath. "I just gotta know. I know about Dad, but Mom… what exactly… happened to her?"

Courtney returned to the living room with a flattened look.

"She just lost it, Case. She had an episode one night and… fell and hit her head. It happened while she was in rehabilitation." Courtney lifted their family photo again. "The home where mom was recovering put a lien on our house as collateral. After she passed, they took the house to pay for her care. I never saw a dime of that money. Next thing I know, two sheriffs showed up at our door and told me I had to leave. I've been on my own ever since."

Courtney handed over the portrait to Casey and continued toward the back. Casey could tell by her drooping shoulders that the last seven years had been hard on her sister, too. She returned the picture to the table.

"Are they buried? Can you take me to see them?"

Courtney stopped but didn't turn around. Her voice hoarsened as she spoke.

"No, Casey, they're not buried, okay? They were cremated. I gave their ashes to Dad's sister, and boarded the first bus out of New York that I could."

Courtney continued down to her room and closed the door.

Casey plopped on the couch in front of their picture. Before the sense of loss paralyzed her, she escaped to the balcony for a smoke. The skyline put her at ease; the view was a far cry from her cell. The relentless sound of city racket was reassuring to her. She closed her eyes and inhaled the crisp night air. It was hard to imagine that less than a few hours earlier, she'd made it out of St. Agnes Prison.

Casey had suffered from bad dreams a lot as a little girl, even after moving in with the Haughtons. Visions of Aunt Patty's extension cord tearing through her skin jolted her awake. If not Aunt Patty, it was Uncle Benny's advances or a crowd of unruly kids chasing her. Sometimes Casey would get away, and other times she'd collapse from exhaustion, pleading for their mercy. In the dream, a group of seven or eight kids would pin Casey to the floor and take turns doing heartless things to her. She'd wake up crying and turn on the TV. The background noise made her feel as if she wasn't alone. She carried her old habit with her into adulthood where a new genre of bad dreams added to her playlist. Her first night home, Casey woke up from three separate dreams, recounting the horror she'd witnessed during her time away. Her latest was a woman who jumped to her death after being denied parole for a third time. The woman had been convicted for killing her brother. For thirty years afterward, she'd dedicated her life to rehabilitation with hopes of getting out before the board shot her down. Casey didn't see the woman jump but saw the mangled body afterward. She'd burned through a whole pack of Kools the day it happened.

With her face mushed into the couch cushion just after

3 a.m., Casey flipped through channels. *Married With Children* was on. Flip. *Sanford and Son*. Flip. "Are you ready to except Jesus Christ as your Lord and Savior? If so—" Flip. She looked toward the back, noticed Courtney's lamp was still on and went to investigate.

She tapped on her sister's door. "Court. You up?"

Courtney was out, her mouth slightly open. She'd fallen asleep reading *Beloved* by Toni Morrison. The book was flat in her lap. Casey eased over to her sister's bedside, careful not to disturb her. Using a bobby pin she found on the floor as a bookmark, she closed Courtney's book and placed it on her nightstand. Casey noticed another framed memory of the two and lifted it to get a closer look. The photo was captioned at the bottom: *Jones Beach. June '79.* The girls had just turned fourteen and were in their freshman year of high school. Together, they'd hooked school to hang out with Courtney's friends at the theatre to watch *The Amityville Horror* until the kids played a mean trick on Casey, prompting Courtney to defend her. When Casey had returned from the concession stand, her arms loaded with goodies, the kids had all changed seats. Courtney was in the bathroom at the time. The girls told her of the switch, but not Casey, believing Courtney would be in on the joke. When Courtney returned and noticed her sister stumbling through the aisles, looking for them, she went off. The girls had been screwing with Casey all day.

"Hold up, so they never told you about the seats?" Courtney asked her.

"Well… no they didn't—but it's okay, Courtney," Casey answered. "Just girls being girls. I'm not offended or anything, if that's what you're wondering."

Courtney went after her friends for stiffing it to Casey. The show hadn't yet started and was still undergoing feature previews.

"So, y'all think this is funny?" Courtney chastised them.

"Courtney, it was just a joke," one girl said. "We're just having a little jab at Casey. Don't get upset. It's all in good fun. Chill out."

"Well, have fun without me—without *us*. C'mon, Casey, we're leaving."

Courtney's friends all looked at each other.

"Are you serious? C'mon, Courtney, we're friends. It's not like that."

"It *is* like that. You didn't pull this trash on anybody else but Casey because you know she won't fight back. Well, I'm standing up for her—for us."

The girls skipped the film and finished their day down at Jones Beach. They waded together in the Atlantic before Courtney convinced a stranger wearing a Polaroid camera around his neck to snap their picture. "Here you go, girls. Hope it lasts you a lifetime." Courtney fanned the flimsy picture until their cheesy faces appeared in print. She passed it over to Casey.

"I'm sorry about your friends, Courtney. I feel bad we had to leave."

Casey's sweetness made Courtney glitter.

"Will you stop apologizing? I should be apologizing to you. You're my sister, man. If anybody's gonna play a mean prank on you, it's gotta go through me." Courtney buttoned up her rant. "Fucking bitches."

Pepsi squirted from Casey's nose. She found it funny when Courtney used dirty language back then. She choke-laughed which prompted Courtney to whack her across the back.

She never forgot that moment or any other time Courtney went to bat for her.

Casey exhaled in remembrance before returning the framed polaroid onto Courtney's nightstand. She twisted the switch to her sister's lamp, tightened up her blanket and returned to the couch for the night.

The Real World

Casey nearly missed breakfast the next morning after finally catching a wink just after 5:30 a.m. She awoke four hours later to the smell of burnt toast and Courtney humming to New Edition. She was fully dressed. A nosy sun cut through her vertical blinds, leaving shadowy silhouettes across the floor of her living room. Yesterday, when Casey had woken up, she'd been surrounded by steel. Today, she was surrounded by the real world.

"Good morning, sunshine," Courtney sang beautifully from her kitchen. Hot grease crackled in the background as she worked the stovetop. "So, are we hungry? Do we want some breakfast?"

Casey rubbed her eyes and sat up. Her voice was still raspy. "We sure do," she said. "You got any sausage over there?"

Courtney dangled a pack above her head.

"Already on it."

Casey stretched and adjusted her bosom before staggering down to the bathroom. She splashed a palm full of icy cold water into her freckled face, washed and dried her hands and returned out front. She stood near the fridge, watching Courtney break two eggs over an iron skillet. Cooling on the countertop were three strips of crispy applewood-smoked bacon. Courtney sliced down the middle of a hot dog and laid it into the boiling lard. She stirred the links inside the grease before pressing it against the surface. Grease exploded from underneath. Beside the toaster was a pair of homemade waffles, syrup, and a jar of freshly-squeezed orange juice. Casey took her seat and waited for Courtney to serve her— she almost dropped it.

"Here you go, ma'am—whew, shit! *Hot-hot-hot.*" Courtney blew at her red hands. "I sent the bacon down to hell, just the way you like it. Satan sends his regards."

Casey shoved a strip into her mouth. She hadn't had a home cooked meal in seven years.

"Thanks, Court." She chomped with her mouth full. "Hey, where's yours?"

Courtney raised her mason jar from the counter. A green, seedy fluid swished inside.

"Th'hell is that?" Casey asked her.

Courtney downed her green drink. She wiped her mouth with her forearm afterward and held it up high for Casey to see.

"Kiwi slices, lettuce, soy milk and green tomatoes. Yum-yum. Wanna try one?"

Casey gagged. "I'll pass. I don't drink stuff that looks like it's been sitting inside of a shower drain for the last twenty years."

"Health is wealth, my dear. Well, enjoy your breakfast. I gotta be at work soon."

"Already? It's our first morning together in seven years—what the fuck?"

"I got bills, son. *Mad* bills. I gotta get these credits cards paid down. New York ain't cheap, you know." Courtney pushed in her chair. "If you don't like my smoothies, perhaps I can offer you an alternative to swine?"

"What for? I'm already a pig. What am I supposed to do? Eat healthy and work out five days a week? That won't work on my big ass, Courtney. Besides, I'm already on a diet plan."

"Really? And what might that be?"

Casey waved around her pack of Kools. "Yum-yum. Wanna try one?" She smiled.

Courtney sighed. "Those things are gonna give you cancer someday—just like Dad."

"Yeah? Well, Dad never smoked and he got cancer. So, what does that tell you? Cigarettes aren't the cause of cancer, Courtney, life is," she laughed evilly. "So, what the hell am I supposed to do all day? I don't know anybody around here."

Courtney reached into her pocket and handed Casey fifty dollars.

"There's a discount shop on Eighth Street. I think they're hiring," Courtney told her. "Add this with your commissary and go get yourself some clothes. Try to find something nice in case you get a job offer. There's a bus stop a couple of blocks from here."

"Ditto, thanks," said Casey. "So, about that green drink… What are you one of those weird fitness people or something?"

"Hey, I'm just tryin' to live. Okay, I gotta go. Quit buggin' me, already."

"Who's buggin' you?"

Courtney pecked Casey on top of her pumpkin head and left.

After breakfast, Casey digested her meal with a cigarette while overlooking the city. Growing up, she'd smoked her first cigarette at fourteen before graduating into a half-pack-per-day fiend. Her habit increased after arriving at St. Agnes. A cigarette in Brooklyn was nothing. In prison, however, cigarettes were a hot commodity. Inmates wagered sticks all the time during dominos or other card games—and you'd better pay up.

Casey exhaled her toxic fumes into the atmosphere while admiring the noise around her. Tenants stomped their feet above her and the couple next door argued constantly. Neighbors talked across from their balconies at one another as if they were on a private phone call. "Yeah, uh-huh, I told Willie yesterday about that no-good-ass son of his—runnin' into my Lincoln with that damn bike," a man hollered from two stories up. "Oh, he got you too? Little retarded fucker. Boy ain't been right since his momma dropped him on his head," the neighbor replied. A bicycle striking the side of a Lincoln was miniscule to Casey's new life, her first morning back. She'd forgotten what it was like to be a regular. She kicked her feet up onto the railing, grateful to be home.

Casey couldn't have foreseen how much the world had changed in seven years. She felt lost as the city bus pushed into the throat of her old stomping grounds. She twisted in her seat, acknowledging the latest signs and billboards. Near a pharmacy was an ad for a rap group named De La Soul; she'd never heard of them. Growing up, she'd listened to Kurtis Blow or groups like Grandmaster Flash and the Furious Five. Further up, she saw a liquor ad with Sean Connery's picture beside a bottle of Jim Bean. She last remembered it as a picture of Marvin Gaye; he had since passed. Behind the pharmacy was a rotting apartment building with charred windows. Casey recalled an old classmate of hers who had lived there. The girl's name was Melanie Thompson. Her family had relocated to Landover in 1981 after her parents separated. Casey stared up at the blackened window, recalling where Melanie liked to sit and admire the busy sidewalk. Before long, the traffic light changed, ending her sentimental moment.

Casey noticed more than just billboards and burnt memories during her bus trip down the block. Gas prices were higher, bus fare was more expensive, and clothes were different, too. Bell bottom jeans were near extinction the last she remembered. People were now wearing Sassons, Levis, Guess and Jordache brand jeans—Courtney wore a pair the other day. One kid had on a pair of jeans so baggy, it reminded Casey of a parachute. Men had stylish high-top fades with parts in their hair, and some were still wearing jheri curls. Women rocked mullets, wolf cuts, curls or finger waves with large hoop earrings. The cars were also different, and so was the lingo.

Casey tugged onto the passenger cord near Eleventh and Baltic Avenue, hoping to get a closer look. *Where the hell am I?* The world had changed without her permission.

Casey stood on a street corner in the middle of Brooklyn like a lost tourist who had wandered from the group. She carried up the busy sidewalk before slipping into a McDonald's bathroom. She stood in front of her reflection, lost. The real world was a scary place, just as Sheena Washington had once warned her. Casey turned on the sink and hovered over the running water. "Get it together, girl," she whispered to herself. "It's fuckin' 1989. What'd you expect?" She splashed a handful of water into her face and moved on, wandering onto Eighth Street toward the discount store Courtney had mentioned earlier. In the window was a "Now Hiring" sign. She took a deep breath and pushed open the door.

The small but loaded shop enthralled Casey—she hadn't seen a store or a mall in person since her teens. She swatted through the discounted racks. Her commissary from St. Agnes at the time of her departure was just over two hundred dollars plus the fifty Courtney had given her. She piled her arms full of outfits, snickering at some of the old fashion giveaways she recalled from her childhood. "Oh, my God." She covered her mouth. Near the back was—no kidding—a platform shoe. Casey lifted it to get a closer look and returned it. She looked for a fitting room but instead found a large mirror. She placed a pair of faded jeans and other items up to her wide figure. She carried her things to the register and placed them on the counter. Her eyes strolled to the "Now Hiring" placard near the front. The clerk on duty was a young Asian girl wearing spongy headphones. Her Walkman was clipped to the side of her jeans, and her music was so loud that Casey could hear it as she walked up.

"Excuse me? Are you all hiring?" Casey asked.

The kid stopped her device.

"Huh?" The kid screwed her face. "What'd you say?"

Casey pointed at the window. "Are you still hiring? The sign?"

"I don't know. What are you asking me for?" The kid shrugged. "I don't do any hiring."

It took everything in Casey not to reach over the counter and behead the thoughtless teen. She hated kids, especially rude ones like that punk kid from the other night in front of Courtney's building with the boombox. The girl rung up Casey's things and held out her hand.

"$44.07. Cash or card?"

Casey thumbed between her eyes before handing the girl the cash. The last thing she needed was a charge for aggravated assault.

"So, are you just gonna ignore that I asked about the hiring sign in the window?"

The girl gave Casey back her change and went to the back.

"Um, hello? Are you gonna help me out or what?"

When the kid was far enough away from the register, Casey grumbled at her. The girl then returned with the store's manager, a middle-aged woman wearing bi-focal glasses. The manager extended her hand to Casey.

"I see you've met my daughter," the woman chuckled. "Mina says you're looking for a job. We do have a vacancy available. Why don't you come to the back? Let's talk."

The manager reached behind the counter for an application and handed it to her. Casey was glad she hadn't gotten into a shouting match with the girl. She sliced her eyes at the kid before following the woman to the back. "Right this way—excuse the mess," the woman said, gesturing. They packed inside a cramped office that was almost the same size as Casey's old cell. She couldn't believe it; she'd been paroled for less than a day and was on the verge of a new job already. She couldn't wait to tell Courtney about it later. She envisioned receiving her first paycheck and began calculating how much rent she could afford to pay. For her first car, Casey wanted a green Ford Mustang with a sunroof.

"Have a seat, dear," the manager offered. "I'm Mrs. Lu, by the way. I'm looking for a new sales associate. Are you interested? What's your name?"

"Casey." She smiled. "I'd love to help out—absolutely."

"Great. I just need you to fill out this application. Afterward, we'll do a short interview and see where things go. When you're done, stand at the door and call my name. I'll be right over."

Casey's hand trembled as she filled out the application. She rushed through the front page and appeared at the door.

"Okay, Mrs. Lu," she called to the manager. "I'm all done."

Mrs. Lu appeared from behind a rack and returned to

the office. "Boy, that was quick!" She entered the office and looked over Casey's application.

"Ahhh," she said. "There's a back side you missed, but that's okay, we'll just fill it in as we go. C'mon, let's get started so we can get you out on the floor."

Casey was in paradise with Mrs. Lu throughout her interview. They laughed like best friends throughout the morning as the manager diverted to irrelevant topics such as last year's presidential race, football, and local politics. Casey didn't care for either, but she was well-informed since she'd had nothing but time on her hands over the past seven years.

"Well, I don't really follow politics like *that*, Mrs. Lu. They're all crooked, if you ask me," she said. "Everything's about money these days."

"I'd have to agree with you there, dear. Gosh, what's wrong with our world today?"

"I wish I knew."

The two conversed for nearly a half-hour about living in the big city. Mrs. Lu said she and her husband owned a laundromat business in Queens and that her brother-in-law owned a restaurant in Manhattan. Casey tugged for a few brownie points by sharing with Mrs. Lu her on-the-spot aspirations.

"Law school? Dear, that's wonderful!" Mrs. Lu celebrated. "I'm trying to get my lazy daughter to practice law. All she does is draw and listen to Run DMC. She's in her last year of high school. Perhaps Mina can use some of your magic. How old are you again?"

"Twenty-four," Casey laughed. "Sure, I'll use some of my David Copperfield on her."

Mrs. Lu nodded her head.

"Ambitious. Well-spoken. Funny. Smart—you're a gem, Casey Haughton. Where were you when we first opened back in '86?" she chuckled. "Okay, let's wrap this up so we can get you on the books. Here we go. Question eighteen. Have you ever been convicted of a serious misdemeanor or felony in the past ten years?"

Casey's smile collapsed. She stared at the store owner.

"Are you alright, angel?" Mrs. Lu asked her. "Did I read that too fast? I can repeat the question if you'd like?"

"Please."

"Sure, dear. Have you ever… been convicted… of a seri-ous… misdemeanor or felony in the past ten years?"

Casey froze again. Her first instinct was to lie, but Mrs. Lu was too sweet of a person and seemed understanding enough.

"Okay, I have—but here's the thing," Casey started to explain right away. "I was seventeen at the time—real young. I got into some trouble—I had a hard life growin' up. Been through foster care and lived in a few different houses throughout the state. But I've changed, Mrs. Lu, I really have. I'd love to have an opportunity to work here, ma'am."

Mrs. Lu's expression changed suddenly.

"Why does this always happen to me? So, I guess that whole thing about law school was a big joke or something, huh?"

"No, ma'am," Casey half-lied. "I really do want to study

law, but law school is expensive, and I need a job to pay for it."

"Sure, you do."

Mrs. Lu ripped up Casey's application and dropped it into the bin right in front of her.

"Please, Mrs. Lu. I won't be a problem, I swear," she negotiated. "I'll mop floors. I'll work midnights—whatever you need. Saturdays. Sundays—whatever it takes. If I make one mistake you can fire me on the spot."

"I'm sorry dear, but I can't help you. Take good care of yourself, okay?"

Casey dropped her head down to her feet. She felt a good cry coming on and got up to leave before it came gushing out. Mrs. Lu followed her out of the office as if she'd just been busted for stealing from the rack.

"What if I bring you a letter of reference?" Casey tried again. "Would that work, Mrs. Lu? How about a trial run? The first two weeks are on me. If you don't like the way I work, fire me. No hard feelings. What'd you say?"

Mrs. Lu opened the door to her shop.

"I'm very sorry, dear. But my husband and I agreed when we first opened this store that under no circumstances are we to hire any criminals. None whatsoever."

"I get that, Mrs. Lu, but I'm not a criminal. It's not like I'm out here robbing the world as we speak, you know. I was seventeen, I made a mistake. This goddamn country robs people every day. Hell, they've been robbing people for centuries. C'mon, Mrs. Lu. Give me a chance to prove to you that I'm worthy. I won't let you down."

Mrs. Lu stood defensively by the door. "Take care of yourself, dear."

Casey exhaled and trudged from the store. As she turned to try to negotiate once more, Mrs. Lu closed the door in her face. *Wham.* She even locked the door. *Clack-Clack.* She walked over to the window and removed her "Now Hiring" sign. Not long after, her rude daughter, Mina, lowered the blinds. Casey stuffed her hands inside her pockets and continued up the sidewalk.

Six

In an alley not far from Mrs. Lu's shop, Casey wept like a mouse. Her shoulders dipped with gloom as she cowered behind a trash truck. She'd never felt so small in her life. In that instance, she wished she was back in her old cell at St. Agnes. At least there she'd have her old job in the woodshop and didn't have to worry about what society thought of her. She reached for her smokes but couldn't stop her mouth from quivering. She eventually gave up and slithered up the busy sidewalk to look for more work.

Every job Casey visited asked the same question. "Have you ever been convicted of a serious misdemeanor or felony in the past ten years?" She even tried an X-rated shop on Upshur Avenue, but the question was still the same. The manager there had the audacity to bring up the store's policy on decorum. "Decorum?" Her nostrils flared. "Dude, you got a fuckin' dildo sittin' on the counter, waving at customers as they walk in—but you wanna lecture me about decorum?" The guy shrugged at her misfortune. "Look, I don't make the rules here. Now which size do you want? The six or the nine?"

Casey shoved open the door and left. She tried a check-cashing place the next block over but ran into a different problem.

"What do you mean you don't have a high school diploma?" A Black woman there asked her. "My God, how on earth do you get by in this world without one?"

"How do you get by in this world *with* one? Casey countered. "I might be a dropout, but I'm not stupid, lady. C'mon, hook a sista up with a job."

The boss squinted at Casey, confused.

"Sista? Wait, you're Black? I thought you was a white girl."

Casey swiped at a box full of miniature pencils on the counter, knocking them onto the floor. She looked around and noticed customers and employees alike all staring back at her as if she was a lunatic. Embarrassed, she picked up the pencils, returned them to the counter and left.

Her last stop was at a furniture warehouse on Grandview. She bypassed the large trucks near the half-open bay and ducked inside. Men howled and whistled at her as if she was Jessica Rabbit. Their chauvinistic vibe was off-putting to her. As she turned to leave, the warehouse manager stopped her. He spoke with an Italian accent and a Cuban cigar wedged at the corner of his warthog mouth.

"Yeah, how ya doin'? Can I help ya with some'm?"

"Are you guys still looking for lifters?" she asked him.

The man looked her up and down. "You got a son or some'm?"

"No, it's for me."

The guy lifted his eyebrow at Casey.

"What's that look for? What do I have to do? Grab at my crotch or something? Do you need help or not?"

"Well, I don't know, I'm not looking for a secretary at the moment. Can you lift a hundred pounds by yourself?"

"Can *you* lift a hundred pounds by yourself?" Casey flipped it back to him. "Not all women wanna be secretaries, you sexist sack of shit."

"Whoa-whoa-whoa. Take it easy."

"No, you take it easy, asshole," she growled. "I could pick up this stupid warehouse on one finger, if I wanted to."

The man busted into a wide grin.

"Well, I do like your temperament—I'll give you that— but not for this job." The man then squeezed beside her. "But, I guess I could make an exception."

The man suggestively lifted his brow at Casey and popped at his suspenders. She nearly threw up inside of her mouth at the thought of entertaining him. She surveyed the other pig workers there and ducked beneath the bay door.

With her hoodie pulled tightly over her head, Casey rode the city bus home with her feet propped in the seat beside her. She leaned her head against the glass, irritated by the day's events. Rejection was a familiar passage in her life's story. She'd tried over thirteen different jobs that day, and each employer turned their nose at her. Mrs. Lu cut the worst. The two had seemed to have a great rapport before Casey admitted her felony conviction. Her eyes teared as she recounted the woman closing the door in her face and removing the "Now Hiring" sign from the window. She yanked her hoodie over her face to mourn. A passenger overheard her soft cries and offered their condolences. "You okay, sweetheart? Are you hurt? Is there anything I can—" Casey turned her back to the concerned rider. She raised her head just in time to notice her neighborhood and pulled on the passenger cord, urging the bus driver to stop.

With her hands stuffed inside of her pockets, Casey trekked through Gardener Heights back to Courtney's building. She bypassed a group of winos in front of a liquor store skipping checkers along a board. "Smile, baby girl," one of them said to her. Casey gave the man an evil look and kept going. Further up in the parking lot, a group of kids were tossing around a football when it suddenly rolled by her sneakers. As Casey went to pick it up, a boy kicked it from her reach. "Ewww, man, don't touch my football!" The boy picked up his ball and used his T-shirt to wipe it off. Casey grumbled to herself and went inside.

It was after 6 p.m. when Courtney finally got in from work later that evening. Casey was lying on the sofa with her face mushed into the pillow watching *Jeopardy!* Courtney entered, removed her shoes and glided into the kitchen, rambling about her perfect day at work. "A couple of us went down to Frank's for lunch—food was amazing—you ought to check it out," she carried on.

Courtney waltzed around the kitchen, closing the icebox with her perfect shape. "So, there's this guy at my job, he says he's from Iowa but grew up in Philly playing basketball before going into the Marines. I think he's feelin' me," Courtney laughed. She bounced onto the sofa beside Casey with a spoon and a small container of Häagen-Dazs mint ice cream. She unfastened her bra from beneath her shirt and dropped it onto the floor beside her. Casey gave her the side eye and went back to *Jeopardy!* Courtney patted Casey on her leg.

"So, tell me all about your day." She beamed. "Any luck out there?"

Casey side-eyed her again.

"That kind of day, huh?" Courtney sliced into her frozen treat with her spoon and placed it at Casey's frown. "It's mint. Your favorite. Hmm?"

With her eyes still on the TV, Casey parted her mad mouth. Courtney wiped the back of her spoon against her sister's lips. She cut into her treat again.

"Remember when we'd eat out the same container with one spoon and watch *Falcon Crest*?" Courtney reminded her. "So, what happened today?"

"Nothin', that's the problem," Casey said. "Just another shitty day—just like when I was locked up. I went to thirteen different places today and didn't get jack. I came close once, but…"

"But what?" Courtney curled her feet beneath her. "C'mon, tell me."

"It's nothin', really. It's just…"

Casey turned her head away from Courtney and began to cry.

"Ohhh, Casey." Courtney placed her snack on the table. She grabbed Casey by her balloon head and pulled her into her lap.

"Down at the thrift shop," Casey sniffed, "fuckin' lady, man. She closed the door right in my face when I told her about my record. I'm not a criminal," she whined. "Son, that shit hurt me to my soul, Courtney, you have no idea. She ain't have to do me like that."

Courtney listened without judgment. She ran Casey's golden hair between her fingers back and forth, gently massaging her scalp.

"I even tried the porno outlet down on Upshur. Even they turned me down. Do you know how pathetic you have to be to not get hired at a porno store, Courtney?"

Courtney snorted, prompting Casey to chuckle at her own misfortune.

"Wait, you did say Upshur, right? Isn't that the porno store down by the pharmacy? The one with the blonde chic in the poster over by the register? Across from the Chinese food place?"

Casey looked at her.

"Wait, you know about that place?"

"What? No, of course not!" Courtney backpedaled. "You know I'm not into that kind of stuff. I was just curious, you know… I'm being serious, Casey, quit staring at me like that. Look, I only know about it because when I first came out here looking for apartments, I was out that way and—"

"Let me guess. You somehow tripped, fell, stumbled

inside and noticed a hot blonde woman on a poster? Right, Courtney, I gotcha. So, what size dildo did you buy? The six, nine, or the twelve-inch special order? Son, that's a lot of meat. Damn, you stretch your shit out like that? Word, they had a turquoise one over by the register. They had this other one called Mr. Ed because it was shaped like a horse's dick. Goddamn thing looked like a science project."

"I do not have any dildos inside my apartment, Casey. Now, chill out on the jokes!"

Casey watched as Courtney went back to eating her ice cream, mad. As soon as she let her guard down, Casey sprung from the couch and raced down the hall to Courtney's bedroom. Courtney dropped her spoon and went after her.

"Oh, my God, you little fucking—I told you I don't have one!"

"Is that why you're chasing me?" Casey laughed.

She dashed inside her sister's bedroom and went to close the door. Courtney forced her arm through the opening, desperately flailing against Casey's mass.

"Just tell me the truth, and I'll leave you alone."

"Casey, GET OUT OF MY ROOM!" she hollered. "I'm not kidding. Now, cut it out."

"No, quit lying to me. I'm gonna find it one way or another, Courtney, so you might as well tell me the truth. Yo, I bet you got one of those Mandingo ones from the Kingdom of Zamunda. Like some *Coming to America* type shit. C'mon, Court, give it up. Where's the royal dildo?"

Courtney busted through the door, forcing Casey to lose

her leverage. She speared her childish sister onto the bed and pinned her arms above her head. Casey wheezed with laughter.

"You probably own the whole shop!" she laugh-cried. "Hey-hey-hey, can I borrow your membership card?" Casey exploded again.

Courtney shoved her into the mattress. Casey laughed so hard that her jaws and belly ached. Her pudgy, freckled face was painted red.

"C'mon, man. Let me up."

"No!"

Casey wheezed again. "For real, Court, let me up. You know how I get when I laugh too hard. That shit goes straight to my ass. I gotta fart, now get off."

"You ain't going in my closet, Casey. I will throw your ass off this balcony and—

Whoop. Casey let go of one right beneath Courtney's nose.

"Are you serious, right now?" Courtney clipped her nose. "Case, what the fuck?"

"I told you to let me up!"

The girls both screamed. Drool leaked from Casey's mouth and onto Courtney's sheets. It was the longest and hardest the girls had laughed together in years. Casey's embarrassing gas problem had first started years ago when the girls were horse-playing at home. Courtney had Casey in the same silly, vulner-able position when Casey ripped one loose from laughing so hard. "Holy mother of Jesus!" Courtney said back then.

After their childish moment together, Courtney finally owned up to her stash. The girls were lying side by side staring at the ceiling with their heads touching.

"Okay, so maybe I own one."

"Only one?"

"*Two*, Casey. Okay? Damn. Dating is just so hard these days, you know. I mean, sometimes I wonder if I'm making it harder than it has to be."

Casey rolled onto her side, facing her. "Well… are you?"

Courtney covered her face.

"Yup," said Casey. "I know that look, you ain't got a clue. C'mere, you." Casey sat upright and now invited Courtney over to her lap. She gently rocked and petted her sister.

"Gosh, you're so serious sometimes, Court. Loosen up, I'm only kidding. Who gives a shit if you own a dildo… or two. It's your vagina. Get whatever size you want. Have a drink. Eat bacon. Go get shit-faced at the bar and have a one-night stand. Live your life."

Courtney whined in response. "Nobody wants me because I'm weird."

"Oh, shut up. You're twenty-four, fit, gorgeous, and have a stable career. Please, any guy worth his salt would be lucky to have you."

Courtney lifted her long face. "Really?" She lit up. "You think I'm gorgeous?"

"Of course, Court. I mean, you're smart, beautiful— and you got some nice titties." Casey squeezed one of them. "Just don't impale your womb too much with your accessories. Save a little space for when the right guy comes along. Otherwise, he's just gonna think you're a hooker."

Courtney smiled.

"I bought the six-inch. Nine was too big," she giggled. "I get your point, though. I needed that. Thanks, Case."

"What else are sisters for?"

The girls hugged, both moaning gleefully in the warmth of each other.

"I'm really glad you're home, sis. You keep me balanced when I get too ahead of myself. I missed that while you were gone. Life gets hard sometimes, you know."

Casey kissed Courtney in her hair.

"Yeah, well, you won't have to worry about that anymore because I'm home now, and I'm gonna find a job, and do whatever it is I have to do to be the best sister I can be. I've got a lot of time to make up for."

"You already have," said Courtney.

She rose from her bed and fetched a towel and washcloth from atop her dresser. She slipped into the bathroom and closed the door behind her. Casey waited a few seconds and crept over to her sister's closet. The second she reached for the knob, Courtney yelled through the wall.

"Get out of my closet, Casey! I can hear you!"

Remember Me?

The parole office where Casey was required to check in was eleven blocks from Courtney's apartment. As a convicted felon, she had to adhere to a strict program and was required to check in bi-weekly. She would also have to provide a urine sample. For even a minor infraction, a judge could revoke Casey's parole status and recommit her to serve the full sentence of her fifteen-year conviction. She could also be recommitted for not having a job since part of her parole agreement was to obtain work. The parole officer assigned to Casey, Mr. Hawthrone, could give a damn about another ex-con with a troubled background. Casey could tell when she first met him what he was about. "Yeah, right, mmmhmm," Hawthrone blew her off. He jotted something in her folder before tossing it onto a stack of others. "Well, you know what's comin' next if you don't find a job in a few months, don't you?" he chuckled. Casey didn't find her situation amusing at all.

Casey went *everywhere* looking for work but to no avail. McDonald's said no. Burger King said hell no, and the manager at the Pancake House on Twelfth and Lattimore laughed when Casey asked if they hired felons. She nearly lucked up at a Chinese food carryout in Bed-Stuy, but the language barrier was too much for her. "Never mind, man. Just forget it," she told the lead chef before walking out. She stopped at a used tire shop three blocks down only to be disappointed once again. Casey had better luck getting hit on by perverted old timers at the corner store near her apartment in Gardener Heights.

"Well, your application looks good and you interviewed well," the manager said. "Do you have a high school diploma or certificate?"

Casey rose from her seat, defeated.

"Nah, but it's all good," she exhaled sharply. "Take it easy, man."

Her bottom lip shivered as she moved up the sidewalk and down the block. Each failed attempt at securing employment was like a knife through her heart as weeks passed without any leads.

Meanwhile, Casey's parole officer reinforced her impending doom. "Well, your urine came back clean *this* time, so you're safe… for now," Hawthrone told her.

Each passing week Casey came up short on a job, the further into despair she slipped. At night, she dreamed of memories from her childhood—kids bullying her, robbing Casey of her coat and sneakers. Unable to sleep, she'd sit out on her sister's balcony and have a smoke or a frosty beer. It was the only highlight of her day. One evening, Courtney came home early from work to find Casey asleep next to four empty beer bottles and invited her for a ride down to the store. "C'mon, let's get you out of here."

Casey dragged behind Courtney at the supermarket. St. Agnes was heavy on her mind as her commissary wound down. She had no car, no money and could barely afford to catch the bus to look for work. She stood beside her sister at the register with a despondent look. Courtney paid for her things with a twenty-dollar bill and offered Casey the leftover change. Casey tucked the few bucks into her pocket. "Thanks, Court. I'll get it together one of these days… I hope."

When the girls returned outside to the car, Courtney noticed a flyer on her windshield.

"Here, I've got a job for you. Looks like you can start tonight."

Courtney handed her the ad. When Casey flipped it over, she noticed it was for a strip club. She crumbled up the salacious poster and hurled it at Courtney's head.

"So, you don't want to be a stripper?" Courtney danced. "Oh, c'mon, I'm only joking, Casey, cheer up. I thought you could use a laugh."

"Ha-ha, some joke. By the way, you lied to me."

"Lied to you? About what?"

"Your stash. I saw your closet, you fucking dinosaur pervert."

Courtney lunged at her. She placed her bag onto the hood of her car and began stalking Casey around the car.

"Yeah, that's right," Casey backpedaled. "Six inches, huh? More like thirty-six inches! That thing looks like a light saber from Star Wars, Court—lights up and everything. Where the fuck did you find that thing anyway? Goddamn. What'd you do? Order from the Stone Age section?

Courtney chased Casey around the car.

"You are *so* dead, Casey—get over here!"

"Nope."

Around and around the girls went. Casey pulled at the door handle, trying to get away from her. Courtney's grocery bag slid from the hood of her car and crashed onto the pavement. She went to lift it and noticed her soggy bag was dark at the bottom.

"My eggs! Fuck!"

"What are you talking about? *Your eggs.* Dildos don't do that. Just don't insert it too—"

"I'm not talking about those eggs, you dummy—look." Courtney held up the bag. "Dammit, Casey. Look what you made me do. Ugh."

Courtney threw her car keys at Casey and marched back into the grocery store. Casey unlocked the car and crawled inside. She leaned back in the passenger seat and kicked up her feet in victory. She reached for her smokes inside her windbreaker before noticing a familiar face exiting the grocery store. She sat up to get a closer look. It was Uncle Benny, her sick-in-the-head uncle from Brownsville. He had wiry gray hair and hobbled on a wooden cane before getting into a black Mercury Cougar. Casey watched him as he smiled and waved at a passing couple. She'd thought he was dead. She bolted from the car and raced after him. Benny fired up his ride and cruised from the lot before Casey could catch him. She turned and ran inside the grocery store. Courtney was at the register, buying new eggs.

"C'mon, we gotta go, sis. Right now!"

"Why? What's wrong? Why are you sweating like that? What happened?"

"Just trust me on this, Courtney, *damn*. Now, c'mon."

Courtney grabbed her eggs at the counter and rushed out of the store.

"You wanna tell me what the hell's going on? Did you rob somebody again?"

"No, I didn't rob anybody, just go out of here and make a right—go! C'mon, we're gonna lose him, Courtney. Go!"

"Lose who? What the hell's going on?"

Casey screamed at her. Her eyes popped out of her head. "GOOO!"

Courtney whipped her Chevy Chevelle from the lot, nearly striking a patron in the process. She hightailed it out onto the main roadway after Uncle Benny.

Casey scowled at the back of her uncle's peanut head as the girls followed him throughout the city. By the end of her tragic story, Courtney was just as determined to hunt down Uncle Benny and beat him with his own cane—maybe even run him over. "I don't care if your uncle crosses the border into Mexico, we'll be right behind him."

Courtney lived up to her word. She followed Uncle Benny from Flatbush to Staten Island, back to Flatbush, Bed-Stuy, and New Lots before he eventually parked in a church parking lot along 56th Avenue. He exited his two-door coupe, straightened his white collar and went inside.

"Are-you-kidding-me?" Casey said. "This nigga is a pastor now? So, I can't find a job to save my soul, but he gets to save his? All the shit he did to me? Oh, so he wants to preach the word of God now, does he? Well, perhaps he ought to meet him."

As Casey went to undo her safety belt, Courtney grabbed her.

"If you go in there and make a scene, you're just gonna go away again. Where's your head at, Case? C'mon, be smart. Let's just keep following him and see where he ends up."

Casey slammed the door and stabbed in her seatbelt. The girls sat outside the church in the lot like undercover cops. They waited over an hour for Uncle Benny to leave. Casey smoked about five Kools during that time, boiling with revenge. "Mmmotherfucker." She jabbed at the cigarette lighter. "I swear to God, Courtney, if you weren't here, I'd be going back up north for murder."

Casey fussed the entire hour, waiting for Uncle Benny to finally leave. She went off again as he exited the church and headed over to his ride. "Where you goin' now, huh? Follow that prick, Courtney—follow him!" Courtney eased her Chevette into traffic behind him.

For two hours, the girls tracked Uncle Benny's movements throughout the city until he finally pulled his car into a complex near Forest Hills. They parked several spaces behind him, waiting for Uncle Benny to get out.

"Hmph. Yeah, you done fucked up now, Uncle Benny. You done—"

Casey looked over and noticed Courtney with her carton of eggs in her lap. She'd removed them from her grocery bag.

"Oh, for sure." She caressed her carton. "It's time to pay the piper, Uncle Benny."

Casey gave her an incredulous look.

"And what in the hell do you suppose we do with those, Courtney? Make him an omelet? I'm not egging his car, man. I wanna snap his fuckin' neck. You know what, th'hell with this nonsense, I'm tired of waitin' around."

She launched from Courtney's car before her sister could stop her. She rushed across the lot toward Uncle Benny. She watched him as he read from his bible inside the car—he hadn't noticed her yet. Casey punched at his window, scaring the daylights out of him. Uncle Benny looked over at her, confused and shaken.

"Get your old ass out the car!"

Uncle Benny slowly opened his door with his hands up as if he was being carjacked. He was even grayer up close. His hairline had declined since she'd last seen him, and the skin on his face was wrinkled and sagged. He'd aged horribly over the years. She looked at his weathered hands and noticed he was still holding his bible. Casey ripped it from his hands and slammed it onto his car. She grabbed Uncle Benny by his jacket and shoved him against the door. *Boom.* The car shook under her power. She yoked him up and slammed him against his ride again. *Bam.* He yowled, doubling over in pain, reaching for his back. Courtney ran over to save Casey from killing him.

"Okay, you've made your point, Casey, now stop it before you really hurt him."

Disoriented and weary, Uncle Benny looked up at Casey, lost. She grabbed him by his old face and pressed.

"You didn't give a shit when I use to cry, remember that?" She talked to him through her teeth. "Used to have to beg you to go away, but you didn't. So, why should I go away?"

"C-C-Casey?" he stuttered. "Little Casey? Is that you?"

Casey threw her uncle onto the ground. He winced as he landed on his old knees.

"You daaaamn right. All two hundred pounds, here in the flesh—and I'm gonna kick your ass up and down this lot for what you did to me, you son of a bitch."

Uncle Benny broke down right in front of her. He placed his head onto Casey's shoe and seeped in pitiful hopelessness. Casey shooed him off.

"Th'fuck off me." She shook her leg. "C'mon, get up. Get up, I said!"

"Please don't hurt an old man, Casey," he begged. "Lord knows, I ain't been right all my life, and I'm payin' for it now. I'm a pastor at a church and—"

She grabbed him by his coat.

"You ain't no pastor! You ain't nothin'." Casey's voice buckled as she tried to talk. Memories of her early childhood in Brownsville fell from her eyes. "What nine-year-old deserves what you did, huh? Answer me!"

"No one does. B-B-But I was a sick man back then, Casey," he sniffled.

"You're still sick. You think because you're a pastor now, that somehow absolves you? Your sins have been washed away? You're a sick piece of shit. Where's Aunt Patty—the bitch? Is she still around? I'd like to beat *her* a few times with an extension cord. Where is she?!"

Uncle Benny hung his head.

"Sh-sh-she passed away three years ago," he sighed. "Ovarian cancer."

Casey trimmed her eyes at him. She could tell by his wretched demeanor that he hadn't slept in fifteen years—about the time she'd last saw him. Casey reached for her uncle's bible atop his car and shoved it in his hand.

"Here you go, preacher—take it," she told him. "Go preach the word of God to your hoodwinked congregation—just do me one favor. Tonight, when you go to bed, thank the heavens that I spared your pathetic life."

"No, that's not me anymore." He shook his head. "I'm different now."

Casey stood over her humpbacked uncle. He shrank instantly.

"You ain't different." She peered into his soul. "From this day forward, you are no longer my uncle. I'm taking back that part of my life. I might be a felon without a diploma or much of a life, but at least I'm real. You're a fraudulent piece of dog shit."

Courtney chest bumped him. "Amen," she said. "Everything she just said. And if you ever dream of molesting my little sister again, I'll egg your car so bad—you won't even recognize it. Now, get out of my sight… *our* sight, you piece of garbage."

Uncle Benny trudged inside his building. Courtney nodded her head, proud of herself.

"Well," she said, "we showed him."

Casey watched as her former uncle went inside.

"Yeah," she exhaled, "we sure did."

Seven

For years, Casey had thought confronting her perverted uncle would make her feel better, but it didn't. She laid on her sister's couch in the dark just after 2 a.m., unable to sleep. Her round face was moist throughout the evening as she reminisced about her past; nothing ever went right for Casey Haughton, she thought. When the girls had first arrived in the lot of their apartment, she'd looked over at Courtney and noticed she was crying.

"What are you crying for?" Casey asked her. "I'm the one with the screwed up life."

Courtney half-laughed. She dried her eyes with her T-shirt. "Because… it all makes sense now," she said. "You're just so much stronger than I could ever be—confronting Uncle Benny like that. I couldn't imagine."

Casey thought about her sister's words all night as she pressed into the sofa. Her life suddenly overwhelmed her. *What's the point of carrying on like this?* Her life had been shit since the day she was conceived. Her biological father barely claimed her, and her momma was a dope attic. Casey never had a straight path until she met the Haughtons. It worked for a while, but she was too far gone to truly appreciate them. The only friends she ever had took advantage of her. "After you get done with him," a boy once told her, "my homeboy in the other room needs a favor, too."

Casey looked over at the sliding glass window of Courtney's balcony, contemplating her demise. She had nothing to live for except for her sister—which would some-day change once Courtney found Mr. Right and started her own family. She slowly sat up and looked over at the balcony again. At seven stories high, Courtney's balcony would make for a clean fall. She reached for her lighter and cigarettes. She placed one of the sticks in her mouth and left the pack behind as a souvenir for Courtney before heading outside.

Casey leaned over the railing to her sister's balcony. Her face was so ugly with tears, she couldn't keep the cigarette in her mouth. It was the kind of child's cry after learning she wasn't good enough to make the local softball team. There was nothing left in this world for Casey Haughton except more hurt; she'd never find a job or instill the peace of mind to overcome her travesty of a life. She tried for her cigarette again and pressed the button on her lighter. *Tff.* She pressed it again. *Tff.* Casey pressed the button repeatedly. *Tff-Tff-Tff.* She hurled the empty canister into the dark and watched until it disappeared. She pondered using Courtney's stove before realizing it was all-electric. She gave up and spattered into the chair—her life was so despicable, she couldn't afford a good smoke.

The sights and sounds of the nightly neighborhood traffic were nothing new to Casey. Cops doubled in patrol cars, harassing streetwalkers. Mindless tenants blasted music above and beneath her, smoking reefer or cigarettes. Occasionally, a whiff of marijuana or cigarette smoke would tickle Casey's nose, making her groan with envy. Lucky for Courtney, she was a sound sleeper and could slumber through an earthquake. Noise persisted throughout the building with stomping feet, crying babies, and loud music. Casey could tell by the bass that it was Heavy D. She stood at the edge of the balcony, hoping to track the sweet cigarette smell and noticed a man beneath her on the sixth floor. Bare-chested and wearing cut-off jean shorts and black slippers with no socks, he sat in a bamboo chair, enjoying a smoke. Casey waved her arms at him like a stranded motorist.

"S'cuse me. Hey. Yo, up here."

The man rose from his chair and met Casey at the edge of his platform. He was tall with sparse bushy hair and a grubby beard.

"Yeah? What's up?"

"You wouldn't happen to have a light, would you?"

The man raised his brow at her. "Depends," he said. "Am I gonna get it back?"

"Of course, you will. All I need is a quick light."

The guy reached into his pocket for his lighter.

"Just try not to drop it—you ready?"

Casey cupped her small hands. "I gotcha, man. I won't drop it, promise."

Underhanded, the man tossed his lighter at Casey—you couldn't ask for a better throw. It bounced off her fingertips, whacked the iron railing and vanished into the night. The man's eyes followed his falling lighter until it was no longer visible. Casey thumbed at her eyes.

"Ahh man, my bad, homie. I had the thing and then… how much was your lighter? I'll pay you for it, first thing tomorrow. What apartment are you in? I can't believe I dropped that shit."

"Please, it ain't nothin' but a raggedy old lighter," he said. "What's your name, sweetheart?"

"Who me? Oh, uh, C-Casey," she hesitated. "Well, it's really Carmen—a lot of people don't know that about me—but everybody just calls me Casey. So, you can call me that." She bopped herself on the head. "Sorry, didn't mean to be awkward."

"Well, I'm Rob. Everybody calls me Rob," he laughed. "You didn't think to try the stove?"

"It's all-electric." She rolled her eyes. "I guess I'm shit out of luck until daybreak."

"Well, maybe not. I got an extra lighter if you want it? I can meet you by the elevators in a few. I got a bunch of those things; you never know when your neighbor just might drop one down the goddamn fire escape in the middle of the night."

Casey couldn't help but laugh.

"Oh, so we got jokes now, do we? Okay, I earned that one. Well, if it's no trouble, and you don't mind. Yes, I'll take you up on the offer. See you in a few."

Casey returned inside to meet up with her new friend Rob. She slipped into Courtney's windbreaker jacket before stopping to straighten her hair in the mirror near the foyer. She headed towards the door before returning to the mirror a second time to check her hair.

A Friend

Bundled beneath Courtney's nylon coat, Casey waited near the elevators for Rob to show up with the lighter. He got off sporting a bulky New York Giants coat, and the same cut-off jean shorts and bedroom slippers she'd seen him in. He smiled as he strolled off the elevator and over to her.

"Hey there, neighbor," he greeted her. "Here you go. Spanking brand new—never even used it. Like I said, I got a bunch of those things."

Casey tossed her jack into her mouth, lighted up and exhaled in triumph.

"You know somethin', Rob," she told him, "man, you got a friend for life. Thanks."

"No problem-no problem," he said. "So, whatcha doin' up so late? And how come I ain't never seen you around here before? You live in the building?"

"Questions, questions, questions," Casey giggled. "Well now, let's see. Hmmm. Well, I'm up late because I have the absolute worst insomnia in the world. You've probably never seen me around here before because I just moved here back in September. I'm staying at my sister's for the time being. So… what was your last question again?"

"You already answered it. So, you're the balcony with all them plants?" Rob scratched his scruffy chin. "The army girl. She drives the blue Chevette, right? I've seen her around. She don't say much—at least not to me. Y'all are sisters?"

"Until the end." Casey smiled. She pinched the orange glow of her cigarette, putting it out. "Well, Rob, I can't thank you enough, but I'm probably gonna head in and—"

"Want a beer, Casey?" Rob reached inside his coat and removed two ice cold cans of Budweiser beer. "I usually like to have a cold one and a smoke down on the first level when I can't fall asleep. I figured a beer and a chat might help. You down or what?"

Casey looked down at Rob's beer and back at him, offended.

"Yo, what kind of chic do you think I am?"

Rob looked down at the beer and back at her, lost.

"It's just beer, Casey."

"No shit, Rob." She took one of the cans from him. "Budweiser? Really? You ain't got any Heineken? You know, the green bottle?"

"Do you see any Heineken in these hands?" he asked. "Beggars can't be choosers—shit, I ain't the corner store. So, you comin' or what?"

Casey placed the can inside her coat and followed Rob onto the elevator. The way things had been going in her life lately, she could use the drink, and a new friend.

"A'ight, but just for a little bit. No funny shit, Rob."

In the dead of night, beneath a murky lamp haunted by moths, the two sipped and chatted along a railed wooden fence out front. Initially, nothing about Rob fancied Casey except his generosity and the fact that she was bored enough to entertain him. He wiggled his toothpick legs back and forth as he talked about his past and how he used to get down in the streets back when he was younger. Casey pretended to be impressed by him. "Oh, for real? Word? Wowww. Son, what happened?" Occasionally, she'd peek at her watch. Casey could spot a bull-shitter from eight penitentiaries away, and Rob loved to bull-shit from what she could tell. He was a nice guy but just as flawed as she was, if not more. When she least expected it, he hurled an intelligent question at her. It was cliché at best.

"So, what's your destiny, Casey? Do you even have one?"

Casey nearly choked on her drink.

"Beg your pardon? C'mon, don't get all philosophical on me now, Rob. We were having a nice discussion about your hood days before you flipped the script. Destiny? I don't even have a damn job."

"If you're scared to talk about some real shit then just say it. Otherwise, answer my question. So, what's your destiny? Where do you see yourself in five years?"

"Where do *you* see yourself in five years?" Casey dodged the question. "I can't see past the next five minutes, the way my life's been lately."

"How come?"

She brushed him off. "It's all good, Rob—I'm cool on that for now." Casey quickly gulped the rest of her beer, and gave him back the empty can. "Well, I enjoyed myself, but I better get inside. It's almost 4 a.m. Thanks for the lighter."

As she got up to leave, Rob asked: "So, how much time did you do in the box?"

Casey turned around, her eyes wide.

"How'd you know?" She sat back down. "What are you, CIA or some shit? Who the hell told you that?"

Rob showed Casey his pack of Kools.

"Ain't all that hard to spot." He shrugged. "Everybody Upstate knows that when you're short on commissary, Kools is the brand to buy. I noticed you smoked Kools when I saw you put one out earlier near the elevators. You did that shit so carefully too, Casey," he chuckled. "You almost stuck it behind your ear, but you didn't. That's a jailhouse move. Plus, when I asked you about your destiny, you tried to run… just like earlier when I first gave you the lighter. I remember when I first came home," he said. "I used to run all the time, too. I didn't want anybody to know who I was, and I still don't know my destiny, either. And last, you said you was livin' with your sister for the time-being. So, I just put two and two together."

Casey's mouth touched her shoe.

"You ought to be a goddamn detective, Rob. Are you always so damn nosy?"

"Observant," he corrected her. "You tend to notice a lot of

shit when you got nothin' but time on your hands… like not having a job, right? I've been there, too."

Casey covered her face with embarrassment. "A'ight, man, you got me," she laughed. "So, where'd you do your time?"

"Benntown. Between Rochester and Buffalo, right on the water," he said proudly. "I started there and then they moved me out to Michigan for a while before I came back. You?"

"St. Agnes." Casey lowered her eyes. "In a little hick city about ten miles from the Canadian border. So, what'd you do? Don't tell me you were a pedophile. Otherwise, I'm gonna take that cigarette and shove it up your nostril."

"I'm not a pedophile, Casey. But I do have a body on my record."

"A body? Damn, son. Well, I guess I can't judge. There's a lot of people I wanted to smoke when I was younger, too. So, who'd you do in and why?"

"You first," he laughed.

"What, are we in grade school? What does it matter? Fine, then." Casey threw up her hands. "I helped rob a little sucka-ass convenience store when I was sixteen… ish. They charged me as an adult. They gave me fifteen years, but I paroled out after seven. So, who'd you kill?"

"Nobody, I was just there and wouldn't say who did it."

Casey looked him up and down as if he was short. "Nah, you gotta do better than that," she laughed. "Why you frontin' on me?"

"How do I know you ain't the feds?"

"How do I know *you're* not the feds?" Casey shot back. "How do I know this beer can isn't connected to some undercover cop van parked three blocks away?"

Back and forth Casey and Rob went before agreeing to call a truce and switch topics. She was shocked to learn that Rob used to play the violin in elementary school and wrote poetry. He blushed when Casey asked him to recite one of his works on the spot.

"Fuck outta here with that shit—stop playin' with me, Casey." Rob sipped his beer to hide his smile. "I ain't recitin' no poetry to you."

"Is that because you're full of shit?" she challenged him. "Last I checked, you're the one who invited me out for a drink. Well, I came, didn't I? The least you could do is let me hear a few lines. Not even for me?"

"Not even for you—nope."

Casey continued to fuck with him. "That's so cute. You're blushing."

Rob sucked his teeth at her.

It was 4:48 a.m. when the two wrapped up their sudden date. They came up the elevator together, laughing like old college roommates. Casey teased him along the way, nicknaming him "Shakespeare Rob." He turned red once again before trying to play tough guy. "Girl, I ain't no damn Shakespeare, don't be callin' me that." Casey stared at him, unimpressed. When she raised her brow at him, Rob grinned and shook his head.

"If you don't get off this elevator—"

"Or else what?" She stood in his face. "You're on the sixth, I'm on the seventh. See, look at you. You can't even remember your own damn floor. Lightweight."

Rob grinned again. "Just try not to drop your new lighter. Maintenance man got enough shit to clean up down in the lot as it is." He beamed at her. "Take it easy, Casey. Maybe I'll see you again."

"Yeah, maybe… or maybe not." Casey jabbed at the elevator button. She teased him once more. "Goodnight Shakespeare—I mean, Rob." She cheesed as the doors closed.

A Low Point

Opportunities remained scarce for Casey despite her attempts to find work throughout October of '89. She drank to mask the pain of her rejection and purposely avoided Rob, fearing she'd fall for him at the wrong time in her life. With each passing denial she faced, the further into darkness she slipped, and the more her insomnia killed her sleep. Her past suddenly showed up, reminding her of how pitiful she was. To avoid Rob, she'd smoke inside her sister's bathroom instead of out on the balcony—until Courtney walked in on her. She stood at the door with her arms crossed. Casey got the message. "Yeah-yeah, I know. *What the hell is wrong with you, Casey? Blah-blah-blah.* I'll take it outside." Casey squeezed by her angry sister and returned to the balcony to finish. Later, when she heard Rob's window open, she put out her cigarette and ran inside.

The little money Courtney spared Casey from time to time was barely enough for a roundtrip bus ticket to look for work. Casey had cleaned out the commissary she'd accumulated as a woodshop operator and relied on her sister each week.

"Sorry, Case, can't do it this week, but you're welcome to the change in my ashtray." Casey scrounged the few coins inside her sister's ride. The girls were sitting in Courtney's car outside of the supermarket. Casey was on her way in to fill out a job application.

"I've got a meeting to get to. So, I can't wait around today. See you back at the apartment later?" Courtney tooted her horn and left. Casey carefully counted out the change and noticed she had $1.87. Cigarettes were $2.01, and a one-way bus ticket home was $1.98. Her lips quivered as she realized she didn't even have enough bus money to make it home. Before she could cross the lot to enter the market, someone removed the "Now Hiring" sign from the window. It took her back to Mrs. Lu down at the discount store on her second day home. She shook her head and headed down to the bus stop.

With coins bouncing inside her hands, she counted out $1.87 for the bus driver—it was mostly pennies. The lady looked down at the change and back at her.

"You're short eleven cents."

Casey's eyes filled with worthlessness. The driver sighed and dropped a quarter into the box.

"You're lucky I'm in a good mood. Hop on. I've seen enough tears for one day."

Casey piled into the front seat behind the driver and rested her head on the glass. She couldn't keep the tears from falling. The driver eyed her from the rearview mirror.

"I don't know what you're going through, but whatever it is, I hope it gets better."

At the end of her complimentary ride, Casey touched the woman on the shoulder. "Thank you," she squeaked before getting off.

Casey reached her lowest point since being home the following week at a Kentucky Fried Chicken restaurant on 38th and Pacific Avenue. She waited behind the building for the assistant manager to come out and confronted the poor woman. Casey had put in an application but hadn't heard back. She barked at the woman in her angry New Yorker accent.

"What the fuck are you tawkin' about—*the position's been filled?* Where's my application? You better start tawkin' lady, otherwise I'm gonna smash your fuckin' head in. Now, where is it?"

"Please, don't hit me, ma'am!" The fragile woman shook uncontrollably. "My son's sick, and I can't afford any more hospital bills. He's got the s-s-sugars. Just found out about a week ago."

Casey looked down at her hands and realized she had the lady by the collar. Near a dumpster was a piece of broken mirror. She noticed her bully reflection staring back at her. Flashes of her childhood flickered on the shattered surface. She gasped and let the woman go.

"Oh God! I-I'm so sorry." Casey covered her mouth. "Let me help you up, listen, I didn't mean to—I put an application in, and I just wanted to—"

"Get awf me!" The woman shoved her. "What the hell

is wrong with you? Are you a crazy person or something? Somebody help!"

"No, I'm not crazy, I'm just desperate to—"

Within seconds, a gang of loyal colleagues came running out with brooms and deep fryer baskets to fend off Casey. She darted down the block before hiding inside a Catholic church bathroom to lose them. She climbed through the window above the sink and disappeared into the city. Later at home, Casey confessed her sins to her sister. Courtney looked at her as if she was a lunatic before making a joke out of her ordeal.

"So, let me get this straight… You got chased by a bunch of angry Kentucky Fried Chicken workers for tuning up one of their employees? What? Was the chicken not crispy enough for you or something? Did the chicken not cross the road fast enough? What the cluck is wrong with you?"

"It's not funny, Courtney!" Casey yelled at her. "God, I feel so horrible."

"You think you feel horrible? How do you think that lady felt, the one with the diabetic son? What were you thinking?"

"Man, I don't fuckin' know." Casey splashed onto the couch and buried her face inside her hands. "Do you think I can go to jail for that?"

"Uh, yeah, if you go around roughin' up fast-food work-ers, I would imagine so. Hang on, there's something else I want to show you."

Courtney went into the kitchen and returned with the garbage bag. She placed it down at Casey's feet. A cluster of beer bottles clanked all at once. She opened the bag and removed several Heineken bottles Casey had creamed over the past three days. "One, two, three, four, five, six, seven, *eight* bottles of beer, Casey? Is it too much trouble to ask if you could save me one?"

Casey counted the bottles with her eyes and lowered her head.

"I'm sorry, Court. I don't mean to be a burden."

"Then don't be!" Courtney blasted her. "Look, I can't sit around and babysit you. The other day, you left cheese curl dust all over my coffee table, and on the floor—and you forgot to flush the toilet *again*." Courtney crossed her arms. "There's spray in there for a reason; use it."

Casey shrunk with indignity.

"I'm sorry, Courtney." Her eyes blurred. "I really am. I'll do better, I promise."

Courtney exhaled, angry at herself for snapping at Casey.

"Well, if you wanna help, take this bag down to the dumpster." She kicked at it. She picked up her work shoes and headed down the hall. "I'll be in my room if you need me." Courtney slammed her door when she got there. *Thoom.*

Casey closed her eyes, overwhelmed by her sister's grievances. She tied up the garbage bag and headed down to the apartment dumpster out in the lot. She hurled the heavy bag inside the dark hole on the side of the large iron canister. She looked up at her sister's apartment window from the ground and ducked behind the box to weep until another tenant showed up to empty their trash and overheard her.

"Casey?" Courtney called to her, concern in her voice. "Is that you?"

She quickly dried her eyes. "Yeah," she sniffled. "I just needed a smoke, I'm okay."

Courtney walked back to where Casey was hiding from the world. In her hand were Casey's cigarettes and lighter.

"Kind of hard to smoke when these were inside on my coffee table. I should've thrown them away—here. You forgot to empty the bathroom trash and the can in my bedroom. Make sure you get *all* the trash next time… ewww, it stinks back here. How can you stand it? Smells like eskimo pussy during July."

Casey chortled at Courtney's crude joke. She wiped her eyes.

"How do you know what eskimo pussy smells like? Quit trying to make me laugh."

Courtney knelt beside her.

"Well, it can't smell all that great, I would imagine. You've been out here almost a half hour. How long does it take to throw away trash?"

"However long it takes for me to fit my fat ass inside that dumpster." Casey removed one of her cigarettes from her pack and lighted it. "I'm probably gonna be out here a while. So, if you don't want any of my secondhand smoke or to see an orca attempt to shove itself inside a dark hole, now is the time to leave."

Courtney rolled her eyes. "Will you please come inside and stop with this pity party stuff?"

Casey exhaled from the side of her face. "I told you, I'm fine."

"Are you upset because I jumped in your shit?"

"No, I'm just… I'm good, I just need a minute, that's all." Casey's eyes hazed again. "Go back inside, don't you have to work in the morning? You don't have to hover over me like this. C'mon, you're blowin' my high, Courtney, go. Is it a crime to have a cry and a smoke? You'd cry too if you were an orca."

Courtney shook her head and left. Casey peeped from behind the bin, waiting for her sister to return inside. That tore into her too. She was so pathetic that her sister came looking for her and knew exactly where to find her: by the dumpster. Casey fiddled with her lighter inside her hand. She put up with the dumpster smell for over an hour before finally leaving. On her way up, she took the staircase, careful to avoid Rob.

Between more bad dreams, failed opportunities, and loneliness, Casey mused over her life the next several days. Her parole officer, Mr. Hawthrone, was still pressing her about finding work.

"Time's running out, Haughton." He tapped against his watch. "You better get a move on. You know what's coming if you don't find something soon."

"Th'fuck do you think I'm tryin' to do?" she snapped on him. "Nobody ever said how hard it'd be to get a job with a felony on your record. What do you want me to do? Become a hooker?"

Mr. Hawthrone shrugged with pity. "Just make sure you list it on your W-2."

Casey picked up her jacket and stormed off.

Meanwhile, at home, the girls were still at odd ends. They battled like a mother and rebellious teenage daughter at times.

"Get up, right now!" Courtney kicked at the couch one afternoon, waking her up. "There's a big grease spot on the stove and shredded cheese near the microwave—go."

Casey climbed off the sofa and went into the kitchen. She looked back to notice Courtney standing over her.

"What about that spot over there?" She pointed near the fridge. "The floor is sticky, too. There's a mop inside the hallway closet."

"You said near the stove and counter. I didn't do all that."

"Well, you live here, don't you?"

Casey sucked her teeth and retrieved the mop from the closet. She scrubbed at the floor like an entitled, stuck-up brat. She returned the mop afterwards and bounced on the couch as if she'd just finished working a ten-hour shift. Courtney rushed over to confront her some more.

"Have you even been out at all today? The last two days? Three days?" she asked her. "Seems like all you've been doing is eating and slugging around."

"I haven't felt up to it."

"Girl, your better get up off my couch and get out there. Don't you have to have a job by a certain time while on parole?"

"I will, Courtney, damn. Why you sweatin' me?" Casey laid back down. She looked up and noticed Courtney was still staring at her. "Whaaat?"

Courtney stormed down to her bedroom and closed the door. Casey mumbled to herself, relieved. "Go read a book or something. Leave me alone. Sheesh."

Eight

The girls were in the middle of yet another heated debate over grease, leftover cheese and unemployment when the phone suddenly rang one early evening in November. The sisters had been at each other's throats all day when Courtney answered the line in a haste. "Who? Casey? Yeah, she lives here… for now!" she snarled into the phone, eyeballing her. Casey noticed Courtney's expression change as the caller carried on. Courtney covered the phone and lowered it. "It's for you," she whispered. "Some guy named Brian? Is this about that job at the porno store?"

Casey dashed to the phone to take it. "Give me that—hello? This is Casey. Who's this?"

"Hi, Casey. I am Brian Joyner. I'm the co-owner of BuBoy's Restaurant on West 44th and 7th Avenue in Manhattan. You filled out an application a few weeks back. Are you still interested in employment with us?"

Casey covered the phone and began jumping up and down as if she'd won the Powerball.

"What? What'd he say?" Courtney asked.

"Remember that new Italian place we saw in the paper? It's them!"

Courtney gasped. "Word? Well, get back on the line before he hangs up—go."

Casey composed herself and returned to her call.

"Hello, Mr. Joyner," she said civilly. "Yes, I remember, and I'm still interested."

"Please, call me Brian. So, you applied for a server position with us? Is that correct?"

"Yes," she cracked. "Are you calling to tell me that I got the job, Brian?"

"Well, no, but I am calling to tell you that we're very interested in you, Casey, and we'd like to set up an interview. But if all goes well, we would love to have you. We have quite a few vacancies, and based on your application, we think you might be a good fit for our restaurant. How soon can you visit us? Are you available this evening at seven?"

"Tonight? At seven?" Casey looked over at Courtney for approval and received a nod. "Sure, Brian, seven is great. See you then."

"Actually, I won't be in, but Todd, our other manager, he'll be there. Good luck, Casey."

When her call ended, Casey screamed in celebration. "Holy shit, I'm going to work!"

Casey grabbed Courtney and danced her around the kitchen. It was the closest she'd come to an interview since Mrs. Lu put her out of the discount store back in September. She pressed Courtney, pecking her with sisterly kisses on her pretty cheeks. "Thank you." *Peck.* "Thank you." *Peck.* "Thank you." Casey grabbed a towel from the hallway closet and glided into the bathroom to freshen up for her new job opportunity.

For the next two hours, Courtney helped Casey prep for her interview. She drafted a list of mock questions to sharpen her interview skills.

"You can't say 'fuck' at a job interview, or you else ain't gonna get it, Case," Courtney said. "Be professional—and don't forget to smile, too."

Later, Casey rehearsed her goofy smile in the mirror with Courtney standing there.

"Will this work?" She stretched her face like a jack-o-lantern.

Courtney palmed her face.

"For now, I guess. You look like Michael Keaton in *Beetlejuice*—we'll work on it."

The stage was set. Courtney heated her favorite hot comb over the stove and took it to Casey's kinky hair. Steam emitted from her scalp like a kettle. While Courtney straightened her hair, Casey painted her nails a pretty, clear polish. Growing up, she'd hated wearing polish or make-up, afraid it didn't fit her pale features or that others would ridicule her. She laid out a beautiful floral dress she'd purchased down at the thrift shop and borrowed a pair Courtney's wedged sandals. Courtney zipped up her dress in the back before applying the finishing touches to her hair. Casey rocked from side to side as she tried to walk in her sister's shoes. "Whoaaa, shit," she giggled. She wobbled down to the bathroom and stood in front of the mirror.

"So, what do you think?" Courtney asked her.

Sparkles formed in Casey's eyes. She covered her mouth with both hands.

"Oh, my God. I-I can't believe it. I look beautiful." She began to cry. "I never *ever* thought I could be beautiful."

Casey turned to thank Courtney and noticed she also had sparkles in her eyes. Courtney began straightening Casey's dress for her.

"You *are* beautiful… except when you cry—you're ugly as shit."

"Shut up!" Casey bopped her.

The girls placed their heads together before Courtney yanked herself away and finished dolling her up sister.

"Okay, now quit the mushy stuff. You're ruining the make-up."

Life In the Big City

Resumé in hand and dolled to perfection, Casey strolled into BuBoy's Restaurant on West 44th and 7th Avenue fifteen minutes early for her interview. She'd borrowed one of Courtney's manila work folders to carry her drummed-up document and studied it during the subway ride over. Casey could still hear Courtney's voice inside her head as she dropped her off. "We got this, right?" Casey nodded her head. "Right!"

She entered through the lobby doors and followed the signage down to the glass elevators. Her stomach rumbled with each passing floor on her way to the top. The building was still under construction with the restaurant set to open before Thanksgiving. Casey's stellar reflection overlapped the busy city night during her trip up. She stopped to gawk at the neon skyline, moaning blissfully at New York City's backdrop. She flailed at a strand of stubborn hair before practicing her introduction. "Hi, I'm Casey. Nice to meet you." She stopped herself to try again. "Oh, hello there!" She smiled this time. "My name's Casey Haughton. It's a pleasure meeting you." *Shit.* She leaned against the wall and exhaled. Casey had never wanted anything in her life more than to walk out of BuBoy's that night with a job. So, she did something she seldom ever did. She clasped her hands together and prayed. "Lord, please," she begged to the heavens. "Just let me have this one." She crossed her big heart and got off at the twelfth floor.

The view from the restaurant overlooking Manhattan at night was so rivetingly beautiful, Casey forgot why she was there. Streaks of colorful lights decked the skyline for miles, the eye of the sun barely peeked over its horizon. Growing up in the city, she'd fantasized of someday moving away, but the view that night changed her mind. Casey had never seen anything so strikingly magnetic in all of her—

"Yes, can I help you?"

Casey spun around, off guard. The welcomer was a young, pregnant Puerto Rican girl with long hair. She looked to be about eighteen or nineteen years old.

"Hi!" Casey waved, surprised. She put on her *Beetlejuice* smile she'd practiced at home with Courtney and walked over. "I'm Casey Haughton. I'm here for my interview."

The girl rolled her eyes and waddled to the back. Casey took the inappropriate gesture in stride and returned to enjoying the view. She wasn't sure of much else in her life but was sure about not leaving there that night without a job. Before long, the hostess returned, holding her belly.

"You're here for Todd, right?" She winced. "Sorry for the attitude. This baby's been kicking my butt. I'm Wendy, by the way."

"Casey." She extended her hand. "How far along are you, Wendy?"

"Too far," the hostess laughed. "So, you're here for the waiter position, right?"

"I'm just *here*, Wendy. But to answer your question, yes, I am here for the waiter job. My goodness. Have you ever seen such a view?"

"Never, and I used to think my grandma's rooftop in the Bronx was great. I'll have to bring my little boy up one day after he's born to show him."

"So, a boy? Oh, cool." Casey smiled. "I always said if I have kid, I'd hope for a boy—not that I want any kids, but that's another story. Do you have a name for your son?"

"Yeah. I'm naming him after his father. But I'm gonna call him Junior."

"Junior," Casey repeated. "I like that." She returned to checking out her new work space when suddenly a man dressed in a brown three-piece suit emerged from the kitchen to greet her. He was an older gentleman with tracks of salty gray in his hair. He reminded her of a gameshow host.

"Casey, right?" He pointed at her, grinning from ear to ear. "Come on over here and let's talk. Brian's been telling me about you. I'm Todd. I'm one of the co-managers here."

As Casey began to follow Todd, Wendy touched her arm.

"I'm not supposed to tell you this, but… welcome aboard," she whispered.

Casey cheesed from ear to ear and walked over to meet Todd at a booth. He waited until she arrived before taking his seat.

"Welcome, Casey. I had a chance to read your application. Your handwriting is fabulous. Boy, are my cooks gonna love you. Where'd you learn to write like that?"

"You'll never guess… prison!"

Todd rumbled at her candid joke and gestured for her to take a seat. He removed a pair of ugly glasses attached to a bootstring and stuffed them onto his face.

"Alright, let's get down to business." He cleared his throat. "What do you got there for me—a resumé? Mind if I look?"

Casey handed Todd her fibbed document. Courtney had put it together earlier while Casey was in the shower. She glanced at it while on the train, assembling a storyline in case she was questioned.

"So, Dominos, huh? Yup. That's how I got started."

Casey kept a straight face as Todd reviewed her resumé. Her pulse rate increased as Todd scratched at his gray hair.

"So, how long did you work at Dominos?"

"A little while… only part-time." She shrugged. "You know… high school."

"Yeah? Where? Which one?"

"West Fellers. They went out of business."

"Really? No kiddin'? I didn't know they had a Dominos in West Fellers."

"Mm-hm."

When Todd went back to reviewing Casey's resumé, she deflated with relief. He closed Casey's folder and handed it back to her.

"Well, I'll tell you what, Casey, I'm impressed." He

removed his glasses. "I like your sense of humor too, and I think you need that in this business. I spoke with Brian earlier and we feel confident about moving forward with you. We're not officially open yet, but we still would like to bring you on and familiarize you with staff and our menus. Is that okay? Would you like to work here? Please say yes."

"Yes!" Casey smiled gleefully. "Double-yes."

"Great. Why don't you come back tomorrow at noon? Welcome aboard, Casey."

The two met outside the booth and kindly shook hands. Todd took Casey on a brief tour of the restaurant. He showed her the kitchen where orders were processed; he also showed her the storage, the freezer, and even showed her how to clock in for work. The place was spacious and finely outfitted with dark wood paneling. He even gave Casey tax forms for her to fill out at home. "Just bring those back tomorrow when you come or the day after. You wanna get paid, don't you?" He winked at Casey and returned to the back.

Casey's prayers had finally been answered. On her way out, she stopped by the hostess desk to chat with Wendy. "See, what'd I tell you," Wendy whispered. "Okay, let me show you the phone system. It's kind of crazy, but you'll get used to it after a while." Casey oohed and aahed as Wendy worked the lighted buttons on the phone.

By the time she was ready to depart, her hands were loaded with tax forms, menus, and other work stuff. Wendy even had one of the chef's prepare red velvet cupcakes for Casey to take home as a welcome gift.

"Thanks, Wendy." She smiled. "Hopefully we get to chat more before you go out." She waved goodbye and returned to the elevators. Before she could leave, Todd came running down the aisles to stop her.

"Casey, can you come back for a minute? I want to introduce you to somebody."

Casey handed Wendy her cupcakes and forms and headed over.

"Well, aren't you just the talk of the town?" Wendy cutely laughed. "Shit, if I'm not careful, you'll end up taking my job."

"Yeah, let's hope not. Don't eat my cupcakes—I'll be back!"

Casey walked over to meet with Todd again. Standing next to him was a guy with the company's insignia stitched on the front of his jacket.

"I forgot to introduce you to our driver, Chuck," Todd told her. "You'll be helping him out with warehouse runs from time to time until business picks up. Chuck's a great guy, he'll show you the ropes and then you'll be issued a key to our van. You do have a license, don't you?"

Casey's soul trembled.

"License?" She hesitated. "Um, no, I don't—but I'm working towards getting one. I've got the book back at my sister's apartment. I just haven't gone to take the exam yet." She panted, running out of breath. "I'm sure I can have one in the next couple weeks—a month at the latest."

Todd rubbed his eyes in disappointment before sending Chuck off.

"Well, I really need another driver."

"I know, and I'm gonna get one soon, I promise."

"*Soon* doesn't do me any good, Casey. We really could use another driver and—"

"How close is the warehouse from here?" She cut him off. "Maybe I can work there until my license comes through? Will that work, Todd?"

"And do what? Fumigate the place?"

Casey's mouth opened but nothing came out.

"I'm very sorry, Casey, but I can't bring you on. Brian and I really need another driver. I wish you the best of luck out there. I mean that. I'll talk to Brian about what happened. Who knows, maybe another spot will pop up. I'll call you if it does."

Casey stared through Todd's eyes and could see herself standing there looking like a damn fool. Her mouth propped open in disbelief. Her heart cracked as she waited on Todd to smile and tell her that the whole license thing was some big hoax. She received her confirmation as he walked off. She had come within a hairline of landing a job and had fallen on her face yet again. Her chest winded tightly, making it hard for her to breath. The feeling was like the onset of a heart attack. She placed her hand against the paneled wall in shock, holding her chest. She prayed, but the Lord didn't deliver. He never did—not when it came to her. Sick, she rushed into the lavatory stall, closed the door behind her and wept loudly. Mascara ran down Casey's face as she fell into a hideous, silent cry. She cried so intensely that Wendy walked in to check on her. Casey could tell it was her because she recognized the shoes.

"I heard what happened. Is there anything I can do?"

Casey splintered again, moaning in stammering gibberish.

"I… j-j-just wa-wanna be *alone*." Wendy shoes suddenly went the other way.

Casey sat on the floor inside the bathroom, clutching her knees. Afterward, she moved over to the sink to rinse away her smeared makeup. She was no longer beautiful and back to being the furious, ugly, fat kid no one wanted. It was the same indignant look she'd worn for most of her battered life. On the way out, she bypassed Wendy along with her free cupcakes near the hostess stand and left without saying goodbye.

At a payphone along a crowded street corner in Manhattan, Casey pressed her wet cheek to the receiver to phone Courtney. She could barely dial the number, her hands shook so gravely. She lost it the moment her sister answered. "I didn't get it!" She boohooed again. "I'm so… I'm so fuckin' done, man. Don't worry about looking for me. I'll be home later." Casey hung up. She crossed her arms over her wide body as the machine deposited her quarter and ambled toward the subway.

With a blank look, Casey gripped a metal handlebar above her head, watching sparks launch from beneath the rail car as riders came and went. She felt foolish for even believing she'd thrive with her felony record. Her mind worked against her. *You tool. You really thought they were gonna hire you?* The more she thought about her latest rejection, the more she regressed to believing that parole was a mistake. She'd never live the simple nine-to-five lifestyle like Courtney, hoping to ascend the corporate ladder. As a felon on parole, Casey was ineligible to vote, own a firearm, travel abroad—or work, apparently. On a poster in front of her was a picture of Uncle Sam encouraging riders to join the military. She couldn't do that, either. Her limited road to success seemed bleak.

On her way home, Casey trolled the city with Courtney's sandals in one hand and a cigarette in the other. It was the only good thing she had going for her in her life, her cigarettes. She smoked one on her way to the subway, two while she waited for the train, a fourth when she got off, and a fifth and sixth during the walk back. Along the way, she spotted a hooker promoting herself to cars at an intersection and shook her head. Even *she* had a job, Casey thought to herself. A wino solicited Casey further up the sidewalk, offering her a good time. He showed her a palm full of crack rock. "Yo baby, you need a hit on somethin'?" She bypassed his invitation for drugged sex and continued beneath a half-shuttered liquor store. She stopped to marvel at a hiring sign in the window of a bakery. Before she could blink, the owner removed the signage and replaced it with a board that said, *Position filled.*

Casey continued toward her building in the distance and stopped as she reached the lot. She stared up at Courtney's balcony on the seventh floor and noticed the living room light was on. She envisioned her sister pacing throughout the living room, waiting to hear what had happened. She parked onto the wood bench, hoping to wait her out. Casey sat in the cool November air for over an hour waiting for the lamp to turn off, but it never did. She eventually gave up and headed inside to face the music.

Casey plodded through the lobby and down to the elevator, defeated. She pressed at the button and waited for a car to arrive. When the doors opened, she noticed a familiar face on the other side.

"Casey?" Rob greeted her. "Damn, where you've been?! I been lookin' for you the past couple weeks, but I ain't seen you." Rob squinted at her. "You a'ight?"

"I've been *good.*" Her voice suddenly gave out.

Rob looked her over. "You sure?"

Casey nodded her head.

"No, you ain't. Get in here." Rob draped his arms around Casey and pulled her into him. She crashed into his chest. "C'mon, tell me what's wrong?"

"Everything is fuckin' wrong, Rob, everything," she sobbed. "Nobody will hire me, and I'm scared of going back to prison 'cause I won't find a job in time. I'm a burden to Courtney. I don't have any money—or a damn license, and I'm a big, fat stupid orca!"

Rob held Casey as she bounced inside his arms. He removed his coat, placed it around her and began rocking her.

"I gotcha, baby girl, I gotcha. Everything's gonna be alright. It's hard out here in this world—but you gotta hold on sometimes, you know? But I gotta ask you somethin' though, Casey. I know I ain't the smartest man in the world, but…

What's an orca? Hell, I ain't never heard of such a thing. They got 'em here in Brooklyn?"

Casey snorted on Rob's coat.

"Well, at least you still know how to laugh, I guess." Rob pressed at the elevator button. "C'mon. Let's get you cleaned up."

Nine

Rob's apartment was nothing compared to the sanctuary Casey had become accustomed to while living at Courtney's. It was cheap and unfulfilling with makeshift furniture to accommodate his space. His wobbly coffee table was propped on books and looked as if he'd got it at a yard sale. Across the room was a janky stereo and a small television which sat atop a metal folding chair. Down the hall, Casey noticed Rob's bed: two mattresses, one stacked atop the other with a worn shipping blanket serving as a comforter. There were no pictures, burning potpourri, or ornate plants decorating his balcony. His minimal setup reminded her of a struggling college student living on gas station coffee and Ramen noodles. Casey stood near the wall, leery of his intent.

"C'mon, let me show you where the bathroom is, in case you wanna—"

Casey jerked her hand away from Rob as he tried to guide her.

"…freshen up." Rob studied her. "Bathroom is in the back. Help yourself."

"You got a pan and some water?"

Rob gave her a dubious look and went to the back. He returned with a pan full of warm, soapy water and a hand towel. He placed it on the floor near the couch and took a seat.

"You gotta come over here to get it."

Casey turned to leave.

"Nice try, Rob. Find another easy girl to fuck. I'm out."

Rob leapt from his couch and over to the door, blocking her exit.

"Wait-wait-wait, now just hold on a second, Casey, hold on. Look, I ain't like that. Hell, I'm on parole, just like you," he said. "Shit, you're the first girl I've had in here in two years." Rob reached for her hand. "I was hoping we could shoot the shit for a little while—maybe a beer or two. On my momma's grave, I ain't tryin' to push up on you like that, shawty. Hell, if you wanna go, who am I to stop you? It's your world, Casey. I just wanted to be a part of it… if only for a little while."

Casey watched as Rob unlocked the door to his apartment and returned to the couch, allowing her to make the decision. He looked down at the pan near his feet and bounced to the far end, hoping to convince her that he was trustworthy. Casey still didn't buy it. Rob then reached beneath his couch and pulled out a raggedy old journal and began to read.

Four walls. Encased behind steel.
Yet, still, the system steals the dreams
of men whose destiny it is to still dream.
We just want the chance to enhance our old ways,

and to see the light of a new day.
But as soon as I got out,
those same dreams suddenly died out.
I cried out, for every door that America
locked and threw away the key.
I just couldn't believe
that after so many years of my captivity,
I couldn't catch a break, couldn't find a job—
but that's my reality, you see.
I guess that's just the way it's gonna be.

—Robert Daniel Barkley Jr. - May, 1987

Rob returned his journal beneath the couch. Casey aborted her suspicions about her neighbor and grinned at him. Like that, she had forgotten about her sour moment at the Restaurant. "There he is, Shakespeare Rob," she called him by his pet nickname, glowing.

Rob lit a cigarette and gave her a dirty look. His softness suddenly vacated the apartment. "I ain't readin' you shit else, Casey, so don't even ask. That's your first and only poem." Rob dipped his smoke into a porcelain ashtray and blew from the side of his poet face. "So, you stayin' or what?" With her arms crossed over her heavy body, Casey locked the door, moved toward the couch and took a seat beside him. When Rob placed his arm around her, Casey quickly sat up. He backed off. "Told you I ain't like that," he said. Casey relaxed and returned beneath his arm. Rob used his foot to slide the pan of soapy water to her.

"I'm not used to being inside of another man's apartment. Been around mostly women the past seven years."

"Wish I could say the same. I've been around men the last twenty."

A slight chuckle escaped from Casey. She rinsed what was left of her runny mascara and the grime from her heels. She dried her face and looked around at Rob's bare walls.

"Why is your place so bland? Don't you have any pictures you want up?"

"There ain't none worth puttin' up," he said. "Moved here right after I got out. Didn't have the credit, so my mother pitched in—God rest her soul." Rob looked around. "That first year is hell when you come home. I was lonely, broke— scared half the damn time." He sighed. "That's how cats end up goin' back in. The world can be a scary place after you've been gone from it for so long, you know. You come back and feel like a damn stranger."

Casey dried her hands with the towel. "Yeah, tell me about it. Everywhere I turn, I keep getting doors slammed in my face." She lifted her pan full of dark water. "Where do I dump this?"

"I got it." Rob took it from her.

Casey waited while Rob emptied her pan full of dirty water. Her feet were still sore from her long fuming walk back to Gardener Heights. She used her unoccupied time to check out Rob's blank setup. It was on her mind to phone Courtney and let her know she was safe, but she didn't want a lecture. If Courtney knew she was hanging out inside another's man apartment, she'd put out an All-Points Bulletin and ask Casey fifty thousand questions when she finally showed up. Instead, Casey reminded herself that she was an adult and did not have to adhere to Courtney's good-girl bullshit and regimented structure. After all, it was 9 p.m., not 3 a.m. The last Casey had checked, she was grown and could make her own decisions. Before long, Rob returned to the living room.

"Well, I was a thinkin' about goin' downstairs to sit near the stoop for a little bit. You down, or you cool on that?"

Casey finally opened up. "Can we stay here instead? It's chilly out, plus my feet are sore."

Rob tilted his head at her. "You wanna stay *here?*"

"Well, yeah. I mean, I don't want you to feel uncomfortable or anything, Rob, I know it's been a while since you've been this close to a girl and all," she teased him.

"Shawty, stop playin' with me," Rob fired back. He walked over to the icebox, fetched two Heineken bottles and offered her one. Casey looked down at the bottle and back at him.

"You got Heinekens?!" she gasped. "Oh, my God, I love these."

"That's why I got 'em, Casey." Rob took back her beer, bit off the cap and gave it back to her. Casey touched her lips, in awe of his soft yet macho persona. Nothing about Rob was attractive on the outside, but his soul was golden. She wondered what else glowed about Rob and decided to stick around to found out. Without warning, he toasted his bottle against Casey's. Suds quickly foamed near the top, prompting her to suck at the tip. Rob stared at her, frozen by the erotic gesture. Casey laughed at him.

"You're leaking." She pointed out. "It's all over your hand."

Rob looked down at his bottle and noticed foam oozing down his hands.

"Shit—I uh—" He paced around nervously. "You still got that towel from earlier?"

Casey giggled at Rob's childlike bashfulness. She grabbed her used towel near the couch and handed it to him. She watched as he cleaned up his mess. She shook her head at him.

"Yeaaah, it's definitely been *a while*, Rob, holy shit."

"Stop Playin' With Me"

Rob must've said it a thousand times that night, but it still sounded new to Casey each time she heard it. The room blinked as the two spilled their guts to one another throughout the evening. Casey dangled her leg across Rob's knee as she reminisced about her wrecked childhood and ended at her shitty night down at the restaurant. She dabbed her eyes, recalling the humiliation she felt after scoring a job and suddenly having it taken away. "I never felt so small in my entire life, Rob, and I've been small before."

Fried on Heineken, O.E. (Old English), and whatever else Rob served her, she dumped her life's story into his lap. The thought of checking in with Courtney had expired hours earlier. Rob used his hand to stroke Casey's thigh, putting her at ease. Each time she got close to finishing her drink, he offered her a new one. "Looks like you need another beer, hang on," he'd say to her. Rob would then return with another bottle. Casey would sip her new drink and continue unpacking her miserable life.

"Man, one time I got beat up for a week straight when

I lived with my aunt and uncle over in Brownsville. It was those kids, man—those goddamn kids. I think that's why I hate kids so much. Makes my skin crawl just to think of raising one, ugh."

"Why'd they beat you up?"

"Who knows? I'd show up and get beat down just for being there," Casey laughed. "By the time I was thirteen, I couldn't fuckin' wait to get out of Brooklyn. I moved in with Courtney after that. Things were going well until… I don't know. I think I just got scared or something."

"Scared of what, Casey?"

"How would I know? I was just a stupid kid." She mulled over it some more. "Then again, no, I'm lying. I think I was afraid of not being good enough. Most of the kids in West Fellers were smart, good-looking, had real teeth. I was just a fat rat from Newark who lucked up on a great situation. I didn't feel like I deserved to be there. I ended up sabotaging myself, and in the process, I hurt the only people in this world who gave a damn about me.

Casey exhaled and sipped from her beer before her reflections could overwhelm her. Rob leaned forward to stump his cigarette butt into a porcelain ashtray. He fanned away his smoke and readjusted Casey's leg on his lap.

"You ever wonder if the shit we go through ain't about us, but for somebody else? I know that sounds fucked up. But who knows, your story might help somebody one day."

"Somebody like who?" Casey asked. "Who could I possibly help in my position?"

"Hell, I can't call it, but what if someday you meet some kid or something?"

"Do I *look* like someone responsible that a kid should take advice from, Rob?"

"Maybe not right now. But that could all change, Casey."

"Yeah, when hell freezes over," she chuckled. "Speaking of kids—you got any? Is there a Mrs. Shakespeare Rob in your life? She into poetry, too?"

He looked at her. "Shawty, stop playin' with me."

Rob's path to prison was similar to hers, Casey soon learned. He told her he was thirty-eight, never married but had two boys (Paul and Ellis) who didn't live with him. Rob didn't work, but he received a check from the government every month. For what, he didn't say, and how or how much, he wouldn't reveal. Rob's father left the family when he was young. His mother wasn't a drughead like Casey's biological mother, but she was a workaholic and worked two full-time jobs which often left him and his three brothers to their vices.

"A lot of shit got put on me when I was young. I couldn't handle it," Rob confided to her. "I'm the oldest, so I remember seein' my father leave. It did somethin' to me."

"What did it do to you?" Casey coupled beside him.

Rob broke down his path to the big house.

"A'ight. So, my mother owned a little .22 and I took it one day. I got into some shit with these boys from around my old neighborhood. Ain't have no business going up there in the first place since I had a baby and a second one on the way. Plus, I was still on probation, you feel me?" Rob explained.

"Anyway, I gave the gun to this homie of mine. We go down to the spot where those kids were, and my man shot one of the boys. I ain't know he was gonna shoot nobody, he said he just wanted to scare 'em. We all ran, but the cops showed up later with my mother's gun. The look on her face, Casey," he shook his head. "She was so hurt that I did that. My man got life, and they stuck me with thirty-three. I made it out at twenty, but I'll be on papers for a while."

"So, where is your mom now? Is she still around?"

"She… died last year." Rob paused to compose himself. "She used to visit me every month until she started getting sick—even when they sent me out to Oklahoma—*and* while she was takin' care of my three younger brothers. She used to call me Robby. So, one day she said, 'Robby, I don't know how much more of this I can do. I'm startin' to slow down.' I knew then I had to get my shit together and come home."

Rob tucked his hands inside his arms. He closed his eyes and exhaled sharply through his nose. Casey could tell how much recounting the story had taken out of him. As she went to hold him, Rob shot off the couch and into the kitchen. "I'm a'ight." He stood near the icebox for an extended time. Casey went over to console him.

"It wasn't like we grew up hungry, my brothers and me," he said. "We had everything we needed. Momma used to drive us down to Jones Beach during the summer. I played music, wrote poetry, and got to do other shit most kids in my building didn't get to do. I was decent in school too, but I still just… still had that darkness about me. I just couldn't shake that shit, Casey."

"I know what it feels like to think that you're worthless, but you're not, Rob. And… if it means anything at all to you, I forgive you."

Rob looked at her, almost offended. "Yeah? Well, you might forgive me, but *I* don't forgive me!" He slapped at his chest. "The world—out there—they don't forgive me. I mean who cares about little old me anyway, Casey, when it's all about—"

Casey grabbed Rob by his scruffy face and kissed him, silencing his rant.

"Shut up, okay?" She smiled at him, holding his face. "None of us are squeaky clean in this life, Rob. We're all just pieces of shit floating down some murky stream, trying to find our way." She eyeballed him. "I said I forgive you. Doesn't that mean anything?"

Rob gazed into Casey's eyes with newfound freedom. He pulled her in tightly, wrapping her inside his long arms and returned a lavish smooch. His long fingers glided down Casey's backside and cupped her apple bottom. She giggled between kisses, backing him up.

"Later, Rob… maybe," she laughed. "I still don't trust you yet."

Rob gave her a defeated look. She could tell by his long face he thought was on the verge of scoring with her. She decided to tease him a bit longer, hoping to test his fortitude. If nothing else, he was great company, a good drink, smoke, maybe a fuck—but she refused to love him. When Rob went for another kiss, Casey backed up.

"We good?" he asked. "I thought that was what you wanted?"

He tried once more and Casey weaved to the other side.

"So, you're one of *those* kinds of girls? You want a man to come flyin' out the sky with a rose hangin' from his mouth? Is that it?"

"Negro, didn't I say later?" she laughed. "It was just a kiss. Put your snake away, sheesh!"

Casey shook her head and returned to the sofa, leaving him dry. She curled onto Rob's couch and invited him over. The night was still young and Casey already had his undivided attention.

"So, we kickin' it or what? You got any Sadé?"

Happy Dust

By 2 a.m., Casey and Rob had compiled a surfeit of cigarette butts, empty beer bottles, and solo cups on his living room table. They burned through Michael Jackson's album *Thriller*, Salt-N-Pepa, Heavy D, Full Force, and a host of other vinyl collections Rob owned. He didn't own any Sadé tapes but claimed he'd buy one soon to accommodate her. "Next time," he said. Casey had forgotten all about calling Courtney, she was so bent. She stood on the arm of Rob's couch, palming the ceiling for balance. "Catch me, Rob, I'm falling. Weeee." She tilted off the sofa and into his arms. Rob caught her and fell backward onto the floor, hard. *Boom.* As he winced in pain, Casey cracked up laughing. "Yeah, you better had caught me. Otherwise, you ain't gettin' shit!" She staggered onto her feet and continued her show. She shook her goodies, backed up on him, and grinded her rump into his meat. "So, you like my lap dancing skills?" she asked him. Rob widened his legs and leaned back. "Love it." He reached inside his pocket and removed a joint of reefer, lighted it and passed it to her. Casey hit Rob's joint, straddled him and held

Rob by his mouth with both her hands.

"Open up."

When Rob opened his mouth, Casey blew her smoke into his puss and kissed him. She dragged her finger across his lip, touched Rob on his flat nose and went back to seducing him. He puffed his blunt and groaned with pleasure.

"Word is bond, you got some moves for a white girl, Casey—I ain't bullshittin'. Who taught you how to dance like that?"

Casey slowly peeled herself back from Rob and gave him a glaring look. She hopped off Rob's lap and tossed herself beside him.

"Th'fuck did you just say to me?"

Rob's face straightened with worry. "I said you dance good for a white girl… I ain't mean it like that, Casey, I mean—you know what I'm tryin' to say, right? Like, you know— 'cause most white girls ain't got no rhythm when they dance—but you dance good—I didn't mean to upset you; I meant it as a compliment. You really can dance, though."

"I'm not white, Rob!" Casey crossed her arms. "Haven't you ever heard of albino?"

Rob's mouth hung open.

"Well, either way, you got some moves… and some pretty eyes, I might add."

Casey sucked her teeth at him and turned her head, pretending not to notice his scruffy face checking on her. Rob pinched Casey's side, prompting her to smile and shoo him away.

"I'm mad you thought I was a white girl, though. Nigga, did I not just sit here and do a duo with you, line for line, to 'Love and Happiness' by Al Green? You couldn't put two and two together?"

"White people like Al Green too, Casey."

Before Casey could complain, Rob wrapped her up and peppered her with kisses and tickly bites to her neck. She squealed, trying to get away.

"Nope. Get off me—get off me." She play-fought him. "I ought to go home for that shit."

"Well, you can't go just yet," Rob told her. "The party hasn't even started."

Rob left her on the couch and went into the back. Casey made herself comfortable by reaching for an old flannel blanket on the floor. Before long, he returned with a small hand bag. Casey slid closer to him and hooked her leg around his, curious.

"What's in there?"

Rob emptied his bag onto the table. A short straw, expired credit card, and a small baggie of cocaine landed on the table.

"Holy shit, Rob," she said. "Don't they piss-test you down at the office?"

Rob plucked at his baggie. "Look, I ain't tryin' to force you into nothin' you ain't comfortable with. But for me—*me?* I need this right now. Between losing my mother right after I came home and other shit I've been through, I guess I never worry about gettin' caught. Ain't nothin' out here in the city for me anyway. If I go back, I go back. But I ain't been caught yet, so..."

Casey hung on Rob's relaxed philosophy. She watched as he sprinkled a chalky line across his table. She stopped him as he lifted his straw.

"Rob, wait, hold up." Casey grabbed him. She stared down at the buzzing cocaine. "Let me go first this time—I'm the one who didn't get that stupid job down at the restaurant."

Rob handed her his straw. He used the old credit card to refine a line proportionate to Casey's inexperience. She placed the straw up to her nose and went to inhale it.

"Th'fuck you doin'?" Rob grabbed her, annoyed by her eagerness. "Man, this shit'll fuck you up, Casey. Slow it down."

Casey nodded her head and held the straw up to her nose. As a teenager, she'd drank alcohol, smoked marijuana, and experimented with acid, PCP, cough syrup and other drugs. She had come close to using cocaine but never had any—afraid the powdery drug was more than she could stand. She once placed a fingertip's worth on her tongue and was amazed how it numbed her mouth. Back then, it scared her from going any further. But now, she was sick of being let down and desperate to find a break from her broken world.

Casey closed her eyes and inhaled Rob's blow. The tiny white particles entered through her nasal passages and quickly absorbed into her bloodstream. Rob patted her back as she gagged and coughed. "You a'ight?" Casey nodded and coughed again, unable to talk. She snorted the remaining small atoms and fell backward onto the couch, gazing at the ceiling. Her dim existence started to illuminate. Feelings of euphoria ignited the dopamine radars inside her brain as she floated with elation. Her past soon became a distant memory. She simmered with the assuredness of a global icon arriving on stage to receive an Academy Award. Every nerve inside her body tingled with pleasure; each limb sensitive to the touch. Her mind went trippy as pieces of her past melted before her eyes. Casey grabbed her head with both hands as if to stop her mind from getting away from her.

"Feel good, don't it?" Rob asked her. Rob's voice echoed as if they were standing inside a subway tunnel. "You sure you a'ight?"

"Yeah, man. I'm good. Th'fuck?" Casey snapped on him. "Quit askin' me that already."

Already resonated even louder inside her head. She closed her eyes and leaned her head back in ecstasy. Her soul burned with the composure she'd been missing all her life.

Rivets of happy dust floating throughout her blood stream, Casey's night at Rob's was a whirlwind of blind fun with brief photographic memories. "Here, now snort this." Rob pushed Casey's head down onto his table to take in a half-line. "Here, now balance it out." Casey downed a shot of Hennessey. At one point, he offered her another hit of reefer. She indulged her narcotic neighbor, hoping to impress him with her resiliency. His apartment shook violently inside her head. The walls inside Rob's apartment closed in like her old cell as bars soon formed around her. A ghostly guard wielding a shotgun showed up. The blurred figment chambered a slug and pointed it at Casey's head. The shadow then laughed at her.

"What's the matter, Haughton? You didn't get your mail this week?"

Casey's dry red eyes popped opened the next morning in Rob's bed. Dazed, she went to get up and realized she was fully naked. She covered her breasts with her arm and returned to bed. Her head pounded ceaselessly, and her loins felt sore and stretched. She touched between her legs and noticed her vagina was bleeding slightly. She stared at her hand in disbelief before her wild night suddenly came back to her: the cocaine, the reefer, the booze—all the result of failing to secure employment for an umpteenth time. She nudged Rob with her elbow.

"Rob? Rob, wake up."

His bullfrog face quickly came to life. His untamed hair was matted to one side. He stretched and climbed off his mattress. He was naked too—still wearing the dried condom he'd used on Casey throughout their extravagant night.

"Oh, no! Tell me we didn't, Rob." Casey covered her face.

Rob smiled smugly. "Yeah, we did," he chuckled. "Don't act like you ain't love it, either."

Casey rubbed her eyes and glanced over at Rob's digital clock on his dresser and noticed it was 9:53 a.m.

"Courtney! Fuck!"

She scrambled for her strewn clothes and dressed herself. Her sober mind reminded her that she hadn't seen or spoken to Courtney since the night before. She imagined her crazed sister wired on coffee and driving around Brooklyn with her service-issued pistol in her lap, looking for her. She scurried through the bedroom in a haste.

"I gotta get back before she kills me." Casey wiggled into her underwear and dress. "Can't believe I was so stupid."

"Why would she be upset?" Rob asked her. "Shit, you grown, ain't you?"

"You don't know Courtney like I do. You think I'm crazy? Try pissin' her off."

"Well, piss off her later. I was just about to run down the street and get us some breakfast. You want some pancakes?"

"No, Rob, I don't want anything—I gotta go. Now, where are my shoes?"

"Out front."

Casey ran into the living room, grabbed her shoes, and sprinted home barefoot. She hauled down to the elevator and mashed the button. She waited a half-second and mashed it three more times. "Th'hell with this." She dashed down the hall, up the staircase and onto the seventh floor, nearly missing apartment 714. She fumbled with her keys before dropping them. She picked them up and dropped them again before finally inserting the right key into the lock. As soon as she unlocked it, the door whipped open causing her to fall to her knees. Her eyes drifted to a pair of fuzzy Victoria's Secret slippers and a pair of beautiful brown legs. Casey slowly looked up and saw Courtney standing beside the door with an indignant look.

"I can explain—"

"So, explain," Courtney cut her off, crossing her arms. "Why aren't you explaining?"

Casey crawled onto her feet, barely able to stand from her bad hangover.

"I should've called. That was bad on my part—being out like that all night and leaving you here to worry. Just give me a chance to explain."

Courtney slammed her door so hard that a picture fell from the wall. As Casey backed into the living room, Courtney stalked, not taking her eyes off her.

"Where… the fuck… were you?"

"C'mon, Courtney. Look, chill out, okay? You're scaring me—"

"Scaring you?!" she yelled at her. "Scaring you? You don't think I was scared last night? Huh? Wondering where the hell you were in this big city, doing God knows what—and with who? Scaring you?" she repeated. "Are you FUCKING kidding me, Casey?"

Courtney backed her onto the couch and stood over her.

"Look, I was upset about not gettin' the gig down at the restaurant. I'm sorry."

Courtney picked up one of her sofa pillows and began whacking her.

"Fuck you—you're sorry, you little—" Courtney threw it at her. "I can't believe you could be so STUPID." She screamed, shaking as she talked. Her voice buckled as she continued. "You're selfish. All you care about is *you*." Courtney lobbed another pillow at her. "Suppose something happened to you? Then what? You better get your shit squared away real fast, Casey, or else!"

Courtney escaped out onto the balcony, leaving Casey to mull. She watched as her sister leaned over the ironing railing. As a little girl, Courtney had rarely cried, Casey remembered, but she cried that day. She edged outside, hoping to smooth things over.

"I'm sorry, Courtney." Casey placed her hand on her sister's back. "I messed up. Look, if you wanna know where I was, I'll tell you."

Courtney turned around. Her eyes were red with tears.

"I don't give a shit where you were, Casey. I just wanted to know that you were alright. You're grown. I get it. You wanna do you—do you. Just don't leave me hangin' like that."

Casey grabbed Courtney's hand and gently swung it.

"Never again," she said. "I guess this whole freedom thing is new to me. I've been locked up like an animal for seven years—takes some gettin' used to being out."

"Well, you better get accustomed to it quickly, 'cause if it ever happens—"

"It won't, Court. Look, I know what I gotta do to keep myself off the radar, and I'm gonna. Just... believe in me, please. You're the only one who ever has."

Courtney squinted her eyes at her. "I'm trying, Casey. I really am." She leaned in. "What's that on your nose?"

"On my nose?"

When Courtney reached for her face, Casey blocked her wrist.

"No-no, I got it. Uh, I mean... I'll check it out. I need a shower, anyway."

Casey rushed inside, down to the bathroom, closed the door and locked it. She couldn't help but recall the skeptical look Courtney gave her. She turned on the light and stood in front of the mirror. On her left nostril was the powdery residue from her good time at Rob's. She splashed a hand full of icy water into her face and scrubbed it relentlessly. She stripped off her clothes and climbed into the shower. She checked her achy vessel again for bleeding and shamefully leaned her head against the wet tile. Casey had never felt so disgusting in her life. She went haywire, scraping and clawing at her freckled skin, hoping to restore what was left of her dignity before realizing she no longer had any. Hopeless, she sat on the floor with her knees pulled tightly into her chest, allowing the boiling waters to consume her.

Ten

Casey's hope diminished the longer she went without finding a job. She had been home for barely two months and was succumbing to the dark rage which had put her behind bars seven years earlier, each failed opportunity pushing her closer to the edge.

She applied for a tank cleaner position at a pet store in Prospect Heights and was shafted. "No way would I touch you, lady. What are you, nuts? A felony?" The manager laughed in her face. "Sorry, but I don't do criminals, sweetheart."

Casey raised her voice at the man. "Don't call me that! I'm not a criminal," she said. "I made a mistake, and I paid for it. I'm out here trying to do what's right just like everybody else." She took her business elsewhere.

A dog walker position turned up nothing as well. Casey had never liked dogs but was desperate. She changed her mind when the owner showed her a photo of a rottweiler. Two days later, she attended a hiring fair at Madison Square Garden and lost it when she didn't get selected for an usher or ticket taker job. Casey stood outside in the rain for over an hour with other aspiring applicants, waiting to be let in. "I can deal with the felony, but you need at least a diploma or HSE. I'm hoping you know what that means? High School Equivalency?" the event's planner asked her. Casey sat on a metal chair inside the renowned arena, scowling at the new hires as they were issued radios and fluorescent vests. Someone tapped her on the shoulder.

"We're about to start training soon, Miss Haughton," the manager said. "I hate to ask you to leave, but we can't allow the public to watch us train. Do you mind?"

Casey snarled at the man. "You want to me leave? Fine, that's all you had to say. Where's your fuckin' balls, man?"

Casey picked up her jacket and blasted toward the exit, full of attitude. She glanced over her shoulder and noticed she was being followed by the planner and a team of indoctrinated new hires. When Casey realized she was the guinea pig for their training exercise, she went ballistic.

"Yo, my nigga, why the *fuck* are y'all following me to the door like I'm some terrorist?! You asked me to leave, and I'm leavin'—now back up off me before I kick your fuckin' teeth out—all of you. I don't even know why I came to this stupid building in the first place."

The group continued to follow Casey down to the exit. The manager bypassed Casey and held the door for her.

"Have a good day, Miss Haughton—"

"Fuck you." She went off again from the other side, cursing the man to hell. "Fuckin' pussy. You couldn't even walk me out by yourself." She cursed at another. "Th'fuck are you lookin' at? Point that radio at me again and watch what happens. I'll squash you out here!"

The man shook his head at Casey and closed the door to MSG. Casey turned and stormed up the rainy sidewalk, mad at the world.

On her way home, Casey stopped by the liquor store. She used the bus money Courtney had given her to purchase a bottle of vodka. She couldn't afford a chaser, so she drank it straight. The alcohol made her act even more foolish than she already was. She sipped her drink at a nearby park, thinking aloud and acting shamefully. She hogged a swing set as a group of teenage kids stopped by to hang out. Casey cut her eyes at the group, daring them to challenge her. She drank from her bagged container, wiped her drunken lips and spat in the dirt, hoping to draw their attention. *Toof.* When the kids turned to look at her, she stood up.

"What up?" She outstretched her arms. "Th'fuck y'all lookin' at, huh?"

The teens muttered amongst themselves and ignored her.

"Y'all want this swing set? I *bet* you won't come and take it," she dared them.

She stumbled back to her seat, glaring at them. Casey waited over an hour for those kids to try her. They happily overlooked her pitifulness before moving along, leaving her disappointed. She waited until they disappeared up the sidewalk and continued home. Holding that swing set was Casey's only victory since making parole. Meanwhile, her shrunken world was only decreasing the more she and Rob became acquainted.

Rob possessed a magnetism about him which made it difficult for Casey to resist. He was screwed up like her but in a different way, and they understood each other. He smoked Kools, complimented Casey's crudeness, was fun to be around, amicable, and the sex was decent enough. Plus, Courtney worked a lot, leaving Casey alone to her thoughts. Bored, she'd end up over at Rob's.

"All you do is fuckin' work. We haven't even been out to the movies yet. Don't you ever like to have any fun?" Casey asked her sister once over the phone during her lunch break.

"Well, you got any money?" Courtney countered. "Fun costs money, Casey—money I don't have. I don't see you creating any 'fun' for us."

Casey hung up on her, hard. She paced throughout her sister's apartment before grabbing her coat and keys and returning to Rob's.

Every time Casey would go to Rob's, she'd promise herself not to return, but it never worked out. Rob was a dead end; a bum at best with an apartment provided to him by the government for an unverified "disability" he somehow claimed. He knew all the tricks of the system and used his knowledge to exploit the process.

"I can't do this anymore, Rob. If I'm not careful, I might turn into you. This is the absolute last time, and then I'm out." Casey snorted a short line of cocaine, chugged the rest of her beer and headed out. She went back to her sisterless apartment and returned a few hours later. "You got any more blow left?"

Within weeks, Casey became addicted to cocaine. She'd do so much coke with Rob some nights that her nose would numb or bleed, and the high was amazing when supplemented with alcohol. Cocaine provided the self-worth she'd been missing since her childhood. Her traumas subsided and were replaced with feelings of intense euphoria. She didn't worry about a stupid job, diploma, driver's license or keeping Courtney off her back.

When sober, Casey was back to being her regular broke self. She stopped checking in with the parole office for her weekly visits, knowing she was dirty and would return to the penitentiary if caught. She was restless, jumpy, and cranky. She jumped out of her skin at Courtney once for loudly dropping a pan into the sink. *Thung.*

"What are you trying to do, give me a heart attack?!" Casey quickly sat up. "What in the hell was that? Sounded like a train crash."

Courtney looked at her, confused. "It's a pan. What else would it be?"

"It's not just a pan, Courtney. Okay? Dammit. You're scaring the hell out of me back there. Did you scare the shit out of your last boyfriend, too? Good Lord."

"Oh, go to hell, Casey."

"Apparently I'm already here!"

Casey whipped her blanket over her head and turned over. Her sudden paranoia didn't end there. She was shaky and ate less which was unlike her. She double and triple-checked the hallway and balcony and was afraid to get the mail from the box in the main lobby. One night while the girls were watching a movie, the neighbors above them invited guests over. The sounds of shuffling feet across the floor reminded Casey of her old prison's riot team surrounding her cell block with guns and tear gas.

"You know what—on second thought—" She stood up. "You go ahead. I don't feel so good. Think I need the bathroom."

Casey picked up her cigarettes and headed toward the back. She closed the door, locked it and sat on the side of her sister's bathtub in the dark. She fired up a cigarette and rubbed between her eyes. Courtney soon showed up on the other side.

"If I knew *Fright Night* would've got to your stomach, I wouldn't've rented it. You're gettin' soft on me, Case. We used to watch creepy stuff all the time when we were little. You good?"

Courtney opened the door and turned on the light. She crossed her arms at her.

"Yes, I'm smoking inside your bathroom after you've told me ten thousand times not to, Court." Casey sighed. "Now, may I please finish my smoke before you yell at me?"

Courtney turned on the vent fan, not taking her eyes off Casey. She braved the foggy smoke and took a seat beside her on the edge of her tub. Annoyed, Casey pinched out her cigarette and placed it inside her pajama pants.

"Can I ask you something?" Courtney looked at her. "This isn't easy to ask, so I'll just get on with it—are you using drugs?"

"Holy shit, Court. Are you for real? *Am I using drugs?* That's funny."

"Well, are you?" Courtney asked again. "Are you gonna answer my question?"

"No, Courtney, I'm not using any drugs. Why would you even ask me that?"

"I have my suspicions." Courtney slapped both her thighs and stood up. "Well, if you say you're not—then you're not. Just thought I'd ask."

Casey's eyes widened. "That's it?"

"Yup." Courtney gave her a presuming look. "I mean, you are my sister, right? Why would you ever do anything to hurt me? I'd have to be a damn fool to even think you'd do drugs, knowing the jeopardy it could put us in. Right or wrong?"

Casey shamefully lowered her head. "Yeah… right, Court."

"Riiiight." Courtney nodded slowly. "Enjoy your cigarette, my dear." She turned off the light and pulled the door shut, leaving Casey in the dark.

Courtney's skepticism messed with Casey's head later that night. She stood in front of the bathroom mirror, scrubbing her face until it came off. She exhaled at the dark patches forming beneath her eyes. The skin around her nostrils was flared and slightly yellow, and her eyes were red. She tossed on her hoodie and went to pay Rob a visit. She told him off as soon as he opened the door.

"Hey, I was just about to—"

"Hey—nothin'," she bypassed his greeting. "Look here, Rob. I can't kick it with you no more. We gotta knock this shit off. I need a job with some real benefits. I don't need any more of *your* benefits. Have a nice life."

Rob grabbed Casey's hand and gently rubbed it.

"Well, can I at least say, goodbye? At least let me have somethin' to remember you by."

Casey entered Rob's apartment and allowed him to bid her a proper "farewell." Afterwards, he offered her some of his favorite dessert.

"Okay, but no more after this. I mean it. I've gotta get back on track."

Drughead

With each hit of blow, Casey convinced herself she could stop whenever she wanted. It was typical addict talk, foolishly believing she could shake off her drug use under her own free will. The high that cocaine gave Casey made her so dependent, she began stealing money from Courtney to supply her habit.

"What do you mean you haven't seen it?" Courtney asked her. "I placed the leftover money from the Chinese food on the counter, Casey. Did you even look?" She bombed her. "It was five dollars and some change. I needed that for gas."

"Look, I didn't see the damn money. What do you want me to do?" Casey gave her shit back. "Besides, what the hell would I do with five dollars, anyway?"

"Oh, I can think of something, I'm sure."

Courtney walked off. She went down to her bedroom and closed her door. Casey returned to the sofa and plopped in front of the TV. She reached inside of her sock for Courtney's gas money and looked at it. She deflated and hid the money beneath a food box, hoping to trick Courtney into believing she'd overlooked it. Less than hour later, Casey swiped the money and went to see Rob.

Rob was a good time, and a relief from Casey's despair. They'd listen to music, smoke reefer, snort cocaine, drink, laugh together, cry together, have sex, and do more cocaine. They talked about everything from eloping to marry at a small chapel in Belize to entering the music business together as partners. Casey would place her big spotty leg across Rob's leg and lay across his nappy chest, fingering his gold medallion necklace. He'd palm her backside, stroking his fingers in the gorge of her spine.

"Okay, so explain this shit to me, Casey." He passed his blunt to her. "How does being bisexual work? Is it a fifty-fifty kind of thing? Like, do you like men and women the same or one more than the other?"

"Both, actually." She took a hit of his joint. "But I think it depends on the person, too. Take me, for example. I'm more like sixty-forty. I like men, but I'd prefer a woman. Make sense? Honestly, everybody's got a little bit of bisexuality in them, I think. Some more than others."

Rob looked at her.

"Yeah, okay. Ain't no way I'm bisexual."

"Yes, you are!" she laughed, pushing him. "I read about it in this magazine while I was locked up. It's kind of neat, the way the author broke it down. He talked about the duality of us as people and how feminine energy works, even in men. For example, a guy can look at another guy and think he's

216

handsome, good-looking, or whatever. Doesn't mean you want to fuck him, you know. Even if you do, hey, to each his own, right?"

Rob didn't blink.

"What the *hell* did you just say, Casey? Duality of who?"

Casey shook her head and went back to her reefer.

Whenever their drug stash got low (which was often), Casey would accompany Rob to buy more. He'd take her to some hole-in-the-wall building surrounded by rotting cars on cinderblocks, gang tags, mounds of trash, dope fiends, boarded up windows, and nodding heads. To get there, they'd cross a railroad track and squeeze between a hole in a wiry fence with barbwire at the top. The first time Casey went along, Rob was holding the gate back for her until it slipped from his sweaty fingers, cutting her across the arm. She had on a T-shirt that day. "Shit, Rob!" She inhaled through her teeth, in pain. "Th'hell is on your hand, Crisco? Watch the fuckin' gate, man!"

Casey and Rob once visited the same drug spot three times in one day. She followed him up the rundown staircase, dodging gummy-mouthed drugheads in her path. "Watch your step," Rob warned her. One user, a middle-aged woman, was so high she'd fallen asleep going up the staircase with the rail still in her hand. The door for Casey and Rob's supplier had no number, only a peephole.

"Wait out here," he'd tell her before going inside. Some mumblings would occur and then he'd emerge with the drugs.

One day, Rob surprised her at the door. "A'ight, you

can come in, but stay close to me—and don't say nothin'. Not a word."

Casey shook her head and followed him inside. She sheltered behind Rob, silent as a funeral. The image she saw that day would forever burn in her mind: jug bottles, soda cans with burn holes, foil, pill bottles, needles, moldy food containers, blankets, clothes, a shitty mattress (literally), cooking pots, eating utensils, and broken liquor bottles—and that wasn't even half of the junk crunching beneath Casey's sneakers. Above all, the worst Casey saw was a young white girl sitting on a filthy sofa attempting to rock her crying baby to sleep. "Sh-sh-sh." The girl looked to be around nineteen or twenty and was pregnant with her second child. Her face looked as if she hadn't slept in days. Her fingertips were swollen and yellow from freebasing, and her fingernails were nibbled back to her cuticles. She bounced her whiny daughter inside her arms, attempting to sweet-talk her. Casey could tell the baby hadn't been changed because the diaper was slugged to one side on the poor kid. It reminded Casey of her Newark days living with her drughead mother. Across the room, Rob put on his negotiator hat, hoping to cut a deal on a decent supply of blow for them.

"Th'fuck do I look like to you? You think I'm stupid?" Rob chewed out his dealer. "That's the same amount I usually buy, G. All you did was chop it down. You're undercuttin' the value on every dollar by overchargin' me at triple the rate. That's price-gouging. That's the same shit those oil companies did to consumers back in the seventies."

Casey couldn't believe her ears. She knew her man was

no dummy, but she'd never heard him articulate himself so passionately. Her head moved back and forth as Rob negotiated with some guy named G. over their shitty deal.

"Man, what? I ain't tryin' to hear all that wack shit, Rob. Forty, take it or leave it."

"Thirty, nigga. Man, I always been loyal to you!"

"Thirty-five."

"Thirty-*two*," Rob raised his voice. "Thirty-two-fifty... ma'fucka."

G. packaged Rob's drugs and placed it on the counter. Rob counted out twenty-eight dollars and placed it next to the drugs. He patted his pockets before looking at Casey for help.

"You still got that five on you?"

Casey smacked it into his hands. "Just hurry up, please."

Rob gave the dealer Courtney's gas money. Casey took one last look around the dealer's shipwreck apartment. She couldn't take her eyes off the junkie mother rocking her baby to sleep. Rob gave the dealer the thirty-three dollars, took his drugs and left. Casey scolded him during the walk back.

"What the fuck was that back there?" She pushed him. "Did you see that?"

"See what?" he asked. "It's only fifty cents, Casey. At least I got it down to—"

"I don't care about the cost, Rob. Did you see that place? How could you not see that girl sittin' there with her baby? That was the most disgusting thing I've ever seen. Why'd you bring me here?" Casey pushed Rob again. "Don't ever do that shit again."

"You said you wanted to come. You didn't have to go in there."

"I was watching your back!" she hollered at him. "You know what, fuck it, from now on, get the shit yourself. I don't ever want to see anything like that again. Otherwise, I'm gonna call the cops on you myself. Is that understood?"

Rob broke into a boyish grin. Casey put up her dukes, prepared to fight him.

"Oh, that's funny? Huh? You think I'm joking?"

Casey swung at Rob, missing him with a wide left. She threw a right, left and another right which sailed by his shoulder. He laughed, easily dodging her shots. Frustrated, she shoved him and walked off. Rob chased her down.

"Casey, wait up."

He followed her up the block and grabbed her from behind. Casey turned and fought him.

"Get your hands off me!" She swatted at him. "You make me sick."

"Okay, Casey. You made your point. From now on, you won't have to go inside. You can stay back at my place, if you want. I'll get it myself."

Casey finally stopped. "You promise?"

"Promise," he agreed. "Look, it used to make me sick too when I first started seein' stuff like that. But that's just the world we become a part of with this shit. It's fucked up, but that's how it is."

Tears were spilling down Casey's face.

"I just… I don't wanna end up like that girl back there. If

that's what it's gonna be then—"

"You won't, Casey—*we* won't. I won't let it happen. Okay?"

As Rob reached for her hand, Casey walked off again. She made it about twenty feet before remembering she'd just put in on a bag of blow and wanted her five dollars' worth. She turned around.

"You comin' or what?"

Addict

Casey slumped on the couch to watch the Macy's Thanksgiving Day Parade live on TV. She sniffled and pawed at her runny nose as if she had a cold, unable to sit still, fiending for a hit of blow. Shifty, she tapped her fingers incessantly at the arm of the couch, bouncing her knee. She glanced over her shoulder repeatedly, waiting for Courtney to leave. The longer she took to ready herself for work, the more unstable Casey became. She paced the living room, went on the balcony, returned inside, bounced her knee, went back outside and returned to the sofa just to tap her fingers once again. She glanced over her shoulder to look for Courtney and noticed Courtney was staring at her. Casey sat up abruptly. "*Whaaat?*" Casey eyes shifted. "Damn, what's wrong now?"

Courtney shook her head and went to the closet. It was the girls' first holiday together in years.

"Nothing about this picture surprises me, unfortunately." Courtney slipped her coat off a wobbly hook. "Just tell me you're close to finding something so that I don't have to—" Courtney patted her pockets, surprised. She sniffed her hand

and looked over at Casey.

"What?" Casey asked her. "What is it? What's the matter?"

Courtney reached inside her coat and pulled out an empty Heineken bottle. A small, empty bag with cocaine residue and soggy reefer flakes swam at the bottom. Casey had borrowed her sister's jacket the other night to visit with Rob and had forgotten to throw away her trash. Courtney marched in front of the TV.

"What's all this stuff? And why is it inside *my* jacket?"

Casey hung her head down to the floor.

"I borrowed it one night and… I should've thrown it away—"

"You're damn right you should've thrown this stuff away! You shouldn't have it in the first place," Courtney growled at her. She looked over the bottle again. "Are you crazy? Aren't you on parole? Don't they drug-test you?"

Casey sighed. "Yes, Courtney."

"Then what the hell is wrong with you? Shit, I give you a place to stay. Feed you. Clothe you—give you money. How do you repay me? By stealing from me—lying to me—and bringing drugs into my apartment." Courtney threw the bottle at her.

Casey looked down at the bottle in her lap and slowly picked it up.

"I wanna know everything," said Courtney. "Where'd you get this stuff?"

Casey continued to play with the empty bottle, picking at the label.

"So, you're not gonna tell me?" Courtney asked her.

Casey shrugged her shoulders. She looked down at her feet, fearful of her sister's wrath. Courtney threw up her hands and went to find another coat for work. She tore through her closet.

"Well, I'll tell you what." She put on her windbreaker. "You better start looking for a new place to live soon 'cause you're not gonna be layin' up in here doin' drugs on my watch. I'll be damned if the cops raid my apartment because of you."

"Nobody's gonna raid anything, Court. I can give up the shit… at any time. I'm just struggling to come to grips with my world crashing all at once. I'm still trying to get adjusted."

"How? By becoming a drug addict?" Courtney asked her sarcastically. "How's that working out for you? How's that working out for *us?* Did you ever think about that? Us? You promised me you were gonna do right, and you did the exact opposite. You lied to me—I trusted you!"

Casey's lips trembled with regret.

"I gotta go, I'm gonna be late." Courtney slammed the door behind her.

The Truth Hurts

"**H**ow did I get myself into all of this?" Casey asked herself aloud in front of Rob. She sat with her face behind her hands. She could still hear Courtney scolding her inside her head as she left for work. A tweet escaped Casey as she began to cry. Rob placed his hand onto her back and rubbed it. "So embarrassing, man—so pathetic. Nobody can be this pathetic." It always bothered Casey to see her sister mad at her, even when they were young. She relived the door slamming and the glimmer in her sister's eyes as she left. She was a stalwart of a troop, unbreakable, hardcore to the brim—army strong. A tear from Courtney was real pain. For Casey, tears were just a part of her little damaged world. Rob sat there listening to her, silently puffing his blunt until he'd had enough. He scooted from his couch and over to his stereo, turned up the volume and returned beside Casey.

"You ain't pathetic," he told her. "Shit, if you're pathetic, then I'm all-the-way fucked up."

Casey chuckled at his junkyard humor. Rob ran his hand beneath Casey's shirt and massaged her fleshy back, gently rocking her. She closed her eyes, marinating in his consolation.

"Well, if you're worried about Courtney throwin' you out, you can always stay here. My place ain't all that, we got a TV, music, and—"

"Do you love me?" Casey looked at him.

Rob's eyes brightened with unease. "Huh?"

"I saaaid…" Casey scooted closer to him. "Do you love me?"

Rob looked down at his cocaine and joint of reefer burning in the ashtray and back at her as if she'd had too much. Casey shook her head, smiled, and removed her shoes.

"Relax, Rob. I'm not *that* high—at least not yet." She laughed and kicked her feet into his lap. "But I would like to hear a poem from you before the night is over. Think you can make that happen sometime tonight?"

Rob cut his eyes at her.

"How about you go to hell sometime tonight. Stop playin' with me, Casey."

She grabbed him by his bearded face and began kissing him. Seconds later, the two were interrupted by a mysterious knock at the door. They pulled away like anxious high-schoolers being caught smooching by their parents.

"Casey, it's me. Open the door." Courtney's voice sounded from the other side. "I know you're in there—I followed you. C'mon, open up. We need to talk."

Casey covered her face, embarrassed.

"Sorry about all this."

She slithered off the sofa and over to the door to answer

it as Rob looked on. She opened the door with the lock chain still attached and peeked at her furious sister.

"What are you doing here, Courtney? I thought you had to work?" she whispered.

Courtney didn't blink.

"Open the door, Casey."

Casey pushed the door shut, removed the lock chain and let her inside. Courtney looked her up and down and entered without saying hello. Her eyes zoomed over the table covered with beer cans and scattered paraphernalia. She gave Rob a culpable look before rejoining Casey at the door.

"C'mon, get your stuff. We're leaving."

"No," Casey told her. "I'll be home later. I'm in the middle of something."

"Like what? Frying your brains out?" Courtney grabbed her by the arm. "C'mon, we're out of here. I'm not letting you do this to yourself."

As Courtney tried to haul her away, Casey fought back.

"I said, no… wait—get your *hands* off me!" Casey shoved her into the wall. Courtney was more shocked than hurt, she could tell. As Rob attempted to get up, Courtney quickly drew her service weapon from her jacket and pointed it at him. He surrendered immediately.

"You know what you doin' with that thing?" he asked her.

Courtney cocked the hammer. "Would you like to find out?"

Rob backed himself onto the sofa, not taking his eyes off her. Courtney de-cocked her weapon and returned it inside her jacket. Casey's eyes widened with surprise.

"That's the third time you've done that to me," Courtney said. "You pushed me when we first met. You pushed me again right before you went Upstate, and you just pushed me now. Hell, you've been pushing me away ever since I came into your life. Well, maybe it's time that I start pushing you away."

"What's that supposed to mean?" Casey asked. "Why, because I'm not like you? Because I don't have an army stick up my ass—pretending that everything is so goddamn perfect all the time?"

"I never said things were perfect, Casey, all I ever wanted was—"

"All *you* ever wanted," Casey raised her voice. "What about me? What about what I want, Courtney? Man, I never get what I want! I'm always last. I never got first dibs on anything. It's always what's left over—and I'm sick of it. I can't be like you, Courtney. I can't pretend anymore." Her voice split. "I'm just in your way, man. I've always been in your way."

"Casey, will you please just come on? You're not in my way. Look, I don't care about the stupid drugs. Just come home. We'll figure something out."

"No, I am in your way," Casey complained. "I'M IN YOUR WAYYY!"

She ran into Rob's bedroom and crashed onto his bed, spent by the sudden visit. Meanwhile, out in the living room, Courtney and Rob argued like two devils over who would take possession of Casey's soul. They barked at each other before Courtney finally gave up and left. Casey couldn't make out all of it but overheard her sister in the end.

"You're dead, motherfucker! You better hope I never see you around Brooklyn." Rob's door thumped from wall to wall as Courtney stormed out. He entered the bedroom seconds later and took a seat next to Casey on the bed. He was unperturbed, with his joint still in his hand, despite having had a .45 Smith & Wesson pointed at his head.

"You a'ight there, Casey?"

She rolled over and looked at him. "Is she gone?"

Rob nodded his head. "Yeah," he said. "At least for now."

Casey faced the wall. "Hmph. Good."

Eleven

Casey slept through most of her next several days at Rob's place, sick. She woke up only to vomit or medicate. For two days, she tried to ween herself off cocaine by replacing her desires with alcohol and marijuana. She shot out of bed and into the bathroom to gag over his bowl. Lines of slimy drool dripped from her curled lips into the commode. She had no food in her system and was so overcome with alcohol that she couldn't pull herself off the floor. "Rob!" she hollered. "Robbb!" Rob sprung from the kitchen and went in to help her. He guided Casey back to bed, holding her up. She moaned, stumbling across his floor with pieces of vomit cake hanging from her lips. He placed Casey on his mattress and cured her the only way he knew how.

"Girl, are you crazy? Two whole days? Here, hit this." Rob poured Casey a line of his magic dust. Desperate to end her suffering, Casey indulged him. The tiny particles entered through her bloodstream, treating her illnesses. Relieved, she rolled over and exhaled as if she'd just had her brains fucked out of her. She hadn't seen or heard from her sister in days.

Casey was so hooked on cocaine, she thought she'd die without it. The physical changes she'd undergone after using the drug nearly every day for months were startling. Her soft, plump face was sunken in around her eyes and her pupils were dilated. She tremored and struggled to sit still. Her nostrils were raw-looking and red, and her nose was always runny. Her skin was dry and flakey.

Rob had changed also and had begun perfecting a new high for them by freebasing cocaine. Using baking soda as an additive, he converted his white dust to a rocky yellowish texture and smoked it. He looked down at his crack pipe with new approval before passing it over to her. "Try *this!*" Casey placed his hot tube to her lips. Her hands shuddered so badly, she couldn't hold the lighter steady. "Light it up for me." As Rob placed the flame up to his glassy pipe, Casey inhaled the vapors. She paused and hit it again before smiling at him delightedly.

Days after their discovery, Casey was napping on Rob's sofa while her boyfriend attempted to string together a decent payment on another hit of crack rock. They had already smoked up his first-of-the-month check and were looking for more money. Rob flipped his couch and pulled out the pockets of every pair of pants he owned. He tore through his bedroom, spilling clothes everywhere, searching for dough. He woke Casey up twice in the same hour to ask her about the sofa. "Ain't nothin' here, man, you already checked," she rasped. Rob went back to tearing apart his bedroom, looking for drug money. Casey turned over and tried to sleep again.

She was nearly out before a knock sounded at the door.

"Casey? It's me." Courtney knocked again. "Are you in there? I really need to talk to you."

Casey kicked her blanket onto the floor, sat up and rubbed her addict eyes.

"I just want to talk, Case. I uh… I miss *you*." Her voice changed. "I never realized how small my place was without you there."

A tear slid down the side of Casey's face. She rose from the dead and unchained the door. She noticed Courtney's eyes were just as shiny as hers.

"Jesus, Casey." She shook her head. "You look like a whole different person."

Casey leaned against the door. "What do you want? I'm trying to nap."

"I just want to talk. Two minutes? It'll be quick. I promise."

"Rob and I may head out in a few. I'll stop by your place after we—"

"You don't have five minutes? Not even for me?" Courtney asked her. "I gave you eleven years. The least you can do is give me five minutes."

Casey rubbed at her forehead. "Wait here a sec." She closed the door in Courtney's face and went to the back to confer with Rob.

"Courtney's outside," she said disinterestedly. "I'm gonna take a walk with her—maybe grab a few of my things. I shouldn't be long."

Rob gave her a curious look. "What does she want?"

"Well, I don't know that yet, Rob, that's what I'm gonna find out. Just wait for me." Casey stood on her tippy toes to kiss him. "I'll try to squeeze a few dollars from her if I can."

Casey went out to meet her sister. Together, the girls trekked down the sixth-floor hallway and up the staircase. Courtney talked during most of the walk.

"So, I've been thinking a lot—about everything. You know I love you and only want what's best for you. You know that, right?" The girls turned down the corridor. "I hope you can forgive me for the other day. But I did that out of love, Casey."

"I know, Court," Casey said. "If it was me, and some strange guy had you by the horns, I probably would've pulled the trigger."

The girls traveled down the hall and stopped in front of their apartment.

"We *are* sisters, and we'll always be that." Courtney removed her keys and unlocked the door. "I packed up your things for you—I even washed them. If you ever need anything, you know where to find me. I'm sorry things didn't work out." Courtney gestured for her to enter.

Casey took a deep breath and let it out.

"I'm sorry, too." She hung her head and stepped inside. As soon as Casey slipped through the doorway, three cops grabbed her. Confused, she began fighting with them.

"Just let them take you, Casey, don't try to—"

"What the fuck is this shit?!" she shrieked while resisting arrest. "Are you serious? Courtney! How could you do this to me?"

The cops wrestled Casey onto the floor and placed her into custody. She kicked her legs back and forth, hysterical.

"I didn't wanna do this, but you made me—"

"Fuck you!" Casey lamented. "You sneaky bitch. You set me up!"

Casey banged her head against the floor, blubbering unintelligently. Her short run at freedom was finally over. With her hands cuffed behind her, the cops hoisted Casey onto her feet and led her out of Courtney's apartment. She hollered and fought like a six-year-old being dragged away from an amusement park. Nosy neighbors peeked from their apartments and watched as Casey took her walk of shame. She slumped forward with her head pointed down at her feet. Courtney lagged at the rear, justifying her excuse for the deception.

"I'm probably gonna hate myself for doing this, but I'd rather see you in cuffs than inside a box. You'll understand someday. You're a survivor, I know you'll be alright."

Cops ushered Casey down the elevator and outside as tenants and bystanders watched her howl in misery. She threw herself onto the ground and caused a scene the second she saw the police car. Casey placed her face into the asphalt.

"Why'd you do this to me? I just needed time. I was gonna do right, Court."

"No, you weren't," Courtney told her. "You never do right. You haven't done right since I've known you. This whole thing has been one great big lie. Between all the drinking and drugging—stealing money from me. Hopefully you learn your lesson this time."

The cops lifted Casey onto her feet. She spat into her sister's face. *Toof.*

"Fuck you, Courtney. You always thought you were better than me. I wish I'd never met your sorry stuck-up ass."

Courtney used her shirt to wipe her face. Casey looked off into the distance toward her old building and noticed Rob standing out on the balcony, watching her.

"Rob!" She called to him. "You see this shit? Robbb?!"

Rob turned and went back inside, leaving her. The cops shoved Casey into the back of their squad car and closed the door. She banged her head against the grated glass repeatedly before ripping Courtney again.

"You stupid bitch. You stupid-fucking-bitch—don't you *ever* come and visit me. I don't have a sister anymore!"

Courtney's soft eyes glimmered.

"Yeah, you should feel bad," Casey poured it on, "turning in your own sister like that. Did they teach you how to be a rat piece of shit in the army?"

Casey blasted Courtney as the officers drove her away. She raved until her sister's image became another spectacle in her shattered world.

Withdrawal

Casey wandered her precinct cell, unable to sit still. She bounced from wall to wall, pacing her confined space like an irritated lioness. She shifted from sitting on the floor, her cot, leaning against the wall and overseeing the small window out into the hall. Casey back-kicked her cell door, on the verge of a nervous breakdown. Hopeless, she splashed into the corner of her cell with her knees tucked to her chest and whined. She returned to her window to negotiate with a passing guard. "Hey, man. How long am I gonna be in here?" The guard ignored her and continued down the corridor. Casey kicked at the door once again. "Did you hear me? I said, how long am I gonna be in this place? What about my phone call?" The guard turned down the hall. Desperate, she tried bending the bars with her hands, veins bulging at her forehead. She stopped to catch her breath before trying again, this time showing her teeth. "C'mon-c'mon!" Casey placed her foot on the door and pulled until her palms turned blue. She gave up and melted to the floor in despair, buzzing for a hit of cocaine.

It was late when the bolt to Casey's cell finally unlocked that night. Two cops entered to give her food and water, concerned she was dehydrated. She swiped at the food tray, splashing one of the guards with her bean soup. "Dumb bitch." *Whap.* The guard socked Casey in the face, dropping her. He kicked her in the stomach so hard that it knocked the wind out of her. He grabbed Casey by her hair, torquing her neck. "Bet you won't get a goddamn thing else tonight!" He pushed her head down to the floor and left. His buddy picked up what was left of Casey's meal, poured it on her and closed the door. She laid there, covered in pain and soup.

Without access to cocaine, the next several days were a blur to Casey. She tottered throughout her cell feeling close to death as she waited to see a judge. Her eye was swollen, and she jerked and spasmed due to muscle stiffness. Her withdrawals were so severe that a team of two cops were assigned to watch her. She mumbled to herself unintelligibly at times, stripped off her clothes and banged her head repeatedly against her cot. It took eight cops to forcibly dress her. She screamed as if they were violating her. "Nooo, you can't do that! Oh, God. Please, no!" The next day, a guard making his rounds peeked inside her cell and noticed Casey was sitting on the floor with blood around her mouth. "Holy shit—hey, Sarge? She's doin' it again!" Casey had stripped off her clothes and gnawed at her forearm. Guards dressed and pepper-sprayed her. They laughed as she howled in agony, scrubbing at her eyes. "Now, the next time you take off your clothes, I'm gonna spray you somewhere else." Casey got the message.

The days passed, but Casey's erratic behavior didn't change. She talked at the wall, leaving guards confused. When she did try to eat, she'd puke or defecate right after. Her stool was loose, runny, and bloody. She curled onto her cot, sweaty and shivering, snot dripping from her nostrils. She ran a fever of 103°F. Occasionally, a weird spaz escaped her. "Quit *fuckin'* yellin' at me, I can't think!" She covered her head with the blanket.

The cops brought in a specialist to check on her. When her conditioned worsened, they tried to dump her on the correctional staff at Riker's Island. By then, Casey had been locked up for six days. Her eye was still badly swollen when COs arrived to take her. A decent guard noticed her state and spoke up. Casey was still out of it but remembered the dialogue.

"Sorry, fellas, but she ain't goin' inside my van with her eye all lumpy like that. Somebody's gotta answer for that, and it ain't gonna be us."

"Th'hell are you guys talking about? I told you that she fell."

"Bullshit. Somebody kicked her ass."

The two sides argued over who would take possession of Casey. In the end, she stayed at the precinct until her hearing date.

"Can you hear me, Miss Haughton?" A judge asked Casey the following Monday during her hearing. She was so wrecked that bailiffs had used a wheelchair to roll her down to the courthouse. Because she had no reportable income, the State afforded Casey a public defender to represent her. The untried attorney couldn't lawyer his way out of a wet paper bag.

Casey slunk to her right, halfway involved, drool leaking from her face as if she was high on tranquilizer. The judge chastised her for violating her parole agreement.

"*Miss* Haughton!" the judge barked. "Ma'am, do you need medical attention?"

Casey slowly shook her head.

"It says here in your file that you haven't followed up with the parole office since October—here it is December. Your toxicology reports stated that during your arrest there was a considerable amount of cocaine and marijuana in your system. What do you have to say to that?"

Casey shook her head again.

"Do you even care what happens to you today?"

"What's the point?" she muttered.

"Oh, so, you can speak?"

"I can hear, too," Casey sassed the judge. "May I please go back to my cell?"

The judge's face tightened with disputation. She closed Casey's thick file and placed it at the edge of her bench.

"One year, Miss Haughton—and let me say this," she began. "I hope you take the second go-around more seriously than you did the first one. You are also hereby ordered to complete the High School Equivalency exam and enlist into drug rehabilitation and anger management—before consideration for parole is given. No more breaks. From now on, you decide your fate."

The judge signaled the bailiffs to remove Casey from her sight. She didn't cry or protest the strict sentence. She rolled down the corridor staring lifelessly at her passing reflection across the tile floor. She glanced at her right hand and noticed it had a slight tremble to it. Casey clenched her fist, hoping to stop it. She turned her wrist, noticed bite marks and did a double-take. She couldn't remember how the impressions got there. The stoic guard looked down at her.

"What?"

Casey showed him her wrist. "How'd this get here?"

The guard pressed at the button. "Try using your imagination."

Twelve

Little had changed when Casey returned to St. Agnes Reformatory Center for her second stint. She slumped beside her chained neighbor during the drive Upstate. The same creepy gargoyles sat atop its castled roof. Casey and her fellow riders stood on the infamous blacktop to await COs' orders as frantic inmates hooted from behind the courtyard fence. They taunted the newcomers with suggestive threats and terroristic fury. Casey had heard it all before. "Oh, shit—look who it is! Welcome back, Haughton!" one inmate shouted. Casey looked down at her feet, ashamed. She was more embarrassed than she was afraid of being back at her old, barbaric institution. A CO checking in names overheard the exchange and doubled back to Casey. She lifted her head and glanced into her smug face. "Couldn't get enough of this place, eh, Haughton?" The CO carried on.

The intake bay where Casey was violated seven summers ago was freezing. She was strip-searched once again and had her private parts invaded by immoral guards. "Open your mouth. Lift your tongue. Side to side. Turn around. Raise your arms above your head. Spread your legs. Squat. Cough. Stand up. Lift your foot. Other foot. Very good. Next inmate, step forward."

COs who recognized Casey from her first tenure wasted no time reacquainting her to life on the inside. "You've certainly filled out over the years, Haughton… but in all the right places. Shit, I like a little extra luggage when I go flyin'," a warped CO commented. Cold and naked, Casey ambled down the line to receive her state-issued personals. "Well-well-well, if it isn't our old pal, Haughton." The prison's property specialist left and returned with Casey's old stuff. "I put it to the side." The lady winked. "You won me fifty bucks, you know that?" Casey snatched her personals off the counter and walked off. The fact that COs had profited on her return made her furious.

With her head titled on her palm inside the cafeteria, Casey poked at her chicken patty dinner later that evening. Her sandwich was still frozen in the middle and had a bone in it. Next to her plate was a glass of water with debris floating in it. She thought about Courtney's drinking glasses and how clean she kept her stuff. Courtney wasn't a great cook but a good one, and her chicken patties were never frozen in the middle. She surveyed the cafeteria and noticed her co-inmates all scarfing down their meals. *Why would Courtney do this to me?* Her eyes misted as she recalled the betrayal. She pushed her tray aside and returned to her cell.

Casey returned to her old survival instincts inside the steel box as if it was her first day. She spoke only when spoken to, sat facing the door and used the end shower when it was available. Her third night back, she saw three women scuffle over a newspaper in her section. That same night, a nineteen-year-old felon got her skull bashed with a metal pipe. The sound was like a metal bat striking cement. The poor kid went down to the infirmary and never returned. Casey knew something was up when guards were sent in to clean out the convict's cell. She couldn't sleep for two nights after the attack. Discouraged, she phoned her drughead-lover hoping for encouragement. She gave her name when prompted by the operator. "Rob, it's Casey. C'mon, pick up." As she waited for him to accept the call, the operator returned instead. "The person you are trying to reach is not accepting calls from this institution." Casey hung up and tried him again but received the same automated response. Not only had Courtney given up on her, but so had Rob. Pain shot to her heart as feelings of betrayal persisted yet again. She escaped to the courtyard for a smoke, hoping to distract herself from her latest rejection.

Casey sat on a wooden bench with her cigarette wedged between her fingers, sifting through her thoughts. She had hoped for a better ending to her year than celebrating another Christmas behind bars. Suddenly, it all came down. She had no hope for a better life than the one she had, no money, no friends—no family at all. She was near tears before a group of rowdy convicts showed up and demanded she give up her table. Casey stood her ground. "No, I'm not fuckin' leaving this table—find another one." Casey went back to her smoke, eyeing the girls, daring them to buck. She had lost more than her fair share the past seven years and refused to give up anything else. The group muttered amongst themselves, nodding at Casey before she eventually conceded. After all, it was just a table—it wasn't worth her life. She dragged her cigarette into the dirt, putting it out, and rose to her feet. "You know what, take it—just take the goddamn table. I'm in enough trouble as it is." Casey took her cigarettes and bad attitude and went to the bleachers on the other side of the courtyard. When she got there, she looked back and noticed the girls were still watching her. She gulped and looked away.

The thought of being mandated to attend rehab and anger management classes made Casey even more upset. *Fuck that stupid judge, I'm not angry,* she convinced herself. She walked into the prison's library the next morning to feel out her workload. She fingered through a few books and rolled her eyes. She spotted another inmate sitting by herself at a table next to a stack of books. Casey's jaw fell to the floor. *Holy shit? All that?* She fixed her face and went over.

"Are you studying for the HSE? Do you have to read all those books?"

The convict looked up at her, annoyed. "It's only eight books."

"Only?!" Casey panicked. "Dude, it's like the whole friggin' library next to your head."

The convict ignored her and went back to work. Casey deflated and left. Further up the study hall, she stopped to observe a group of prisoners dissecting their dilemmas. At the head of the class was the therapist. She sat with her legs crossed and her hands folded on her lap. Casey watched from the hall, careful not to draw attention to herself.

"I shot my boyfriend," the killer openly admitted. "I'm in here for life because of that." Casey's throat closed as the woman recounted the details of the homicide and her past which led up to her boyfriend's murder. The killer's origin was disastrous: alcohol, drug use, absentee parents, and a bad temper. Her tragic upbringing had the same recipe as Casey's.

"Believe it or not, Savannah, you might be serving a life sentence, but your life isn't over," the therapist told her. "That's where I begin with my all students, recognizing that whatever sentence you were handed—there's no period at the end of it, unless you put one there."

Casey turned her nose at the woman's flawed philosophy and kept going. Life without parole *was* a death sentence, no matter how the therapist sliced it—sorry, Savannah. Casey was too bullheaded to sit with a bunch of lifers recounting how she got there. The answer was simple: Rob had turned on her, Courtney was a rat, and that was that.

On the way back to her cell block, Casey bypassed an open doorway and felt a sharp blow to her back. The pain depleted her voice as she fell onto all fours. Before she could look, three inmates dragged her inside of a dark room and obliterated her. "Beat her ass, I'll watch the door," one of them ordered. The two girls pummeled Casey mercilessly, wailing on her from so many directions she couldn't defend herself. One inmate had her in the headlock position while another shot uppercuts into her face. A third inmate kicked her in the ribs, dropping her. She could barely cry out. "Somebody help me!" Casey curled into a ball on the floor, waiting for the annihilation to pass, but it didn't. They dragged her across the floor by her hair, tore off her clothes and poured feces on her. Crawling, covered in shit, she grunted miserably as she stumbled on all fours, trying to get away. Her masked assailants stood over her. One of the girls yoked Casey by her hair. "Next time, give up the table, bitch." Another kicked Casey square in the jaw, knocking her out.

Speechless

Casey awoke from her assault hours later inside the prison's infirmary smelling like Dial soap. Her face and head looked like a balloon. Her lips were the size of Polka sausages and her jaw felt tight. She peeked through the slit of her red eye and noticed a sickbay of other injured patients. One convict across from her was being treated for cancer and another was a healing amputee. Each time Casey moved her eye, her head throbbed. She moaned, hoping to get a nearby aide's attention but was ignored. As she tried to sit up, a current blitzed through her tender body. She tried to scream before realizing her mouth had been wired shut. She patted her cabled jaw and yowled in distress. The aide looked over at Casey and went back to assisting other patients.

"Heard you the first time. One second."

Desperate for assistance, Casey peeked at her bedside table and noticed a shiny bell sitting there. She grabbed the golden device—hurt like hell—and waved it around like a child. The aide left her patient's bedside and walked over.

"Do you need more pain medicine?"

Casey grunted at her nurse, unable to speak. The nurse lifted her chart and looked at it.

"But you just had pain medicine less than an hour ago. It's every four hours."

Casey bounced in despair, whimpering.

"I know, and I'm going to do everything in my power to keep you comfortable, okay? I'm Sydney," she introduced herself. "Listen, try not to move a lot or else your jaw might buzz on you. Doctor says it's a moderate break but should heal fine. I left that bell beside your bed in case you need anything. There's also pen and paper if you'd like to write."

Casey lunged for the pen and scrap paper next to her cot. Wincing, she scribbled on the pad and held it up for Sydney to read.

How long will I be here?

"At least until your jaw gets better. You've got some other things we need to take care of too. I'd count on spending your Christmas down here with us." Sydney smiled.

Casey scrawled again.

I'm so fucking over this life shit, man.

The pen slipped from her hand and rolled onto her cot. She pulled her blanket over her head and bawled through her teeth. Crying even made her jaw ache, but she couldn't help it. She turned to her side and squealed, done with it all. She was tired of the system, tired of prison, feeling unlovable, Courtney's betrayal, Rob's betrayal, and life in general. She soaked her cot that afternoon, hysterical. Sydney gently pulled Casey's blanket from her head and kneeled beside her.

"I'm gonna get you through this. I just need you to work with me. Will you work with me?"

Casey shook her head.

"No? Why not?"

Casey fetched for her pen to write.

Do you have something I can take so I never wake up again?

Sydney looked at her. "C'mon, you don't really mean that, Casey. You don't—"

Casey turned her back. She pulled her blanket over her swollen head and returned to despair. A tear trickled along a cut at the bridge of her nose, burning her. Sydney touched her arm.

"I'll check on you later. Get some rest."

Time idled for Casey during her stay in the infirmary. She spent her Christmas cooped up beside battered convicts, staring out into the gray. Her meals were repulsive vegetable smoothies and water at room temperature. For pain medicine, Sydney mashed her pills into a white dust and sprinkled it inside a tin mug with a swig of saltwater. "You ready?" Using her straw, Casey would then slurp the chalky fluid. The bitter taste made her squinch in disgust. "One more. Here we go. We'll let this digest and then I'll come back to do your exercises. Wouldn't want you to get stiff."

Casey hated the taste of that medicine, and she hated being in the infirmary. She spent the rest of her holiday glaring at jolly inmates with envy as they celebrated with ginger ale and banana loaf bread. Not being able to talk killed her.

Casey was so discouraged, she asked Sydney to face her bed toward the wall, away from her peers. "Are you sure about this, Casey?" Sydney whispered. "That wouldn't look so good to the other girls in here." Casey scribbled into the paper, nearly tearing it. *I don't give a shit!* She slammed her pad onto the floor, causing a scene. Sydney shrugged and moved Casey's bed. "Is there anything else I can do for you?" Casey turned her back to Sydney, signaling there wasn't.

Days before the new year hit, Casey faced the wall as inmates traded war stories, pictures and letters from back home, reminiscing better days. A woman with her leg amputated at her knee led the chorus. Everything was wrong with her from what Casey overheard: hepatitis, HIV, diabetes, high blood pressure, and lupus. She proudly smoked her cigarettes like a weary old combat veteran.

"This here is my granddaughter, Ava," the woman said. "Her mother—that bitch, I had her when I was twenty. That's me holding her back in 1959. She's got the same eyes, just like my—"

Casey waved her bell over her head and returned it to her table, interrupting them. The room went quiet. She could feel the room staring at her before Sydney walked over.

"Yes, Casey. What is it?"

She handed her a note. Sydney read it and give her a defiant look.

"No, Casey, I won't say that. I'll find a nicer way to tell them to… quiet down."

Casey was the worst patient there. Once, when Sydney

tried to apply a new dressing to her wrist and tied it too tightly, Casey went into a mumbling fit.

"Excuse me?" Sydney backed off. "Did you just call me what I think you just called me?" Casey turned her head. By then, Sydney had had it. She tossed her things into her bucket.

"Fine. Do whatever you want, Casey. Face the wall away from everybody. Ring your bell. Write your nasty messages—because the way I see it, the only way out of here is through me and the rest of the nurses here in the infirmary." She picked up her bucket. "If you want to lay here and die, that's up to you." Sydney returned to the far end of the room, away from her.

Casey spent New Year's Eve staring blankly out into the courtyard, mum with gloom. When Sydney showed up to change her bandaged arm, she didn't blink. "Is that too tight? Would you like to work on some of your speech therapy or not?" Casey didn't move. Sydney exhaled, finished the job, and walked away, leaving her there to rot. Casey stared into the gray sky, contemplating her life.

She thought about Courtney a lot during that time, how quickly their paths had diverged after her conviction and where her life was headed—where it had been. She thumbed at her eyes, feeling sorry for herself. That night, Casey did something she seldom ever did: She prayed. Prayer never seemed to work against Aunt Patty's extension cord or Uncle Benny's advances. Prayer had failed Casey her whole life, but it had to work that night. Moving her lips, she prayed not to see the new year.

Not only did Casey's prayer fail her once again, she was the first patient up early on New Year's Day, 1990. Using the window as her mirror, she noticed her healing face and shook her head. She stared up at the ceiling disappointed but feeling somewhat less achy than she had the previous couple days. Her jaw was still wired, and her mouth didn't ring as badly when she moved.

In the window, she captured a glimpse of Sydney in the back, writing in what appeared to be a ledger. Casey watched her, studying her aide's gentle nature, recalling their previous couple days. Lucky for her, Sydney was a lot more patient than Courtney was. If Casey was half the jerk to her sister she'd been to Sydney, Courtney would've tossed her off the seventh-floor balcony. The thought made her chuckle—the first since she had returned there. With her bum wrist still wrapped, she hoisted herself upright, using her bell for support. She sat at the end of her cot, taking small breaths. Her legs were weak but operable. She looked across the room and noticed her aide watching her. Sydney quickly went back to writing in her ledger. The two had conversed little since she'd laid down the law. Since then, Sydney would show up at Casey's bedside with a look of boredom. "You need the bathroom?" She'd help her down to the restroom and back without the same politeness as before.

Casey continued to observe Sydney while her aide pretended not to notice she had gotten up all on her own. Unassisted, she sprouted from her bed and wobbled across the room. She used her bandaged arm to pull up a wooden chair close to Sydney's desk before collapsing in the seat beside her, looking for endorsement. Sydney continued to write. Casey forced herself to talk, abbreviating her sentences to nullify some of her pain.

"Sorry," she spoke through her wired teeth. "Been a real jerk, lately."

Sydney lifted her head.

"It happens. Thank you, Casey." Sydney went back to filling out her ledger. Casey noticed her aide's salty face and knew she'd torched that bridge. She cut her losses and rose to her feet to leave. Before she got far, Sydney called to her.

"So, how'd you end up down here, anyway? Did you get in a fight?"

Casey returned to the chair.

"Yeah, I got jumped," she sighed. "Boy, did they kick the shit out of me—three of 'em."

"Three? Hmph. Well, that's not a fair fight. Did you get a few licks in?"

Casey looked at her. "I just said they kicked the shit out of me."

The two laughed at Casey's misfortune. She rubbed at her tender jaw and winced.

"Well, I just wanted to say sorry for everything. Besides, it's annoying talking to me right now. I sound like such a dummy."

"Please, I had a patient once who was wrapped like a mummy from head to toe. She had her jaw broken on both sides, and I could still understand her," Sydney said. "I'm sure

I can handle a small break. Besides, talking is good therapy for you. I'll admit, it's also nice to have some company for a change."

The two looked at each other glowingly. Casey had despised Sydney before their brief exchange that morning. Through conversation, however, it was easy to see why the other patients were so fond of her. They chatted on and off throughout Sydney's shift and became so amicable toward each other that Sydney stayed one hour afterward. Casey talked so much that day her mouth ached. She bugged her new friend for a favor just as she was about to leave.

"Can you move my bed back before you go?" Casey asked her.

Sydney lit up with astonishment. "Well, excuse me," she laughed. "Sure, I'd love to help you with that—but only if you pitch in."

"Pitch in? Girl, I can barely stand—but okay."

Together, the two returned Casey's bed to its original position. Sydney did most of the lifting while Casey used her mass to guide the steel frame. Sydney fluffed Casey's pillows and gestured at the cot.

"There you are, my dear. Anything else?"

"I'll take a cigarette and a Heineken… and a bedtime story while you're at it? You got a light? I lost mine when I got jumped. How about a nail clipper? Fuckin' nails look like Dracula's."

Sydney lifted her eyebrow. "Don't you think you're asking for a bit much?" she chuckled. "Later, Casey. We'll talk tomorrow."

Casey watched her new friend leave, not taking her eyes off her. When Sydney got to the door, she looked back, tucked in her curious grin and left. Casey smiled and waved before grasping her injured jaw. Her face pounded for the rest of the day.

Thirteen

Originally from Connecticut, Sydney Saunders began working at St. Agnes in the fall of '88. She was the youngest of two older brothers, both of whom were doctors with their own private practices. Sydney's father was a cardiologist, and her mother worked as a pediatrician. Medicine was the family business in the Saunders household, although Sydney wanted no part of the complex field. "Even though I was around medicine my whole life, it wasn't my path," she told Casey once during therapy. "I really wanted to study art, but Dad said artists don't make anything. So, I studied nursing to shut him up. Worst mistake of my life." According to Sydney, her career in medicine had been a conundrum of politics, disappointment, and hard luck. She pulled and stretched Casey's arm, explaining her patchy upbringing.

"My folks are total asses when it comes to the field. My dad says that nurses are lazy doctors who dodged medical school. He lost his shit when he found out I was going into nursing. I became the new black sheep of the family."

Casey exhaled. "I know all about black sheep, unfortunately. Well, at least you finished nursing school. That's something to be proud of, right?"

"You would think! I got into this huge fight with my family when they learned I was being offered a job up here in Esseltown as a prison nurse. They thought I was too talented to waste my time providing care to convicted felons. They wanted me to own a practice in Manhattan like my two older brothers, but that wasn't my thing. So, I came here instead."

"Hmph," Casey grunted. "That's fucked up."

"Yes… it is fucked up." Sydney dropped her extra wrap into her bucket. "My dad had this saying—I never forgot it. He'd say, 'In medicine, Sydney, if someone is sick but has limited insurance, we do what we can. But if someone is sick and has great insurance, we do all that we can.' Now isn't that screwed up? Everything is about money these days."

"Always," Casey concurred. She rotated her wrist to check out Sydney's wrap job. "Well, I don't know what your family is barking about, but I see a great nurse standing in front of me."

Sydney touched Casey on the tip of her nose and returned across the room. Their gentle patient-caretaker relationship bloomed during Casey's time in the infirmary. They swapped stories of their pasts, both candid about their struggles with alcohol and drug usage. It shocked Casey to learn that someone as sweet as Sydney had used drugs.

"Absolutely!" she admitted. "Well, I've tried some stuff. Not everything, thankfully. You?"

Casey giggled. "Maaaan, I did it all."

Casey and her aide became so friendly that Sydney carted her around in an old wheelchair for a change of scenery. She was still having trouble with her knee from the attack and couldn't walk far. She teared up one Sunday when Sydney showed up with a wheelchair. "Wanna go for a ride?" she asked.

Casey's eyes blurred as they rolled down the hall. "Why are you so nice to me, Sydney, when I'm such a bitch? Can't you tell?"

Sydney turned at the end of the corridor. "Bitches need help too, Casey."

By February, Casey's jaw had finally healed enough for doctors to remove her hardware. She sat in front of the mirror, moving and flexing her jaw as Sydney flanked from behind.

"Well, at least my teeth made parole," Casey joked. "Now, if I could just get my wrist and knee to cooperate. Then again, I think I'll milk it a little longer." Casey winked at Sydney's reflection and beamed as her friend turned pink.

"Well, just don't milk it for too long. There are other sick patients here at St. Agnes who need my help." She pinched Casey on the chin and returned to work.

Sydney was a gorgeous woman with beautiful, long strawberry hair. She had a tattoo of a butterfly on her upper right arm and her hands felt soft and moist. Casey noticed that whenever Sydney worked with her, she didn't wear latex gloves. "How come you wear gloves with everybody else except me? What if I got cooties?"

Sydney laughed at her. "Do you ever shut up?" she asked.

At night, Casey would fantasize about kissing Sydney's soft lips. She'd lock her pillow tightly in her arms, imagining herself rolling in the grass with her aide down at Central Park. She'd pet it as if she was stroking Sydney's strawberry hair before kissing her lover goodnight.

Casey also grew protective of her special friend. One day, an older, grumpier convict gave Sydney hell because her soup was cold. "Are you a moron? Do you know what soup is? Soup is supposed to be warm—not cold."

Casey got up from her bed and hobbled across the room.

"If you want it warm, why don't you try shoving it up your ass and see if that helps." She wobbled back to her bedside and glared at the woman. Sydney stopped by later to thank her.

"Thanks for the assist earlier with Meriam," she whispered. "We're not allowed to swear at the inmates, but I sure as hell was thinking about doing it. I feel bad for Meriam sometimes. She's been through a lot."

"Fuck Meriam," Casey growled. "Want me to beat her ass?"

"She's old, Casey."

"I don't care! I'll hit that bitch so hard she'll shit out her pacemaker."

The girls giggled before Sydney returned to finish her shift.

By late February, their time together had come to an end. Casey had fully healed and could get around without limping. They commemorated her recovery on the loading dock beneath a silver awning, sharing a smoke in the rain.

"You're alright, Syd. I almost wish my jaw was still broke

so that I could stay with you."

"Well, perhaps we ought to break it again?" Sydney shook her fists at Casey. "I should break it, anyway. Why don't you have a high school diploma or HSE? What are you waiting on?"

"Hell to freeze over," Casey laughed.

Sydney took away Casey's cigarette and put it out.

"I'm being serious. What's the problem? Do you need help?"

Casey shoved her hands inside her pockets. "What's the point? I'm still a criminal, regardless of my education—or lack thereof. I can't win out here."

"What are you talking about, Casey? You've got your whole life ahead of you."

"What life, Sydney? I've been a reject since the day I was born. What good is a high school diploma gonna do for a bum like me? Hell, I feel safer in here than out there. At least I know what I'm dealing with. Three hots and a cot plus health insurance. All paid for by the State—you can't beat that. Out there, there's taxes, homelessness, and expectations... family? No way, man. I'd rather take my chances in here."

Sydney shook her head. "You're locked up in two cells: St. Agnes, and the one inside your head," she told her. "What's really the problem, Casey? Is it fear? Is it Rob? Is it Courtney—"

"Do NOT mention her fucking name to me!" Casey hissed at her.

Sydney stared at Casey, unimpressed by her sudden tantrum.

"Do you love your sister at all anymore?"

Casey snatched her cigarettes and matches off the deck.

"Son, I just told you not to mention her name, didn't I? You know what? I think I'm gonna head back to 3G. I'll see you around sometime, Syd. Peace out."

Sydney blocked Casey's path.

"Th'fuck are you doing? C'mon, get outta my way, Sydney. I'm not playin'."

"Or else *what*? You gonna hit me, Casey? Do you really hate your sister that much? For God sakes, after everything she's done for you and—"

"Look, I can't do this right now, Sydney, okay? Please, just move. MOVE!"

Sydney gave her a daring look. Casey clenched her fists, preparing to strike her former aide. She was so tight with rage that her hands turned red and steam whistled from her ears. Sydney turned her head at Casey, offering her a free shot. Casey didn't take it.

"Look at you," said Sydney. "You're an even bigger wuss than I am. You're all bark and no bite, Casey Haughton. When are you gonna grow up, huh? When are you gonna start owning your own shit and stop expecting others to carry it?"

Casey sunk her head. "But I'm not asking anybody to carry my shit."

"Then why'd you come back here? You couldn't do any better out there?"

"Nobody would hire me. I kept gettin' kicked to the curb everywhere I went."

"Bullshit. Everybody faces rejection, Casey, even college graduates. You didn't try hard enough because you're lazy," Sydney fussed. "Yeah, that's right. Instead, you conned your sister into moving to Brooklyn, punked out on her couch, got hooked on blow and then got pissed when she dropped a dime on you. You're soft. You're a chump. You're nothing but a soft chump."

"I'm not soft—and I'm not a chump."

"Prove it then. Prove me wrong by taking the HSE. Prove me wrong by accepting that what happened between you and Courtney was—"

"Son, quit sayin' her name, already! So fuckin' annoying, I swear to God, man."

"Courtney-Courtney-Courtney-Courtney-Courtney," Sydney challenged her. "What are you gonna do about it, Casey? When are you gonna stop playing the victim? You've been a victim your whole life—don't look at me like that, you are. When are you gonna start giving a shit?"

"I *do* give a shit."

"No, you don't. Because if you did, you wouldn't be here—a second time—with a cracked jaw, blaming your sister, the system and the rest of the world for your problems. You might've been dealt a bad hand, but at least you still got a hand. So, own it… you fucking soft chump."

Casey wiped her eyes. Everything Sydney said was right, and she knew it. "So, what do you think I should do then? Since you obviously know everything."

Sydney reached for her hand. "St. Agnes is hosting the

HSE in a couple months—take it. I know what's on there, I can help you study for it. Whatever books are not here, I can get from the library near my apartment. I just need you to show up. What do you say?"

Casey reached inside her pants for her cigarettes. She tossed one between her lips and exhaled in irritation. As she went to spark up, her small flame kept blowing out. Sydney placed her hands around Casey's stick, allowing her to light up.

"And quit smoking so darn much," Sydney told her. "Your lungs are gonna look like shit by the time you're thirty. So, are you studying for the HSE or not?"

Casey glared at her. "The cigarettes are non-negotiable." She thumbed at her forehead, took a long pull and let it out slowly. "If I'm gonna do this, you gotta be with me all the way, Syd. I'm pretty sure I'm gonna be an asshole too, just so you know."

"I deal with assholes all day, Casey. One more won't hurt."

"Good. Judge says I'm supposed to take anger management and rehab classes, too."

"Whaaat? You? Angry? You don't say!" Sydney chuckled.

Owning It

Casey sat in the back of Dr. Matthews's class, steaming about her new agenda. She slouched in her chair, yawned with boredom, and sat with her head slanted inside her palm the first couple days. She had double the work since both Sydney and Dr. Matthews assigned her homework. Her first day there, she noticed that Dr. Matthews hugged all her students before class.

"Welcome, dear. You must be—"

Casey sidestepped her. "Casey," she gruffed under her breath. She took her seat, eyeballing the woman with cynicism. Dr. Matthews shrugged off her cold shoulder and returned to greeting the other inmates.

Part of why Casey hated her new teacher was because she was too damn happy. She was a chubby white lady with bushy blonde hair and rosy makeup. She looked like Robin Williams in *Mrs. Doubtfire*. Casey saw her as another phony from the criminal justice system who could give a rat's ass about an inmate's future. Each day, Dr. Matthews scribbled a word or phrase on the board for the class to discuss. Casey's

264

peers spent three hours dissecting its meaning while she lurched in the back.

"Okay, now that we all have said it individually, let's say it as a group." Dr. Matthews dictated. "Is everybody ready? Here it goes. One-two-three—"

"*I am angry, and it's okay.*" The class shadowed each other like indoctrinated dummies.

"Very good, class!" Dr. Matthews clapped. "Today, everybody gets a gold star."

Casey thought of a lot of things to do with that gold star. Before long, her jovial teacher put her on blast. It was her third day in the class.

"You there, in the back. Casey, right?" Dr. Matthews asked. "Are you awake?"

The class full of twenty-five inmates all turned and faced her. Casey sat up straight before cutting her eyes at the woman, annoyed.

"Yeah, what's up?"

"For two gold stars and two pieces of Jolly Rancher candy, in your own words, define 'integrity' for us and what it means to you."

Casey pinched between her eyes, trying not to kill her teacher.

"Doing the right thing, I guess? Even though nobody's looking?"

"Interesting. How about an example?"

Casey gripped the edge of her desk. She hated being the center of attention and replied candidly.

"Well, being here sucks, for one, but I gotta be here. If I had it my way, I'd be on my cot right about now flipping through a *Playboy* magazine with a honeybun in one hand and a cigarette in the other. I probably speak for most of us here when I say that we're all here—not because we want to be—but because we screwed up. And the only way out of this hell hole is through this class. Hope that example worked for you."

Dr. Matthews's cheerful look turned cold. She traveled across the room with her eyes locked on Casey. She stopped in front of her desk. Dr. Matthews reached inside of her dish and placed two pieces of Jolly Rancher candy onto her desk. Casey looked down at the candy and back up at her.

"Good answer." Dr. Matthews gave her a fake smile and returned to the front.

Casey had little time to complain under Sydney's watchful eye. They met on Mondays and Thursdays in the prison's library throughout late February and into March.

"Let me see your workbook from class."

Casey handed over the booklet Dr. Matthews assigned to her. She had also returned to her old gig in the wood shop. Between work, studying for her diploma and Dr. Matthews's class, she kept busy. Sydney gave Casey a list of books from the library to check out and page numbers to read for each.

"Whoa-whoa-whoa, are you serious?" Casey flipped through one of her assigned books. "You want me to read from 146 to 275 by Sunday night? That's 129 fuckin' pages, Sydney. Do you know how long that's gonna take me? Are you out of your mind?"

Sydney calculated Casey's math.

"Very good, Casey, that is exactly 129 pages. Just make sure you read it all. We're gonna have a quiz on it the next time I see you."

"Quiz?" Casey panicked. "Man, I haven't had a quiz in over ten years. You can't do that!"

"Sure, I can. Now go before I give you more."

"But-but-but—"

Sydney shooed her off.

Casey went stomping from the library that day, but by Sunday she had read all 129 pages and passed Sydney's quiz with flying colors. By the end of their second week, Casey had bodied over five hundred pages ranging from English, social studies, mathematics, and world history. Meanwhile, her weakest subject was still Dr. Matthews's class. She called on Casey every day to participate, inviting her to the board to write or partake in group discussions.

"Casey, my dear, why don't you come forward and define what 'intuition' means? C'mon up and show your peers that beautiful handwriting of yours. Come-come."

"I can define it from back here, if you don't mind."

Dr. Matthews gave her a stern look.

"I insist you define it up here." She held up a piece of yellow chalk, urging her forward.

Casey scooted from her chair, sucking her teeth. She plodded to front of the room, took the chalk from Dr. Matthews's hands and scribbled on the board. She dropped the chalk into the tray, wiped her hands and returned to her desk. Dr. Matthews turned to read her answer.

"Great. Now explain to us what it says. Up here, preferably."

Dr. Matthews hammered her with intuition questions all afternoon. Casey's days of skating by were over. She called on Casey six times that day and ten on the next. By the start of their fourth week together, Casey walked into class and noticed Dr. Matthews had moved all the desks closer to the board. She marched up to her teacher and demanded answers.

"What are you trying to do here, Dr. Matthews? Drive me insane?" she whispered. "Did Judge Applewhite send you here to ruin my life? You think this is a joke?"

Dr. Matthews ignored Casey and greeted the class.

"Good afternoon, everyone," she said. "I just want you all to know that Casey—" She touched Casey's shoulder. "—has volunteered to define our new word of the day, 'ambition.' So, let's all give her our undivided attention. Go ahead, Casey. Whenever you're ready."

"Wait a second, I never said—"

"Don't forget to write your answer and explain to us what it means," Dr. Matthews interrupted her. "Go on, Casey. No need to be bashful."

"How about I just show you guys instead?"

"Even better." Dr. Matthews leaned on her desk. "Show us what ambition means."

Casey dragged her desk to the back corner of the room. As it scraped across the floor, her convicted classmates giggled and snickered at her. Dr. Matthews gave her an indignant look. The war of mind games had just begun with the score tied at one-one.

"Ambition," Casey gestured at her desk, high on sarcasm. "When I came to class today, it was my ambition not to be social. Ambition is like a desire, want, or need someone has. Today, I desire not to be fucked with. Ambition." She cheesed and took to her seat.

Not all the books Casey needed for her HSE were in the prison library. So, Sydney would get them for her at the local one near her apartment. She'd smuggle the literary contraband into the facility and bring them with her during her meet-ups with Casey.

"I'll need 'em back in a couple weeks, or else I'll get charged," Sydney would tell her.

Whether during her break at the woodshop, out in the yard, cafeteria, or in her cell, Casey's head was in a book. Her four preparatory subjects were: Reasoning through Language Arts, Science, Mathematical Reasoning, and Social Studies. She read so much that her eyes ached. Occasionally, Sydney would sneak away from the infirmary to check on her. Her cute face reduced the monotony of a routine day. Casey noticed how closely Sydney would sit beside her during their sessions. She'd dangle her foot, striking Casey's leg repeatedly or would sit so closely that her necklace between her breasts would show. Casey's curiosity bested her one afternoon. The two were in the middle of studying fractions.

"Syd, do you mind if I… ask you something?"

"Yes, Casey, I am," she answered straight away.

Casey turned red with timidity. Since a teenager, she'd always been sheepish about discussing her sexuality. She covered her face and laughed.

"How'd you even know what I was gonna ask?"

Sydney interlaced Casey's hand with hers and looked in her eyes.

"Now, you know the other reason I'm estranged from my family. Sad, huh?"

"Wait, your family gave you the finger because you bat for the same team? That's so messed up. Courtney can be a dick sometimes, but she never blinked about me being bisexual. She's a real gem, Sydney—you'd love her, and she was always so damn supportive and…"

Casey stopped herself as her sister crossed her mind.

"Oh, my God." Her eyes began to fizzle. "I've been ruining that girl's life ever since we were thirteen. All she's ever wanted to do was support me, and I took advantage of her." Casey gasped. "What's wrong with me, Sydney? I had it made, living with her… and now it's all gone."

Sydney grabbed Casey by her double chin and kissed her.

"Well, that just means it's time for a fresh start, don't you think?" Sydney kissed her again.

Casey had kissed girls before and had even dated one. But for some reason, Sydney's kisses felt more sincere and put her at ease. Her soul departed each time their lips connected, liberating her from the enslavement of her own self-consciousness.

Their courtship began that afternoon inside a medical supply closet which only Sydney owned a key to. Her sex was spellbinding and generous as she properly introduced Casey into the world of human anatomy. Sadly, their flame extinguished as quickly as it began to heat up. One week into their wooing, the prison's riot team showed up at Casey's cell demanding answers. She was lying on her cot reading a book by Zora Neale Hurston. She slipped it beneath her pillow.

"For God sakes, what is it now?" she snarled at them. "You guys tried this nonsense the last time I was here. Look, I am not trafficking any drugs into St. Agnes. Now, if you don't mind, I have a test to prepare for."

The lead CO, a lieutenant, lifted his mask.

"We're not looking for drugs this time," he told her. "We're looking for books. Are you in possession of any books that don't belong at this institution?"

Casey chuckled with surprise. "You're actually serious! You want my books?"

"Step aside, Haughton—"

"*You* step aside," Casey growled. "You ain't gettin' my books. I've got my HSE coming up in April. If you wanna bust my ass for that, go right ahead."

The lieutenant turned to confer with his team. They backed off and pushed up the corridor. Seconds later, Casey's cell door opened. The lieutenant stepped inside find removed his helmet, attempting to reason with Casey over the violation.

"I'm just trying to do a job here, Haughton. That's all."

"Yeah? Well, so am I." Casey's lips quivered. "What do you need *my* books for?"

The lieutenant stepped closer and lowered his voice. "Look Haughton, Sydney's already in enough trouble as it is. If she's lucky, she won't have to end up in a cell beside you. It's illegal—what she did. You both know better."

Casey's demeanor changed at the mention of Sydney. She turned to deliberate with herself before eventually collecting the six books her friend had trafficked into the prison. Her face was wet with mourning.

"If I give you the books, will you leave her alone?"

"I'm here to do a job, Haughton, that's it. Sydney's got her own mess to sort out with her super and the warden. Come on, give me the books before my captain shows up."

Casey sighed and handed over the books. "What's gonna happen to her? Can I see her?"

The lieutenant counted the stack of books, ignoring her.

"I'm going to need that Zora Neale Hurston, too. The one you hid under your pillow."

Casey returned to her cot and retrieved it. She was so scared of what was to come that her hands were shaking.

"Thanks," he said. "I really am sorry, Haughton. But if I don't do my job, I won't have one. I've got four kids. I'll try to smooth things over so that this blows away."

The lieutenant turned and left. It was the paltriest violation Casey had ever been guilty of: SWB—Studying While Black. She crashed onto her cot, fearful of what the prison staff would do to Sydney for attempting to help her. On top of that, with her best reads now gone, her chances of passing the HSE were slim. She cried all night, scared for her friend. Even when Casey tried to do right, life chastised her. Sydney showed up at her cell the next morning with a box full of her things loaded in her arms.

"They fired me," she drooped. "But I guess it isn't too bad. They're not gonna charge me, and I got my books back. It could be worse."

Casey placed her hand onto Sydney's.

"Sydney, I am so sorry for this. I almost wish I never signed up for that stupid HSE. If I didn't, you'd still have a job. What are you gonna do now?"

Sydney placed her box onto the floor.

"Are you kidding me?" she whispered before looking over her shoulder. "I fucking hated this place until I met you. I'll bounce back, and you will too."

Sydney reached into her shirt and slipped Casey a folded note.

"What's this?"

"A list of books down in the library that could help," she told her. "No matter what happens... all the way, okay? Don't stop."

Casey stuffed the note inside her shirt.

"I won't. Thanks, Sydney. Take care of yourself."

Sydney patted Casey's hand and left. She watched as a guard down the hall escorted her friend and ex-aide through the double doors. For twelve weeks, Sydney had looked after Casey, treating both her wounds and her heart. Their rocky beginnings fostered into an unlikely friendship before dissolving under the system's crushing power.

Casey returned to her cot to look over Sydney's note again. The message smelled like the citrus perfume she liked to wear. She placed the note up to her heart, allowing it to absorb into her soul. She felt somewhat invigorated by all that she had accomplished so far, despite the separation. Later that morning, Casey checked out the list of books on Sydney's note.

Fourteen

Passing the high school equivalency examination was the single most important component for Casey to get another crack at daylight. Her stomach boiled all morning at breakfast as she waited for the clock to strike 8 a.m. on Saturday, March 24th. The room where she was scheduled to take her exam was full of hopeful convicts looking to redeem themselves. One test taker, she noticed, looked to be around eighty years old. Casey shuddered as she overheard the woman share the gist of her 1937 conviction with the test administrator. "When I go up to the gate to meet Momma," the old woman hacked, "I'm gonna show her my diploma." The bittersweet proclamation was beautiful and tragic.

Casey plopped at a vacant desk occupied by a test booklet, Scantron sheet, and pre-sharpened pencil, ready to work. The exam featured over 230 questions ranging from the five sections she'd spent the past month preparing for: mathematics, language arts, science, social studies and world events. Each section was graded on the spot through a machine. The units were all timed and required an overall score of sixty percent to advance. Test takers were given five hours and not allowed to leave the room (not even for the bathroom), according to a rep there from the New York Board of Education.

"Any questions?" the woman asked. She looked down at her stopwatch and waved them on. "Good luck, you may begin."

A wave of papers turned all at once as the inmates zeroed in. Meanwhile, Casey was still stuck on the part about not being able to use the restroom. She was fourteen seconds into her test and about to burst.

The first portion of her exam was social studies and world events. The first question asked for the exact month, day and year of Dr. Martin Luther King Jr.'s assassination. Casey penciled "B" on her scantron for Thursday, April 4th 1968. She only remembered the date because she once helped Courtney do a book report on Dr. King. The next question was trickier: *What year did the American Civil War begin, and what year did it end?* Casey tapped her pencil against her desk in doubt as failure entered her mind. She distracted herself by flipping through her test booklet and noticed she had 228 more questions left to go. She exhaled and returned to the front, but the question was still there. She fussed to herself. *How the hell should I know? I wasn't born in the 1800s.* A light bulb went off inside her head as she reviewed her choices; A: 1861-1865, B: 1959-1975, C: 1950-1953 and D: None of the above. She smiled, penciled "A," and moved on to question three.

Casey blasted through the rest of phase one and finished well before the time limit. She strode to the front of the room and handed the administrator her Scantron. The woman placed it into the machine, recorded her score and gave it back to her. Casey shifted left and right, hoping to see how she did. The admin shielded her grade book.

"Um, can I help you?" the woman laughed. "You passed, have a seat."

"Ooh, is that my score? Eighty-seven? Holy shit, Batman—and I thought I was a dummy this whole time. Is there any way I can use the bathroom before we start round two? I didn't know the rules. I probably shouldn't've drunk all that orange juice. My bladder's about to rip."

The admin trimmed her eyes at her.

"Or, I could just hold it in… and stay here and chat with you." Casey cheesed. "So, I was thinking about applying to be a test proctor someday. What's the requirement to—"

"Hurry up—"

"Thank you!" Casey glided across the hall to tinkle and returned to start round two. Thanks to her, the admin had to now allow other test takers to relieve themselves. Out of the sixty hopefuls there, only two failed the first part.

Phase two was even easier than the first, Casey thought. She shaded in her answers as if she was holding a paint brush, brimming with confidence. She even stopped midway to reminisce about her time there with Sydney Saunders. Strangely, she hadn't left a way to contact her. Casey kicked the thought from her head, surmising that their brief romance would've likely ended the way every other relationship in her life did. She finished number one again and strayed to the front of the class, overconfident. The admin placed it inside the machine and handed it back to her.

"Too close. I almost kept it. Have a seat."

Casey's happy-go-lucky expression waned.

"Really? How close was I?"

The admin pointed at the red ink in her ledger.

"Sixty-two," she whispered. "Look, this isn't a race. Take your time. It's only gonna get harder from here. See you in round three."

Casey lumbered back to her desk, worried. She came within a hairline of failing her HSE and ditched the arrogance.

Phase two washed out half of the test takers there. Inmates protested their scores to the admin. "Fifty-eight? It's two goddamn points! You can't curve it?" The saddest dismissal was the eighty-year-old from earlier. "I'm sorry, you didn't make it. You need at least a sixty," the admin told her. The old woman didn't cuss or contest her score. She snailed from the room before eventually disappearing down the corridor. Casey saw herself through the eyes of the old convict and readied herself for the next round.

Math and science had never been Casey's strong suits in school. She hated the trickery and stern rules. She hated even more that phase three would count as one score instead of two. She was clueless at times and often distracted. Not to mention her hand was sore; it was still stiff from the attack months ago. Discouraged, she considered giving up. She paused to mourn before noticing the admin staring back at her. The woman looked over at the clock on the wall and back at her. Casey shook off her demons and returned to work. Science was a natural disaster for her. She was so lost on the biology portion she reverted to childish games like "Eeny meeny miny moe" as her guide to the correct answer. Before she knew it, the admin called a halt to the test. "Time's up, ladies. Please bring all Scantrons forward."

The line to turn in Scantrons might as well have been the line for the electric chair. The admin shocked and stunned inmates' aspirations. "Sorry, not good enough this time. See you in six months." Casey watched from the back of the line. *Six months?* "It's not me, it's the machine, ladies," the admin explained. "You need at least a sixty or better. Next person, step forward."

By the time Casey made it up front, the machine had eliminated eleven inmates. Her hands trembled as she turned hers in, and her eyes fogged as failure seemed imminent. When the admin placed her Scantron into the machine, the device made a weird grunting sound before spitting it out. Casey blotted her eyes with her prison shirt.

"So, you said the state offers the HSE every six months, right?" she asked.

The admin reviewed her Scantron and recorded her score.

"Yes, ma'am… but only if you didn't pass." The admin grinned at her. "You made it, Haughton. See you after the final round."

Hell had finally frozen over. It was the needle in Casey's haystack she had been asking for her entire life. She scored a ninety-one on her phase three—well above the benchmark.

She gasped in amazement before busting loose in front of the test admin.

"Oh, my God," she squealed as she covered her mouth. "I really *am* smart."

The woman handed Casey back her golden Scantron.

"Child, please. You ain't hardly dumb. But you will be if you don't get your behind back to your seat for the next round. Now, go away."

Casey rushed back to her seat for the final round, crying tears of joy.

The last section was the cruelest: thirty-five questions; twenty were true or false and the rest required written answers. The index finger on Casey's dominant hand was puffy and red from hours of penciling in bubbles. One of her written questions asked for her plans following commencement. The eraser on her number two pencil had diminished beneath the metal, so she crossed out her errors.

I hope to someday leave this place behind for good, find a job and stay clean. I want to study family law since my situation wasn't so good growing up. Maybe ~~reunited~~ *reconnect with Courtney, my* ~~adopted~~ *sister. I miss my sister so much. We haven't talked in so long. I sure hope she's good.*

Casey reread her answers quietly to herself. The more she saw her ambitions spelled out in front of her on the page, the more eager she was for a fresh start. She thought back to 1982, wondering how her life would've turned out if she hadn't decided to participate in the robbery. A tear left her cheek and splattered onto the page as she powered through the rest of her exam, seeing herself in a light she could never have imagined. She submitted her Scantron and test booklet, and waited for the official verdict. The announcement came sooner than she expected.

"If you hear your name, please stand," the admin announced. "Sarah Winslow. Kellie Griffith. Elsa Johnson. Elizabeth Enright. Tyra Butler. Lynn Jones. Casey Haughton. Virginia Madison. Charlene Gregory. Please stand if I called your name."

Casey and her fellow inmates slowly rose from their seats.

"Congratulations. You all passed."

The room was ecstatic. There were tears of joy and pain for those who had made it to the final round but fell short. Casey stood there with a subdued look, silenced by her great feat. Out of sixty test-takers, she was one of nine graduates. The admin walked over to congratulate the St. Agnes graduating class of 1990. She handed the awardees mock diplomas, wrapped beneath a golden ribbon, a stand-in before their real diplomas arrived.

"Congratulations, Haughton. You made it. How do you feel?"

Casey gazed around the room at her peers all celebrating. Receiving their diplomas restored a sense of self-esteem which had gone missing. For Casey, receiving her diploma meant something different.

"Miss Haughton? Are you there?" the admin giggled. "I said, you made it."

Casey looked down at her phony certificate.

"No, I didn't," she said. "I'm still behind. Hell, I've been behind the last eight years."

"Well, you'll get where you need to be in due time. Listen, the HSE isn't the easiest test to pass. It's one of the hardest in the nation. You should celebrate."

"What am I celebrating exactly? The fact that I'm back at this place again? That my sister probably hates me for ruining her life? Oh, I know! Maybe I ought to celebrate that I'm a scumbag-fuck who destroys everything she touches—what the hell is it that I am celebrating?!"

The room went silent under Casey's wrath as inmates and the test admin looked on.

"I'm sorry, I just… I can't do this." She handed back her fake diploma and left.

Self-Loathing

asey paced near the phones, debating whether to call Courtney to apologize for last December. The thought of basking in the good news about her HSE subsided as she reached the box. She picked up the phone, returned it onto the hook and lifted it again, unsure. She practiced her lines. "Hey, it's me, I was just…" She stopped herself. "About December. You know what, Court, how about we start fresh? What do you say?" Casey banged her head against the wall, lost. She dialed her sister before she thought of something else stupid to say. Her heart tremored as an automated voice answered with a familiar message: "The number you are trying to reach is no longer in service." The phone relaxed inside of Casey's hand before crashing onto her shoulder. The girls had always fought throughout the years but would make up, until now. She stared at the phone box, speechless with hurt. She slithered back to her enclosure watery-eyed.

Casey rotted on her cot, mulling over her reality, indifferent to her latest achievement. In the real world, diplomas were a dime a dozen. Commencements were celebrated with family and friends. By twenty-four, most people were already working towards a career, apartment, car note payment, or looking for love. Casey was still hoping to find out who she was.

Days later, Casey was summoned to the auditorium for a cap and gown fitting to walk with her fellow alumni. She stared at her pale, round face in the mirror with a hapless look. She removed her cap and gave it back to the seamstress. "You don't want to walk?" the lady asked. "No, I don't, and I don't want to be here anymore, either." Casey unzipped her robe, balled it up, dunked it inside the box with the others and left.

Weeks after acing her HSE, Casey filtered into Dr. Matthews's class and moved her seat to the back. By then, she had been a student there for six weeks but still wouldn't concede. She defied her teacher with the same shitty attitude which had kept her in the hole for most of her dented adulthood. On their last day together, Dr. Matthews made a bold prediction.

"I have this fear about you, Casey Haughton," she said. "You're a smart woman, but you've got this thing where you think the world owes you something because you're sad. Well, guess what," Dr. Matthews told her, "nobody cares. You can keep making excuses for your mistakes or learn how to make miracles from them. I know this class is a court thing and you'd rather not be here and all that—I get it. But your toxic outlook on things is detrimental to your future."

Dr. Matthews zipped up her work bag and started toward the door.

"I never had a future, Doc," Casey blurted out. "Sorry for wasting your time."

Dr. Matthews turned around. "Well then… Do you want one?"

Casey played with a spot inside of her hand. She flicked her shoulders like a child.

"What do you mean, you don't know?" Dr. Matthews dropped her bag. "My God, Casey. Don't you want to live at all? Doesn't your life mean anything to you outside of here?"

Casey rolled her lips to keep from tearing up, but her eyes betrayed her.

"I am *waiting*, Casey!" Dr. Matthews raised her voice. "Now, what is it that you want out of this world? What does your life mean to you?"

"I don't knowwww!" Casey shouted. She buried her face beneath her shirt. "Please, just go. I've already wasted enough of your time as it is."

Dr. Matthews cruised over to her pupil's desk, her pumps clicking against the floor. She stopped in front of Casey's desk.

"I am not leaving here until you give me a better answer, young lady," she said. "For God sakes, Casey. Where's your hope? Where's your family? Do you have any?" Dr. Matthews slowly uncovered Casey's face. She held Casey by her pudgy chin.

"Look at those beautiful eyes," she said. "Filled with so much despair."

As Casey tried to look away, Dr. Matthews repositioned her pupil's gaze back on her.

"I don't have any family. I don't have any hope."

"Oh, bullshit." Dr. Matthews used her sleeve to dry Casey's face, holding up her chin. "Because somebody in this world needs you," she said. "But first, Casey Haughton needs to find out who Casey Haughton is before she can expect others to appreciate her. Catch my drift? You're probably one of the smartest students to ever take my course, Casey, but maaan, you sure are stubborn. Some days I wanted to beat you with a chair!"

Casey laughed at her own bullheadedness. Dr. Matthews glowed at Casey. She placed her hand onto her pupil's shoulder.

"You know, this is the most I've gotten out of you in six weeks. I can tell you've got a real soft spot in there, but it's covered up—with what, I don't know."

"A beaver built a dam over it," Casey chuckled. "Sorry for being such a jerk to you. I wish I could take it all back."

"Apology accepted. C'mere, you."

Casey left her chair and stood up to hug Dr. Matthews. As her teacher's arms embraced her, Casey felt another storm brewing from her heart. It was a much-needed hug. She held onto Dr. Matthews for nearly two minutes.

"Am I holding you up, Dr. Matthews?" she asked her.

"No, not at all."

"Good, I think I'm gonna lose it again."

Dr. Matthews squeezed Casey even tighter, allowing her to exhale. She held her like a mother would a daughter. Afterwards, the two accompanied each other out into the hallway and said their goodbyes.

"Well. I've got to be honest with you, Casey. You failed the course, but you passed the final exam with flying colors," Dr. Matthews told her. "That was quite the presentation back there—best I've seen all year. Think you can keep up the momentum for your remedial?"

"I'll give it a shot." She shrugged. "Besides, where else am I gonna go? They won't let me out until I pass. I'm sure I can do better."

Dr. Matthews patted Casey on the arm and shuffled up the hall, her heels clicked until she vanished in the distance. Casey returned to her cell to prepare for her fresh start.

A Fresh Start

Casey sat atop her favorite table out in the courtyard enjoying a smoke, gazing at an official copy of her high school diploma. She rubbed the letters of her crispy certificate in disbelief, tracing the letters of her name. Rather than participate in the ceremony that day, Casey celebrated with an ice-cold Dr. Pepper, a Payday candy bar, and her Kools. She cautiously returned her document inside its cardboard casing and gazed out into the mountainous backdrop. Her private moment was soon interrupted by a group of inmates wanting her table.

"You mind movin' to the other table?" one girl asked. "Couple of my homegirls wanted to play dominoes here. We got a big group comin' by in a few."

Casey glanced down at her diploma and up at the condemned felon before hopping down. She put out her cigarette.

"Sure, knock yourselves out." As she headed across the field, the same inmate called to her.

"Yo, you forgot somethin'."

Casey turned and noticed the woman was holding her diploma and returned to get it.

"This you? Word, you probably don't wanna leave that lyin' around here. You know how this place is. You know how to play dominoes? We could use another player."

"Well, I guess I do owe you one, right?" she giggled. "One game shouldn't hurt."

"Haughton!" a CO hollered at her from the tower. "Forget about that stupid game for now. You're needed down in the mailroom right away."

Casey rolled her eyes at the guard.

"Hold my seat," she told the thoughtful convict. "I'll be back." She rushed inside.

When Casey arrived down at the mail room, she was greeted by the riot control team. She glowered at them from the door. Each time they showed up, her valuables were either destroyed or seized. The team's lieutenant walked over to greet her. Casey gave him shit before he could speak.

"Let me guess, my heroin shipment just arrived." Casey crossed her arms. "What the hell do you guys want now? I'm still waiting for my house made of popsicle sticks to get replaced. Do you know how long that took to create?"

"That was under a different regime, Haughton." The lieutenant unbuckled and removed his helmet. He reached inside his vest pocket and handed Casey an envelope. "Here, take this."

Casey looked down at the envelope and back at him, suspicious.

"Th'fuck is in there? Tear gas?"

"Do you want it to be tear gas?" He raised it again. "Go'on, take it."

Casey took her letter from the already-opened packaging and began to read. Her eyes skimmed to the center of the page.

…Thus, in lieu of your recent good behavior and completion of the High School Equivalency examination and mandated rehabilitation class, the court hereby reinstates your previous application for parole. Effective Monday, April 30th 1990, at 2 p.m. under the following guidelines and restrict—

Casey reread the judge's ruling several times over, mystified. She giggled to herself as disbelief gushed from her eyes. A slight smile appeared on the lieutenant's face.

"I'm sure Sydney would've been proud," he said. "I want your cell cleaned out two days before your departure… unless you'd like to stay a little longer?"

"No way, man. My time's up!" Casey laugh-cried, covering her mouth. "I'm going home. I'm actually going home, I don't believe this. Thank you, Lieutenant."

Casey stuffed her letter inside her shirt and went to visit Dr. Matthews. She was scheduled to begin her remedial class the week of her release from prison. She rolled into her old teacher's class to show off her letter. Dr. Matthews was eating her lunch and working on a crossword puzzle.

"Dr. Matthews! Dr. Matthews!" Casey busted through the door, flailing her letter about. "I'm going home. Look!"

Dr. Matthews looked over her letter. "Well, I can't say that I'm all that surprised. You deserved the early release. Your final presentation was spot on. I made sure I noted that in my letter to Judge Applewhite."

Casey put two and two together.

"Hold up. You ratted on me? Yo, I thought I failed the class?"

"You did," Dr. Matthews laughed. "But I felt your presentation at the end was worthy enough for me to write a letter asking the judge for some leniency. I'm glad it all worked out. Stop by and see me if you're ever in Esseltown."

Casey glanced down at her letter, shocked by her teacher's faith.

"Sorry, Teach—" She shook her head. "—but I think I've had enough of Esseltown for a while, if you know what I mean. I'll write you sometime."

Dr. Matthews returned to her lunch. "Whatever works." She smiled. "Take care of yourself, Haughton."

Casey ran to her cell that afternoon with her letter and diploma. She launched onto her cot, kicking her feet, overjoyed by the day's events. Across from her cage, the sun found its way through a section of glass, spiraling a radiant glow which beamed throughout her cell block. "Oh, my God, I'm going home! Ahhh!" She rolled around. For once, it was a good day.

Fifteen

The duress of real-world problems discouraged Casey as she attempted to make her final trip home from the big house. With Courtney out of the picture, she faced the arduous task of finding transportation home on her own. The State ordered her to serve the first six months of her release at a transitional house somewhere in Brooklyn. Casey was skeptical until an inmate schooled her.

"It's like a little mini-jail, but it ain't," the inmate told her. "You check in, you check out. You gotta be in by a certain time unless you're at work—then it doesn't count. They give you a small room with a door, privacy. It's like an apartment with other tenants there. Enjoy it while it lasts, though. It ain't forever."

Casey solicited another convict's opinion and received a different response. "Depends where they put you," the killer told her. "Most of those places are poorly run—you'd be better on the street, in my opinion." Casey hadn't needed a halfway house or the streets last year when she was first released. She'd had Courtney's couch.

Out of the eleven cab companies Casey researched in the phonebook for the Upstate area, no one was interested in driving her back to Brooklyn. "Lady, that's past Albany!" one dispatcher said." Nobody would help her. She mulled for days, worried she'd have to give up booty on the side of the road to some creepy truck driver named Dale just to get a ride back to the city. She waited six days and phoned back her last contact with a different plan. "Albany, New York? Sure, we can take you there. May I have your name, please?" the dispatcher asked. Casey cupped her hands over the speaker so no one could hear her. "Yes: Margaret Wilson."

Casey's next urgent call was to the parole office. For her second stab, the court assigned her a new parole officer. The man's answering machine message reminded her of a gruff, coffee-sipping foreman with three ex-wives. *Beep.* "Jack Woods. Leave a message." Casey hung up, nervous. She took a walk, returned and dialed again. A woman answered this time. "Sure, may I ask who's calling?" the secretary asked her. "Uh, Haughton. C-Casey Haughton," she stammered. The secretary transferred her immediately, tossing Casey into the fire. The line buzzed as if she'd phoned a slaughter house. Casey was surprised to hear a different name when her new PO answered.

"Miss Jacqueline Woods, who is this?"

Casey went silent. *Jacqueline Woods?* She wasn't sure if "Jack" was short for Jacqueline, or if the secretary had mistakenly transferred her to a Jacqueline when she really needed a Jack.

"Yes, I'm looking for a… Jack Woods?"

"This is Jacqueline, how may I help you?"

Casey froze again. "So, do you mean like, Jack as in Jac-queline, but everybody-calls-me-Jack-but-my-real-name's-Jac-queline… Jack or is it the kind of jack that you—"

"How-may-I-help-you, caller?" the woman said to Casey as if she was slow. "You're speaking with Miss Jacqueline Woods. Do I need to spell it out for you?"

"No, sir—ma'am. The court sent a letter here that was—"

"Last name?"

"Um, Haughton. H-a-u-g—"

"I know how to spell, Haughton, sweetheart. Who was the magistrate?"

"Magistrate?"

"The judge. Who was the judge? Your last judge, Haugh-ton?"

"Oh, sorry. Um, Applewhite. A-p-p—"

Music suddenly started on the other end of the phone as Casey waited for Miss Woods to return. Her short fuse kept her off balance throughout the call. She twirled the phone cord between her fingers, her heart still out of her shirt.

"So, you're my little dopehead parole violator, huh?" Miss Woods suddenly returned to the line. "Well, if you think you're gonna run the streets under my watch, sticking straws up your nose, you've got another thing coming. How long were you a crackhead before you got pinched?"

"I ain't no damn crackhead," Casey raised her voice. "I've got plans, Miss Woods."

"We'll see how long that lasts. Everybody talks a good game until they get out. Everybody's flying straight, going to law school and converting over to Islam. Let me tell you something, if you take as much as a sneeze, I'm gonna know about it. You work for me now, Haughton. Just try me. I'll bust your ass back into the cell. We clear on that?"

Casey talked through her teeth, mad. "Crystal."

"Good. Now, write this down. 132 East Arbor Street, Brooklyn, New York. That's the halfway house you've been assigned to. The place is called Fellowship House."

Casey jotted the address onto the back of her court letter. "Got it."

"Good, write this: 288 South Chambers Avenue. Fourth floor. Suite 329. That's my office. Report there on the day of your release. My office number is 212-561-7878. I'm in Monday through Friday until 5 p.m. and late on Tuesdays. If you run into any problems, you call me right away. Any questions?"

"No, but I wanted to talk to you about a transportation issue that's—"

"Not my problem. Figure it out. Have a good day."

Miss Woods hung up on her. Casey looked down at her chicken-scratch notes. Of all the parole officers she could've been assigned, the State had sent her the devil.

Margaret Wilson

It was after 2 p.m. when St. Agnes opened its steel doors for Casey Haughton on Monday, April 30, 1990. She was two months shy of her twenty-fifth birthday. Casey left with a small bag of toiletries, a few clothes, her prized diploma, and $170 in her commissary. In her pocket was a half-eaten Payday candy bar and her Kools. She waited along a grimy roadway under the sizzling sun, watching for her cab to arrive. Her T-shirt had melted to her porky body as heat radiated from the pavement. Her pits were runny and salty, and her hair a clumpy mess. She swiped her oily forehead with her hand and rubbed the excess fluid onto her jeans. Across from her on the side of the road was a mileage sign for New York City. It would take her more than a week to hike 352 miles across the state. She grew impatient, waiting for her ride to show. "C'mon, dammit," she sighed, irritated. She plugged a cigarette into her mouth and went for her lighter. Before she could light, a yellow cabbie came speeding up the roadway and pulled beside her. The driver had thick bushy eyebrows, a heavy beard and beige skin.

Casey could tell he wasn't American.

"You Wilton?" the foreign driver asked.

"It's *Wilson*," Casey corrected him. She jiggled the door handle. "You gonna let me in?"

"Where's money? You have?"

"Of course." Casey flashed her short stack. "Okay, I told you my name. What's yours?"

"I am Javier. So, you give me money now?"

"No, that's not what I agreed to over the phone," she lied. "We agreed to half upfront, and the rest at the end. Didn't they tell you this, Javier?"

As confusion and worry appeared on his hairy face, Casey poured on the bullshit.

"C'mon, Javier. Open the door," she bullied him, pulling at the handle. "It's hot out here. You want me to turn into a homecooked meal? Let me in."

When Javier unlocked the door, Casey hurried inside and closed it. His air-conditioned ride felt like a spent hydrant on a ghetto street in July. He turned around to face her.

"You give me half now and other half in Albany? Yes?"

Casey played him again.

"Albany? What the fuck is wrong with your job, dude? I told 'em Brooklyn."

Casey feigned an attitude as she reached inside her pocket. She counted out $125 and slapped it into Javier's hand.

"Here, man—here. This is *ridiculous*. Forget it. We'll sort this out later, just drive."

"No-no, no drive to Brooklyn. Too far. Only Upstate."

"Upstate? Dispatch said you guys go there all the time, Javier."

"Dispatch say?"

"Yes!" Casey raised her voice. "It's conflicting information, and it's false advertisement. You can get sued for that shit. You know what, just forget it, alright? Next time, tell your dispatcher to try a new headset or something. Fuckin' lady is nuts."

Casey was the one who was nuts. She was trying to stiff Javier on her cab fare. He scratched his thick beard as he counted his money. Casey eyed him closely, hoping he'd take the bait. She pressed him again.

"Oh, my God, Javier! Really? Would you make your mother or sister walk in this heat? I'm pregnant, for God's sakes. I'm pretty sure your boss would want you to do the right thing."

Javier scratched his head again, overwhelmed.

"Okay, I take you," he agreed. "You pay me good, Wilton. Yes?"

"Of course. As soon as we reach Brooklyn, I got you, homie."

Casey relaxed as Javier finally drove off. She fell back into her seat and sighed with relief. She had no idea how she was going to pay him.

Javier made Casey feel uneasy as they moved down the highway. He eyeballed her from the rearview mirror with his thick eyebrows. Casey stayed in character. "What?" she barked at him. "Dude, I told you I'm gonna pay you. Chill out." Javier mumbled something in his native language and carried on.

They stopped at a rural gas station in a township called McConklin, New York. "You pump, I'll pee," she told him. "Don't leave me, man. You promise, Javier?" Javier held up his right hand as if he was under oath. "I promise. No leave. I check air in tire first then get gas."

Casey unfastened her seat belt and rushed inside. She went straight to the food counter and ordered two chili and cheese hot dogs, chips, and a drink. When Javier walked inside, she ducked and zipped into the bathroom with her food. She worried that if Javier caught her stuffing her face, he'd know she had extra money and would bug her for it.

With her back pressed against the door, Casey absorbed her food like a neanderthal. She'd skipped breakfast at the prison that morning, fearing that a jealous convict or an overzealous CO would try her on her last day there. Satisfied, she threw away her trash and rinsed the evidence from her hands. A knock sounded at the door. "Yeah, one second," Casey told the querying patron. She washed and air-dried her hands and opened the door. Javier was standing on the opposite side.

"ATM?" He pointed over at a sign in the window, overly excited. "You can get money now. Pay me, no problem. I take you where you need to go, yes?"

Casey looked over at the sign and stalled.

"Oh, that's for Discover card. I use a different bank. Besides, their fees are too high."

Javier thumbed his eyes in frustration. Casey placed her hand onto her driver's shoulder and squeezed. She played the poor guy like a cello.

"Quit worrying so much. As soon as we get to Brooklyn, I got you. Okay?"

Javier sighed. "Okay, Wilton. Too far already. You get me good, yes?"

"Son, I got you. Just give me one second, I think I need the girl's room again."

Casey waited for him to leave and bought herself a pack of Starburst candy and a book of matches. She stuffed them inside her pockets and headed out. When she got outside, Javier was standing next to his cab with his arms folded across his chest.

"You buy candy and hot dogs earlier, I watched you," he fussed. "You have money. You lie. You eat a lot, Wilton."

Casey flipped it on him. "I am *pregnant*, Javier!" She popped her neck at him, fake-upset. "Way to make me feel insecure about myself, dude—thanks. Thanks a lot."

Javier's tone quickly changed. He opened her door and helped her inside. Casey impersonated an overly-dramatic, soon-to-be mother.

"You are so cruel, you know that?" She reached for her door and slammed it.

It was just after eight o' clock that night when Javier's cab arrived in the city. Casey had pimped him for 352 miles. Finally, she was home. She sat up in her seat, admiring Manhattan's exquisite glow as soft trumpet music emitted from the car's stereo. She gazed at the twinkling lights, wondering where Courtney could be. Her gut brewed with tension as Javier's cab merged into the busy lights off in the distance. Casey had one last crime to add to her rap sheet before the night would end: Theft of Services (NY Penal Law 165.15), punishable by a maximum of one year in jail and/or a fine of one thousand dollars. She double-knotted her shoestrings and laced her toiletry bag around her wrist. She hated the thought of playing roulette with her freedom again but was desperate. "Pull over by that ATM over there, Javier," she told him. Javier eased his cab in front of a NationsBank at the corner. Next to the ATM machine was a long, narrow alley.

"Okay, wait here, I'll get the money."

When Casey reached for the handle, the door didn't budge. She pulled it several more times, nothing. Javier turned around to face her.

"What are you doing, man?" she panicked. "This isn't funny, Javier. Now, cut it out!"

Javier turned off the motor.

"Nice try, Wilton." He smiled devilishly. "I come with you. We get money together. Soon as you pay, I go home. Is deal?"

"Okay. Fine. Just open the door. You're scaring me, man. C'mon, open up."

Javier got out and walked around to let Casey out. She pounded the seat with her fist. *Shit.* She crawled out as if everything was normal with Javier flanking from behind. She walked over to the device and stood in front of the screen.

"Do you mind? How about a little privacy, Javier?"

He cut his eyes at her. "No more games, Wilton. Pay me money."

"I will—now back up!" Javier took two short steps back, not taking his eyes off her.

Casey looked him up and down and returned to trolling at the machine. She reached inside her shirt, pretending to stuff her bank card into the device, watching him through the mirror strip above the machine. The moment Javier turned to check his running cab, *bam*, she bolted down the alley. Her toiletries clattered together, chopping into her side as Javier chased after her.

"You fat bitch!" he bellowed in his native accent. "You fat fucking bitch. You stiff me!"

Casey hauled to the other end, pushing as fast as her big legs would take her. As a youth, she'd developed great speed from getting chased home by bullies. She ran up Baltic Avenue and killed it up the road, dodging between cars. Javier attempted the same feat and collided with a passing cyclist, taking him out of the race. Casey scurried down another slim alley, jumped a fence and disappeared into the city.

Fellowship House

Casey arrived at her halfway house just after 9:40 p.m., disheveled and weary from her run. She verified the address provided by Miss Woods and ascended the staircase, bypassing a group of dice shooters on the side of the building. She peeked through the thick glass doors, surveying the inside. The building's decor reminded her of a dentist's or doctor's office in its former life. Inside the lobby were couches with tables full of magazines and children's coloring books. A television set was anchored to the wall. In the corner near the restroom was a fish tank that looked as if it hadn't been cleaned since the Civil War. Scattered along the walls were signs and visual reminders of visiting hours and prohibited drug use. A guard sat at a desk in the middle of the room with his boots kicked up, flipping through channels. Casey pressed at the call button on the door's frame to get his attention. The bell chimed like a ringer from the 1930s. The guy looked over at her and went back to watching TV. When Casey pressed the button again, the man ignored her. Irritated, she banged at the glass with her palm. *Bap-Bap-Bap.* The guard grabbed the microphone from his desk and spoke into it. His voice blared like alien garble.

"Visiting hours are over. Come back tomorrow." He went back to watching TV.

Steam blew from Casey's ears. She was tired, dirty, and had a deranged cab driver somewhere out in the night looking for her. She jammed her thumb into the button again, holding down the ringer and pounding at the glass. The guard finally got up and met her at the door. He looked young and full of himself.

"Come back tomorrow."

Casey pressed the button again, holding it down. The man covered his ears.

"Stop doing that shit!" he yelled at her. "Who are you looking for?"

Casey finally let go of the call button. She reached inside her bag, removed her court-ordered letter and slammed it against the glass for the man to see. *Thonk.* The guy tilted his head to read it.

"It's after curfew."

"No shit, Sherlock. How about you quit being a dick and open the door?"

The man returned to his desk and pressed a button, unlocking the door. Casey ripped it open and walked inside. The asshole guard placed a clipboard on the counter for her to fill out. He was still wiggling at his sensitive ears.

"Here, just fill out these sections."

Casey dropped her toiletry bag on the counter. Deodorant

and other hygiene products rattled together. When the guard placed a pen beside her, she snatched it and began to write.

"Sorry, I thought you were a visitor."

Casey continued to write, ignoring the rude jerk's attempt to be nice. She slammed the pen onto the clipboard and picked up her bag.

"Where's my room? Up these stairs or what?"

The man reached behind him for a key to Room 6.

"It's on the right. If you need anything, my name's—"

Casey walked off before he could finish. *Fuck your name, dude.*

The co-ed sober house where Casey was assigned was an extension of the prison system. Doors were locked, bars were on every window and the place was ousted with signage reiterating the building's visiting hours and curfew time. On the bottom floor was a tiny kitchenette and a small table for six. A man wearing a tank top with jeans and a tie-back durag over his head leaned against a wall on one foot, smoking a Black & Mild cigar. He eyed Casey with interest as she passed by.

"Say there, baby girl? So, what they pinch you on, huh? Stealin' some guy's heart?"

Casey batted her eyes at him.

"Murder. Stabbed my husband in his sleep and set fire to the house. You single?"

The guy scurried from her path. She moved down the slender hallway, entered her miniature room and closed the door behind her. She turned on the light, leaned against the wood and exhaled with relief. Finally, she was home.

The cramped space where Casey was assigned was short of accommodating. Her hospice-looking bed looked weak and unsteady. The mattress smelled like sex, and her white sheets were yellowy. An old, ugly TV with a cracked screen was mounted to its wallpapered walls. She dropped her toiletry bag onto the floor and walked over to her window. She peered out into New York's night life and noticed a familiar landmark from her past. "Son of a bitch, I don't believe it," Casey chuckled to herself. Directly across the street from her window was the same building that had once been the liquor store she and her old crew tried to rob eight years earlier. The store had since been remodeled into a vacuum repair shop, but its old signage was still attached to the roof. For however long she was assigned there, Casey would have the pleasure of reliving her senseless decision. She twisted the handle to her shade, sparing herself from the irony. With her long day nearing its end, she emptied her raggedy bag full of toiletries, grabbed a towel, and lumbered across the hall for a hot shower. She moaned with ease as the waters beat against her freckled skin. She placed her head onto the tile, giggling in disbelief. "Right across the street, though?"

Sixteen

A sharp knock sounded at Casey's door early the next morning, startling her awake. She shot up and looked around, uncertain if she was dreaming until the disruptor knocked again. She fell backward onto her bed and grunted with discontent. The visitor pounded once more. *Boom-Boom-Boom.* Casey whipped the covers over her tired head. "Go away!" she shouted at the door.

There was a long pause before the visitor knocked a fourth time. Casey stuck her head out the side, thinking it was the prick guard from the main desk. "Haven't you ever heard of beauty sleep, man? Go bother someone else." She fluffed her pillow and rolled over. The disruptor knocked a fifth time.

"You're not gettin' rid of me that easy, Haughton. It's Miss Jacqueline Woods, your parole officer!" she snarled through the door.

Casey was on her feet by the time she heard "officer." She'd forgotten to call Miss Woods after her chaotic night.

"Oh, my God! I-I'm so sorry, ma'am. One second, please."

Casey fingered through her wild hair, gurgled a lid full of

mouthwash, spat it into her trash can and raced for the door. She answered wearing panties and a long T-shirt.

Waiting for her on the other side was a short dark-skinned woman with hatchets for eyes, and a mole on her left cheek. She had a parted box fade with tribal earrings like Shabba Ranks. She stood between two Twin-Tower-sized cops. She split her eyes at Casey like an angry mother there to pick up her bad child from school. Casey slowly backed inside her room as Miss Woods and her entourage entered without permission. Her PO signaled at the two cops.

"Cuff her, right now," Miss Woods ordered.

The two cops swarmed Casey, grabbing her arms. Their wide hands felt like meat hooks, tearing into her skin.

"Wait-wait-wait, what'd I do wrong? What am I being arrested for?"

"Parole violation. Why else? Have a nice trip back Upstate, Haughton."

"Back Upstate? I just got in last night. Give me a break."

The cops hooked Casey up again, she couldn't believe it. She'd been on parole less than a day and was already headed back to the big house. She thought she'd gotten away with stiffing Javier, the cab driver from last night. The two cops placed Casey under arrest and sat her on the bed.

"You were given specific instructions and you disobeyed them. I told you to call me the second you arrived in Brooklyn and you didn't. This is not Burger King, Haughton—you cannot have it your way."

Casey's voice wavered as she tried to explain. "I know I

let you down, but I've got a good excuse. I didn't get in until after nine, and I was so dead, I honestly forgot. Please, ma'am. Don't send me back. I-I-I just got my diploma," she stuttered. "How can I make anything in my life right if I'm locked up all the damn time?"

Miss Woods exhaled with displeasure. She signaled at one of the cops to unhook Casey before asking them to wait outside. Casey sat on her bed, relieved.

"You were *this* close, you know that?" Miss Woods gestured. "No employer is gonna feel sorry for you because you can't follow directions. Moving forward, I expect full cooperation out of you. I'm not your friend. I'm not your colleague—I am your parole officer, understood?"

Casey rubbed her wrist. "Okay, I got it. Jesus, you act like you just busted me in Vegas at a roulette table or something. I am where you wanted me to be, aren't I?"

"Honey, we are looong way from where I want you to be. This is only the beginning."

"Well, it felt like the end just a second ago. Gosh, I wish everybody would just get off my damn back. I'm doing the best I can."

"Well, your best is not good enough, Haughton. If this is the best you've got, maybe it's time to change your approach. Don't you want better for yourself? Or, do you want to come back out here and become another crackhead, criminal drug addict—"

Casey leapt to her feet. "Don't call me that! I ain't no crackhead, and I am not a goddamn criminal. I paid my dues already—and I'm tired of paying extra. Don't call me that, Miss Woods."

Casey splashed on her bed, mad. Miss Woods looked her up and down.

"That sure seemed to strike a nerve," she said. "Do you even know what it is you want in this world? Well, do you?"

Casey wiped her eyes with her shirt. "To survive, what else?"

"To survive? Shit, half of the people out here are doing that already. You can't do no better? I saw your test scores, Haughton. You're not a stupid woman. Only someone with goals can pull off a decent score like that—and sit up straight when you talk to me," she ordered. "Girl, I am not playing with you. I said *sit up…* and look at me when I'm talking to you, young lady."

Casey sighed as she sat up on her bed and looked directly at the mad woman.

"Get those tears out of your eyes. You'll be twenty-five soon, not five—and put on some damn clothes. Straighten your hair. You look like one of these hookers out here roaming the streets at night. Show some class."

Casey fetched for her sweaty jeans from last night. She put them on, tied her hair into a ponytail, and returned to her bed with a defeated look.

"You're worse than my teenage daughter. Where's your parents? You got any family?"

"I don't have any family."

"Why not? Did you run them off with your drug problems?"

Casey hung her head. "Look, I ain't no better than any-body else, but nobody else is better than me either, Miss Woods. I got my baggage just like everybody else. At least I'm dealing with my shit—as pathetic as I may be."

Miss Woods nodded her head at Casey, impressed.

"Good answer. So, what are your goals?"

"To survive. To finally make it."

"What else?" Miss Woods asked her. "C'mon, Haughton, think. Everybody's trying to survive out here. Hell, it's New York City."

"Well…" Casey paused. "I would like to see my sister again, Courtney. We've been falling out the past eight years. I was hoping to make up for that."

"Really? And what makes you think Courtney would want that?"

"Why wouldn't she want that? I'm her sister."

"You can't just walk in and out of people's lives whenever you feel like it. Even family members get tired of that. I'd bet my apartment that Courtney is tired of waiting for you to grow up."

Casey deflated as Miss Woods turned to leave.

"Just what I thought. This was your one and only freebie. No more excuses. Your next check-in with me is at my office in a week. If not, I'll drive you back to St. Agnes myself… in my trunk!"

Casey snorted until she noticed Miss Woods clip her eyes.

"That's your problem," she said. "This isn't a joke, Haughton. You're already on thin ice. Lock it in… before I lock you up. See you in a week." Miss Woods closed the door behind her.

Revived

Casey hit the streets with newfound purpose after her close call with Miss Woods. Despite her efforts, the results were the same as last year. For every job she queried, she was turned away. "Sorry sweetheart, no felons. Congratulations on your diploma, though," a lady told her. Casey's first day home ended with her discouraged, staring up at her ceiling fan as it rotated throughout her room.

By day three, she contemplated breaking the law again so the State would send her back up north. She missed the routine and stability that being an inmate provided; she felt safer there than in society. Her life was dog shit. She sat on her window sill with a beer bottle, stewing up rage as she stared out into the Brooklyn lights. *Why did I even come back?* She staggered from her window, using the wall for support. She wobbled to her nightstand, noticed her disgusting reflection in the mirror, and lost it. Her wild hair covered her face. She pounded on the wood. "Look at you… you're a fuckin' disgrace. No wonder your sister didn't—" She backhanded the bottle onto the floor, shattering it.

The sound startled her as she fell backward onto her bed, holding her ears. Her head spun as she curled into a ball and crashed into a mumbling stupor. Casey woke up early the next morning half hung over and noticed the shattered bottle from the night before. She swept up the spent glass, showered, and went out to face the world.

At a Brooklyn phone booth, she turned through a raggedy phone book, searching for her last name in hopes of tracking down Courtney. She worried that her sister had moved out of the area. Courtney had never been fond of city-living and had only moved there for her. Casey traced her finger down the page, hoping for a miracle. "Haas, Hamlin, Hampton, Hazel, Hughes." Not a single Haughton was listed. She closed the book and returned it to the shelf. A passing bus stopped at the street corner nearby. Casey noticed in the window that the bus was headed for Gardener Heights. Suddenly, it dawned on her: Rob, her old lover. She raced toward the bus, nearly mowing down a passenger as they attempted to board. "Hey, watch it!" the angry rider shouted at her. Casey piled into the front row of the bus.

Thinking of Rob stoked a rage in Casey. She hated him for introducing her to blow, not to mention turning his back on her after her second stint. He had sweet-talked her, fucked her, lied about having her back, and then dumped her when the cops showed up. He used his cocaine to control Casey which ultimately led to her and Courtney's fallout. Rob was nothing more than a smooth-talking bully and a con artist.

The more Casey reflected over her past year, the angrier she grew. With her nostrils flaring, she hopped off the city bus and canvassed the lot of her old building. She looked for Courtney's blue Chevette and noticed it was gone—that made her even more ticked off. She looked toward Rob's balcony on the sixth floor and noticed the sliding glass door was open. Casey remembered he liked a hit of reefer in the mornings and would leave his window cracked. She bolted inside, bypassing the sleeping security guard.

Casey was out of the elevator before the doors fully opened. She trooped down to Rob's apartment and stood at the door. His stereo was on, and there was an eviction sign posted on his door. She imagined Rob was in there, high on reefer and cocaine, slugging around. Casey beat at his door if she was the cops.

"Yo, Rob!" she yelled. "I know you're in there, you coward, it's Casey. Man, your window's open. Open up this door right now!"

When Rob didn't answer, Casey kicked it. *Thump.*

"Ohhh, I see. You in there with another bitch? Is that it?" She kicked it again. "That's some weak-ass shit you did to me last year—blocking my calls from Upstate. You took advantage of me. You doped me, fucked me, and now I'm gonna fuck you right back. Open this goddamn door, Rob or else I'm knock it down!"

Casey pounded some more. She pressed her head against the door to listen but could only hear Chubb Rock playing in the background. She dropped to her knees to look for any movement inside Rob's apartment before quickly jerking her head away at the stench. Casey covered her nose with her forearm. She stood up and was greeted by an elderly tenant from across the hall. The woman held a section of newspaper over her face.

"Good luck gettin' him to answer," she said, squinching her face. "His mailbox is so full, the mailman started giving me *his* stuff. The hell with the mail, they ought to do somethin' about that smell. I called the rental office. Somebody's on the way up to do a welfare check. I tried knocking a day or two ago, but I couldn't get an answer."

Casey stared at the woman with an astonished look. She looked back at Rob's door. The rotting odor stunned her again.

"You got a name, sugar? I'll tell him you came by if I happen to see him."

Casey looked back at the woman. "Don't bother." She turned and left.

Casey sat at her window that night, still in shock over her gruesome discovery. She'd arrived at Rob's apartment seeking revenge and left feeling sorry for him. She imagined her ex-lover dead on his bathroom floor with a pipe next to his moldy carcass. It bothered her well into the night. She counted her lucky stars and made it a priority to find Courtney before it was too late.

By the weekend, Casey was ready to pack it in. Hungry, she entered the grocery mart on Coventry Avenue and stuffed her pants with tuna fish cans, rolls, soap, tampons, and a chocolate candy bar. She hurried back to her room and dumped her stolen goods across the floor. She whimpered as she picked up the tuna can and realized she needed a can opener. "Oh, come the *fuck* on!" She hurled the tuna fish can behind her bed. A passing tenant noticed Casey depressed and offered her some advice.

"Next time, get the ones with the pull-tops," the ex-con chuckled. "You ain't gotta steal, though. We each get two meals a day. It's down in the kitchen. Make sure you claim your meals, though. Otherwise, somebody else might—"

Casey leapt over the pile of stolen merchandise, clearing it in a single hop. She shot down to the kitchen and noticed a tray with her name written on it. She rushed back to her room, ripped off the lid and went to town. Inside was navy beans, carrots, and a pork chop smothered with gravy. She bit into the cold flesh, grunting with pleasure, chewing with her eyes closed. She stopped upon realizing her food was cold. "Ewww, yuck!" Casey returned downstairs to warm up her meal.

With nourishment no longer a concern, money was still an issue in Casey's world. While out looking for jobs one afternoon, the sky dumped on her. She stopped at a street vendor selling umbrellas and removed her wallet. "You got anything under $2.50?" The seller reached beneath his stand and handed Casey a newspaper. "Nope, but you can have this. I already read it—keep the change." Casey continued her job hunt with the sports section covering her head. By the time she made it to the edge of the block, she dumped her paper for a cardboard box she found near a garbage compactor. The box lasted for three blocks before it split in half on her. Soaked, she rushed inside of a nearby coffee shop for relief until some pencil-necked guy with a zit stuck to his nose ushered her out. "Sorry, these seats are for paying customers only. You gotta leave." She sighed and left.

Casey stood near a watery bus stop, unsure of her next move. Beside her was a professionally dressed woman (with an umbrella). Casey watched the woman with her side eye. She contemplated jacking the lady's umbrella and running off until Miss Woods entered her thoughts. The woman beside her signaled for a cab. Rushing, she dropped her leather purse in the roadway. Casey picked it up and went running after her.

"Ma'am? Excuse me?" Casey kindly called to the woman. "Ma'am? I think you—"

"Hey, back off!" the woman shouted. "I was here, first." The lady slammed the door as the cabbie sped off up the block.

Casey unzipped the woman's bag, looked inside, and noticed a wad of cash and several credit cards. She casually zipped up the bag and returned to the coffee shop with the geeky manager. The man confronted her as soon as she walked in.

"Hey, what are you doing? You can't just—"

Casey bypassed the manager and went into the bathroom. She locked the door behind her, unzipped the fallen purse and removed the money. Her eyes ignited at the cash as she thumbed through the crispy bills, counting nine hundred dollars. She smiled and pocketed the money. On her way out, she tossed the lady's purse into the can. The manager was waiting for her at the door as she walked out.

"You can't be in here unless you're a paying customer—I told you that."

Casey pulled out her stack, peeled off a twenty and stuffed it inside his apron.

"Remember this face. Because when I come back tomorrow, I want the biggest cup of cawfee you guys have, and I want *you* to brew it. Think you can handle that?"

Casey patted him on his acne cheek and left.

Outside, she peeled another twenty and gave it to a waiting cab driver. "Manhattan, please."

Queen for a Day

With her feet crossed comfortably in the chair across from her at a Red Lobster and a bib covering her bosoms, Casey crushed two lobster tails, a half-pound of shrimp, curly fries, green beans and a scoop of jasmine rice for lunch. Dessert was a shopping spree at the Macy's on West 34th Street. She helped herself to some cute outfits with matching shoes (they were on sale), umbrella, and a rain jacket. She tried on *everything*, modeling in her new threads. She left the store and made it three blocks before remembering she didn't have anything to wear for a job interview and returned to buy three more outfits. She wobbled into a fancy, Asian-owned salon with her arms covered in bags. She placed them onto the floor at the counter as a worker greeted her.

"Yes, help you?"

Casey showed the woman a one-hundred-dollar bill. "What can I get for this?"

An army of staff swarmed Casey before ushering her to the back. They placed cucumbers over her eyes and covered her face with weird creams before rushing her into the pedicure chair. She tittered as workers prodded her soles with odd devices. It was the first time she'd ever had her nails professionally done. She marveled at the jadish color, wiggling her fingers and toes. "Neat, I love it!" She tipped the salon an extra fifty and left. On the way home, she saw a vagrant digging in the trash for food and offered him the same tip. "Here you go, my man." Casey gave the guy fifty dollars. Close to home, she stopped at a Pizza Hut and ordered herself a large pepperoni pizza with extra cheese and a two-liter of Dr. Pepper for her dinner. She then signaled for a cabbie and returned to Fellowship House. Casey had so much stuff to carry that even the driver had to help. Her day of royalty was short-lived, however.

Casey sat with her head propped between her hands later that night, depressed. Her pockets and belly were full, but her heart still felt heavy. She missed Courtney dearly and reminisced the few times they laughed together when she first came home last year. She stood at her window, staring out into the blinking city lights, a few hundred dollars richer but still poor overall. She showed up for her appointment with Miss Woods the next morning with a hopeless look.

"So how are things coming along your first week back?" her PO asked her. "Got any prospects to share?"

Casey gave her bleak look. "I'm a felon, Miss Woods. The only prospect is me fuckin' up again." She looked down at her feet. "Can I go back?" she mumbled.

Miss Woods sat up in her seat. "Excuse me? What'd you just say?"

Casey fiddled with her hand, avoiding the question.

"So, you're givin' up on me, huh? After a week? Is it really that hard for you, Haughton? Or are you just too chicken shit to be somebody in this world? Which one is it?"

Casey kept her head down. She was done with living on the outside and wanted no part of this shark tank society or its responsibility. Miss Woods got up from behind her desk and walked over to her. She motioned with her hand.

"Get up. Get out of my chair," she demanded. "Right now."

Casey slowly rose. Miss Woods skinned her eyes at her.

"Now, you listen to me, young lady. You will *not* quit on me. I won't allow it! And the reason you can't quit on me is because... you don't have my permission to." A gentle glow appeared on her face. "You got that? Now, you get out there and you fight back. Don't you let this world keep you down. C'mon, you got this. If you can survive seven and a half years in a place like St. Agnes, this world ain't got nothin' on you."

Casey smiled back. She didn't know if Miss Woods could spell "smile."

"You're right, Miss Woods. I won't quit... at least not yet, anyway. I'm gonna march into every building on this block and demand somebody give me a job. And if they don't, I'll set the goddamn thing on fire."

"Yeah, let's not do that," Miss Woods giggled nervously. "But I like your attitude."

Casey left the office that morning feeling encouraged

despite being a jobless insomniac with no sister and little hope. As she crossed the lot, Miss Woods called to her from her office window on the second floor.

"Do you like kids?"

Casey turned around and found her at the window.

"Kids?" she hesitated. "As in children? Like, little people?"

Miss Woods gave her the dummy stare. "Do you like kids, yes or no?"

"No. I hate kids. They're awful. Why?"

Miss Woods dropped a card from her window down to Casey. It sailed left and right, evading her as she attempted to reach for it. She picked it up off the ground and turned it over. On the front was information for a local YMCA.

"You said you needed a job, right? There you go."

"Can't I just get the gas chamber instead?"

"I'm not asking, Haughton." Miss Woods straightened. "I know the guy who runs it, his name is Bruce. He runs a gym on the weekends for young kids to keep 'em off the streets. His assistant quit on him last week. Go down there and give him a hand until something better comes along. It's a volunteer gig, so don't expect to be paid. Work whatever schedule he gives you."

"But I'm not good with kids. I mean, look at me. I'm a big scaredy cat who still sleeps with the TV on because I'm afraid of the dark. I still use a bib when I eat because I'm messy, and sometimes I forget to flush. I'm not exactly the mentor type, Miss Woods."

"Then become one—just go. Anything else?"

"Yeah, is the firing squad still an option these days?"

Miss Woods closed her office window. She pointed up the road, ordering her to move on. Casey stuffed the card in her jeans and walked off. She hated kids.

Seventeen

Casey slogged down to the YMCA on Warner Street the next night with her eyebrows slanted in irritation. She couldn't fathom the thought of working at a rec center with kids… for free! She rounded the corner of her new gig, saw a group of kids, got anxious, and went in the opposite direction. *Nope.* She made it halfway down the block before remembering what had happened to Rob last week. Without any structure in her life, she feared she'd end up on drugs again, or worse.

Casey played it safe at first when she arrived to start her new job. She peeped from behind a parked car, watching as parents passed off their minions at the front door. A man with a jheri curl fade like Al B. Sure! high-fived kids at the entrance. Casey swallowed her pride and pushed down the sidewalk, dragging her feet to get there. She stopped at a lamppost several feet away, waiting for the man to acknowledge her.

"Picking up or dropping off?" he asked her.

Casey hung her shoulders and walked over.

"Dropping dead." She extended her hand. "You Bruce?

I'm Casey Haughton, Miss Woods's latest victim. She said you needed help for tonight?"

Bruce reached for her hand.

"Jacky said you'd be here. She always keeps her word," he said. "It's not as bad as you think, Casey. I promise, by the time you leave from here tonight, you'll want to come back. They're a good group, you'll see."

Casey gave him a bland look. "So, about that group… Do you have a like a trap door or someplace where I can take a smoke break?"

"They're good kids, Casey. I just need some help for a few hours while I handle some paperwork for a field trip later this summer."

Casey peeked through the window at the group of devil incarnates racing across the gym floor. There were basketballs going, jump ropes, arts and crafts, hopscotch, and juice drinks everywhere. She backed against the wall like a frightened skydiver.

"Jacky said you had a lively personality." He grinned. "I'll show you around and then—"

"Wait a minute, Bruce, *shit*." Casey peeked through the glass again. "How many kids are you expecting tonight?"

"Twenty-five. Thirty. Maybe thirty-five—this ain't nothin'. I'm hoping to get up to sixty before summer ends. Seventy-five, if I'm lucky."

"SEVENTY-FIVE?"

"Of course, Casey. You can never have enough kids off these streets."

"Right now, I wish I was lying *in* the street, Bruce. Hopefully a big Mack truck will drive over me." Casey shook her head. "C'mon, let's get this over with."

The YMCA Bruce ran was a converted warehouse space donated by the city, and Casey's first real-world job ever. After her brief introduction, she cowered on a metal folding chair in the corner, watching the kids play. Bruce stopped by to check on her an hour into her shift.

"Told you it wasn't all that bad," he said. "Shoot a few hoops, if you want. You don't have to sit here all night. Some of these kids got game though, Casey. Choose your battles carefully."

Casey gave him a dirty look. "I'm fine right here, Bruce, thanks."

A basketball suddenly rolled over to her chair. Casey stopped it with her foot and picked it up as a boy ran over to get it. "Yo, can I get that back?"

She gave the kid back the ball, glaring at him with distrust. She checked her watch and noticed it was 8:24 p.m. She was due to stay at least until midnight. Bruce bothered her again.

"Casey, over here!" He waved to her from across the gym. "I want you to meet somebody."

Casey rose from her seat, not hiding that she was annoyed. She noticed Bruce kneeling beside a cute little girl with bubble ponytail holders in her hair. She looked to be around eight or nine and was distraught with tears.

"She lost her favorite comb. Can you help us out?"

Bruce asked her. "It has her initials on it: V.A.B. Can you look around?"

"V.A.B.," Casey repeated. "Got it."

Casey searched high and low for that comb. She checked both the bleachers and even out in the parking lot. Nothing. She investigated the girl's lavatory with the same luck. On the way out, Casey passed by a garbage can and noticed a pink comb handle buried between the wreckage. She shook the can a couple times and noticed the comb had the little girl's initials on it. The comb was covered in rolled tissues and other unsanitary debris. "Sorry for your luck, kid." She turned off the light and left.

When Casey returned to the gym and noticed the little girl being consoled by her peers, her heart melted. She returned to the bathroom to recover the wasted comb. She stood in front of the can with her hands on her hips, plotting how to retrieve it. "You're killing me here, kid." Casey removed her belt and used it as a lassoing device. It took her fourteen tries until she finally got it. The girl's comb was covered in stringy hair. A half-eaten lollipop was wedged between its teeth. Casey transported the comb over to the sink for a thorough wash and placed it beneath the automatic air-drying machine. She fanned the damp comb, went back into the gym, and gave it to the girl. Her precious face lit up, and so did Casey's.

"Here you go, sweetie-pie." Casey patted her head. "Next time, you may wanna—"

The kid ran off before Casey could finish.

"Um, you're welcome!" Casey giggled. "Little sassy-ass—did you see that, Bruce?"

"Sure did," he laughed. "I wouldn't mind Vanessa. It's her last night here, anyway. She's been strange ever since her parents split up. Where was the comb?"

Casey put up her hand. "Don't ask."

To Casey's surprise, she survived that night. She passed the time by putting out other small fires involving the kids. When a boy's Doritos got stuck in the vending machine out in the hallway, she launched her hefty shoulder into the side of the box. *Boom.* Seven other bags of chips fell out along with a Twix candy bar. She pocketed the Twix for herself and entered the gym with her arms loaded with snacks. "First come, first serve!" The kids all rushed her at once.

Afterward, Casey saw a little boy without a snack and made a deal with him. "Tell you what, man," she told him. "I got this Twix, right. I'll give you one, and I'll keep the other. We'll have a race to see who finishes first." Casey handed the boy one of her chocolate bars. "On your mark. Get set. Go!" Casey let the kid beat her. She then took a wet paper towel and wiped his face for him. The kid turned his head as she tried to help him. "Boy, if you don't hold still—quit movin'!" she threatened him. Bruce didn't seem to mind at all.

At the end of her shift that night, Bruce called the kids over to say goodnight to Casey. They huddled around her as if she was a campfire.

"Okay, kids. Miss Haughton is leaving us for the night. What do you guys say?"

"*Thank you, Miss Haughton*," the kids all chimed at once.

Casey teared with gladness. "Aw shucks, you guys. Y'all are gonna make me cry. Thanks for lettin' me hang out. You all be good, okay?"

"*We will.*"

Bruce walked Casey out front and held the door for her. He followed her out into the night and closed the door behind him.

"So, do you have another night in you?" he asked.

Casey turned around, still beaming from earlier. "Me?" She laughed nervously. "You want me to come back?"

"Only if you want to, but I can't pay you right now. I'll see what I can do about that soon, though. What do you say?"

Casey stared at Bruce, shocked that someone had offered her a job.

"Uh, s-s-sure. Thank you, Bruce… thank you so much. I'll let Miss Woods know."

"She's Jacky to me, but yes, let 'Miss Woods' know that the kids all loved you." He winked at her. "See you tomorrow night. Same time."

Casey waited for Bruce to return inside and grinned from ear to ear before skipping down Warner Avenue into the heart of her city.

"Damn little goof balls, I swear," she giggled. "So cute."

Casey glided through her first weekend down at the YMCA with ease. By the end of her second week, she let the kids call her by her first name and had most of their names memorized along with their aspirations. Kennedy wanted to be the first Black female president. Aaron had dreams of playing in the NBA. Esmeralda wanted to become a singer, and David wanted to be a cop. "Word, I wanna shoot bad guys like this, *bang!*" He pointed his pretend gun at Casey. She gently lowered his weapon. "Not all bad people need to be shot, David, okay?" she giggled. "Be a good cop, don't be like some of these assholes that are out here." Casey hopped off the bleachers and moved on to a new group.

Bruce made things easy for Casey. He let her curse since most of the kids there were already using bad words, and he let her choose her own hours since she wasn't being paid. Casey offered a different proposal. "I'll work whatever hours you need, Bruce. Just feed me, that's all I ask." Bruce lived up to his word. Every night Casey showed up for work, Bruce had her meal. "I got the crunch wraps you wanted, Casey. Extra cheese with green peppers, and a large Dr. Pepper." Casey gave him two thumbs-up. "Much obliged. Thank you, sir."

The kids all got a kick out of Casey's ability to connect with them. They had her playing hopscotch, Double-Dutch, pick-up basketball, and a few girls even asked if Casey would do their hair for them. She also let the girls play in hers. They chortled at her crude but affectionate dialogue.

"Yo, what the hell are you little sausages doing?" she barked at them once. "Didn't I say don't touch that? Now, put it back before I put you down!"

For the older kids, she spoke a great deal about her time at St. Agnes, hoping to discourage them from the path she once took. They hung on her every word, encircling Casey near the bleachers. "See this scar here? That's from when I got my jaw broken. If you guys don't already know, I talk too much sometimes. Man, I couldn't talk for six whole weeks." Later during her shift, a fight nearly broke out when two boys got into a dispute over a basketball game. Casey climbed off the bleachers and took away the ball.

"Now, nobody's playin'. I don't even see what the big deal is, honestly. Lamar, you suck. Your three-pointer is some shit, and *you*—" Casey pointed at another kid. "—you can't even spell 'basketball', much less 'ball'. So, I'll just take this into Bruce and have him donate it. Peace out."

The boys set aside their differences and went after Casey. They chased her from one end of the gym to the other until she collapsed, goofy with exhaustion. She laid across the bleachers afterwards, out of breath. By the end of her first month at the YMCA, Bruce removed Casey's training wheels.

"I won't be here next Friday night, but I'll be in later to close," he told her. "Can you handle things while I'm out? I left some money for you in the drawer. Can you get pizza? There's a Pizza Hut not far from here."

The Friday after, Casey munched on Pizza Hut and downed Dr. Pepper soda with her feet crossed on top of Bruce's desk, watching TV. Occasionally, a kid would show up to bug her about a stuck ball inside the gym.

"Dude, that's *three* times tonight. Y'all are killin' me with this shit," Casey complained. "Do I have to get rid of all the balls? I'm trying to watch a movie here." She snatched Bruce's push broom from the janitor's closet and headed into the gym, fed up. Casey swore they were doing it on purpose.

"Okay, where is it?"

The kid pointed at the stuck ball between the rim and backboard. The kids all snorted and giggled, covering their mouths as Casey prodded at the jammed ball, mumbling to herself.

"Son of a BITCH, I don't believe this." She swung her big broom and missed. "Well, don't just stand there, gimmie a chair or something."

One of the boys brought Casey a metal chair for her to stand on. She punched at the basketball so hard, it sailed into the air. The kids struggled to contain themselves.

"What the hell is so funny?"

"You!" The kids all burst out in collective laughter as she stormed off.

The next night, Bruce introduced the kids to dodge ball. He showed up at the gym with a bag full of burgundy rubber balls. Wearing a sick grin, Casey paid them all back for the previous night. "Got your little ass!" *Thunk.* She bopped a boy across the back. "Yo, Lamar. Remember me? I got your basketball right here." *Thunk.* Unbeknownst to her, a kid had targeted Casey's wide behind. *Bap.* Casey grabbed her rear end and jumped. "Ow, you little… shit!" The whole gym laughed, including Bruce. She picked up her rubber ball and chased the culprit around the gym until he gassed out with laughter. He called a timeout, motioning with his hands. "Nope!" she told him. Casey whacked the boy senseless with her ball, busting him across his back and side. "Keep fuckin' with me, here?" The kid was hysterical.

By the end of May, Casey had completed her first full month down at the YMCA, and the kids all loved her. She loved them too, but she still wasn't making any money. One night after the kids had cleared the gym, Bruce asked her to stay behind. It came as a surprise since he'd normally let her cut out a few minutes early.

"I've got some bad news, Casey," he sighed. "I can't let you volunteer down here at the YMCA anymore—I'm sorry for this. I'll call Jacky and let her know."

Casey chuckled at her poor luck. "Great. I'm probably the first person to ever get fired from a volunteer gig. I don't believe this."

"I know. I wish I could keep you on as a volunteer, but the thing is—"

"Forget it, Bruce. Just... forget it, okay." Casey exhaled, disappointed. "Well, thanks for the opportunity, I guess. Can I at least visit every now and then?"

"You can visit whenever you want, Casey. In fact, I'd like it if you visited more often. How does $140 every week sound?"

Casey's jaw fell to the floor. "Excuse me?"

"So, I'll take that as a 'yes'?"

"Hell yeah, it's a yes!" Casey laughed. "I'm glad you said something because I was about to beat you down inside this office—firing me for no doggone reason. Thank you, Bruce."

She reached out to shake her boss's hand. He handed her a pocket schedule for June, tax forms, and a building key.

Outside, Casey stopped to breath in the air of triumph. For every failed shot at life she'd taken early on, her one little victory made it all worth it. She looked around, wondering to herself how proud Courtney would be to see her finally working—doing something with her life. Before her past could diminish the moment, Casey pushed up the sidewalk into the night.

Employed

Casey tucked her work shirt inside a pair of tan khaki shorts and double-checked herself in the mirror. She brushed her kinky golden hair and applied a touch of makeup before using a towel to wipe it off—she was enough. When she was young, she hid her albinism by wearing jeans or long sleeves and would use her allowance to buy darkening creams from the store. As an adult, she'd sheltered her broken spirit with cocaine, rage, and alcohol. She wiped the last smudge of her phony mask from her corner lip, turned off the light and left.

Before work, Casey rode the city bus down to the Department of Motor Vehicles and applied for an ID card to cash her paychecks. She made a second pitstop around the corner and waited in line to receive a study guide for her learner's permit. The clerk handed Casey their latest manual, dated June 1990. "Good luck, ma'am," the clerk told Casey. She dropped her book in her bag and returned to the bus stop in time for work.

Casey worked five days a week down at the YMCA, and

Bruce paid her extra on the weekends. Her first paycheck was for $424.29. She ran into the first check-cashing spot she saw and went nuts when the guy there charged her fourteen percent. A woman waiting in line offered her some advice. "You ever heard of a bank? Try there," the lady suggested. "It's free, and you can have your money deposited straight to your account without any extra fees."

So, Casey did just that. She strolled into a NationsBank and opened her first savings account. When the teller asked what she did for a living, Casey replied delightedly, "I'm a mentor and summer aide down at the YMCA on Warner." The teller handed her a deposit slip. "Well, congratulations on the new job. Come see us again."

Casey's first big assignment was to help chaperone a bus full of youths on a trip to Times Square. Bruce handed her a clipboard with fourteen inquisitive thinkers on ship. She studied the list, hoping to memorize each student's name. The lead chaperone was an older guy named Artis. He was knowledgeable but dry and no fun whatsoever. So, the kids looked for Casey to entertain them. She'd give the kids a dirty look or say something crude to get them going. "Whatever dude, I saw your game last week. You can't hoop worth a damn." The whole bus laughed, including the victim. Throughout the trip, the kids talked smack to Casey and she'd talk smack back. She was also keen about steering the group away from her past mistakes.

"Yo, Casey? You got any brothers or sisters?" one girl asked her. "Are they like you?"

Casey looked at the young girl. It was one of the few times she straightened up around them.

"Yes, Emely, I do. A sister. But we haven't spoken in a while."

"What's her name?"

"Her name's Courtney. Like I said, I haven't spoken to her."

"How come?" another boy asked. "Y'all beefin'? Who started it?"

"Nobody started anything, Jamal, okay?" Casey laughed. "Sometimes, it's just like that, I don't know. Well, we used to be close but… never mind, just forget it."

"How come you wanna forget it? Don't you love your sister?"

The more pressure the kids applied, the more Casey backpedaled until she finally hit a wall. She shrunk in defeat, unable to avoid their straight questions.

"Of course I love my sister, guys. But I'm not sure how she feels about me at this point. I uh… I wasn't such a good sister to her, even though she was to me. I fucked up. I got into trouble when I was sixteen and got sent away. I came home last year and went back." She shook her head. "I was in a real bad spot last year, y'all. I was on drugs, drinking a lot, angry all the time. It was bad, man." Casey stopped to catch her breath. "Look, nothin' makes my day more than to see y'all laughing at my crazy ass. Just do me a favor, stay in school. Stay away from stupid people. Stupid people make you do stupid things, and if you got good family, love on them… the way I should've loved on Courtney when I had the chance. I'll leave it at that… excuse me."

Casey got up from her seat and moved toward the back. The trip down to Times Square was quiet the rest of the way.

When Casey wasn't at work, she missed her little sausages. She'd slug inside her room at Fellowship House sleeping, watching TV, or studying her driver's education booklet. Even if she did pass the exam, she didn't have a car to practice in or someone to help her. Bored, she started showing up at the YMCA on her off days just to get out of her room. Bruce was working on a first aid report one evening and did a double take as she walked in. He stopped her in the hallway.

"I thought I gave you the night off?"

"You did," Casey said. "I was just in the neighborhood and thought I'd stop by in case you guys needed anything. Y'all good?"

Bruce lifted his brow at her. "We're good… How about you? You doing alright?"

"Oh yeah, like I said, I just thought I'd drop in and you know, see what's happening on this end. I'm fine. Everything's good, Bruce, really."

Casey walked into the gym, ending the discussion. She walked by Bruce's office a second and third time during her next off days. The fourth time it happened, Bruce called Casey into his office and closed the door.

"I can't afford to pay you any more than your normal time, Casey," he said. "I appreciate you wanting to help, but we've got plenty of staff on hand."

"I'm not asking for any compensation, I just wanna hang out."

"But you don't have to."

"But I *want* to," she corrected him. "I've been in a steel cage for over a third of my life, Bruce, forgive me if I want to make up for that." She sidestepped the boss and entered the gymnasium.

On June 15th, Casey celebrated her twenty-fifth birthday down at the YMCA with the kids; she was scheduled off that day. She didn't tell them it was her birthday because she didn't want a show. Watching the children play reminded her of Courtney—she'd celebrated her birthday three days before. When Bruce walked into the gym and saw Casey braiding hair, he shook his head and went into his office. She shook her head at him, too.

Casey stayed late that night to help Bruce clean up. She beat him to the punch, clearing out the gym full of balls, jump ropes, and other athletic equipment. "I got it, Bruce. Don't worry. You sit down, relax." When their night ended, Bruce pulled her aside.

"I heard about Times Square a couple weeks ago. One of the kids told me all about it. Is it true you don't remember the last time you spoke to your sister?"

"Is that a crime?" Casey became defensive. "No, it's not true. I do remember."

Bruce moved to the edge of his desk and folded his arms.

"Is that why you've been coming in here so often lately on your days off? Look, Casey, I know what you're going through.

There's help here if you need it. You don't have to do this all by yourself. You need to rest and have your days off."

"But what if I just want to spend my days off in here? Shit, it's not like I got any family or anybody else." Casey pinched between her eyes and sighed. "You know what, I'm sorry. I don't know why I'm even trying to fight you over this."

"It's okay, Casey, if you wanna come—come. I can't stop you from visiting. I just want you to know that I'm here if you ever need to talk."

"Duly noted. Thanks." She threw on her hoodie and left.

Casey laid on her bed later that night, puffing on a cigarette. She had everything going for her now: a job, a booklet to study for her learner's permit, a savings account, and a warm bed to sleep in. But still missing from her world was Courtney. Guilt filled inside her eyes as she slung her head. The more she thought about the past year and her life before that, the worse she felt. On her nightstand was a card that a couple kids down at the YMCA pitched in to get for her. *You are great person and fun to be around!* the message read. Casey burned the card with her cigarette until a hole appeared. *I'm none of these things*, she told herself. She dropped her charred card into the bin and turned off her room light.

Eighteen

Casey continued to feel like an imposter all throughout June and into early July. The only time she was happy was when she was working. One night, a local news station threatened a severe storm so Bruce closed the gym early and sent the kids home. "What are you looking all sad for? You're still gettin' paid for a full day," he told her. Casey didn't care about the money. She didn't want go back to her crawl space at Fellowship House where insomnia from past traumas awaited her. When Bruce offered her a ride home, Casey lied and told him she had a cab coming. "Yes, Bruce, I'm sure. Thanks for the offer, though." She waited for him to leave, zipped up her coat, and braved the storm.

It poured for two nights in a row over New York after Friday's first big splash. Few kids showed up to the gym on Saturday and Sunday which gave Casey time to teach a kid named Camilia how to braid hair. "Okay, now you try. Remember, start with three strands." Casey sat in the metal folding chair, allowing the eleven-year-old girl to practice on her head.

While beauty school was in play, Casey was also detangling a kid's shoestring. The boy's name was Joshua, and he was albino like her. "How'd you get this many knots in one shoestring?" she teased him. "Are you a crazy person? Take off your shoe." The boy removed his shoe and handed it to her. Casey snatched it from his hand and playfully trimmed her eyes at him. He broke into a cute smile. "Beat it, you. Come back later." The boy ran off, hobbling around the gym. The few kids that showed up that night taped to Casey as if she was a celebrity. Nothing was off limits.

"Yo, Casey, what was prison like? Was it bad?" one kid asked her.

Casey kept her head tilted as Camilia played in her hair.

"Hell yeah, it was bad. That's why you don't need to go. That's why nobody needs to go—*easy* there Camilia, I'm tender-headed."

Casey entertained her small party with some details about the prison world. She ad-libbed the food part of her story, hoping to get a rise out of them.

"Sometimes there's no food, and you have to go out into the field and dig for bugs."

"*Ewww.*" The kids all grimaced in unison.

"Yeah, I know. One time I caught this big-ass beetle, and I bit off its head. Little joker was still crawling around in my stomach. It gave me bad gas. So, they had to put me to sleep and cut open my stomach to get it out. Wanna see the scar?" The kids all gathered to check out Casey's scar. She grabbed the closest kid to her and gave him a noogie. "Gotcha, you little shit!" she giggled. "Y'all crazy? Do I look like the type that would eat bugs? Just don't go to prison, okay? That's all you need to know." The kids all groaned in united disproval. Not long after her beetle story, another aide showed up in the gym to inform Casey she had a visitor waiting for her in Bruce's office.

"Visitor? For me?"

With her hair half-braided, she headed to the main office. She looked through the glass and saw Miss Woods and Bruce together. She hurried inside.

"Miss Woods? What brings you out this way?"

"One of my responsibilities as a PO is checking up on my parolees, like this old knucklehead here." She nodded at Bruce. "How long's it been now, Bruce?"

"Ten, fifteen years?" he said. "I went to juvy when I was a youngin', but old Jacky got me straight. Isn't that right?"

"Somewhat. But back then, it wasn't Jacky was it?"

"Lord, no!"

The two laughed together as Casey looked on. She aspired to reach the same level of respect with Miss Woods someday. After their laughs, he got up from his seat.

"Well, I guess I'll let you ladies talk. Good seeing you again, Jacky." He closed the door behind him. Casey turned to face her PO.

"Is everything alright?" she panicked.

"I don't know. Is it? You tell me because I already heard Bruce's side of the story."

Casey looked through the glass at her boss, confused.

"I-I didn't know Bruce had a story," she stuttered. "Did something happen?"

"Yes, something did happen. He called to tell me how much of a dedicated aide you've been down here at the YMCA. Figured I'd stop by and see for myself."

Casey sighed with relief. "Well, he ain't lying."

"Hope not." Miss Woods went inside of her bag and extended a white envelope. "I've had this for a while, but I think it's time to finally let it go."

Casey reached out to take the envelope.

"What's in here? Birthday money?" she chuckled. She noticed Miss Woods wasn't laughing. Casey opened the envelope and noticed a slip inside with an address. She read it aloud:

"132 Holmes Place, Apartment 319, Queens, New York. Hmmm. What's this? You're not sending me to another halfway house, are you? C'mon, Miss Woods. It's a ten-minute walk from here to Fellowship House. Don't transfer me—I'll never get to work on time."

"It's not a halfway house, Casey." She hesitated. "It's Courtney's address."

Casey stared at her.

"Listen, um… I know all about sisterly bonds and how delicate those can be. I have a sister in Philly. We don't talk much either, and it's mainly my fault. At least you've been willing to bend, I wasn't when I was your age. I think if you apply the same determination that you've shown me and the YMCA, perhaps you can rebuild what you once lost. Sometimes people deserve a second chance, wouldn't you say?"

Casey's eyes glittered. "Or a third, fourth, or fifth... as much as I've screwed up." She laughed. "Thank you, Miss Woods. But what if Courtney wants nothing to do with me? What if she hates my guts?"

"She probably does. But it's never too late to ask for forgiveness, Casey. If not, at least you can finally move on with your life... the way I did." She started toward the door and stopped. "If Courtney asks, don't tell her where you got that. Good luck, Casey."

Queens

Casey stood at the corner of Holmes Place and Nasir Street where Courtney now resided, acknowledging her high-rise building. A cop foot-patrolled the courtyard, moving along an assembly of amateur musicians congregating near the entrance. Unlike Gardener Heights, the construction appeared fresher and its maintenance was tidy and recent. She surveyed the colossal structure and assessed that Courtney had been doing much better since the girls had split up. Casey approached the building and looked for a call button with her sister's name. Her heart skittered when she saw *Haughton C.K.* at the bottom. Only Casey and the people who printed Courtney's birth certificate knew that her middle name was Kimberly. She buzzed upstairs and waited for a response. Seconds later, Courtney sweetly chimed into the speaker. "Yesss?" Her sugary voice made Casey even more doubtful about showing her face there. She was sunshine; Casey was shit.

"*Yesss?*" Courtney sang again, kind but impatient. "Luke, I am your father!" she breathed into the mic like Darth Vader, giggling. "Suit yourself. Peace."

Casey stared at the box, afraid to answer. She could hear it in Courtney's voice, she was doing well without her. She placed her finger up to the call button and pulled it back. The last thing Courtney needed was her life being wrecked again by her. Casey kissed her finger and touched her sister's nameplate as if it was a tombstone.

"You're in a better place now. You don't need me screwing up your life anymore. Take care of yourself, love. See you on the streets."

As Casey turned to leave, Courtney returned to the box.

"Casey," she said plainly, her voice flat and lacking sweetness. Casey returned to the wall and pressed the button.

"Courtney? How'd you know it was me?"

There was a long pause on the other side.

"Hello?"

The mic clicked on. "C'mon up." Casey took a deep breath and entered the building.

Everything about Courtney's new building signaled that she was better off than she had been with Casey around. The inside was clean and smelled like fresh paint and a security guard roamed throughout the building alert and vigilant, unlike in Gardener Heights.

The closer Casey made it to Courtney's apartment, the more her stomach simmered with nervousness. Her mind raced as she made her way down the hall. *Will she ever forgive me?* Casey wondered. She hesitated at the door of Courtney's apartment before finally knocking. The bolt suddenly detached as Courtney answered. She was lean and pretty as ever. She peered into Casey's soul, impeding the doorway, not saying a word.

"Hey, Court." Casey broke the ice first. She lowered her eyes and raised them to see Courtney still glaring at her. "I know you're probably wondering what in the world am I doing here, and I'll get to that, if you'll let me. Can I come in?"

Courtney moved to the side, not taking her eyes off her. She closed the door behind them and followed Casey into the living room with her arms hiked onto her toned hips.

"How did you find me?" she asked.

"I uh… I followed my heart and it led me here." Casey looked around at Courtney's place at the familiar furniture pieces and other aesthetics of Gardener Heights. She noticed right away there were no pictures of her. "Nice place you got here. Can't say I'm surprised, though. You've always done well for yourself."

Courtney somewhat lowered her guard, leaning against the wall.

"Would you like something to drink?"

"No, thank you."

A weird pause occupied the room as the sisters traded obstinate looks, forcing Casey to cut into the awkward air between them again.

"Oh yeah, I got my diploma. Plus, I'm working as a summer aide now—with kids! Can you believe that? Me and kids? I never thought I'd see the day."

"Hmph… where at?"

"The YMCA on Warner. I'm studying for my learner's

permit, too. Hoping that'll open up some more doors for me eventually."

"Yeah, hopefully."

Courtney returned inside her shell, unphased by any of Casey's recent accomplishments. Casey cut to the chase and got to the real meat of why she was there.

"Courtney, listen, I uh… Look, nothing can fix last year or any time before that. I'm smart enough to understand that, and I'm not here trying to—"

"Then why are you here, Casey?" Courtney cut in. "You still haven't even told me how you got my address, or what it is you're doing here. Enough with the small talk already, I'm busy. What's up? What do you need?"

Casey carefully walked over to her.

"I just want us be sisters again."

Courtney sprung from the wall and into the kitchen. She distracted herself by tidying up, leaving Casey near the foyer. With her back facing her, she ripped into a dirty pan.

"*Be my sister again*—wow, Casey." Courtney chuckled. "I've always been your sister, that'll never change. But I learned recently that sometimes even your own family you've got to love from afar, you know." Courtney tossed her pan into the rack, busting a glass in the process. She ripped her dish towel from the stove lid and swiped the shattered glass into the bin.

"Can I help you with—"

"No, you cannot help me with anything, Casey. Just… wait a minute."

Casey waited five minutes for Courtney to clean up the

broken glass. She tried to keep the momentum alive by making frivolous talk, hoping to convince Courtney she was living a clean life.

"Yeah, so the kids down at the YMCA—I wasn't sure about it at first. But they're a good group, you know. Respectful, kind, fun to be around. I thought all kids were just little rug rats until I met them. I helped chaperone a few on a trip into Times Square. Pretty cool, I'd say."

Courtney ignored her. She rinsed her hands and returned out front.

"Well look, I appreciate you dropping by, but as you can see, I'm kind of busy right now."

The formal shift rocked Casey to her core.

"I understand, Court. I get it."

"Do you? Really?" Courtney asked her. "Because I don't think you do, Casey. Come to think of it, I don't think you *ever* got it."

"I can't change what happened last year, the year before that, or any other time, Courtney, but I know who I am now, and I know how much I messed up. I swear to you, I'm on a totally different page now. I'm nothin' like who I used to be."

Courtney clapped her hands. "Congratulations on being an adult. What, you thought you could just show up today with your diploma and a job, thinking I'd fall all over you?"

"I never said that, Courtney."

"Then what are you saying? Why are you here?!" Courtney yelled at her. Her lips shook as she talked. "Dammit, Casey, you broke my heart. Ever since—" She stopped to catch her breath. "You've been stabbing me in my back since the day you showed up in my life! Why, Casey?"

Casey crumbled right there.

"Well, I'm sorry about that, Courtney, really, I am." She stopped to wipe her eyes. "Someone was stabbing me in my back, too. Shit, everybody was stabbing me in my back. My biological parents. The schools I went to. Every city I ever lived in—every house! Every house except the ones where you were there. I didn't know what I had until I met you and your family, but by then it was too late—I was too far gone. You're the only light I ever had, Courtney. Every place else has been dark for me."

Courtney stood there, unimpressed. Casey's monologue sailed through her.

"You shouldn't have come here. I think you need to go. You may have changed, but so have I. I'm sorry, Casey, but I can't do *this* anymore." Courtney gestured. "I just… I can't."

Casey's spirit cracked with rejection. She honored her sister's request with a gentle nod and headed out. Courtney opened the door and invited her into the hallway.

"Please don't come by anymore, Casey."

Casey exhaled sharply. The moment was heavy with hurt as she accepted her fate. She kissed Courtney on her wet cheek, passed through the doorway, and turned around.

"Since you've been seeing me at my worst for most of my life, I just thought that I'd show you me at my best." Casey sunk. "Take care, Court."

Casey left without looking back.

Finding Casey

Casey called out sick from work for two days after her fallout with Courtney. She slept since being awake was too depressing. The only time she was on her feet was for a smoke or to relieve herself. She even contemplated returning to Gardener Heights to see Rob for a hit of cocaine before remembering the stench from her last visit. She knelt by the window with her chin on the ledge, replaying her sister's last words inside her head. *Please don't come by anymore.* It hit just a little bit harder each time she recalled it.

On her third day, Bruce sent two aides from the YMCA to check on Casey. When she noticed her co-workers walking up the block, she rushed down to the front desk. "I'm not here, if anybody asks," she told him. She ran back to her room and closed the door. Less than five minutes later, she watched as her colleagues went down the block. She lowered her blinds and returned to her bed. An hour into her angry nap, Casey awoke to two voices yelling outside her door. She recognized one of the voices.

"Ma'am, I can't do that unless there's foul play suspected

or a special circumstance. That's illegal. I could lose my job. She still has some privacy rights, even as an ex-felon."

"Rights? I don't give a shit about her *rights*—I'm her parole officer. Open this door!"

Keys jingled as the building manager unbolted the door for Miss Woods. She entered Casey's room and closed the door behind her. Without word or warning, she marched over to Casey's bed and ripped off her blanket.

"Get up, right now—before I help you up."

Casey slowly sat up, taking her time. When Miss Woods grabbed her arm to assist her, Casey pulled away like a stubborn teenager. Miss Woods grabbed her again.

"What is wrong with you, girl?" She talked through her teeth. "Why you do you insist on doing everything the hard way all the time?"

Casey gave her a depleted stare.

Miss Woods lowered her voice. "What happened? What did Courtney say?"

Casey shrugged. "It doesn't even matter anymore, Miss Woods. Can't believe I was so stupid to believe she'd wanna see me again after everything I put her through."

As Miss Woods sat next to her on the bed, Casey stared down at her feet.

"It looks like Courtney made her choice. You've got to move on."

"But I don't *wanna* move on!"

"So, what are you gonna do next? Curl up and die?" Miss Woods raised her voice again. "It wasn't your choice, Casey, it was hers. Now, I talked to Bruce earlier and he wants you back at the YMCA tonight. Get up and get down to that gym, or else I'm gonna to take you out of here in a pair of cuffs—pick one."

Casey rose to her feet. She dawdled over to her dresser and looked for something to wear, barely interested. Miss Woods walked over and pushed her drawer closed.

"What about those babies, Casey? Huh?" she reminded her. "Those are your babies down there. Not mine, Bruce's, or anybody else's—yours. Those kids need you."

Miss Woods reached inside her purse and placed an envelope in front of her.

Casey's damp face brightened. "What's that?"

"You tell me," she said. "Go'on, take it."

Casey reached for the letter. Her name was spelled as "Miss Kaci Howtan" on the front of the envelope. Inside was a letter. Her eyes blurred as she began to read:

Dear Kaci, we ~~mess~~ miss you. Get better so we can play ~~dudge~~ dodge ball again. Little Sausages

Casey placed the letter to her chest and wailed, jerking with gratitude.

"You keep saying you don't have a family, but you've got a family right there at that YMCA. You follow what I'm saying?"

"Yes, ma'am," Casey moaned, wiping her eyes.

"Good. Because we can't always choose who our family members are, but we can choose the kind of family we want. Your whole life you've been looking for a family to plug into. Maybe it's time you create your own family."

Miss Woods placed the empty envelope onto her dresser and started toward the door.

"Don't you quit on me, Casey… not yet." She pulled the door shut behind her.

Casey wiped her round face and reread her letter. She hadn't noticed it at first, but at the bottom was a picture of a wide stick figure with gold hair, surrounded by kids. She taped the letter onto her wall above the bed. She stopped to glow at the warm illustration. "My little sausages," she sighed, shaking her head. She fetched a towel from her nightstand and headed for the shower.

The closer Casey made it to the YMCA, the more relieved she felt about her fallout with a lot of things. She was tired of life happening to her and of becoming a victim of her circumstances. She was through with waiting around for change and decided to become the change. Miss Woods was right—everybody had a choice. She reported to work on time in her crispy khakis and polo shirt. She entered the facility and went straight to Bruce's office. He got up from behind his desk and extended his hand. When Casey reached for it, he grabbed hers with both of his.

"Bruce, I'm really sorry about—"

He waved her off. "Nope. I don't want to hear it," he stopped her. "As much as you do for the YMCA, Casey? Please. You were on sick leave. I put it down on your timecard."

"But I don't have enough leave accrued, I just started here a couple months ago."

"You-were-on-sick-leave," he reiterated. "Besides, you needed the rest anyway. All those days you've been coming in off the clock? Don't worry about it… are you alright?"

"Yeah, I'm good." Casey shrugged. "You know, hangin' in there. Thanks, Bruce."

She walked over to his office window and peeked through the blinds. As was typical on summer nights, there were basketballs going, jump-roping, arts and crafts, dodge ball, and crocheting all at once. Bruce joined her at the window.

"Did you get the letter?" he asked her.

"Dude," she laughed. "Gosh, I'm getting choked up just thinkin' about it."

"Well, don't choke just yet," he said. "Wait here."

Bruce opened the side door to his office and blew into a sports whistle around his neck. The kids showed up within seconds and formed a tight circle around him. Goosebumps covered Casey's skin as she anticipated her grand return to the gym.

"Okay, you kids!" Bruce yelled. "I got a surprise for you."

"Is it pizza?" one boy shouted.

"Even better. Y'all ready? C'mon out, Casey!"

Casey pushed through the double doors and into the gymnasium. When the kids all noticed it was her, they stampeded in her direction, knocking Bruce down. Casey ran around the gym, forcing her pupils to chase her. "She's running; get her!" Casey sprinted around the gym, dodging her little sausage people. She picked one boy up and spun him like the blades of a helicopter before setting him down and finally giving herself up. They surrounded her on the bleach-ers, not letting her out of their sight.

"Where've you been at, Miss Casey? Dang, it's been like three weeks."

"Three weeks? Try three days… did it really feel that long?"

"*Yes,*" the kids synced collectively.

"Well, I'm sorry guys, but I had to rest. I was sick."

"Sick with what, Miss Casey?" another kid asked her. "Sick of us?"

Casey grabbed the boy and placed him in a headlock.

"Are you kidding me? Of course not. I could never get sick of you guys." She let him go. "Y'all are my family. Didn't you know that?"

"*We are?*"

Casey surveyed their young faces and spoke life.

"Well, yeah… We're like one big happy family in here, you know. I learned something today, and I want to share it with you guys. See, we can't always choose who are family members are, but we can choose the kind of family we want." She surveyed their enlightened faces. "Make sense?"

The kids all looked at each other, lost. Casey could tell it went over their heads.

"Never mind," she laughed. "I know it doesn't make sense now, but someday it will. Just put that in the back of your mind for about another ten years, you'll see." Casey looked over at Bruce and winked. "Okay, you little sausages, I'm back. Now, go away before I get the dodge ball out!"

The kids scurried from the bleachers and returned to their devices as Casey watched them. Seconds later, Bruce pulled up beside her.

"But we can choose the kind of family we want, huh?" he repeated. "That was deep—I'm stealing that one. It's great to have you back, Casey." Bruce returned to his desk.

"Shouldn't have left in the first place," Casey muttered. She went back to watching a game of pickup basketball.

Nineteen

Casey anxiously waited to receive her score on her learner's exam with New York's Department of Motor Vehicles. She watched as the woman behind the desk removed the top of her red-ink pen. According to her name tag, the woman's name was Mary. She wore peach-rimmed glasses and had silver hair. "Alrighty, Miss Haughton. Let's see how you did." She peeled back the top page and began. There were twenty questions total, and Casey needed at least an eighty-five percent or better to pass.

Mary tapped her pen against the desk as she reviewed Casey's exam. She made it through the first page without a single markup. At the bottom of the second page, Mary marked a big red "X" next to questions nine and ten. Casey computed the math in her head and grasped she could come away with a ninety percent. Mary cleared the third page without any markings and glanced at Casey as she made it to the final page. Halfway through question seventeen, she went back to page two and looked over nine and ten again. She cancelled her red X's and initialed them both before returning to page four. Mary then flipped through Casey's test and placed a big one hundred percent at the top, circled it, and signed her name at the bottom. "Congratulations, Miss Haughton. Perfect score." She smiled. Mary handed Casey a card with a number printed on it. "Head down to licensing on the other side, so they can take your picture."

Casey took her card and grinned. "Thank you, Mary."

In the licensing line, there were four novice drivers ahead of her, all teenagers. They cheesed after receiving their permits, showing them to family members or friends. When it was Casey's turn to take the picture, she tried to hold back but exploded into a goofy smile as the flash went off—she couldn't help but gush. She looked at her card afterwards and noticed her Disneyland smile and that her eyes were closed.

"Would you like to retake it?" the cameraman asked her.

Casey looked down at her happy, chubby face and declined. "Nope, I'm good. Thanks." She tucked her learner's permit inside her wallet (behind her bank and health insurance cards) and headed out to the bus stop. It arrived less than a minute later. She paid her fare, hopped on, and sat at the front of the bus before checking her watch. It was 9:09 a.m. She was due for her weekly check-in with Miss Woods in less than an hour.

With more than fifteen minutes to spare, Casey entered Miss Woods's suite and arrived at the receptionist desk. "I'm here for my ten o' clock with Jacqueline Woods," Casey told the lady. The receptionist got up from her seat and went to the back briefly before returning with an empty cup and a form for Casey to fill out. "Jacky says you're early, but here. When you're done, head back."

Casey filled out the same dull questionnaire she did every week. "Have you had any contact with law enforcement since your last visit? If yes, please explain." *No.* "Have you used or had any exposure to any illegal narcotics since your last visit?" *No.* Casey answered the other twelve invasive inquiries and returned her clipboard. She picked up her small cup, went into the bathroom to pee and returned with her container sealed and dated and headed back to Miss Woods's office. She showed off her learner's permit once she got there.

"They said it was the highest score they had all week." Casey grinned. "Crazy, huh?"

Miss Woods looked over the laminated card and gave it back to her.

"Keep up the good work," she said. "By the way, thanks for arriving early. So, how are things? Have you heard from Courtney?"

"Not since we last spoke. I'm maintaining—still hurts, though. But my new family down at the Y? They got my back. I'm refereeing this dodgeball tournament next Friday, right before the kids head back to school. Bruce and I are thinking about putting together a tutoring program for kids throughout the school year. I'm a dropout, but I'm decent at math and world history. English sucks. Makes me wanna throw up, yuck!"

Miss Woods nodded her head.

"Well, that's certainly noble of you to want to give back. Let me know how I can help… Oh yeah, before I forget, congratulations on your sobriety, Casey. You told me last week, and I forgot. That's what happens when you get old," Miss Woods chuckled. "How long has it been now?"

"About eight months or so. It feels good to be clean—and on the right side of the law, for once," Casey giggled. She glanced at the frame on her PO's desk. "Hey, Miss Woods? Can I… ask you something personal, if you don't mind?"

"Shoot."

"You said you had a sister but that you two don't talk? How come?"

Miss Woods leaned back in her chair and exhaled.

"That's a looong story for another day, Casey," she sighed. "But the short of it is that we never got along, ever. After getting to know me throughout this process, I'm sure you can understand why that is."

"Did y'all have a fight or something?"

"No, we just never got along. I'll leave it there. We call during the holidays, or if the kids have stuff going on—I always try to make it to those. She lives with her family in North Philly. I've been trying to get her to move from that place for years—place is like a war zone. Anyway, like I told you before, I know all about family dynamics and how complicated that can be. I thought I saw an opportunity for you to reunite with Courtney, so I wanted to give you that option—once I knew you were worthy of it. Unfortunately, like in my case, it didn't work out. But we still gotta move on."

"Do you think it'll ever work out between you and your sister again?"

"No, but I can live with that now. Before, I couldn't."

"Really?" Casey asked. "I don't think I'll ever get over it."

"You won't. You'll just get older and grayer and time will push it further into the dirt. That's usually what happens. Pain never goes away. It just gets buried beneath the surface." Miss Woods rose from her chair. "Well, I got another parolee to see in a few. See you next week. Tell Bruce I said hello."

At the bus stop, Casey studied her facial features on her learner's permit. Eight months ago, she remembered her face looking skeletal and patchy from cocaine use. She'd since turned her life around and was working towards helping young kids do the same. Somewhere in the bottom of her heart, she still had a sister in this wide world, but was now striving to build a new family. Moments later, the city bus arrived. She climbed on and noticed it was empty.

"Where you headed, young lady?" the driver asked her.

"YMCA on Warner." She waddled toward the back as the bus pulled off and splashed into a chair. The driver eyed her in the mirror.

"Long day?"

Casey kicked her feet into the chair next to her. "Just gettin' started."

By August of 1990, Casey's had amassed $802.47 in her savings account. Down at the Y, she was promoted to the rank of Third Supervisor. The change bumped her pay up an extra $1.65 every hour. On her nightstand was a pamphlet for community college. It was on her agenda for the next year, provided she could still afford it after her lease was approved. With a bonnet covering her hair and a Kool burning in the ashtray on her window sill, she painted her toes a pretty emerald color in front of *Young and the Restless* on the TV inside her room. With school to start the next week, it was the night of the dodgeball tournament down at the YMCA. Casey was due in early because of the number of kids expected to show. She placed her wet toes in front of her fan, reached for her cigarette, and went back to shouting at the TV. "Oh, my goodness—and you're gonna go back to that prick? After all the shit he just put you through? Women, I swear to God!" She sucked on her cigarette and returned it to her ashtray. Outside, the hallway phone began to ring as the tenant across from her went to get it. He knocked on her door.

"Telephone, Casey."

She swung her feet from her bed and walked on the side of her heels to answer it. Before she could take the call, her neighbor pushed up on her about a job.

"So, who's that? Is that Bruce? The guy from the YMCA? You think you can talk him into hookin' me up with a job?"

Casey covered the phone.

"If you don't get the hell off of my back—asking me about a job," she whispered. "Please, you got a rap sheet taller than the Empire State Building. Bruce wouldn't hire you. Even if he would, I'd tell him not to."

The man sagged. "That's real cold, Casey, real cold."

Casey gave him the Heisman pose as he walked away. "Hey, Bruce. What's up?"

"You're still coming in tonight, right?"

"Of course, I am. It's the last Friday before school starts, and the big dodgeball tournament. You know I ain't missing that."

"Well, I got some bad news—just wanted to give you a heads up before you got here. You're not refereeing tonight. I'm gonna sit you down for this one. I got another employee I wanna try out. I need to see if they're worth their salt."

"You don't need me to sit out just so some rookie can prove their salt, Bruce," Casey told him. "Besides, I'm dodgeball champion. You can't do that. It's in the rule book."

"C'mon, Casey—"

"C'mon my foot, Bruce," she protested. "Alright, fine. I'll step aside *this* time. But tonight, I get to choose where we get the pizza from, and I ain't locking up the gym—and I'm not sweeping, either. I swept three nights in a row already and my back's still stiff."

"Any other demands?" Bruce laughed.

"I'm sure I can come up with something," she chuckled. "So, who stuck me for the refereeing gig? Is it Artis? Yo, it *better* not be Artis, Bruce! Dude is older than Jesus. Dude is so old that his social security number is one. He can't keep up with those kids like I can."

On and on Casey went, ribbing on her colleagues down at the YMCA. After her call ended, she returned to her room to finish painting her nails. Before leaving that night, she wore her referee shirt beneath her clothes, just in case. "Th'hell with Bruce, I'm still the ref."

Casey entered the YMCA that night and continued with her usual business, but her replacement referee was a no-show. She met with Bruce to receive her assignment for the night, helped set up the gym and visited with both teams to offer some last-minute tips. The kids all seemed shocked Bruce pulled her from calling the match.

"But why would Mr. Bruce do that?" a kid asked her.

Casey's answer was simple. "Because he's the boss, guys, that's why. Look, some day when you get old enough to hold a job, you'll understand. Just do your best, whether it's me or the Jackson 5 out there, okay? We straight, y'all?" She fist-bumped each of the players and returned to Bruce's office.

"Okay, I wished everybody well." Casey crossed her arms. "Now where's this stupid referee? They should've been here by now. See, I told you. You've should've let me ref the game, man. The show would've been on the road by now." She showed him her ref shirt. "Look, I'm ready to go. It's the kids' last night before school, and we got 'em sittin' around with their thumbs up their butts waiting on this special 'ref'," she air-quoted. "What up with that?"

Bruce changed the script. "Change of plans. I'll referee tonight, but I need you to fill in for one of the teams."

"Fill in? Bruce! I'm still sore from the other night. There's like a whole section of skin still missing from my ass. I thought you said I wouldn't have to compete?"

"I know, but I need two adults for this one to add a little excitement to the tournament. The other aide is on the way, I'm gonna stick them on the opposing team. Take it out on them. They'll be a little late, but we can still get started."

Casey picked up one of the dodgeballs and spun it on her finger.

"Good. 'Cause I'm gonna smoke 'em," she said. "Then I'm comin' for you!"

The two teams assembled in the gym on opposing sides with Bruce now as the referee. Casey knotted her shoestrings and tied her hair into a ponytail. She squatted and stretched, preparing for heavy combat. She walked into the middle of the gym, threatening the other side. "I want *you*, chump!" She pointed at one boy.

The kid gave it back. "Yeah, whatever, Miss Casey. You don't want none of this."

Bruce surveyed both sides before lifting his whistle. "On your mark… get set… go!"

The kids each dropped their weapons and faced the main door. Dodgeballs vibrated the gym floor all at once—all but Casey's. Confused, she turned to Bruce.

"What the hell's going on, Bruce? What are you trying to—"

Suddenly, Miss Woods entered the gymnasium with Courtney standing beside her. Casey covered her face with both hands. Her dodgeball fell to the floor.

"Oh, my God!" she shrieked. "You guys didn't. You didn't!"

Casey sprinted to other side of the gym and squeezed Courtney as her little sausages all cheered. Courtney's voice splintered as she tried to talk.

"Is there room for one more?"

"Are you kidding?" Casey wiped her face. "There's always room for you, Courtney. Damn, yo, like, what are you doing here, son?"

"I followed my heart… and it led me *here*. Maybe from now on, I should follow my heart more often. I should've followed it when you showed up at my place."

"I'll say," Casey giggled. She turned to see the entire gym in awe. She held onto her sister's hand and held it as she told her story. "I uh… I'd just turned thirteen, and I was livin' in Flatbush before I moved to West Fellers. I had nothing… or no one." Casey composed herself. "I met Courtney and her family that summer. They took me in, gave me everything, and I blew it. It took me a long time to figure out where I went wrong. But it wasn't until I came here to this gym that I really got it. I owe everybody in this room—everybody."

Miss Woods touched her on the shoulder.

"No need to thank me. I saw that you were trying extremely hard to change and wanted to make sure Courtney saw this side of you."

"Yeah, because I still hadn't gotten over the old side!" Courtney laughed. "But when Miss Woods called me and asked to meet, I knew that it was for real. Keep going, Case. All the way."

"Does this mean I get to be your sister again?" Casey asked.

"Maybe." Courtney picked up one of the dodgeballs. "But first, I think I need restitution."

Thunk. Courtney bopped her on the head with the ball. The whole gym roared.

"You ought to try a brick the next time." Miss Woods shook her head.

"Oh please, my head is not that hard."

Courtney bounced a second ball at Casey's forehead. It ricocheted and rolled across the gym. The kids all laughed again.

"You sure?" Courtney laughed. "Goddamn cinderblock with eyes, from what I can tell."

Casey picked up another loose ball and began chasing Courtney around the gym as Bruce and Miss Woods proudly looked on. Before long, the kids joined in and all hell broke loose during that tournament. There were bodies flying and balls hurling throughout the gym. At one point, Casey thought to get even with her PO and raised her dodgeball at her. Miss Woods gave her a dirty look. "You fire that thing at me, and you'll be back Upstate by midnight." Casey backed off and continued her match.

Life had always been a tournament for Casey. She'd been beaten by the system and routed by both the streets and problems with substance abuse. She'd been knocked down in every fight she ever had—most of which she lost. In front of her sister and her new family down at the YMCA, Casey won that night.

Better Late Than Never

On a warm late summer's afternoon, Casey's headphones blared repulsively as she entered Miss Woods's suite for her weekly appointment. Last year, she was a drug addict. This year, she was undecided about which apartment to rent, which car to buy, and whether she wanted to take French that semester or the following spring. She was a week out from taking her road test and receiving her driver's license. Although Casey had gotten off to a late start in life, her future appeared bright. She danced and rapped out the lyrics to Rob Base and DJ E-Z Rock's "It Takes Two," ignorant to the other riders in the elevator. She continued her racket as she exited onto the second floor and shimmied down the hall, gliding to the front desk. She shouted over her music as if she was at Yankee Stadium.

"Good afternoon! I'm here for my ten o' clock with Miss Woods! Is she available?!"

The receptionist gave her the evil eye. Casey removed her Walkman and turned it off.

"Sorry, Mrs. Gerry. Is Jacky—Miss Woods available?"

Mrs. Gerry glared at her. Casey went back there anyway. "Thanks, Mrs. G."

She didn't wear her headphones, but she rapped and played the drums on the way down to her PO's office. When she got there, Miss Woods was on the phone. Casey quietly closed the door behind her and took a seat in the cluttered space. While waiting, she surveyed the office and noticed a bookshelf loaded with criminal law books dating back to 1976. Inmate files were piled on top of older inmate files. Manila folders heaped high beside another chair with even more files. On Miss Woods's desk was a picture of two young boys. As she went to reach for it, Miss Woods moved her picture—still on the phone. Casey sat tightlipped until her PO ended her call.

"How many times have I told you not to touch the stuff on my desk? Next time you're gonna pull back a nub."

"Sorry, Miss Woods. So, are those your kids?"

"Nephews."

"How old are they? What are their names?"

"None of your business, Casey," Miss Woods laughed. "Lord, how in the world does Courtney put up with you? If I was your sister, I'd cut out your tongue. So, how are things down at the Y? Are you getting on Bruce's nerves, too?"

Casey threw her arm over the chair. "I get on everybody's nerves. It's my job. Bruce doesn't seem to mind. I'm working overtime tonight and Courtney's taking me driving. I got my road test coming up soon. I wanna be sharp."

Miss Woods shook her head. "I feel sorry for the people

of New York. So, how have you girls been getting along? Are you playing nice with each other?"

"Of course, we are. We're like peanut butter and jelly, me and Courtney."

Outside from the lot, Courtney laid on her horn.

"Will you excuse me for one minute?" Casey went over to the window. "Whaaat?"

"You said five minutes!" Courtney yelled.

"Ten minutes. Clean the Tootsie Roll out of your ears. I'll be out in a second."

"How about I clean *your* Tootsie Roll? You little smart-mouthed bit—"

Casey closed the window and returned to her seat. Miss Woods rolled her eyes.

"Peanut butter and jelly, eh?"

"We're working on it. Looks like it's gonna take more time than I thought."

"Take all the time you need. I sure wish I would have. See you in a month."

"A month? I thought it was every week?" Casey asked her.

"Would you like for it to be every week? I'm throwing you a bone. Now get lost."

Casey got up to leave. "Thanks for everything, Miss Woods."

"Jacky."

"Huh?"

"You can call me Jacky," she said. "But if I ever have to be Miss Woods again, you know what that means don't you?"

Casey cheesed at her PO. "I think I like Jacky a lot better. See you next month, ma'am."

Casey headed outside to meet up with her sister. When she got there, Courtney was pacing back and forth beside her hooptie. She raised hell as Casey walked up.

"You got some nerve closing the window on me like that," Courtney fussed. "You said five minutes. Next time you're gonna be walking."

Casey held out her hand. "Keys, please."

Courtney handed over her keys. "I can't afford any accidents right now. Bills are through the roof as it is." She crossed her arms. "And don't go stomping on my brakes. I got a little bit of padding left to go, and I need that to last until my paycheck in October. I'm not dicking around, Casey. And don't forget, I only got liability insurance, so don't go running into anything."

"Oh, my God, Courtney! Son, you sound like somebody's momma."

Courtney clipped her eyes at Casey. "Just don't crash my shit and we'll be fine."

Casey couldn't drive worth a damn. She smashed the accelerator and jammed Courtney's brakes, jerking her throughout Brooklyn. She had a heavy foot, and the reaction time of a ninety-year-old man. She rocked Courtney all the way down to the YMCA, oblivious to the jeopardy she put her sister in. "Pothole, Casey... Pothole, Casey!" Courtney warned her. *Thump-Thump.* "Yo, did you not see that big-ass pothole back there?" Casey needed more than just a new foot. She needed glasses, too. She whipped Courtney's car into the YMCA lot. She pulled up so closely on the cement block that she scraped the front bumper. She put the car in park and faced her sister.

"So, how'd I do? Not bad, right? Right?"

Courtney glared at her. "Well done, Casey, marvelous! Mom would be so proud," she lit up with sarcasm. "Go'on, get out. We'll practice more later. C'mon, get out. Go to work."

Casey unbuckled her belt. "Hmph. Well, Bruce loves my driving," she said. "He even lets me practice in the van when we go pick up the kids."

"Great, go kill Bruce. C'mon, I'm late. Get out."

Casey reached in the back for her bag, not realizing it was unzipped. Her *Better Homes* magazine fell onto the driver's seat. Courtney picked it up and began flipping through a section Casey had bookmarked.

"Philly?" Courtney gave her a puzzled look. "What's out there?"

"Eh, just a thought."

Courtney handed over the book. "I thought you weren't allowed to leave the state?"

"Today, I can't. But there's always tomorrow. And from now on that's what I'm fighting for. Tomorrow." Casey dropped her book inside her bag and zipped it. "Later, Court."

She looped her bag onto her shoulder and went in to start her shift.

The End

Epilogue
Five Years Later

Another eviction notice was stapled on Casey's apartment door in South Philadelphia when she returned from grocery shopping that evening. She ripped off the foreboding memo, stuffed it inside her pocket and trudged into her apartment for the night. Two months earlier, she'd been laid off from her job as a waiter at a seafood restaurant and was in dire need to find work again.

Casey had migrated to South Philly two summers earlier after Bruce lost his non-profit with the city and was forced to shut down the YMCA. She needed a job back then, too. Before returning to his native Pittsburgh, he told her about a school in the area he used to work at before starting his own non-profit. "It used to be Brooke's Rowe Elementary for a time, but now it's an alternative school for troubled kids. Check it out if you're ever up that way." Casey checked it out the first week she moved to Philly but didn't get a good vibe.

She drove by in her car and gasped at the abhorrent sight. On its walls was a cracked mural which looked as though it hadn't been touched up in decades. The windows were all barred and there was grass sprouting between sections of pavement. In the corner lot was a rotting school bus missing all four of its wheels. She shook her head and drove off. Later, she called her sister to complain about the school.

"What's the name of it again?" Courtney asked her.

"Medgar Evers… Secondary School, I think?" Casey said. "It doesn't matter anyway because I'm not going back there. Place looks like an ancient crematorium from the 1700s."

"Secondary School, eh? I'll call you back. I want to look it up on the internet."

"Why do you have to call me back?"

"Because I can't use the internet and talk on the phone at the same time, Case. America Online doesn't function that way. I'm still learning how to work this thing."

"Great, just great. They can send fuckin' radio signals into space, but you can't talk on the phone while using the internet. So stupid—I thought it was 1995?!"

"I'll call you back, okay? Bye."

Courtney didn't call Casey back that night. She called during her lunch break the next morning. Casey was curled up on her sofa, circling jobs to check out.

"Okay, so I saw the school. Doesn't look bad on the website, from what I can tell."

"Oh, it's bad, trust me. You aren't suggesting I go back there, are you?"

"Well, what else are you gonna do? You've been struggling to find something suitable since Bruce lost the Y. Besides, wouldn't you rather work with kids? Isn't that what you want?"

"It's not the same, Court. That YMCA was special to me, and so were those kids." Casey sighed. "Fine, I'll check it out tomorrow… even though I'm not expecting anything grand."

When Casey returned to Medgar for her second visit the following day, she noticed the mural had been repainted, the grass was cut, and the rotting bus in the back lot had been removed. She pulled to the side of the road and got out to investigate. She gaped at a beautiful painting of Medgar Evers, Rosa Parks, Dr. Martin Luther King Jr., Malcolm X, Muhammad Ali, and Black Jesus with his arms around Emmet Till. The image triumphed with Casey. She whipped out her cell phone to call up Courtney.

"Courtney, yo!" she began. "Son, you ought to see this mural. It's so dope. Makes me wish I was a bad kid just so I could go here. Oh, shit. Let me call you back. There's a guy in a suit comin' out. I'm gonna go talk to him." Casey closed her flip phone and jogged across the roadway with a manila folder hugged against her blazer.

"Excuse me, sir?" she called to him. "Sir? Do you have a second?"

The guy walked and talked. "Not for long. Late for a meeting." He waddled from side to side like a drunk duck. "Can you make it quick?"

"I can try." Casey walked alongside him. "You guys are an alternative school, correct?"

"We are. What's it to you? Who are you, anyway?"

"Casey Haughton." She leapt in front of the fast-moving fat man, stopping him in his tracks. She peeled off a copy of her typed resumé and handed it to him. "I was just wondering if you guys are looking for any kind of help at all? I worked at a YMCA in Brooklyn for about four years with troubled youth."

The man gave Casey a look of annoyance. He set down his brief case, removed his glasses from his coat pocket, stuffed them onto his face and reviewed her resumé, eyeing her periodically throughout. He handed Casey back her folder and walked off.

"Sorry, I don't have anything."

Casey followed him, pestering the man. "Maybe not today, but eventually, sir?"

"Nope."

"How do you know? Someone could quit or get fired tomorrow."

Casey tailed the man all the way out into the lot like a desperate news reporter. She watched him as he removed his suit jacket and tossed it into his pickup truck. He turned around to see her still standing there and went off.

"For God sakes, lady, what the hell do you want from me?"

"A job, or at least an interview," Casey persisted. She handed him her folder. "Who painted the mural by the way? It's beautiful. Don't you think it's beautiful, sir?"

The man swiped his face and reached out to take her folder. "Alright, I'll give it a second look. I'll call you if I change my mind."

"Can I have your name?"

"Thomas."

"Thomas, what?"

"Thomas Levy."

"Okay, Mr. Levy. Thank you, sir. I look forward to—"

Bam. Mr. Levy closed the door in her face. He fired up his truck and bolted from the lot.

Later that day, Casey called her sister to tell her about her harassing ordeal.

"He's not going to call you, watch," Courtney said. "Why would you annoy him like that, Case? That guy is gonna wipe his ass with your resumé."

"Negative. He's callin' me tomorrow with a job. That guy's sole purpose in life is not to be hassled. He's gonna call because he knows I'll show up there every day at the school and bug the shit out of him. A little reverse psychology tactic."

"Yeah, it's reverse, alright. I sure hope this little experimentation of yours works. Otherwise, you're gonna be selling pussy on Philly's south side for rent money."

"I'm not selling anything. I'm telling you, that guy is calling me tomorrow."

The next day, Mr. Levy called Casey's phone. She glowed with arrogance upon realizing it was him. "Interview? Uh, sure. I can be there before noon." Casey jotted down some info and hung up. She called her sister afterward to gloat. When Courtney didn't answer, she left her a long voicemail. "Yeah, boyeee!" she shouted into her phone. "Told you, you can't fuck with me. The guy called and offered me an interview. What?!" Casey slammed her phone shut.

Not only did Casey get hired that same day, but Mr. Levy offered her a 3.5% pay increase from where she'd left off at the YMCA. He brought her on as a school counselor and administrative aide. It was double the work, but Casey didn't mind at first. She was back to mentoring youth and she'd saved herself from eviction. By the end of her first month, however, she realized she'd bitten off more than she could chew and was already looking for a new job.

The kids at Medgar were nothing like the little sausages Casey had taken under her wing back at the Y. They were dangerous, unsparing, and disrespectful—some with worse backgrounds than hers. Students brought to school guns, switchblades, or drugs to sell. Casey jacked up a freshman one morning who passed by her office with a bulge beneath his shirt.

"Yo, my man? C'mere a second."

When the kid came into her office, she lifted his shirt and removed a black handgun tucked inside his waistband. "What are you doing carrying this thing around?"

Casey depressed the magazine release, dropping the full clip onto her desk. She racked the slide, sending the chambered round flying into the wall. "Now get out of here before I rip your guts out." The kid rolled his eyes at Casey and walked off.

She took the empty firearm into Mr. Levy's office and placed it on his desk. His eyes widened with terror. "That's the fifth one this week, Levy. I took two, and Mrs. Warren three. Did I mention that your music teacher caught a kid with a machete? Sir, you've got to do something."

Mr. Levy did nothing. Not only was the principal useless, but most of the staff at Medgar were corrupt and unprofessional. Some, like Mrs. Hawkins on the fourth floor, stole money from the students. When Casey reported the matter to management, the boss blew her off. She returned to work after a sleepless weekend to learn that her co-workers had ousted her. When she entered the break room the following Monday to heat her lunch, her colleagues all got up and left. It happened again on Tuesday, Wednesday, and on Thursday. By Friday, she visited the music teacher there, Mrs. Patterson, to find out what was going on. "You're stickin' your nose where it doesn't belong, and it's pissing everybody off. Quit trying to be the hero, Haughton. There ain't no hope here."

Casey got no sleep that weekend. She contemplated quitting Medgar altogether until Courtney talked her out of it. They talked for over two and a half hours on Friday, an hour on Saturday, and for three hours Sunday night. She threatened to leave on each call.

"I wish I had some dynamite, pipe bomb or some other kind of explosive device. I'd strap it to that school and blow that shit to kingdom come."

"Then you'll go back to St. Agnes and die by lethal injection. If not, you'll probably end up in a psych ward wearing one of those white jackets."

Casey deflated into the phone.

"Look, Case, if working with kids is your thing, fuck those staff members, you know?"

"These aren't like the kids I dealt with at the Y, Court. They're like little grown people with tempers and tantrums and guns and… bombs and shit." She rubbed at her forehead, frustrated. "You know what? I just remembered something. There's a zoo here in Philly. I'll wipe up goat piss before I step foot into that place again."

"Caseyyy—"

"No, fuck that, I'm not going back. Quit trying to encourage me, for once."

"Well, cleaning up goat piss doesn't pay the rent. Look, every job you go to is gonna be shit. My job sucks, too. But you're good with kids. That's your thing. Don't let those people run you out of there. Someday that place is going to be better, and it's going to be because of you. Will you at least sleep on it?"

Casey pouted like a seven-year-old. "I would, if I could actually go to sleep. Fine, I'll think it over some more, but I'm not making any promises. I'm serious, Courtney. I've just about had it with that goddamn school. I'm gonna hurt somebody in there if something doesn't change."

"Sure-sure. Okay, I gotta go. My ear is burning. Call me tomorrow after you get off."

Casey laid there after her long call with Courtney with her face smushed into her sofa, contemplating whether to return to work. She finally fell asleep just after 5 a.m. and missed her alarm clock. Her cell phone went off three hours later, waking her up. It was Mr. Levy.

"Hey, where the heck are you?"

"I'm sick," she fake-coughed. "Sorry, I thought I called you. I'll be in tomorrow."

"You can't. I need you here today. I'm in a real jam here, Casey. I got this kid—his name's Leonard. His mother just dropped him off. He got expelled for wiping some kid's face across the floor of Franklin High. The staff's all gone to that trip down at the city zoo. I don't have anybody to watch him."

Casey paused. "I-am-sick, Levy."

"I know, but you've got to make it in this time. Leonard needs you."

"No, Leonard needs Jesus."

"And *you* need a job," Mr. Levy threatened her. "Now get in here and get this boy and we'll call this whole mix-up even. On the double, Casey." He hung up on her.

Casey was furious on her way into work that morning. She took her sweet time getting there, stopping for breakfast, and running a few errands. She entered the main office of the school just after noon and bypassed her project child for the day. He was sitting at her desk, bored. He rolled his eyes at her and went back to writing in his journal. Casey went straight in to see the boss.

"Okay. I'm here. Where is he? Is that him at my desk?"

"No, he's outside tarring the roof, Casey. What do you think?"

She looked and noticed the boy was still writing. She

could tell right away that the boy wasn't like any of the other kids she took under her wing.

"What'd you say his name was again?"

"Leonard. He's a transfer from Franklin. His mom works for the postal service, and I'm not sure what his dad does. Hell, I'm surprised the kid's father is even in the picture."

Casey slowly turned around. "What's that supposed to mean?"

"Oh, come on. We know it's only a matter of time. If we're lucky, he'll turn out decent enough for us to ship him back to where he came from. If not, he'll turn into one of these other soon-to-be statistics we've got running around here."

Casey walked over and placed both her palms on Mr. Levy's desk.

"If it wasn't for that kid being right outside your door, I'd be on my way back to St. Agnes." She stormed out of her boss's office and stopped in front of the boy.

"C'mon, kid. Let's get going. I'm Miss Haughton," she introduced herself. "Looks like you and me are kickin' it for the rest of the day. We're gonna head down to Room 206 for a while. That cool with you?"

Leonard rose and shook Casey's hand. She noticed he had a weak grasp and wouldn't give her any eye contact.

"Please to meet you, ma'am," he said quietly.

Casey knew nothing of the sweet boy, but she instantly liked him. He was tall with short bushy hair and carried a Trapper Keeper notebook. After they got the key, she opened the door and invited him inside Room 206.

"Well, it looks like we're gonna be here for a little while in case you wanna—"

Leonard quickly went inside and sat in the back before returning to his journal. "—not say anything," Casey giggled. She closed the door behind her.

For nearly a half hour, Casey tried conversing with the boy without any luck. As she talked, he'd look up at her as if she was a weirdo and then go back to writing inside his journal. Fed up, Casey got up from her desk and went back to surprise him. The boy was so buried in his journal that when he noticed her watching him, he jumped. He shielded his journal the way Casey used to shield her food tray back in prison.

"Can I help you? I'm kind of busy." He shook his head and went back to writing.

Casey glowed at his innocence.

"You know, that is the most you've said to me all afternoon. So, what arc you writing? Ooh, pretty handwriting. Can I see? I promise to give it back."

The boy handed over his poetry journal for Casey to look in. She noticed as she was reading his works he fidgeted with his hands. She could tell he was worried about what she was reading. She turned through a few of his latest pages and stopped at this poem:

You look nothing like what you've been through.
Leonard G. Robinson, Jr.

Casey reread the poem a second and third time; it resonated with her. She read through more of Leonard's works, lost in his brilliance. She gave him back his book.

"You write beautifully, Leonard. That was impressive."

The kid smiled at her. "Really? For real?"

"For *real*, Leonard." Casey smiled back at him. When she did, the boy got nervous again and looked down at his book, but he wouldn't stop smiling.

"Actually, it's Junior. Oh, and thank you… ma'am."

"Junior, huh? Well, alright then, Junior. I'm Casey. Everybody calls me by my first name. So, you can too, if you want. You good, man? You don't have to be so shy. I don't bite, okay?"

"Neither do I."

For the rest of the afternoon, Casey and Junior bonded over movies and rap music. They ended their afternoon together by sneaking out to get Dominos and watching *Fresh Prince of Bel-Air* on a TV Casey stole from the library. When it was time for Junior to leave, Casey walked her new friend to the door. "Wait here, okay? I'll be right back." She rushed down to the teacher's lounge and took Mrs. Patterson's six-pack of sodas and gave them to Junior. "Now, you've got dinner for tonight. See you tomorrow, Junior." He went out the door and climbed into a rusty Buick Skylar with a woman Casey assumed was his momma. She waved as they drove away.

Once she got home, Casey called Courtney to tell her about her day.

"I met this kid today named Junior. He's fourteen, and he writes poetry. Yo, he's so dope! He wrote this poem, I memorized it. Check this out. It goes, 'You look nothing like what you've been through.' Isn't that great, Courtney? You really ought to meet him. Man, I don't even want kids, and already I wish he was my son." She laughed. "I can't believe he got expelled! I wonder how a boy that sweet could end up expelled? It doesn't make sense. I'm gonna make sure nobody lays a finger on that kid. If they do, I'll beat 'em all up—including the principal." On and on Casey went.

Acknowledgements

Thank you for reading *Finding Casey*, the third book in the Beyond Poetry series. The creation of this title would not be possible without the continued support from family, friends, and the many fans who helped make this series special.

About the Author

Nathan Jarelle is an author and poet from the Washington, D.C. metro region (DMV). In his spare time, Jarelle enjoys reading, family time, traveling, and of course, writing. For signed copies, business inquiries or to check out his latest works, visit or subscribe to his website at: www.natejayreads.com. Jarelle's works are available wherever books are sold.